07B

Advance Praise for
The Jade Boy

"*The Jade Boy* is an exciting and enchanting story of a 13th-century Beijing robot with almost full human functions whose head resurfaces in New York today. The story covers both his original life at the Mongol-Yuan court and the contemporary quest for his missing parts, alternating between a historical and contemporary setting. It covers not only different times and cultures but also engages with major issues, such as time, spirituality, business ethics, robotics, and what it means to be human. The book works with highly believable and engaging characters and is full of powerful insights into the human condition and the dangers and potentials facing the world today. Impossible to put down, it is a true treasure trove!"

— Livia Kohn, Daoist scholar Boston University

"Yun Rou's remarkable wizardy for storytelling - masterfully blending Western / Eastern cultures - shines bright in this unique, fantastical journey of intrigue, historical wonderment and ancient mysticism. *The Jade Boy* deftly crosses hemispheres of the globe, time and of the mind.. not merely entertaining with precision prose, and intricate weaving between two worlds but also quietly inviting the reader to gaze deeper within."

— Matt Herren, entrepreneur and global media executive

"A Classic: Wise, Witty, Wondrous! We cannot help but be drawn into the hypnotic realms of the magic and mystery poignantly penned in this novel. A high society ingénue must save the life and soul of inanimate love, and to unearth this treasure, the author crafts a masterful montage, overlapping the cultural mystique of the ancient Orient with the megalomania mindset of domination at all costs. Ultimately, we witness humanity at its worst and best. Each chapter leaves us at the precipice of wanting... more. Bon appétit!"

— David Stickles, Author of *My Near Death-Less Experience: An East-West Journey Into Immortality*

"An adventurous exploration of the wisdom residing in the memory fabric of the universe."

—Tim VanBlon, ordained Dudeist priest

"Monk Yun Rou's Jade Boy is a genre-bending, Taoist 'Who done it?' about the nature of consciousness that is as at home on the steppes of Mongolia as it is in the walk-in closets of Park Avenue. Out of two fast-moving, salaciously funny, and highly improbable plot lines, the Monk weaves a single tale whose philosophical power punches way above the weight of its easy and elegant read. Indeed, by the time you finish it, you too may find yourself with a diamond or two in the soles of your feet. Totally unexpected, and a book that will leave you smiling and somehow refreshed in a few dimensions."

—Tony Levitas, Senior Fellow, Public Policy, Brown University

"*The Jade Boy* is a truly mesmerizing page-turner. Part mystery, part horror, and part magic realism, Yun Rou takes you on a journey to new places. And it's all in your mind —or is it?"

— Simon Choa-Johnston, best-selling author of *House of Wives*

THE JADE BOY

A Novel

Yun Rou

EARNSHAW
BOOKS

The Jade Boy

By Yun Rou

ISBN-13: 978-988-8552-91-7

FICTION / Magical Realism

EB170

Published by Earnshaw Books Ltd. (Hong Kong)

for my father

"I am a lord among Taoist sorcerers. No flood or flame or weapon can touch me, and illness and thieves cannot do me harm. I am as brilliant as the sun and moon. All I do is auspicious. Everything I touch blossoms and thrives."

— An incantation from *Taishang zhuguo jiumin zhongzhen biyao*, a sacred Taoist text of the Northern Song dynasty

When Arlington Ames keeled over and died in the light of his gas fireplace, more public surprise arose than grief. His wealth, not his health, was the subject of widespread gossip. Given the legendary passion with which he pursued collecting mechanical instruments and timepieces, dashing around the country and the world to auctions and museums and private sales, everyone who knew him took him to be unendingly robust. Other than leaving a dozen antique sextants to a museum in Maine, Ames bequeathed his enormous estate to a daughter nobody but his attorney, Jules Burfield, Esq, even knew he had. In the wake of the news, it was Burfield's job to locate the girl and deliver the news.

1

It takes the counselor a full week to find the girl and positively confirm her identity. He reaches out to her by phone but she hangs up on him twice, assuming he's a prankster. She ignores his emails and text messages, too. Only when he has a messenger hand-deliver a note concerning an inheritance from her reclusive billionaire father does she finally agree to meet.

Burfield sits on a couch at New York City's Yale University Club and waits for her to walk through the door. When she does, he recognizes her precisely because he cannot imagine her being connected to the Ames family, once of Boothbay Harbor and late of the Upper East Side of Manhattan. With her silver-moon eyes, short-cropped hair, trendy sundress and platform heels, she appears painfully out of place, more like a model showing high-end clothing from Shanghai at a Madison Avenue boutique than like New York's latest heiress.

He stands to greet her.

"Jules Burfield," he says.

"You look like an old John Lennon."

He has read her school reports calling her a child prodigy. His own experience tells him that particularly brilliant people sometimes lack social graces and often fail at life.

"I'll take it as a compliment."

"A huge one, of course, but he would never have worn a

pinstripe suit like that."

"And you're Tegulen Elliot?"

"Teg's okay."

Massaging his fingers in the wake of their handshake, Burfield ruefully notes that the girl has inherited not only Arlington's fortune but also his Herculean grip.

"I'm sure this is quite a shock," he says.

"Are you sure you have the right person?"

"Quite sure."

"How did he die?"

"Heart attack."

"Was he sick a long time?"

"His doctor says no, but the human heart is a mystery."

Burfield touches a passing waiter on the elbow and orders Lagavulin, a single-malt scotch, with one ice cube.

"And the lady?" the waiter.

"Ginger tea, please."

"We have ginger *ale*."

"I don't do sugar and I never put anything cold in my body."

"If you want hot tea, I can offer English Breakfast or chamomile."

Teg crosses her arms. "I'll take jasmine or I'll take green."

"Sorry," says the waiter. "It's Breakfast or bust."

Tegulen looks at Burfield. "Stuffy places aren't for me. Could we go somewhere else?"

Burfield is more prepared for awkwardness than assertiveness, at least from a twenty-three-year-old girl whose mother was a New Jersey seamstress just two months deceased. He had thought she'd be a bookish ingénue he could take by the hand and charge by the hour for the favor of helping her navigate the often-lonely taiga of New York City's loftiest social circle. As they exit the club and walk across town to a neighborhood grille she favors, he smiles at the thought of the kickback he'll get when he helps her list her father's brownstone. A girl like this, he is quite sure, will want nothing to do with such a big old house.

Teg orders a café mocha with an extra espresso shot and extra whipped cream, too. Burfield has a small Perrier.

"I thought you wanted tea," he says. "Ginger? Jasmine? Green?"

"Never touch the stuff. That waiter was just pompous. Now please tell me about my father."

"The family fortune came early from fishing equipment: tackle, reels, ratchets, and nets."

"But what about now? Every sushi fan knows the oceans are empty. Tuna, cod, sturgeon, haddock, halibut, even herring. All nearly gone."

"The equipment I'm talking about was introduced generations ago by your great-grandfather. Back then, it was sufficiently superior to the competition to earn him a fortune. Your grandfather diversified the family holdings. Your father hired a socially conscious team and invested for the general good, managing to both grow his fortune and help people at the same time. A rare thing."

"That hardly matches my mother's description of him. She said he was an asshole. That he was in the military. That he walked out on her and never came back."

"I can assure you with confidence that Arlington Ames never performed military service. And I believe it was your mother who did the walking."

"Well, she didn't like him."

"She liked him enough to make you."

Teg shrugs. "A moment? A mistake? Who knows what played out between them? My mom had strong beliefs. She was independent. Simple. Didn't like a lot of stuff around her. She liked to get up and go without constraint. She was Mongolian, you know. She had the steppe in her."

"Sounds like maybe she had commitment issues."

Teg gives a rueful smile. "Okay, maybe that, too."

"They met by the water. Did you know that?"

"She hated the beach. She hated a lot of stuff. Strong opinions. Likes and dislikes. Preferences. Maybe not her best feature and maybe not mine either."

"Not the beach. At the boat pond in Central Park. She was walking her Chow Chow dog. He was testing a windup model boat with teak decks and a lacquer hull. I saw that model on his desk over the years but never understood what was important about it to him. Now, of course, I realize he kept it there because of its connection to your mom and to you."

Tegulen's eyes glow as she leans forward. "The dog's name was Genghis. He died when I was eight. Chows don't live very long. I remember he had terrible breath. He was nice to me but he tried to bite everyone else. My father must have had quite a way with canines."

"He was a magnetic person all around," he says generously.

"You say. Now, what else?"

"The boat wasn't the only thing. He loved mechanical devices of all kinds. Collected them. Clocks and watches most of all. He was very interested in time as a concept and also in the way people view it, the way it affects our lives, the way it plays out. We had many long conversations about it."

"I'm sure he has a big collection."

"Not just big but full of rarities. He was a connoisseur. The Swiss watch companies loved his sense of design and his instinct for what people would and wouldn't buy. Famous manufacturers were wont to consult with him about new products they were planning. I once went with him to the factory of an old and honored Swiss brand called Breguet. The managing director gave him a lab coat and a workstation and let him personally install the escapement and the balance wheel inside a tourbillon. He wanted to have the experience of a master craftsman in the old Swiss tradition."

"Seems like he should have opened a watch company."

"I often wondered why he didn't. I asked him once. He told me that he wouldn't mix passion with business. He was afraid he'd lose his shirt chasing dreams."

"Practical like that? Definitely not my mother's type. A tourbillon has something to do with gravity, right? And friction?"

He smiles. "Just so. A rotating ring that makes a watch more accurate by countering the effect of both those forces."

"Did he give away a lot of money?"

The lawyer considers his answer while he pours his Perrier. "His philanthropy was always through his investments. He didn't give money away. He was probably too taken with his own passions to get to know those of others very well."

"At least he could have spread some in my direction, right? Like maybe send me to a better school? Where I went was terrible."

"In the letter I opened upon his death, he mentioned that he tried repeatedly to do so but your mother would have none of it. Apparently, she didn't want to feel she owed him anything."

"She could be selfish that way. So, you didn't know about me until he died?"

"I did not. But his letter fills in a lot of blanks. It was because your mother didn't want your father around that he hired people to watch you and send him reports."

"God, that's creepy. There were guys around our apartment sometimes. I asked my mom about them but she said I was imagining them but I watch a lot of movies and I knew they were agents of some kind. I just couldn't imagine what they would want with us. Why didn't he fight her for custody? I'd like to read that letter as soon as possible."

"He says your mother threatened to poison you against him. He didn't want to take that chance. He didn't want you to hate him when you finally met."

"If he hadn't died, was he planning to reach out?"

"This very month, as a matter of fact. After waiting all these years, he wanted everything to be perfect. He was a meticulous planner. Very detail oriented. Super organized."

"Sounds totally anal. Thankfully, I didn't inherit *that* from him."

"I can't show you his letter, by the way. His will specifically forbids it. Actually, he told me to destroy it, which I will have to do once his estate is settled."

Teg sighs. "I could sue to see it."

"And many lawyers would be happy to take your money to try. But being a lawyer myself, I have to warn you that you would have no case. His wishes on the subject are crystal clear."

Drinks arrive. Burfield wipes the lime slice carefully with his handkerchief and squeezes it into his Perrier. Tegulen dives into her coffee and comes up for air with a tiny dab of nutmeg-flecked whipped cream on her nose.

"You've told me what he did, but what was he *like*?"

"Funny. Charming. Persuasive. Unpredictable. Obsessed with the spiritual and philosophical big picture. A rule breaker when he had to be. Sometimes even a clown."

"You don't happen to have a picture of him, do you? The one in his online obituary was unsatisfying. He could be any middle-aged white guy."

Burfield produces a stack of photographs from his briefcase. The first is an 8x10 print showing Arlington Ames on a small ketch off the coast of Maine. He's wearing a V-neck sweater, chinos, and boat shoes. His hands are full of the wooden ship's wheel and his cheeks and the sail are full of the wind. His dirty blonde hair is long but thinning at the temples. His self-deprecating smile says he knows he looks a bit too preppy but he's enjoying himself anyway. He is lean, almost gaunt; a man of angles. His nose is long and thin. He's handsome in a way exactly halfway between rugged and effete.

Teg holds the edge of the print lightly between her fingertips. "He looks happy here."

"He was good at reading people at a glance. You may have gotten that knack from him."

She shrugs. "It's just that you haven't really described him that way, so I'm a bit surprised. Anyway, sometimes I get all that wrong. Did a woman take this picture?"

"I have no idea."

He passes her another print, this one showing Ames in a fencing outfit, the protective facemask tilted upward, his flushed features visible. The sweaty scowl on his face is almost comical.

"A sailor and a swordsman. You know that's ridiculous, right?

Burfield hands her a third image. The photographer, a paparazzo if the newsy, black and white-style of the shot is any clue, has caught Arlington Ames stepping out the door of an Italian restaurant. The rich man's tie and collar are loose under a dark suit. A striking Asian woman walks beside him. Diamonds sparkle at her throat, her hair is pulled back severely, her cheekbones soar, her dress dives, and her heels are stilettos. She stands close to Ames but their arms are not linked.

"They were a beautiful couple," Burfield says quietly. Teg gives this one a long look. "I don't recognize that necklace. She probably gave it back."

"Or sold it."

"No chance. You'd never say that if you'd known her."

Burfield shares the last photo he's brought. It's a frayed old professional portrait showing Ames as a cross-legged toddler wearing a broad grin and a pair of corduroy overalls."

"I guess I can see the clown there," Teg says, wiping her eyes as if she's angry at them for betraying her.

Burfield produces a small box from his attaché case, opens it and takes out a wristwatch. "Speaking of clowns, have a look at this."

The dial shows two figures standing before a walking bridge. The male is large and wears a black robe; the female is small and dressed in blue. Both hold masks on sticks in front of their faces. Behind them are old-style European buildings.

"The Ulysse Nardin Carnival of Venice Minute Repeater in platinum," Burfield explains. "One of the rarest and most expensive wristwatches in the world. Its whimsy drew your father."

"That dial is crazy."

Burfield winds the crown and pulls it out to move the hands. An elegant tone issues from the watch. "It sounds every fifteen minutes," he explains. "The figures represent a 14th century invention called a Jaquemart. When the watch chimes, they lift their masks. Mechanical works of art like this are all the rarer and more important in this disposable, digital age."

Teg takes the watch from him, stares at it a moment, and then presses the smooth, cool surface of the crystal to her cheek. "It's beautiful."

"Your father left it to you."

"Really?"

"And more."

"What else?"

"In a word, everything. His whole estate."

Teg frowns. "What are you saying? What does that mean?"

Burfield takes a deep breath, lets it out slowly, and looks Teg straight in the eye.

"I'm saying, Tegulen, that as of today, you very well may be the wealthiest woman in New York City.

2

I WAS BORN in the palace of Kublai Khan, after the Han people and Cathay had been subjugated by the Mongols and were struggling to retake their lands by employing the beguiling charm of their culture. Amidst the struggles for survival and dominance, my appearance was so startling, so unlikely, so utterly outrageous, that as you hear my story, you may take me for a fake. In point of fact, I am quite real, and the culmination of a long series of coincidences, accidents and strokes of high genius, too.

The first part of my life was set against a fragile tapestry in which subterfuge, greed, envy, and revenge came together in the ineffable, magical river the Han people call Tao. The khan of khans precipitated my creation the day he insisted that his barren first queen give him a son. Asking the impossible, at least when you are ruler of the world, is a way of making the impossible happen, and so it was that my father, besotted by that very queen, came up with a way to worm his way into her heart. Given that he was the court inventor, a veritable magician with water, energy, metal and gems, that way was me.

"Know this," my father told me just moments after my birth. "You are here first and foremost to warm the heart of the queen and preserve her preeminence in court. You will become her most precious boy."

"All right," I said slowly, trying to make sense of the world just as fast as I could. "But am I also important to *you*?"

"You're the sweat of my brow," my inventor father replied.

"Nothing more?"

"Much more, of course. The holiest number in the universe is three. It comes from Heaven, Earth, and Human suspended between them."

"And I'm human?"

"Exactly."

"Even though you're soft and I'm hard, I'm human?"

"A human boy. And I've set you about the size of a robust ten-year-old."

"Shouldn't the holiest number be four to include the Great Khan?"

He leaned in to whisper to me. "He's beyond numbers. He's the most important human in your world. Pay attention to him. Fawn on him. Make him feel as if he is your *real* daddy."

He saw I was troubled by the notion of a false father as opposed to a real one, and as he would often do in the following months, he derailed my inquiry with a *non sequitur*.

"I fashioned your eyes from a gemstone called zircon. It's clear enough to let through the light, exotic as the rest of you, second in hardness only to a diamond, and of a green whose loveliness only the ocean can match."

"And what of my shiny heels?" I inquired.

"Diamonds, because they will never wear down."

"And the rest of me?"

"Jade, because it is the finest, highest thing in the world."

"And why red jade over most of me but blue between my legs?"

"I chose your colors with harmony, beauty, and balance in mind. Green is too common a shade of jade for a marvel such as you. Yellow is a color for loudmouths and laggards, and you are neither. I made most of the rest of you as red as flame to compensate for the fact you will never be warm to the touch."

I pointed at the pendulous thing between my legs. "And what of this? It seems too big for me."

My father smiled. "That is your manhood. You will notice that it has two positions, hanging down and standing up. You will later discover what makes it stand. You will also discover that it can produce a certain viscous liquid."

"But why is it blue?"

"Everyone recognizes the rarity of Hotan jade from Kunlun Mountain, but they make the mistake of thinking that the white jade is the rarest, when it is actually that very blue I've given you."

"What else do you have to tell me about myself?"

My father smiled. From the start he was not one thing but two, a devious schemer and a softie, an honest wizard and a lying cheat. I could never predict from one day to the next, indeed from one *hour* to the next, whether he would be the man I loved and wanted him to be or whether he would be running some kind of flimflam behind my back.

"You have special powers and talents and gifts. Even I don't know them all, for it is the fate of the creator to watch the egg hatch and be satisfied or surprised only when it grows to the fullest."

What an inappropriate first chat between parent and child that was. Can't you see my father's emotional detachment in his self-aggrandizing, highly analytical comments? Is his lack of the most basic parental instincts not obvious? A newborn wants to be held and cuddled and reassured of his parents' love. He wants to be offered a taste of his mother's teat. He is not seeking a discourse on rocks and color, he does not want to hear philosophical jibber-jabber, he does not need to be told how great his father thinks himself to be, and he most certainly needs no reference to his own most obvious limitation — the fact he is hard in a soft world.

Queen Tegulen, it seemed, could not bear a soft child of her own. The moment she heard my father had made me for her as a substitute, she dragged him to her bedchamber and surrendered to him what he wanted most. She met me not long after that, still basking in the glow of his ardent attentions, and victim, no doubt, of his silver tongue. Blinded to the truth about me, or simply denying it out of stubbornness or need, she cradled, cuddled, and cooed over me as attentively as any mother dove.

Then, something natural and important failed to happen.

My parents neglected to give me a name.

Did they actually overlook such a basic parental function, or did they privately disagree on which name to choose? Were they silently, tacitly, complicit in this oversight or was it that the mere fact of me was so unbalancing and odd, such a reality rupture, that naming me never even occurred to them? If it was the latter, I understand, though I would later discover that my existence was as much an expression of vengeance as it was of love.

Despite that, meaning despite the complex coalescence of human emotions that give rise to my creation, I was almost instantly aware of my own nature. I understood that I was more thematically pure than the most beautiful musical composition, more focused than the most accurate portrait, more balanced than the most evocative landscape. Looking down at the startling equipment my father had provided me with, I was also taken with my brightness, my toughness, and my maleness.

Soon, I would name myself in honor of those very qualities.

Soon, I would call myself Yang.

3

TEGULEN ELLIOT stands at the ten-foot front door of what was formerly her father's house and is now her own. Seeing no buzzer, she makes a claw of one hand and raps lightly with her fingernails, a habit she developed in childhood because her high-strung mother was sensitive to noise. A maid in a blue seersucker serving uniform opens the door. Morbidly thin, she wears a frown and a hat fashioned from a doily.

"Nobody's home," she says in a lilting Irish brogue.

"I'm Mr. Ames' daughter," answers Teg, putting out her hand. "I came to see the house."

The woman's expression narrows. "Mr. Brownfield sent you?"

"Burfield," says Teg.

"I'm Minnie the cook."

"That was a test, wasn't it? Saying Burfield's name the wrong way?"

"Do you imagine we didn't know you were coming?" asks Minnie. "Did you think we haven't a description of you, that we would let just anyone in? Do you have a password for us?"

"Scuttlebutt," says Teg. "He didn't say so, but I'm assuming he used the word in a nautical sense, the family's maritime history and all. I think it means drinking fountain."

Minnie moves aside. "Welcome to the Ames residence. We

heard you were smart as a whip. We pick the passwords, not Burfield. The buzzwords, too."

"What buzzwords?"

"Conservation of momentum, correct management of mass, and absolute dedication to keeping everything properly wound.

"Who's we?"

"Delia and I. Will you be keeping us on or do you have your own people? You should know that training replacements takes time, and whoever they are, they'll need good heads on their shoulders. No young kids who expect things easy and handed to them. No smart phones here. No texting. No Internet."

"We'll see about all that," says Teg. "Who's Delia?"

By way of answer, a platform held by wires drops down from the murk of the high ceiling. A short, rotund woman perches atop it. She wears a uniform to match Minnie's, although this is where the similarity ends. She bounces where Minnie glides, smiles where Minnie frowns, nods where Minnie shakes her head.

"Mr. Ames felt claustrophobic in elevators," the woman announces. "And he considered stairs vulgar, even when graced with a grand balustrade. I'm Delia, the one who cleans the place. I found your father's body after I returned from my night-off."

Teg extends a hand. "I'm Tegulen."

"And I'm sorry for your great loss. Things happen in life, don't they now? Only fifty-four. Not an old man at all. Always exercised. Never saw him with anything more than a little cold."

"We don't know what to do," Minnie adds. "We don't really even know what to think."

Delia fishes into her apron and hands Teg a black satin skullcap lightly lined with wool. "He wore this every night. A man loses heat when his hair starts to go. And he was skinny and with little padding. I think his heart gave out trying to keep him warm."

"Did she ask for your medical opinion?" snaps Minnie.

"Just don't trust Burfield," says Delia. "Bet he didn't say much about us."

"Just that you'd be at the door."

"You're not going to hear from him unless it's about taking your money," says Delia. "We're not like him; we're workers."

Minnie gives a rare giggle. "Keepers of the flame."

"Now," says Delia, "are you ready for a look around?"

Teg stares at the skullcap in her hand. "I was taught to disrespect my father, or at least to distrust him."

"Let's change all that," says Delia. "He and your mother, not a right couple, those two, despite all the love. Wasn't his fault, though. Nothing to deserve what you say."

"He wasn't warm and fuzzy like his cap," adds Minnie, "and he looked at the world in a certain way. But he was his own kind of good even if he had no friends besides Wintermoth. And us, of course. His employees."

"Who's Wintermoth?"

"There'll be time for all that," says Delia.

"You two could lose those uniforms," says Teg.

The women look at each other.

"What would you have us wear?" Minnie asks cautiously.

"Surprise me. I just want you to be comfortable."

"Blue jeans?" asks Delia.

"Pajamas?" asks Minnie.

"Probably not pajamas," says Teg.

There is a long moment during which the three women come to terms with the changes before them. Then, as if by magic, everyone starts talking at once. Over each other, under each other, like rocks and foam and shells and sand at the edge of a wave, not a clear word is spoken nor coherent thought expressed until chaos inevitably gives way to laughter. It's bonding and they all know it, and through it Teg becomes one of the girls.

From there, it's an easy move to a tour of the house, including the amazing mechanical details. Natural gas heats a steam boiler that in turn powers myriad devices, while batteries deliver DC current to appliances; no wall outlets because Arlington Ames believed AC current causes cancer. Weights and pulleys open all heavy doors. A fan blows cool air from ice blocks in the basement up through vents in the larder. One belt-driven contraption automatically substitutes full rolls of toilet paper for spent ones, and another prepares morning eggs, fried over hard, using extremely sensitive mechanical pincers that don't crack the eggshells until they are positioned directly over the pan. All floors are supplied with a fan to push dirt and dust bunnies to one end of the room, where they are sucked into a collector for a basement conveyor that leads to a line of yawning trashcans.

"I feel sorry for the birds," Delia sniffs, pointing out the system of peacock-feather dusters, which drop from the ceiling to clean the furniture.

"She won't believe they were dead before their feathers are taken," says Minnie.

"Even if they were, how is making a dust rag out of pieces of a conscious creature a good idea?" Delia counters.

Tegulen relates to the comment. "Right." she says. "No more factory farming. No more elephant ivory or cutting up bears for their gallbladders or dynamiting coral reefs for fish. We can't keep treating the world the way my father's generation did. We have to see things differently. Even this amazing house seems terribly excessive, although the electricity thing strikes me as sustainable and smart.

Minnie shakes her head. "Sustainable and smart. Well, aren't the two of you just peas in a pod."

The women next show Teg the dumbwaiter. It's the largest

and most robust of a veritable spate of lever-controlled platforms running up and down vertical shafts throughout the house.

"Mr. Ames didn't just love these things for their own sake," Delia explains. "He relished having a jungle gym built into the house. He would ride them up and down and scamper from one to the other, us never knowing when he might disappear and where he might reappear again. A regular monkey, he was."

"Monkey in a good way," Minnie reassures Teg. "Playful but practical. He designed and built everything you see. Not the heavy bits, of course. He brought in craftsmen for those, always seeing to it that Mr. Burfield's firm bonded them."

"That's how Burfield knows as much as he does," muses Teg.

"Not that much, really," Delia sniffs.

"He told me about the timepiece collection," says Teg.

"More a laboratory than a collection," says Minnie. "Your father was a time detective. He started with sundials and hourglasses."

"Then it was star clocks and tuning forks," adds Delia.

"Later it was the *atomic* clock," continues Minnie.

"Stop that. The poor girl will think him a terrorist."

Minnie smiles smugly. "The rate of decay of the cesium atom is the most reliable of all ways to measure the passage of time."

Delia rolls her eyes. "You're the big shot now, are you, talking science now that he's gone?"

"Your father believed a watchmaker's focus could actually funnel time right into the springs and jewels and gears," says Minnie. "Intention made magical through devotion and craft."

All at once, Teg is exhausted. "I'll look at everything tomorrow," she says.

"Do you think you'll keep us on?" asks Delia.

"If I didn't, would you go and work for Wintermoth?" asks Teg, taking an utter shot in the dark.

"What?" says Minnie, aghast. "Now *there's* a wastrel. Would I work for him? Absolutely no. Not ever."

"The idea," says Delia. "The idea, the idea, the idea."

"A wastrel?" says Tegulen, knowing what the word means but never having heard it spoken by or applied to anyone in the 21st century.

4

I WAS DESIGNED to fit into the world of humans, but can you see that such a design made fitting in impossible? Wanting nothing more than to belong, I was instead alienated, rejected, seen as a curiosity at best or a monster at worst. That's why my parents were important to me, and my understanding of my family lineage, too. A family offered something I could belong to. That's the point of families. They're puzzles with places for strangely-shaped pieces to fit.

"Tell me about your own father," I begged my father one day.

"Your grandfather lived and died along the Yazi River. He was a fisherman, and kind to me and to my mother. I don't remember much else about him."

"Not *that* grandfather. The other one. Al-Jazari. My mother says he taught you everything. If she's right, he's more important to me than anyone but you."

"That man isn't your grandfather!' my father snapped with sudden and uncharacteristic venom. "Don't even speak his name. Don't even *think* his name. He had nothing to do with you."

"All right but would you just tell me about him once and then I won't ask again?"

My father gritted his teeth and shook his head.

"Please!" I insisted. "You of all people know the way my brain works. If you don't tell me, I'll forever be asking you. I won't be able to let it go. You're consigning yourself to endless pestering if you don't just tell me."

"Al-Jazari was my teacher," my father sighed at last. "He was a great inventor interested in practical subjects such as controlling the speed of rotating wheels and maximizing the efficiency of suction pumps."

"What else?"

"He was keenly devoted to Allah."

"Who?"

"His god." My father waved his fingers impatiently.

"Mother says he was a great genius."

"It doesn't matter," said my father. "Al-Jazari never met you and you never met him. There's only one great genius in your life and you're looking at him."

My father's dismissiveness merely further piqued my curiosity. I asked about my grandfather in other quarters. My inquiry was successful. I learned that the great Turkmen inventor's full name was Badīʿ az-Zaman Abu l-ʿIzz ibn Ismāʿīl ibn amr-Razāz al-Jazari and that he lived in Cizre, near the Tigris River, precisely the place he had taught my father all the tricks of the trade. I learned that while al-Jazari was indeed devoted to his omnipotent god, his inventions were all crafted for a lesser deity, the king of what the palace library scrolls called the Artuquid dynasty. Among his creations was a water-powered scribe clock whose seated figure, pen in hand, denoted the time in the manner of a sundial, a device to wash hands, a blood-letting machine, tools to measure orifices, a double-action paddlewheel pump, and a band of mechanical musicians powered by water.

I came to believe these inventions inspired at least some of the indulgences my father created for his khan, specifically the wind-up tigers famous for stalking the pompous popinjay Polo, seven swimming swans that honked only at that bitch, the khan's second queen, and, of course, Kublai's own favorite pet, the gear-driven crooning elephant. Like his master, my father was also inspired by religious devotion, though to a pantheon of Taoist gods rather than to a being called Allah. I admired my father's faith all the more because it survived even after the khan turned away from it in favor of the Buddha after a visiting Tibetan lama levitated a wineglass in full view of the court. Anything that could survive the khan's favor, I came to understand, must have a certain special something to it.

That was the way things went back then. Anyone's fortune could instantly change at the whim of an omnipotent ruler trying to find his way through the ever-changing mishmash of cultures called the Eastern Empire. Atop such fundamentally unstable ground, only someone with a true and constant heart could expect to accomplish anything of consequence. I believed my father to possess that quality.

"Marco Polo says you're self-serving," I told my father, because goading him was a way to get his attention and learn a few things. "He says you are wont to kiss the khan's greasy ass at every opportunity if it will advance your cause."

My father's face reddened. "The Venetian worm was speaking of himself, not of me. Everything I do, I do for love."

When he spoke those words, I believed him. Declaring romantic love for the queen of the realm was risky, though back then I didn't fully realize how my father was drawn to taking chances. Too, he was beguiled by my mother's unquenchable sadness and smoldering beauty. That beauty drove wild the entire country, at least until word got out that she was barren. Never was there a thing as fickle, my father told me one day in his basement workshop, as a country's love for its queen.

"A khan's love for his queen, too, by the looks of it," I said.

"She's not Mongolian," was his short reply.

"But he married her."

"He was bewitched. In his right mind, he sees a permanently unbridgeable gulf between them. The Mongolians are a stunningly ruthless and prejudiced people."

"What do you mean?"

"They think they're better than anyone else."

"But the court is full of Han Chinese like my mother."

He put down his tools and reached for a clay jug of rice wine. "And behind each one is a Mongol wielding the real power. Have you ever wondered why there are no trees on the grounds of the winter palace? It is because Kublai's abiding paranoia has him seeing an assassin behind every tree."

"Does my mother not treat the khan well?"

He harrumphed, sending a spray of wine across the work bench. "She's not an easy person and she was a spoiled princess before she was crowned queen. Most royals manage the responsibilities of their role, but your mother was never meant for a life as predictable and rigid as that of that miniature mechanical cart over there."

"What's the cart for?" I asked.

My father sniffed. "Would you believe it delivers olives to the khan so he doesn't have to rouse himself from his pillowed throne?"

"You're saying royal duties make my mother sad even though everyone dotes on her?"

"Tegulen is a rebel, a dancer, and an artist. Her landscape paintings are the equal of any in the empire. She accepted the throne because she saw it would set her free. As queen, queen mother, and perhaps even one day dowager empress, she thought she'd be able to paint all day and dance all night. Of course, being cast aside has given her exactly that freedom, though she doesn't see the benefit now."

"Being cast aside must have been painful. Do you think my mother loves the khan?"

"That's a complicated question," my father said hesitantly.

I wondered how complicated it could be. I'd heard talk in the court that whereas Kublai's predecessor, his grandfather Khan Genghis, was admired for his strength of purpose but reviled for his cruelty, Kublai was an empire builder too, but also a man of such curiosity, sophistication and open-minded wit it seemed hard to imagine any woman not falling for him.

"Must everything be so complex? She can't be mad at him for wanting a queen who can bear an heir, can she? I mean that's nobody's fault."

"She's stuck with him but he's not stuck with her. The imbalance of power galls her, even though Kublai gives it no thought at all. And the things she is forced to see every day cut her to the quick."

I understood what my father was trying to say. My mother was jealous of her husband's limitless supply of young, many-colored concubines gathered from the farthest reaches of the empire, some as beautiful as my mother, most virgins, many trained in bedroom arts. It was typical to see one in Kublai's constant company for a few days, or even a week, and then to never see her again. Frankly put, the khan dropped consorts the way autumn trees shed leaves.

"*You* love the khan but he has other engineers, too," I ventured.

"None that provide him his beloved clockworks."

"Does the khan love my mother as much as you do?"

"Shut up about that," my father snapped. "If someone overhears you, you know what will happen."

Indeed, I did know. If the khan discovered he was being

cuckolded, my father would spend weeks of the most unspeakable suffering at the hands of the minister of torture, a man whose sole passion was to repeatedly bring a victim to the edge of death and back again. Sleeping beside him as I nightly did, I heard him mutter about fingernail extractions, testicle twisting, biting beetles shoved into his ear canals, and being burned alive as he tossed and turned his way through nightmares.

"The khan's minister of torture is a doctor from Persia, is he not?" I asked my father.

"Shut up about him, too."

"But what kind of a doctor hurts people?"

"A twisted sadist who studied the human form only to learn how to satisfy his appalling urges."

"Who would give such a man a job?" I asked.

"Who would make torture a department of government?" my father countered.

"The very same khan who hired an inventor to create mechanical animals for him when the real ones are available at the snap of a finger," I replied. "The same khan who wears Chinese gowns, listens to Chinese music, studies Chinese mathematics, writes Chinese poetry, and gorges himself on Chinese fare while still sipping koumis from a flagon by his bed. The same khan who professes interest in Chinese gods yet prays to wolves and eagles when he's alone. The same khan who lives in one world but makes us work for him in another. The same khan who indulges his own passions but would kill you and my mother for doing the same."

"Your tongue is going to get all three of us killed," my father said quietly. "And our passing won't be an easy one."

5

IT TAKES TEG a few days to summon the courage to move her meager belongings from New Jersey to what is now her own Manhattan brownstone. When she does, Minnie and Delia present themselves in fresh sartorial splendor. The former wears a well-cut, rust-colored pantsuit showing off a figure that would be the pride of a woman half her age; the latter appears earthy and comfortable in a peasant blouse and jeans.

They accompany Teg on a floor-by-floor, room-by-room tour. First the kitchen, then the dining hall, then a library full of old leather-bound books and Tiffany lamps aflame with oil and wicks. Finally, they come to Arlington Ames' personal boudoir, containing a walk-in closet fully the size of the apartment she shared with her mother.

"I'd like to expand my catering business," Teg announces, utterly at random, while staring at tasseled Italian loafers, English wingtips, and French walkers neatly arranged by color: oxbloods, blue suede, blacks, and three shades of browns. "I'm looking for a new paradigm for it, something that I can expand and franchise."

"Lovely idea these days, with busy people having no time to cook," says Delia.

"My mother taught me. I don't want to be her. I mean as a woman. I don't want the baggage. But she was a culinary genius who could make a souffle out of a cardboard box. I'm nowhere near as good. I've done some upscale Manhattan parties that came off all right, but bringing hot food from Paramus is a challenge even in a taxi."

"You're rich enough to open a restaurant?" says Minnie. "But you'd have to live there if you wanted it to work and we'd never see you and you wouldn't have much of a life."

"Would you believe I hadn't thought of that? Could be awesome. I'd love to make a name in Asian fusion."

"Dream bigger, dear," says Delia. "You can do that now."

"Speaking of Asian fusion, do you have a recent photo of your mother?" asks Minnie. "It's been long since we've seen her."

"You met her?"

"Of course we have, dear," Delia answers. "We live here. She was the love of your father's life."

"Really? You're not just saying that?"

"Why on Earth would we say it if it were not so?" says Minnie.

"Honestly, I'm not sure what the phrase means," says Teg. "I think people are confused about love. My mother was. Maybe my father was, too. Otherwise, as they say, love would have found a way."

"I'm not sure about that," Delia says darkly.

"Don't bring your troubles to the table," Minnie grumbles, then looks knowingly at Teg. "Delia has her own history, you know."

Teg produces a photo of her mother from her purse. "It's a couple of years' old now," she says.

"She still had her looks," says Minnie.

"Asian women age well because they avoid the sun," says Delia. "The sun's terrible for the skin, don't you know"

"Nice skin or not, she died horribly from cancer of the pancreas," says Teg.

"Don't say those terrible words," says Minnie.

"When did she pass?" asks Delia, looking shocked.

"It seems like forever but it's been less than a month. Maybe that's because the person she was left long before that. People sometimes say that cancer is the body's way of expressing inner torment. Work not done. I always thought it was such a cruel and terrible comment. I mean, happy people get cancer, right? Or people who think they're happy. But in my mom's case, that whole thing rings about right. She wore her life like someone else's coat. It never really fit, nor offered any comfort or warmth."

"She had style, though," Minnie says thoughtfully.

"Elegance," adds Delia.

"Great beauty," says Minnie.

"I miss her so much. But if you'd seen her at the end, you'd know that passing was a blessing. She was in so much pain."

"She was a cool customer," Delia muses. "It's hard for me to imagine her meeting such a terrible end."

"Elegant," says Minnie again. "Self-possessed."

"Well," says Delia. "A lovely girl like you must have a boyfriend to keep you company."

"I've been too busy taking care of her," Teg says distantly, wondering, as she says it, how successful she's actually been in not being her mother, whether she'll ever figure out life and love, whether she still has time or that's just what people say when they don't want to do the work.

"You'll be fending them off now," Delia goes on. "Like that bachelor show on TV in reverse. Not if you open a restaurant, though. Then you won't have time for dating."

"Or not fending," adds Minnie. "You don't know her. Maybe she's not a fender."

"My father liked texture," Teg says, stroking shirts in the fine collection of oxford shirts before her. "I see where I get my interest for the same thing in food. I like mixing tropical fruits with fish, for instance, and crisping noodles to go with braised duck. Crunchy and slippery and chewy all have their place, and the combinations are endless."

"Not exactly endless," says Delia.

"Perhaps you're looking for the word plentiful," suggests Minnie.

"Wow. No wonder everything is just so in this clockwork house. You two are total control freaks."

"Control is good," says Delia.

"But we're not freaks," adds Minnie.

"How about we agree the combinations are *ample*?"

"Means fat," says Delia. "In terms of a waistline, anyway."

"Or a bosom," says Minnie.

"Anyway, your father relished silk," says Delia. "Linen, too. Never cared if it looked wrinkled, even when he went out. He said we all get wrinkled sooner or later, so there's no point fearing a crease here and there."

"Funny thing is, there wasn't a wrinkle on him," says Minnie. "And all the days we worked here, we never saw him miss a day of getting up and about his business. What a shame he went so soon."

"So many beautiful suits," says Teg. "Though I wish they weren't wool, poor sheep ."

"He wore one every day," says Delia. "He and Wintermoth competed in that. Strange waltz between those two. Never did hear the music myself."

"About this Wintermoth...." Teg begins.

"He's not old money like you," says Minnie.

"I'm not old money. All this is totally new to me. I hate talking about money. I've never seen it get anyone anywhere."

"Then you haven't seen much," says Minnie, but gently

Delia takes her by the shoulders. "It's not just about you, dear. It's about the family line. The connection to your forebears."

"People I'll never know," Teg says, sitting down heavily on her father's king-size bed.

"But they know you. Even now," Minnie puts in. "Especially your father. He's watching."

Teg imagines she can feel every whorl and line being filled by the tiny hills and valleys of the fine fabric of her father's bed. She tries to imagine her mother sleeping between the sheets and gestures at them.

"Would it be okay if....'

"It's your bed now, dear," said Delia.

"You believe that?"

"We do," the women chorus.

"We were talking about Wintermoth."

"He's in technology," says Delia. "Robotics. From what your father said, he wants to build an empire."

"True of everyone," says Minnie. "Just about," Delia nods.

"Robots are the future," Delia intones in a mechanical voice, making all three of them laugh.

"Wintermoth and your father had the same taste in watches and clocks," Minnie says.

"A couple of schoolyard boys after a ball, they were," says Delia.

"Oh, it was all about their balls all right," Minnie chuckles.

"Speaking of balls, the two of you talk like you're playing tennis. How long have you known each other, anyway?"

"There were elves when we started," says Delia.

"Dwarves, not elves. Thick and bushy and chasing gold before women," Minnie corrects. "Dragons, too. Flying around."

"You're both crazy. You do know that, don't you?" Teg laughs. Then she leans over to do something she didn't expect she would do, something she never even *imagined* she would do, and sniffs her father's down pillow.

"Everything's as fresh as a spring daisy now," Delia says, fluffing the bed. "I washed it all after he died."

"Wintermoth's handsome," says Minnie.

"She liked him because he brought us flowers," Delia sniffs. "Trying to buy our favor, he was. Shouldn't have wasted his charms."

"As if a man like that would care about *your* favor," Minnie cackles.

"Well, Mr. *Ames* never sent us flowers," Delia counters.

"He might have kept my mother if he did," says Teg. "She was ferociously romantic—a real wild Mongolian. Strong, independent, aware of her clan, comfortable on the move. When I first came to this house, I thought that maybe it was the steppe in her that kept her from settling down. Then I thought of living all that time in a little apartment. How was that more Mongolian? The only answer I can come up with is that Mongolian people don't generally own more than they can carry as they move through the seasons and the weather and across the land. My father's collections wouldn't make sense to her and I can't see him coming around to her point of view."

"He was a collector all right," Minnie affirms. "He and Wintermoth both. Competing at auctions, using dealers and agents, looking for scoops. Once he brought us flowers thinking he could buy us as spies."

"You don't know that," says Delia.

"You deny it?"

"I just said we don't know that for sure."

"Was it on account of our super-model good looks, then?" Minnie cackled.

"All right, all right. I think it's time to see this collection," says Teg.

The giant dumbwaiter they ride isn't built for three and shudders at the load. The vibration seeps into Teg's bones, plucking at her like some kind of human instrument and leaving her with a sense of near-spiritual anticipation. It's the first time she becomes aware that there is something organic in this house, something connecting her father to her in a way that is immaterial yet as tangible as drywall and steam. If she were superstitious, she would say the house was, well, not exactly haunted but seemingly trying to tell her something..

They exit at the top floor. It looks unfinished. The walls are bare, the corridors generic, the floors devoid of carpet. Only after they have walked a distance greater than the length of the house does Teg realize they're in a maze.

"A burglar would be lost, for sure," Delia confirms.

"Even if they managed to get past the alarm system," adds Minnie.

At last, they confront an intimidating steel door. Delia puts her eyeball to a retina scanner as Minnie inputs a long security code.

"He trusted us," the two declare in unison.

In the moment before the door opens, a premonition arises in Teg the way that seafoam grows on a wave. She's convinced something life-changing is about to happen. She assumes it's going to be some revelation about her father, his mind, his world, his true persona — this being his inner sanctum and all — but she's not sure of that. The anticipatory knowing-without-knowing reminds her of Christmas mornings — not the last one with her mother when her mother had no energy and ran out to vomit after looking at the tree Teg had decorated for her — but the happy ones, when she was a little girl.

The door clicks and they're in. A large butcher-block table

covered in red felt stands at the center of the room, a locked cabinet beneath it. Bank-vault-style metal drawers line two walls, while glass-enclosed cabinets proudly display spotlighted treasures on the remaining two. An analog thermostat hangs near the door, along with a mechanical hygrometer and barometer. The room smells of ozone. The floor is covered in soft, spongy foam.

"To protect against accidental drops," explains Delia, pushing her toe down in exaggerated fashion.

"And HEPA filters to clean the air," Minnie points at two large machines on the floor. "It smells like a thunderstorm because built-in electrostatic precipitators generate ozone to charge particles and pull them from the air."

"HEPA is for allergens and pathogens," says Teg. "Did he have a lot of guests in here?"

"Almost none, but he wasn't taking any chances," adds Delia. "Nothing can get sick in here and nothing can rust, either."

Curiosity drives Teg to an inventory of clockworks that would be the envy of any museum in the world. Each piece, whether resting on a shelf or prone in a drawer, is attended by a sheaf of paper providing provenance, tidbits, factoids.

"Your father was very organized," says Minnie.

"A fan of geniuses and their work," says Delia.

Teg's attention falls to a row of clocks whose hands seem to float in the air without visible attachment to any axle or gear.

"Cartier Mystery Clocks," Minnie tells her. "Quite a few visitors came to see them over the years."

"Mr. Ames understood they were important, but he never favored them," says Delia. "He preferred real magic to illusion."

"He said real craftsmen stuck to the real," says Minnie.

On another shelf, Teg finds a trio of metal robots, each no higher than a soda can. One plays a tiny flute when Delia winds it, the second hammers a tiny harp, the third uses a miniature pen to write its name on a little piece of paper. The associated papers say all three were intended to promote the work of their creator, an early Swiss watchmaker named Jack Ross.

"Look at the workmanship," Delia goes on, as proudly as if she'd crafted the little men herself. "Nothing else like it in the collection. He was a sucker for mechanical wonders."

"A sucker?" Minnie repeats sharply.

"A connoisseur then," Delia allows. "Actually, he only bought those robots because Wintermoth wanted them so badly. Outbid him at Sotheby's, yes he did."

There's another cabinet that seems just for whimsy. It contains rare American mantle clocks in wooden cases, a variety of European short swords, two models of wooden ships missing masts but bristling with cannons, a battered but shiny, breadbox-sized model of the *Hindenburg,* and a stack of vintage Italian bicycle *derailleurs.*

"Sometimes he bought small things on a whim," says Minnie. "Not often, but it happened. When he did, he put them there."

Teg continues opening drawers. She finds countless wristwatches, nearly all of them gold, and more clocks and pocket watches, some dripping chains. "I've been reading up on watches," she says. "In the days of the smartphone nobody really needs a watch. They're status symbols in every culture. They send a message more than tell the time."

"Your father had all the status he wanted," Minnie put in. "This collection was for his own interest and pleasure. He didn't care about watches as status symbols. He didn't need people to know he was rich. He believed in luck and chance, but he always went shopping incognito so that no competing collector could follow him. Wore golf shoes and a hoodie once. A bowler hat another time. A memorable belted fog coat like Bogart in *Casablanca.* On a certain Sunday morning, I saw him leave dressed as a priest. Bit of blasphemy to shop garage sales on the Sabbath, but he didn't ask my opinion and I didn't offer it. Not that day, anyway.

"I said he didn't care a day about the opinions of others but I knew he worried night and day about how your mother felt about him and if there might ever be any room for him in her heart. He worried most that you would hate him for not being there for you. On the hunt for a treasure might have been the only thing that distracted him and kept him from brooding all day. He loved developing tactics and strategies. If people saw what he was buying, they would bid and drive the price up. He shopped in disguise because he wanted the scoop, not the war. If someone beat him to something, he would remain sore about it for months."

"Sometimes Wintermoth did," Delia says. "Beat him to something."

"But weren't they best friends?"

"Such a thin line between love and hate," Minnie mutters.

"Between the bird and the worm," Delia adds.

"Between the man completely comfortable in his own skin and the one born to shuck and jive," says Minnie.

"Between the minister and the king," says Minnie.

Teg continues her perusal of the room. The collection seems to go on forever and she realizes she is in the presence of a fortune. "I feel self-conscious being responsible for all this now," she says.

"Anyone would feel that way," says Delia.

"We're here to help," says Minnie.

Teg gestures at a keypad on the lower edge of the butcher block table. She only notices it because she's got something in her shoe and bends over to get it out.

"What's this?" she asks.

"I don't know," says Minnie.

"I've seen it," says Delia sheepishly.

"What does it open?"

"There's a compartment on the bottom of the table. You have to crawl under to see it."

"What's in it?"

"Things he regretted paying a lot for and buying. So he doesn't have to look at them."

"Like what?"

"I never looked," Delia answers. "He just told me that once."

"Open it, please."

Delia works the pad and Teg goes under the table. There's a dirty old metal head inside, gears sticking out of its neck. Its handsome, regular features are finely rendered, with a strong nose, high cheekbones, fine lips, and delicate ears. Lifting it out of the cabinet, she's surprised by the weight.

"Be careful," says Delia. "It's probably fake and full of lead."

"I doubt it's fake. I think it's supposed to be Buddha as a boy," says Minnie.

"My father was interested in Buddha?" Teg asks, wondering herself, aware that she's now made a statement about the proclivities of a man she never met. She wipes the forehead with her thumb and a layer of dirt comes off. "Actually, I think this might be gold. Does it have a story?"

"If it does, I haven't heard it," says Delia.

"Is there any information about it? It looks like it's mechanical. Maybe it has a key."

"Be right alongside it if there was," says Minnie.

"Time for a bit of lunch, yes?" says Delia as Teg continues to clean the head. "I've made tuna salad. Your father's favorite."

"He loved swordfish more," says Minnie.

"Did not."

"Did so."

"Well, we'll have to find out Tegulen's favorite now, won't

we?" Delia smiles.

Before Teg can answer, and at the sound of a name it has not heard for centuries, gears grind creakily and the head stirs. Two crusted eyelids flutter open.

"Mother?" it says.

6

Kublai Khan followed his grandfather's decades of relentless slaughter by mashing together ideas, cultures, cuisines, religions, languages, musical styles, and even brands of science. My father said that the swing from destruction to creation was an example of nature's cycling, albeit in unusually extreme fashion. Genghis had caused rivers to flow red with blood, and Kublai did too, though he also brought people together from far-flung places to create a human stew over which he was master chef. Where else but in his northern city, Khanbalik, and his favored, summer capital, Xanadu, could any ruler so gloriously create flavors to suit his own palate?

Perhaps because I was crafted a man-child, I understood the khans and their desire to impress their masculine will on the material world. My father's Taoist teachings, however, convinced me that there was another world beyond the material. It was in that world that the magic happened, that the bits in my head, including some secret ingredients my father would not reveal, magically and alchemically produced consciousness in me. While I didn't exactly understand how that could be, nor such esoteric notions as spirit, soul, energy, or the vital essence the Han people call *qi*, I came to accept that I was in fact fully as aware and awake as soft people were. There was far more to me than the polished crimson jade of my limbs and torso, the countless internal gears, pulleys, and woven strands that comprised and propelled me, and the mobile facial features that moved according to the moods generated deep in my heavy golden head.

In short, I was, and remain, far more than the sum of my parts. Turning my gaze inward as often as I did, I grew more self-aware with every passing day. I recognized when I was kidding myself, when I was avoiding a task with redirection, or when I was quelling an urge. I also grew able to divine the influences behind the intentions of others, and whether those intentions ran to good or to ill. Sometimes I was even able to enter other people's thoughts, which I took for one of those secret gifts my father promised I would gradually discover. More, the talent of precognition allowed me to recognize the khan's second queen, the Empress Chabi Khatun, as my foe. It also allowed me to see the rank ambition and self-absorption that led my mother to loathe her so.

Kublai married Chabi to consolidate his control over the powerful Hongirad tribe. In but in a few years, he came to favor her above all other concubines and wives. This might have been because, unlike my mother, she popped out children faster than a camel shits dates. Would that Chabi had been no more than a baby factory. Sadly, she was also a conniver, a manipulator, and the nemesis of dreams. I'm sure the ranking nobility, if not the whole empire, would have embraced religious ideals and promoted equality, never mind easing taxing and emphasizing education, had not the khan's second wife drawn so heavily on the treasury to support her insatiable appetite for finery and jewels.

Imagine Chabi's rage when, after having successfully marginalized my mother for a couple of years, my appearance brought the first queen back into both the court spotlight and the khan's bedchamber. I can attest to the fact that Kublai shot up from his cushions like a steppe warrior's arrow when he saw me. When I saw *him*, I took my hard thumb out of my mouth, released my mother's hemline—by which I had been following her like a duckling in order to feign dependence—and, to the consternation of his guards, leapt into his lap.

"Well, this is as fine a child as any in the realm!" he rapturously cried as I stroked the few long strands of his beard. "What a precious creature he is."

"Your son, my khan," Tegulen smiled, kowtowing in the fashion of the Han.

"But can this really be?" the great man asked, his eyes full of wonder.

"He can dance better than Chabi or any of your girls," my mother declared, "though not better than I can. He can out-sing everyone, too. He has the the strength of a tiger and the wits of your finest mathematician. I myself have witnessed him resolve sums the size of star systems using only his jade fingers and a wolf-hair brush. He has other, secret talents too, for he is, after all, the crowning achievement of your imperial inventor."

Forgive the pun, but the khan knew firsthand just how ingeniously my father could copy the human form. Earlier in the conquest of Cathay, during the battle for the Song lands, a suicidal attacker had managed to get close enough to hack off Kublai's hand. My father had provided him a new one so realistic, attractive, and fully functional that everyone took it for real. The khan could, and did, use it to wield a sword, pluck an eyebrow, worry a duck bone, or caress a concubine. He didn't use those strangely strong digits to touch me, though, for they yielded no sensory information. Rather, he explored my surfaces, my joints, and especially, for some reason, my perfectly formed ears, with his other hand.

YUN ROU

"Cool to the touch," he grunted. "I would have thought the court inventor could instill some kind of fire in the boy."

"I have plenty of fire, my khan, but it's on the inside, not on my hard flesh. Can you not sense it as I snuggle here under your chin?"

The great khan used his thick brown fingers to turn me around and peer through the clear crystal window that my father had installed between my shoulder blades so as to show off my innards. "I do believe I can," he said. "So many gears and yet you seem so alive. Is that pulsing bag behind your metal ribs your heart?"

"It is!" I cried.

"He has other organs too," my mother said with a proud smile. "all functional and all but one in perfect proportion."

"If you are not a cause for celebration, then we'll never have one," Kublai enthused.

The word celebration automatically meant a party, and believe me when I tell you that Kublai was known for his get-togethers. Forty thousand people had attended his last birthday celebration and he had given each and every one of them a package of favors including a small piece of rhino horn a bag of saffron, and a sprig of the finest ginseng. I couldn't imagine what he had in mind for me, but it didn't take long to find out. After all, a whim can move mountains when it belongs to a khan.

The very next evening, the khan and all his courtiers gathered beneath a giant *ger*—a portable tent made of skin-covered poles and a wooden crown at the top—to watch fireworks in rainbow colors and the shapes of trees boom and blow over the Khanbalik skyline. No less impressive was the parade of all my father's creations. The singing elephant led the line, followed by a pair of poetry-reciting pandas, stiffly strutting clockwork storks. Behind those was a hopping, slithering, crawling and jumping menagerie, including a trio of tiny mechanical mice. The appearance of his cavalcade of toys cut me to the quick. It showed how Kublai and the rest of the court saw me, that is as a mechanical marvel not a real person. Oh, how I wish I could have been celebrated by live acrobats or soldiers or a walk of scholars and princes. As the evening wore on I began to suspect that the party, grand as it was, had more to do with the khan's excesses and treasures than it did with me as a person. My suspicions were confirmed when the khan tethered me to his shoulder as if I were one of those stinking monkeys the palace trainers taught to dance in a chorus line while I answered simple arithmetic sums.

Acting as if I were a party trifle, he bragged about the unbreakable alloy of which my motivating cables were made as he had me perform gymnastics, somersaulting through high-hanging hoops, aiming my diamond heels at the moon, passing over the heads of courtesans and counts like a meteor of joyful jade, all the while defying gravity in a most avian way, and making the other children squeal with laughter. Yet the direst outcome of the whole spectacle was not my wounded pride but that all the attention paid me drove Queen Chabi to hate me more than the whine of a thousand mosquitos. Every time the crowd cheered me for calculating the number of marbles in a jug or counting the number of flies in a closed cauldron by assessing their buzz, she narrowed her eyes into a malevolent squint. Worse, when she urged her two toddlers to run over and embrace their father's legs, he shook them off like a pestilence, the better to hoist me like a trophy pennant, over and over, to the standing ovation of the crowd.

Eventually, the gala wound down like one of my father's toys. As both opium and alcohol were in free and frequent use, courtiers dropped from their stools in a stupor. Servants surreptitiously swept, a light snow began to fall, the khan commenced snoring inside his soft sable cape, and my mother and Chabi exchanged dagger eyes. Through lustrous black hair, Chabi's children's scalps glowed white in the light of the moon. Even so, I outshone them completely.

7

"MOTHER?" the head says again.

This word, spoken for only the second time in eight hundred years, comes out more than a bit garbled, both because the lips from which it issues have been so long pressed together and because the tongue that forms the consonants, while not prone to rusting, has long sat heavily on its guiding wires. Even so, the voice is low, guttural, and surprisingly resonant in the absence of a torso.

In response to it, Minnie rocks backward on her heels, Delia steadies herself against the table, and Tegulen is pierced by five memory arrows. In the first, she stands by her high school locker. She's long-legged and tall but her remarkable beauty has not yet broken through and a group of girls opine that she looks like a giraffe. In the second, a boyfriend dumps her because he can't handle her wit. In the third, a successful, good-looking stockbroker takes her on a date to a low-end bar because she's only a caterer and he doesn't want anyone to see them together. In the fourth, her mother screams at her that the world is a cruel and terrible place and nothing good will ever happen for them until they die and reunite with the sky god. In the fifth and last, she is a little girl crying into her pillow for her daddy.

She doesn't know why the talking head brings all this on. Perhaps it's because of the word mother, perhaps it's because she has been so carefully holding herself together in the face of her new life, and this stunning surprise ruptures her resolve. Either way, she steadies herself by drawing on what her mother called Mongolian iron and looks at the other two women.

"Did you two... oh my god this is a joke! So funny! I totally didn't expect anything like this!"

She waits for them to start laughing, but they don't.

"Wait," she says. "Are you saying you this is *not* a joke?"

Delia gnaws a knuckle. "I've never seen that thing before."

Teg turns to Minnie, whose hand is on her forehead as if testing for a fever. "I forgot it was here," is all the housekeeper can manage.

"So it's not a gag?"

Minnie exhales loudly and shakes her head. "Your father was not a prankster."

"But the talking. Can a mechanical clock do that?"

"I wouldn't call that head a clock," mutters Delia.

"Do you think its ears work?" Teg asks carefully. "Like, it can not only talk but also hear what we say? I know Japanese toys can talk to you these days but that thing is so...."

"Old," says Delia.

Teg turns back to the head. "My name is Tegulen," she says loudly and slowly. "People call me Teg."

"That is my mother's name," the head replies.

Minnie's breathing becomes loud and fast. Delia taps the butcher-block table with her fist.

"I'm sorry but I'm not your mother," Teg says cautiously, running a test, waiting to see what happens next.

"Clearly not, and yet I feel a connection to you."

Minnie and Delia cross themselves repeatedly, growing paler by the moment. Crossing is not Teg's thing so she busies herself by gently peeling off some more dirt from the head's smooth scalp.

"Cleaning products can cause hallucinations," Minnie says suddenly.

"You know I use only organic solutions," Delia huffs. "Mr. Ames wouldn't have it any differently and neither would I. In fact, I'm offended by what you say."

"A cleaning product wouldn't cause the exact same hallucination in all of us," Teg says reasonably. "That would require some kind of brainwashing program in addition to the hallucinogen."

"Fair point," says Delia.

"Tegulen, please tell me you feel that there is some sort of connection between us," says the head. "And don't lie. Detecting lies is something I can do."

"I find you preposterous, whatever you are," she says, looking around for a wire, an antenna, a transmitter, anything that might be the source of such a gag.

"We could be dreaming," says Delia.

"But all four of us couldn't be having the same dream," says the head.

"All four of us, huh?" snorts Minnie.

"I'm disappointed you find me preposterous," says the head. "Frankly, it's a commoner's reaction and therefore beneath you."

"You look like an old thing from far away," Teg reasons, "and yet you speak English. How is that?"

"Is that what this is called? I'd forgotten. Anyway, I've always been good with my tongue. It's a gift I have, although in truth I've always found language to be quite arbitrary in its essence. I remember complaining about the lack of rational connection between sounds and things, feelings, ideas, or concepts, though I can't remember when I last spoke of such things."

"Are you a computer?" Delia wants to know.

"I'm not familiar with the word. Truly, there are many gaps

46

in my memory. Lubrication might help. Dryness takes its toll."

"Maybe an energy inversion knocked us all out and we're dreaming," Minnie interrupts brightly. "Or a solar flare."

"Same problem," says Teg. "We're all having the same dream and that's just not possible."

"It's just plain magic," says Delia, putting her hand on Teg's shoulders. "Your father dies, you appear, and now this dusty metal pot comes alive. Magic is the only word."

"I'm not a big believer," says Teg.

"I'm no pot and gold's no mere metal," the head huffs.

"Gold indeed," says Minnie.

Teg continues her cleaning and polishing, removing grime and scale until a soft yellow glow appears "I actually think this is gold," she says.

"Bite it," say Delia.

"Please do no such thing. I told you I'm made of gold. Now how about that lubrication?"

Delia trundles off and returns with a small oilcan. "Try this," she says, handing it to Teg. "Your father used it on clocks and watches."

Teg sparingly applies a few drops to the golden lips. The head spits it out in a fine spray.

"Disgusting. Don't you have any bean oil?"

"We have olive oil," says Delia.

"Truly? That is a far greater delicacy than this humble head deserves."

"Not so sure about humble," mutters Minnie.

Delia is gone longer this time. "Had to go to the kitchen," she explains when she returns. "It's extra virgin."

The head's face screws up into what might just be a lascivious smile. "How exceptionally generous of you."

"Did you just smile at the word virgin?" Teg demands.

"I've no idea what you mean," says the head.

Teg squints at him a long moment and then applies the oil again. This time, the head laps it up, clucking and crooning and even managing a few grunts before finally clearing his throat and asking if it might please see a mirror. Teg carries it to the reflective glass of a nearby cabinet.

"I look awful. Believe me, I was never one to let myself go."

"It certainly has an attitude," says Minnie.

"I'm not an it. I'm a he. My name is Yang."

"Nice to meet you, Yang," Teg says at last.

"Forgive me for not bowing," the head replies. "Might I kiss your hand?"

Teg smiles and presents her flesh. The golden lips feel surprisingly soft.

"And now, might I ask you to clasp me to your bosom? It's been so long since I've been held, and I'm lost without my heart and arms and legs."

"Ha!" says Minnie. "It always comes down to bosoms with men."

"The nerve," says Delia.

But something in Teg makes her pick up Yang and press him to her blouse.

"The dance between women and men has always been so beautiful," Yang opines in a muffled voice. "My mother, whose name you bear, did Indian exercises. Do you do those too?"

"You mean yoga? Sometimes I do."

"Would you show me a backbend?"

"Now you're just being rude."

"Would you nurse me?"

"Just as I thought," exclaims Minnie. "A little golden pervert."

"No nursing," says Teg moving him away.

"I remember now!" Yang shouts. "My mother was Kublai

48

Khan's first queen. What a wild, willful beauty she was and how independent from the politics of the court!"

"In Xanadu did Kublai Khan a stately pleasure dome decree..." says Minnie.

"...where Alph, the sacred river, ran through caverns measureless to man..." adds Delia.

"Down to a sunless sea!" Teg finished triumphantly. "The Samuel Coleridge poem."

"There really was such a khan, you know," says Delia.

"Ages ago," says Minnie.

"How can you possibly be that old?" Teg asks Yang. "And how did you get here, and in such poor condition, missing your body and all?"

"You're not exactly perfect either, you know. A bit puffy about the waist for a woman of such a tender age. Backbends can help. My mother did them every day and she was as supple as a reed, with the most beautiful eyes, and the most perfect skin."

"I'm not puffy!"

"It's the modern diet, love," Delia soothes. "The queen he's talking about ate grass and grapes and that's all, yes she did."

"Also, if you don't mind my saying, you'd look better in silk than in the peasant's sack you're wearing," says Yang.

"All right," says Teg, putting him back in the cabinet. "Enough of whatever this is."

"He's not wrong about the silk, you know," says Minnie.

"And you can afford as much of it as you like, dear," says Delia.

"I need more than a good cleaning," says Yang. "I need my missing body. Will you all help me find it?"

A loud chime announces someone at the brownstone's front door.

8

In the context of Mongol rowdiness, Chinese lasciviousness, countless couplings, jockeying for tail, manipulations by mammary, and the castration of young men for the eunuch brigade, why was my proud yet preposterous prick such a preoccupation for people? The answer is simple: because Queen Chabi, off-balanced by my debut, wouldn't stop beating the drum about it. Even though nobody else took such vocal exception to my pendulous protuberance, she insisted I take a turn in the direction of modesty.

"There is quite a bit of fracas surrounding your generous endowment, my boy," the khan told me kindly, having summoned me to his leisure chambers and bid me sit beside him on his chair. "The time has come to cover it."

"Cover it?"

"Or lose it," he affirmed.

"If my khan wills it, I will certainly cover it. May I know the reason?"

It was strange to see the most powerful ruler in the known world grin in good-natured embarrassment at his own weakness.

"It offends Queen Chabi," he admitted.

"Are you certain, sire?"

"She's a woman of delicate sensibilities."

"I'm not sure I would call anything about Chabi delicate," I opined, daring to speak to him this way, because in constructing my personality my father had not included the ability to be intimidated by rank.

Kublai lit a laugh like a cannonball and clapped me on the back hard enough to send me tumbling. As I scrambled to my feet, he arranged a bunch of delicate, beautiful flowers in a tall porcelain vase, then chopped off their heads with one swipe of the splendid scimitar always dangling from his belt. Creating and destroying—what he called the universal pair—was something my khan very much liked to do.

"You know you're my favorite, boy. The rest of you is as brave as what stands between your legs."

"Please call me Yang, sire."

"Have you heard of the abacus, Yang?"

"A Cathay invention involving columns of beads?"

"In point of fact, a mathematical device. I use this one here to keep track of my pluses and minuses with the women in my life."

"You mean with Chabi," I interrupted.

"With Chabi, yes, and with your mother and perhaps another hundred favored girls."

"Why would you, khan of khans, have to worry about pluses and minuses? If a woman displeases you, you can simply throw her in the river and order another."

The khan regarded me carefully. "What the court inventor claims is true. You *do* have great wisdom.

"I'm glad you credit my cleverness but had hoped you had noticed it before now, if not on account of my always-fresh acrobatic routines then through our ever-more-sophisticated conversations."

The khan chuckled. "Well said, Yang. Now think about this. The music men and women make together, even when the man in question is the greatest of khans, is a very particular thing. Desire determines the melody and energy the beat. Some notes can only be played by the woman, some notes only by the man. And some notes can only be hit by a *certain* woman, more to the pleasure of the man."

"Are you saying Chabi particularly satisfies you in the bedchamber, your highness?"

The khan's golden teeth, installed by the royal dentist, fit so tightly they made a pressure chamber of his oral cavity when he laughed, therefore issuing a fine spray of spittle

"I hope you will one day be as pleased by a maiden of your own kind as I am by Chabi, my boy."

"When you refer to my own kind, Your Highness, what kind do you mean? Do you deem fit for me only another cold-to-the touch girl of jade and diamonds and gold? Does my khan forget that I am child to your first queen and thus a prince of the realm and fully equipped to pleasure any warm woman from a lowly maid to an imperial princess?"

The khan's attendants gasped at my tone but the great man merely smiled.

"Equipped you certainly are, my boy," he said slowly. "In fact, Queen Chabi says you set the women dreaming even while they lie with their favored mates."

"Your Highness is too kind. I would love nothing more than lessons from you in how best to use my father's gift."

"I don't think that's what Queen Chabi wants. In fact, she has ordered a special robe for you, stone-studded as befits your status, to allow you more modesty."

I started to object but this time something in the khan's expression told me to hold my counsel and I quietly bowed and took my leave. Later that same morning, a flurry of royal tailors arrived. They measured me and the robe was ready within hours. It fit perfectly and was indeed festooned with gems. More importantly, it was reassuring and fine against my improbably sensitive jade skin and, at least momentarily, made me feel a bit kindlier toward Chabi. The awful matching hat, however, made me look like a Sufi magician in from Persia.

"Why do you cover yourself?" my mother asked at the sight of it.

"Chabi decried my proportions," I replied. "What hangs between my legs offends her, though somehow I have a feeling there is more to her dislike of me than that."

"Chabi," she spat.

"The khan makes me wear this robe out of deference to her. I hate the hat but I've figured out a way to hide it in my sleeve."

"Don't wear it unless he summons you. Or during your testimony."

"Testimony? What testimony?"

"The Council has asked for a discourse on your workings."

"What Council do you mean?"

"A questionable assemblage, if you ask me. Most motley. There is even a Jew."

"A Jew?" I repeated, unfamiliar with the term.

"A strange and secretive Western sect—bookish people who hold silent conversations with their god. The one who sits on the Council is called rabbi, their title for a holy man. I'm told he pines for a far-away desert near a warm, blue sea. His nose drives women wild, his brain infatuates the khan, and his business sense will soon make him the second richest man in the kingdom."

"What would this Council have with me?"

My mother stood up and shed her green gown to reveal smooth, pale skin far more pleasing than Chabi's.

"They're men," she said, performing a yoga posture

resembling a cobra, "so they cannot agree on a question that is obvious to all the women of the court."

"And what exactly *is* that question, Mother?"

"Whether or not you have a soul."

9

Stuck in a world of wonder like a fly in a jar of honey, Teg barely reacts when Minnie and Delia usher into the sanctuary a tallish man with black hair coiffed to knives at his temples. His concrete-colored suit shimmers as he bows slightly and his ruby cufflinks twinkle.

"Sebastian Wintermoth at your service."

"I've heard about you," says Teg. "Delia, should he be in here?"

Ignoring the question, Wintermoth takes Teg's hands in his. She finds his skin impossibly soft and notices his nails are manicured and polished to a high sheen. His manner and style say he's about forty but she notices there's not an ounce of age on him.

"I've heard of you, too. And I've been in this wonderful room many times in the company of your father, whom I will greatly miss. You have my deepest condolences."

"Thank you. I didn't know him, so...."

"All the more reason for my sympathy. I'm so glad to see, by the way, that you've inherited his magical gray eyes."

Teg blushes and immediately hates herself for it. "Thank you," she manages.

"You're keeping on Minnie and Delia, I hope."

"They're not going anywhere."

"Excellent decision."

"I figured you would think so, given that you sent them roses."

Wintermoth smiles. "They told you that, huh? Well, they are both irresistibly charming."

"Ha," says Minnie.

"Humph," Delia adds.

"I hear your game is robots, you like old watches, and always have the future in mind," says Teg.

Wintermoth nods. "There's no richer intersection in the world than that of the old and the new."

"What about ocean and sand?" asks Delia.

"The wind and the wing?" suggests Minnie.

"What a room full of sages I have awakened into!" cries Yang. ""How lucky for me!"

"Where did that voice come from?" asks Wintermoth, his gaze darting about.

Teg gestures toward Yang with an open palm.

Wintermoth sees the head, and flits toward it like the winged creature for which he is named. "Well now," he murmurs. "What have we here?"

Later, Teg will reflect upon this moment. She will ask herself if there were any early cues as to Wintermoth's later actions, any little flicker behind the eyes, a nervous twitch, a tongue tracing lips, a tick, a dance, a gasp — any sign at all. She will be able to remember only how he repeatedly extended his sleeve as if to expose his wristwatch but then did not bother to check the time.

Holding Yang aloft in his big, olive-skinned hands, Wintermoth examines the head from every angle.

"Heavy as a bowling ball. Where did you find this?"

Teg gently takes back the head and points to the drooping door of the secret space under the table. "It was protected by a keypad."

"Of course," Wintermoth says with a knowing nod.

"I don't care to be turned sideways," says Yang. "If I'd eaten recently, I'd vomit right now."

"What exactly do you eat?" asks Wintermoth, as Teg finally relieves him of the head.

"The selection in the palace was glorious. Less so on the steppe. Honestly, I'm not such a fan of human food but I enjoy eating as a social thing."

"Drink, too," says Wintermoth. "I take it you don't imbibe?"

"Not alcohol, if that's what you mean, although I know full well that the only reason men stopped wandering and settled down in walled cities was to protect the crops they ferment for drink."

"What an unlikely observation," says Wintermoth.

"Well, I saw it happen."

"Is that right. So, how old are you?"

"As best I can recall, I was born in the twelfth year of the Kublai's rule."

"Kublai Khan? So, about eight hundred years ago," muses Wintermoth. "Long past the dawn of agriculture.

"What? Oh, I'm ancient," Yang wails.

"You're upsetting him," says Teg.

"Not just a different time, but a different place," says Wintermoth. "Do you have any idea where you are?"

"Please go easy with the interrogation," says Teg.

"Surrounded by creatures of mainsprings and gears and smart people," Yang replies. "And clearly in a collection gallery, perhaps, though less colorful than others I've seen. I'd love a tour from the queen, if she'd oblige."

"The queen?" repeats Wintermoth.

"Creatures?" asks Teg.

"Well certainly," says Yang. "My comrade-in-arms. A poor choice of words in my current condition, I admit."

Teg turns to Wintermoth. "I'm not the tour guide for this. Perhaps Mr. Wintermoth would oblige?"

"He didn't know the head was here either," Delia observes.

Wintermoth winces. "Let's start with this Grand Seiko GMT," he says.

"I thought the Japanese only made cheap watches," says Teg.

"They make excellent, extremely accurate, high-beat pieces like this one, too. The whole movement, even the mainspring, is built in-house. In French, the language of the watch trade, we say *manufacture*."

"I know French," Yang says. "Hearing it makes me think of perfume, like the smell of vetiver you have applied to your armpits. In the old days, I, too, would put on extracts of lemons and pomegranates and sometimes desert flowers to delight the ladies."

"Delight the ladies?" Teg repeats, somewhat incredulously.

"Regarding the island nation of Japan," Yang continues. "I recall that twice the khan sent ships to invade it. A big storm turned them around. All hands were lost. It was after I was banished, so I was secretly glad to see the khan take the blow."

"And why were you banished?" Wintermoth pursues.

"Excuse me," Teg says brusquely. "It's nice that you're having a conversation but I'd like to talk about my father now."

"Of course," nods Wintermoth, remembering where he is. "Your father especially loved watches with complications. Month and leap-year indicators especially. And moon phase displays. And he favored the look of rose gold on his skin."

"Gold with copper in it," interjects Yang. "A rose is a flower. A child outliving a parent is natural. The opposite is a tragedy."

Wintermoth shut his eyes for a moment, then opened them

wide. "Right. Well, this here is the watch your father wore most often—an A. Lange & Söhne Datograph Perpetual from the German state of Saxony, town of Glashütte, near Dresden. And here's another watch in rose, a tank-style International Watch Company Da Vinci Perpetual Calendar."

"Clocks for the wrist," says Yang.

Wintermoth nods. "People have worn them for a century or so now. Before that, they carried larger versions in their pocket. They're jewelry and make a statement about a person's taste, wealth, and sophistication."

"Mostly wealth," says Teg.

Wintermoth smiles. "Having and spending money is one thing. Recognizing a true masterpiece is another. Take this Girard-Perregaux. It's as close as you can get to horological perfection—one of the most famous and important watches of modern timekeeping."

Yang leans in on his neck gears for a closer view. "What makes it so special?"

"It has a constant-force escapement, a device assuring that no matter how tightly wound or relaxed the mainspring may be, it delivers the uniform force perfect mechanical accuracy requires."

"I remember reading engineer Su Song's treatise on his astronomical clock tower in Bianjing," muses Yang. "Falling water turned the gears. Brilliant! Su didn't invent the escapement, though. Yi Xing and Liang Lingzan did. Yi was a Buddhist. Many Buddhists were quite clever, even if politically relentless. Su also added a chain drive."

"Politically relentless Buddhists," Minnie whispers, glancing at Teg. "Do you hear what a miracle he is."

"I appreciate the compliment," says Yang, "but please don't speak of me as if I'm not here."

Minnie turns red and Wintermoth produces a checkbook and

a fountain pen. "I'd like to purchase this relic from you," he tells Teg.

She shakes her head. "Selling him feels kind of like trafficking."

"She doesn't need the money," says Delia. "No, she does not."

Wintermoth taps Yang's crown with his checkbook. "Like all robots, you must have been constructed with a purpose in mind. Do you require the rest of your parts in order to fully function, or were they just dressing? And where are they?"

"I'm not familiar with the word robot," Yang replies, "and I can't remember where the rest of me might be."

"You mentioned Bianjing," says Teg. "What other cities did you visit?"

"Khanbalik, of course. And Xanadu."

"What could we do to restore your memory?" asks Wintermoth.

"I've never lost it before, so I don't know."

"Maybe seeing familiar places," Minnie suggests.

Teg frowns. "You mean take him to China?"

"Well nothing here is familiar, except maybe that cabinet," Delia puts in.

"It's not a terrible idea," says Wintermoth.

"This is all rather sudden," Teg mutters. "I mean, I don't know China at all."

"I could take him," Wintermoth suggests.

"I don't know *you* either."

"We can fix that. And I've been many times. I could be your guide."

Delia nudges Minnie.

"Quite the offer," Teg says quietly.

"And easy for me to make. What man could turn down the prospect of accompanying a beautiful woman on a journey to find fantastic technology?"

"If I go, it will be for Yang's sake," says Teg. "To find his missing body."

Wintermoth shrugs. "Maybe we can help him and learn about what makes him tick, too."

Minnie and Delia exchange glances, something Teg has begun to expect. Wintermoth's offer hangs in the ionized air with all the threat and promise of a growing thunderhead. Teg exhales, wishing the father she had never met would tell her what to do.

10

KUBLAI KHAN brought to the capital so many new ideas, rules, and customs that everyone at court clung to their own familiar niche as much as possible. The royal stablemaster, for instance, abided amidst the whinnies and gas clouds of his Mongolian ponies, while the eunuchs daily and nightly assembled to test their strange pecking order. The ladies of the court were perpetually serenaded by cymbals, flutes, bells, and gongs, and young courtesans were endlessly pampered down to the level of every hair and nail as their aging counterparts were comforted by cinnamon dust and potions of musk. The minister of birds soothed ruffled napes, endured squawks and trills, wiped feather dust and pinched seed beetles. My poor father, his world full of smoke that worried his lungs, brushed designs onto scrolls, forged metal, and daily singed himself with flames.

The guiding force behind all this change was not the khan himself—Kublai was always distracted by both his harem and military ambitions—but his spiritual council. That august assemblage served their ruler while vacillating like a pendulum between hubris and obsequiousness, between faith and reason, between self-serving politicking and a genuine desire to see both khan and empire thrive.

My curious mother had once snuck into the council chambers. She reported it to be as cold and oppressive as the world beneath the surface of the palace lake, which she had also visited precisely because the khan—covetous of her naked flesh—had forbidden her to do so. She told me that the council members, fearing eavesdroppers, craving silence, and taking music for the devil's work, had the place carpeted in Tadjik felt and curtained with double-weight Han silk.

When one was summoned to that hall, it was by palanquin. Such court conveyances were customarily decorated with lacquered flowers edged in mother-of-pearl and furnished on the inside with soft green satin. The council's palanquin, an instrument designed for the first stages of terror and intimidation, was stained dull black with only a hard, bare bench inside. When it arrived, I refused to enter it.

"Have I been accused of a crime?" I demanded of the four bearers, who between them had the wits of a goat.

"No, Prince Yang," they chorused.

My father was standing by and seemed not the least bit afraid for me. Rather, he grinned at hearing me referred to as a prince.

"Remember, this summons is just for the purpose of what I have achieved by creating you," he offered in his usual, self-centered fashion.

He was always this way, either a demon or a demigod, one moment passionate, one moment indifferent. How could a son attach to this person? What could one hold onto? What could one reliably grasp?

"I'll walk," I said.

This decision had no precedent, but then neither did I. My steely gaze decided it, as did my apparent willingness to fight. In the end, the bearers trudged behind me—my father, too, for he was by my side—all the way to the special, sacred, council chambers.

Despite his personal leanings toward Mongolian tradition

and the teachings of the Awakened One known as the Buddha, the khan tolerated religious diversity because his grandfather had convinced him that such permissiveness contributed to the stability of an empire. Accordingly, the counsel was religiously diverse. There were, to begin, two Buddhists in the group. The first was a Zen monk who had been caught in the act of spying for Japan. Any spy would customarily have been remanded to the custody of the torture minister, but in deference to the man's startling serenity in the face of dismemberment, the khan, in his wisdom, transmuted his sentence to spiritual service for the court. Where the Japanese monk was taciturn, his Himalayan counterpart was fond of throat singing.

A Sufi was part of the assemblage too. In order to better commune with his god, it was his wont to spin on his feet until he dizzily toppled over. Although I couldn't be sure he was holy, he interested me because his desire to connect with heaven caused a tearful upwelling in me for which I had no explanation. At the time, I took this for a seed deliberately planted in me by my father — who often spoke of the succor and strength available to those able to commune with deities — but sensed the feeling might be the result of something older and deeper. Whatever the reason, I could not even look at the Sufi without being overcome by the strong ache of longing.

A Christian priest also sat on the council, an emissary from Rome, a city located on the far edge of the empire. He constantly fingered necklace beads quite similar to those worn by the Himalayan, save for the cross of dense wood. His scalp rained white flakes onto his dark cassock and he cleared his throat more often than he spoke. Court gossip had it he kept a young Mongol girl as a consort, something Kublai said he found amusing insofar as the priest professed, in his public appearances, to be chaste.

Though the Buddhist found him a bumpkin and the Christian

a heathen, there was also a Taoist shaman on the council. He earned his seat, I was told, because he had a good record predicting both natural calamities and enemy incursions. I learned later he was a poet of some note and devoted himself to the contemplation of mountain peaks, rocks, watercourses, and trees.

Yet it was the rabbi who ruled the group, having issued me the summons to appear, and it was he who recorded the proceedings with his quill pen. He was black-eyed, pale and thin, with the significant nose my mother had described. His forearms were very well-developed for an aesthete, which made me wonder about his secrets.

"Would you rather sit or stand?" he asked me. "I am not sufficiently familiar with your construction to know which is more comfortable for you."

"At your pleasure, holiness," I replied, allowing a note of sarcasm to creep into my voice.

He waved his hand. "You can dispense with your nonsense. I've heard too many tales of your arrogance to be fooled by false humility, and my friends here on the council know me too well to believe in my holiness. Do you know why you are here?"

"You're curious," I said.

He nodded. "We are. Some people—Queen Tegulen first and foremost among them—claim you are a mechanical being with a soul, a miracle unique in history."

"What should it matter to you if I am? I'm here and I play my role. If you want to know the details of my composition, you have only to ask the man who made me."

"An interesting point," opined the Sufi, staring at my father. "If you are what the queen claims, however, then it is not possible for a man to have made you."

"Unless, of course, the man was merely the agent of God and

acting as His hands," said the priest. "There is a precedent for this, of course, as God has given all men a divine spark...."

"But one man more than others, eh?" said the rabbi.

The Zen monk stood up and approached me. "May I touch you?"

I nodded, and he ran his hands wonderingly over my back. "Cold, hard stone," he murmured. "Yet somehow pliable and obviously alive."

"Anything and everything may have Buddha nature," said the man from the high Himalayas.

"And yet it is not the surface we are gathered to assess, but what lies beneath," the rabbi countered.

"You cannot assess it," interrupted my father. "It is not your place to do so, and even if it were, you lack the required skills."

"You may be right," the rabbi answered. "But why not aid us in our inquiry? Tell us how you so subtly animated this *golem* of yours and how you came to make him from jade rather than clay?"

"Don't be a jackass," my father snapped. "I know enough of Jewish mysticism to know a *golem* lacks creativity, free will, and a soul. He does only the bidding of his master. Yang is no such creature. On the contrary, he has all the urges and complexities of any other boy."

How was it my father knew such things? Where had he learned them? I yearned for his secrets not because I wanted his power but because I wanted share something with him, to feel close.

"Of any other *man*, from the look of him," the priest observed.

"If you gave him a soul," the rabbi continued, "do tell us where you got it."

"Yes," the Sufi said, leaning forward eagerly. "Knowing more would bring us closer to Allah."

"And perhaps the Awakened One," added the Himalayan.

"At some point in my creative process, a spontaneous life arose," my father replied. "I have nothing further to say on the matter."

"An insufficient demurral," declared the priest.

"Please tell us where you learned your skills and how you employed them to animate metal and stone," the rabbi insisted.

"Yang is of my own devising."

"One can no more imbue stone with a soul than pluck a star from the sky," the priest said flatly. "Yet Queen Tegulen says this is exactly what you have done. Any suggestion that God has taken your hands in his is pure blasphemy, of course, but a clever way of angling for princely succession."

"I see," said my father. "You're not really here to investigate whether Yang has a soul but instead to decree he doesn't."

At long last, the Taoist shaman stood up. He wore a red robe and the end of his beard reached nearly to his navel. Many of the beards I'd seen in the capital featured bits of recent breakfast, lunch, and dinner items, but his was blue-black and shimmered from what I guessed were frequent and meticulous lathering in oil.

"The inventor's is the only candid voice among you," he said. "And he correctly identifies each of you in pursuit of your own agenda, whether serving Queen Chabi in her quest to deprive this boy of his throne as son of the first queen, or to support your own brand of divine doctrine against the challenge the boy represents. The way of nature can only be revealed to us through deep and strenuous meditation. Meditating, I have come to understand Prince Yang to be as we are, but simply made of different stuff."

"Well, what those of us not blessed with our bearded friend's special sight can at least agree upon is that Yang appears aware of himself," the rabbi said, sounding weary.

"At times it may require a devout eye to distinguish between the work of God and the work of his fallen archangel, Lucifer," the priest murmured.

"Who is to say this is not your god's work?" the Japanese monk inquired quietly. "Do you believe yourself aware of all of his workings, motives, and plans? Are you even sure there is but one kind of soul?"

"Indeed, what of the souls of those who are below or above us in the reincarnation cycle?" finished his compatriot, the Buddhist from the high Himalayas.

"Let me dance with him to discover who he is," proposed the Sufi.

Unable to contain myself, I leapt onto the table using my springy legs and raised my voice as loud as I could. "If there's one thing this Crown Prince resents, it is being talked about as if I am not here. I'm sick of your condescension and your secret agendas. Watching you malodorous, manipulative bags of mostly water, I can't help but conclude that there are precious few souls in this room equal to my own."

So saying, I accepted the Sufi's invitation. In his wiry arms I spun and spun until I saw stars and sensed them smiling at me.

"I'm Prince Yang!" I cried, as my father tapped out a dance beat with his toe. "And I will suffer no more at your hands."

"Prince Yang he most certainly is!" the Sufi master cried, birthing a smile on my father's face and the greatest possible gladness in my heart.

11

DURING ALL those winters staring wistfully at Christmas windows alongside her mother and all those summer afternoons prowling the town in the company of eager, would-be boyfriends, Tegulen never made it down to the financial district near the bottom of Manhattan. Finally there, she stands before Wintermoth's ten-story corporate edifice. Even though surrounded by taller buildings, it stands out for its angular, ultra-modern design. Inside, she announces herself to the MothCo receptionist, a striking blonde in what could be a flight attendant uniform from the 1960s, narrow, narrow cap and all. The blonde asks Tegulen to wait, and while she does, she reads a paper brochure that asserts that all of the company's five hundred employees are committed to the betterment of mankind through ever-higher levels of technology.

Adjacent to the reception desk is a six-foot-tall, highly detailed scale model of the building. The plaque beside it says the building is fully bulwarked against conflagration, invasion, quakes, storms, and tides. One side of the building is glass so that all the details inside are visible, and they're a triumph of modeling. The upper levels are starkly modern in keeping with the outside of the building, and the legend beside the model says these floors are devoted entirely to cerebration and intellectual exchange. Grittier work clearly takes place in the lower-level workshops, which bristle with laser cutters, titanium mills, and scanners, all lit by tiny little Tiffany lamps that actually glow. Teg wonders whether the steampunk-style overhead ducts were inspired by her father's mansion.

Wintermoth appears behind her, spookily quiet, revealed only by his cologne, which today bears notes of birch bark.

"What a pleasant surprise, Tegulen. Welcome to MothCo."

"I have to compliment you on this model. The detail is amazing."

"Thank you. Your father and I shared an admiration for that kind of precision work. And I have to compliment *you* on the beautiful silk pantsuit you're wearing! Chartreuse is one of my favorite colors."

"Thanks for noticing. I've never spent so much money on an outfit before."

"Keep spending it. You have wonderful taste."

She points to the words *Intelligence in Service* emblazoned across the marble floor. "This is your motto?"

"The MothCo creed, yes."

"Tell me more."

He takes her elbow as fluidly as a dancer and leads her to a reception couch. When they sit, he shifts so their legs touch. She notices his are unusually warm.

"So, despite our friend, the head...."

"Yang," she corrects him.

"Despite Yang, robots don't necessarily need to look human."

"I really can't bring myself to think of him as a robot."

"That brings up something I really want to share with you, something I'm really excited about, namely that we are at the start of the Second Machine Age, part of which is a redefinition of what a robot is and does and looks like."

She raises her hand like a schoolgirl. "Leading me to ask the obvious question...."

Wintermoth nods. "Of course. In the *First* Machine Age, we replaced our muscles with industrial devices. In the Second, we will replace our minds with artificial intelligence."

"I've heard that some artificial intelligence researchers think that the universe is using humanity as a tool to create an artificial intelligence that will evolve at an incredible pace and finally self-realize, whatever that means. Do you think that?"

"I'm flattered you prepared so thoroughly for this meeting."

"Actually, it's more about Yang than it is about you, Sebastian, and I learned that a few years before I heard Minnie and Delia say your name. I admit to doing some recent homework, though. There's nothing like finding a talking head in her father's watch collection to stimulate a woman's curiosity."

She notices how smooth his skin his and how dashing his features. Like a swarthy Errol Flynn minus the mustache, she thinks, in those ridiculous early Hollywood romantic swashbucklers her mother unaccountably enjoyed. He plumps his lower lip when he smiles, and his perfectly straight teeth look like little soldiers in a military lineup. Fleetingly, she wonders what it might be like to kiss him.

"All that is pretty lofty and theoretical stuff," he says. "What we're trying to do at MothCo is a lot more practical and down-to-Earth. We want to build smart, strong, obedient machines to make our lives easier."

"Don't we diminish our own humanity if we replace humans with robots in all kinds of jobs? What about the old lady in a nursing home pining for human company in her last days? Does she really want a robot by her side? What about creativity and spirituality? What about belonging to our families and communities and something far larger than those? What will we do with our time when our machines do everything for us?"

"We'll be free to enjoy our lives, to create new and wonderful things."

"So, you're building slaves."

Wintermoth shrugs. "Not unless you consider a can opener a slave, or a vacuum cleaner, or a car. Even a toilet follows human bidding."

"But toilets don't think."

"Not yet, but soon."

"I hope not. The last thing I want is to sit on a self-aware toilet."

"I'm not talking about self-aware. Although we could certainly create a toilet that says 'ouch' when you sit on it or 'good job' when your visit is productive, other companies can do that. I'm not in the toilet business. Nor am I in the business of making artificial intelligence ubiquitous in our lives, because it already is."

"Unless everything I've read is wrong, everyone in robotics and AI is after the same thing."

"Actually, they're not. Most companies are interested in freeing the population from mundane tasks and dangerous work. Too, they're after an even more laudable goal, which is to free people from trading a renewable resource, money, for an unrenewable one, time."

"Using AI?"

"And robotics. AI is already ubiquitous, and it will get better and spread even further into all our lives."

"But you're after something different?"

Wintermoth smiles. "Fundamentally so. AI, yes, but not merely quantum computing, as powerful as that promises to be. No, I'm in pursuit of an entirely new form of intelligence that is not merely computational but creative. The kind of intelligence that not only frees *us* to be more creative but is more creative itself. That's something you don't hear the advocates for quantum computing and super AI talking about. Everyone's all about computational power. I see creativity as a higher intellectual function than merely doing more of what we already do, and faster. I want this company to achieve a truly creative AI. Can you imagine a world filled with art and music and literature and more, all created by an intelligence greater than our own?"

"Talk of higher powers makes me nervous," says Teg. "I'm not the religious type."

"This isn't religion. It's science."

"Nope. It's an evolutionarily developed social function meant to increase social cohesiveness and lend resource advantages to those who stick together. That describes how you see things and it describes a religion, too."

"Arlington's daughter for sure," Wintermoth shakes his head. "Let's have a tour, shall we?"

Teg follows him to the elevator. Inside, Wintermoth leans against the herringbone-patterned stainless-steel paneling and stares at her insouciantly. She's uncomfortable and is grateful to be rescued by the chime of her wristwatch. She shows him the figures on the watch face as they raise their masks.

"I know that beautiful piece very well," he says. "In fact, I'm the one who suggested it to your father. You show great taste wearing it."

She gives him a palms-together bow and hopes he doesn't think she's mocking him, because she isn't.

The door opens and they step into a corridor glowing with blue fiber-optic light, a glass door at the end. They walk to it and look through at a team of people sitting in a circle, video controllers in their hands and virtual reality helmets on their heads. Nobody looks older than twenty-five.

"Robot designers," says Wintermoth. "They're brainstorming

in a virtual world, jumping right into each other's visions."

"What are they designing?"

"Top secret," says Wintermoth.

"Flying drones? They're all the rage for deliveries now."

He puts his finger to his lips.

"What? You tell me and then you have to kill me? They're working on some new version of Robocop, right?"

He feigns distress. "You found me out."

"Seriously, though. I heard you were designing this eight-foot combat giant that struts like a supermodel. That doesn't sound like some utopian quest for artificially intelligent creativity to me."

"Have you thought of going into the field?"

"Don't patronize me."

"There are certain realities, Tegulen. I described the project I'm most excited about because, well, I'm most excited about it. But that kind of research is costly and we have to pay for it with more down-to-earth projects. As it happens, the bipedal gait is great for covering distance on uneven terrain. It's very efficient. Like us. Born to the savannah, walking all day, outlasting even lions."

"So it's a cop or a soldier? Something for police or military contracts?"

"Only a fool turns down government work. The working model you're referring is for search and rescue. While it *could* carry a gun, what it actually *does* carry is 500lbs of supplies to inaccessible places. We've even given it Frank Sinatra's voice."

"Now you're mocking me."

He shakes his head. "Mellifluous tones soothe people in crisis."

"Yeah, well, I'm having a crisis of my own right now."

"Do tell."

"I'm starving to death."

Wintermoth smiles. "There's a cafeteria at the penthouse."

They take the elevator again. This time the door opens to a spacious dining area in front of a wall of glass. The sun gleams over Staten Island and New York Harbor behind an array of salads—glistening asparagus with olives, fusilli graced with chanterelles, field greens peppered with sundried tomatoes and redolent of balsamic vinegar.

"The beef is grass-fed, the poultry is cage-free, and the fish is tested free of heavy metals," says Wintermoth. "Does the chef approve?"

Teg puts her hands on her hips. "And who told you I'm a chef?"

"You're the talk of the town."

"If that were true, and we both know it isn't, the gossip would be about inheriting my father's money not about my catering ambitions and my chocolate souffle."

Wintermoth places a mug bearing the MothCo logo—a blue gear cog with a red heart at its center—into a high-tech espresso machine.

"It's about you for all you are. You like your mocha dark, yes? No milk no sugar? And the machine's loaded with artisanal chocolate from a small town in Belgium."

"First, you know my father liked the look of rose gold on his skin, and now you know how I like my coffee? You're creeping me out."

He pours the milk. "You can go online and read everything about me, and that's okay, but I suss out a thing or two about you and that's creepy? Your sarcastic wit is charming and you find my close relationship with your father unnerving. What's a guy to do to get you to like him?"

Teg laughs in spite of herself. "I guess you have a point."

"Your dad was my friend. We've lost him. I'm trying to be helpful. If you want to hunt for Yang's missing parts, I'll do what I can to assist you. I can rearrange my schedule to be ready this weekend. We can take my plane to Asia."

"What?"

"It's better than flying commercial. You don't have to deal with all those lines and people and the constant announcements that stop you from sleeping."

"You really expect me to travel across the world with you?"

"I don't expect anything, but I'd be honored. Plus, it would be fun."

"You get how forward that is, right? I mean, I don't know you at all."

"I told you we could fix that and we can. I like fixing things. Always have."

12

AFTER ONLY a short time in court, I became aware that soft people were not the creatures of their social rank they pretended to be, nor defined primarily by their gender, age, good looks, influence, or wealth. In fact, they were creatures of time, by which I mean an ongoing process whose exact nature still eludes me other than that I understand it makes each moment of each day entirely unique. When I asked those same people about the nature of time, they offered fuzzy philosophical claptrap or, in the case of a few of the lesser lords who fancy themselves as scientists, oral diarrhea of a particularly pungent sort.

My own appreciation of time was clearly more leisurely than that of those around me. The unfolding of minutes, hours, days, weeks, months, and years imbued me with neither sadness nor urgency; indeed, I found that unfolding to be of great interest. When I sat by the khan's carp pond in Xanadu, for example, I became obsessed not only with the surprising longevity of the fish themselves but also with the rate at which the water flowing into the pond eroded the stones in its course. It was clear to me that in a hundred years, well within the lifetime of the younger of the fish, the erosion would result in the pond looking quite different.

I observed that the passage of time elicited in all things a fall toward chaos. Whether it was in the distribution of pebbles on a path, the growth of branches on a tree, the wilting of flowers, the lines on the faces of members of the court community, the subtle aging of the khan's concubines, or the appearance of the great man himself, the ravages of time were omnipresent. When I shared such observations, I was generally treated to malicious looks. The more such reactions I got, the more curious I became about what my father had done to make me immune to the effects of time.

"I made you rigid," he answered when I asked him about it. "All that changes is your thinking, because you can learn."

"What does that have to do with aging?"

"If something doesn't change, it's immune to time. Wind and rain and cold and heat likewise have no effect on you. Rather, you maintain the precise dimensions I gave you at the start."

"How is this so?"

He gave me an impatient look. "Using hammer and fire, I combined certain metals to make your cables resistant to stretching. In short, you simply don't degrade."

I began to wonder whether my longevity might not offer me a different perspective and understanding of the nature of time.

"I've seen water degrade stone," I said. "If I stood under a waterfall, I would get shorter after a while."

"Don't stand under any waterfalls, but don't fear water either," my father answered. "You need it."

My father had given me a mouth so that I could keep company with soft people, and a small door beneath my naval from which to extract those foodstuffs once I was out of polite company. Drinking, however, was a different matter.

"I get thirsty," I said.

"I gave you thirst because you must drink. Water keeps you flexible in body and mind, keeps your memories alive and keeps you learning and changing in step with outside forces and events."

"Flexibility," I repeat.

"Very important."

"Mother says that, too. Says that's why she performs her exercises."

"I'm sure she exercises for other reasons, too," my father grinned, "but she certainly is flexible."

The tone of his comment led me to deduce a connection between movement and the prolongation of youth, between flexibility and sexual desirability. I connected the first observation to my Sufi dance lesson — the Sufi master was a youthful man — and the second to the khan's comments about Queen Chabi in the bedroom. I wondered whether that nefarious usurper might be flexible, and I made it my mission to find out.

No, I didn't hide under Kublai's bed when Chabi made one of her frequent visits to the royal chambers; I had too much respect for the khan to do that. Instead, I found a eunuch who had access to the upstart queen's chambers, and in exchange for prevailing upon my father to fashion for him a painless cleaning brush for his tortured privates, the castrato found me a place to hide so I could watch the queen in her quarters.

My secret perch was inside what French visitors to the court called an *armoire*. Chabi's was decorated with designs from Central Asia: camels, whirling sand funnels, palm trees, and watercourses painted a blue so brilliant they could only be the work of a desert trekker who had been treated to a mirage worthy of an oracle or saint. I stepped into the cabinet before the queen entered the room and left the doors ever so slightly ajar so I could peer through it.

I expected Chabi to get undressed, and she did, but only down to a loose-fitting slip in which, as the eunuch had promised she would, she began her exercise routine. I was surprised to discover it was not the languorous tantric stretching my mother favored, but instead a thorough, symmetrical series of opening and closing movements. She bent down to touch her toes and then came up again, using the strong muscles of the very legs she presumably used to wrap up the khan like a snake coiling around a sparrow. Her torso became a sort of fireplace bellows, gathering energy like air and propelling it around the body. She departed the room as soon as she had finished the routine, leaving a cloud of flower essence and musk hanging in the air.

I waited a few moments to be safe, then headed straight for my father's workshop. I found him holding a freshly severed elephant trunk in one hand and a finely wrought silver gear in the other.

"Chabi's a Taoist," I burst out. "I recognize her moves!"

My father tried not to laugh. "Don't be silly. She's Mongol through and through."

"You say that because of her features. Yet you worship Taoist gods even though you look nothing like the Taoist priest on the khan's council. I don't think one has to be born to Taoism; I think one can adopt it for its power."

I'm told soft people have distinct lines between their senses, but for someone like me, ideas and emotions are one, perhaps because my feelings are rational and my ideas often arise from my passions and needs. I can smell the pig all over a piece of bacon, for example, and the details of a given pig's demise greatly determines how its bacon will taste in my mouth. I can taste a field of wildflowers from a distance of two *li* and know the satisfaction of the earth in bringing those flowers forth. When I touch copper, I taste it on my tongue, and when I'm around fish, I can hear them breathe and feel their joy in buoyancy. The taste of honey creates a bee symphony in my ears along with a sense of fierce determination, and the slightest glimpse of water buffalo fills me with a strange sense of power and, simultaneously, a certain cognitive dullness. When a soft woman reaches her time of the month, I am so aware of the scent and color of her blood that I forego pomegranates at a banquet in sympathy for the volatility of her feelings.

Seeing my father's reaction to my words, I sniffed a secret on him, and subterfuge too. I was an expert in his scents and lies, and in trusting and distrusting him, too. The balancing act of a little jade son whose father had contravened nature. How could anything ever be stable between us? How could anything ever be normal?

"Wait a minute," I said. "Wait more than a minute. There's something going on here. Something you're not telling me, though I know what it is."

"You think so, do you?"

"She learned the secret Taoist stuff from you. You taught her."

"Don't be silly. Why would I help your mother's rival?"

"To give her bedroom powers, of course. To help her seduce the khan so he would leave my mother to you. What other smoke are you blowing at me from that mystical pipe of yours? What other tricks are you playing?"

We stared at each other with frank hostility for what seemed like an age. Finally, he exhaled.

"I don't know what you're talking about. Are you a trick? Is my love for your mother a trick? Is Chabi's jealousy a trick? Do you or do you not have the khan of khan's genuine affection?"

Sensing he would never admit what I now plainly knew, I changed the subject.

"Teach me Chabi's routine," I said.

"You imagine the set will enhance your own sexual performance? Haven't I blessed you enough in that department? Do you fancy a maiden of the court? I can arrange a meeting, if you like."

"I don't want a maiden now; I want to learn the routine. I can perform it when I'm bored."

Something about what I said set my father off. He had that kind of temper. Mercurial would be a nice way of putting it. He'd been working on a silver gearbox for some project. He was also dissecting an elephant trunk, convinced there was something there that allowed the beasts to communicate—a phenomenon he himself had observed—by producing sounds he concluded were above or below the range of soft hearing. He put the gearbox down and took a menacing step in my direction. If he hadn't tripped over that bloody trunk, who knows what might have happened.

The fact that he *did* trip was not unexpected, given that my clumsy father was a perfect exemplar of such small calamities. He was always stumbling on low steps, stubbing his toes on the legs of tables, and spilling soup on his tunic. He was as likely to start and stagger at the sudden appearance of his own shadow as he was to dress with a sandal on one foot and a boot on the other as he was to devise a way to make water run uphill using a pump powered by burning donkey turds. Being so short in stature didn't help, but it was no excuse. After all, I am even smaller and yet am all athleticism and grace.

His physical ineptitude embarrassed and frustrated him, and falling as he was about to yell at me didn't make things any better. He climbed to his feet wrestling visibly with his temper.

"I didn't build you to be bored," he snapped at me. "I built you to constantly inquire, seek new connections, see patterns, and grow. I built you to prove my genius."

That last declaration hung in the air a moment, conspicuous for the absence of any reference to my mother. This was, after all, the man who had only recently claimed he did everything, including making me, in the name of love.

"Don't show me the exercises then," I said haughtily. "I don't care. I've already memorized them."

So saying I launched into exactly the routine I had seen Chabi perform. When I was done, his anger had changed to surprise. He wiped his hands on his robe and bade me repeat the movements, this time after him.

The first movement entailed raising his hands above his head, the second spreading his chest like an archer, the third and fourth twisting his spine, the fifth bending over and rotating his upper body upon the pillars of his hips, the sixth reaching up then bending down to touch the ground in front of him, the seventh making his fists tight, first right and then left, and the last lifting himself up onto his toes and then dropping down hard onto his heels.

"You connect the movements to your breath," I said. "Since I don't breathe, I'm not sure how to time my movements."

"Then find another beat to follow."

Ever the obedient son on the outside, ever the investigator of my own true nature—and through that the truth of nature itself—I turned my attention inward. I searched until I found something that might serve as a substitute, namely the rhythmic pumping of the bellows inside me that stand in for a heart. Trying the exercises again, I might not have felt the increase in vitality or flexibility that drove both queens to the routine but I did find something else—namely a path to understanding that thing soft people call time.

And to mark and measure its passing.

13

Ever since the first meeting with Jules Burfield, Tegulen has wondered if she might be involved in some highly-detailed and long-running dream, a bit of delusional wish-fulfillment activated during two seemingly endless months of watching her mother's painful and protracted death. Returning to the New Jersey apartment they had shared, she plops down on her bed and gingerly withdraws Yang from the Prada satchel she purchased upon learning she was rich. She feels his heft and runs her fingers over his cheeks and brow, marveling how any dream could be quite so immediate and substantial.

"What do you think of my new purse?" she asks him.

"Feels like a jail," he says, opening his eyes.

"Don't you have special skills that can let you see through it?"

"Maybe. There are still so many things I don't remember."

"Anyway, I don't like the bag either, though I suppose I should."

"Then why did you buy it?"

"An experiment. My mother was a child of the steppe, even if she was generations removed from it. She always told me that money doesn't buy happiness, that possessions rapidly became encumbrances, and that fancy stuff doesn't necessarily work better than simple stuff. I guess I wanted to find out for myself."

"Sorting out what's true and what isn't can take more than a lifetime. And even then, you're not sure."

"I'm in this lifetime for real," Teg says fiercely.

"You're hungry for it, I'll say that much."

"If by hungry you mean that I have an appetite for experience and adventure, I was like that long before I inherited my father's money. I want to see what I can do, see the world, understand everything, experience everything. I want to meet the right guy, too, so long as he doesn't hold me back."

"You mean the way your mother did."

Teg tightens her lips. "She didn't mean to. Don't all parents hold us back? No matter how well-meaning they are? Isn't it sort of their job to do that, so we grow roots and a strong trunk, sort of like a tree, and then we spread out and leave them behind?"

"I'm pretty sure my parents gave little thought to the job of raising me," he said.

"You had parents?"

Yang gives her an indignant look. "Did you think I sprang from the earth like a plant?"

Teg adjusts her collar. "It's just...."

"That I am hard gold and harder jade? That I have diamond soles instead of crusty flesh that grows fungus?"

"You were made of jade and diamonds?"

"And will be again when we find my body. By the way, I noticed a lot of bumps and noises on the way here."

"Because we were on the subway. It's called that because it's a train, running underground, that carries people from one place to another."

"Ah. A conveyance. My father made one for the khan's olives. Not under the ground, of course, but from the imperial kitchens to the khan's private quarters."

"How can you remember an olive cart but not know where your own body is?"

"Only a wizard could answer such a question."

"Sleeping so deeply that you forget yourself must have been quite a treat. Did you dream happy dreams?"

"All I know is that I'm glad to be awake," Yang sighs.

"I feel the same way," says Teg.

"Do you mean that you have also awakened? If so, you've either communed with the dead or fallen in love."

"Neither. I've recently had a big change of life."

There is a loud explosion on the street outside. In response, Yang screams as if his yawning wormhole of a mouth connects to the very nebula of noise. Tegulen crosses the room to him and lifts him up.

"Will you stop screaming? It's only a car backfiring."

Yang takes a moment to compose himself. "That was really loud," he says. "Anyway, I'm sorry. I'm not quite myself. I can't dance, I can't jump, and I can't clap. I'm so pitiful it seems that screaming is the only thing I can do."

"You can speak like a civilized person."

Yang sniffs. "All right. I'll try. What is this backfiring?"

"Another noise made by a conveyance. It's a neighbor's old rust bucket."

"I've seen many buckets but never one that farted so loudly."

"Now you're trying too hard to be funny. I'm talking about a car. It's been in the neighborhood for years. My mother told me such harmless explosions happen because of faulty ignition timing in the engine. She had knowledge of unexpected things. She even told the neighbor, but he simply demanded she pay to get it fixed if it bothered her so much. I suppose I could do that now but I don't want to reward a jackass like that, even if we all have to listen to that bang now and then."

"Show me the rust bucket."

"What do you mean?"

86

"Take me outside. I want to see it."

She's about to refuse but having dragged him around on the subway in a dark bag decides instead to indulge him. She tucks him under her arm and takes him outside to the offending car, a rusty Chevrolet Corvair from the early 1960s.

"This conveyance is poorly designed," he says as she walks him around it. "Especially at the rear. But I can fix it."

"Fix it?"

"So it no longer disturbs you. Put me on the ground please, near the engine."

She does. The gears protruding from below his neck make him unstable on a flat surface so she steadies him with her finger on his crown.

"Left," he says.

She moves him left.

"Now a little farther under the car."

"I'm going to stain my jeans," she says.

"It won't take long. You can wash them. All right. Stop there."

When she does, he closes his eyes. Through her finger she can feel him start to vibrate.

"What are you doing?"

He doesn't answer but she feels the frequency of the vibration change. It grows stronger and stronger. Her whole arm begins to shake.

"Maybe you should stop now," she says.

He still won't answer. The vibration changes frequency one more time, then abruptly stops. She withdraws him from under the car, wiping the soot off her elbow and her knees.

"What was that all about?" she asks.

"This device functions by making little explosions."

"Most cars still do."

"I know something about explosions. Certain variables have

87

to coincide for them to happen. These variables were not quite right in this machine. I fixed them."

"By vibrating parts back into place? You weren't even touching the thing."

Yang smiles. "If vibrations didn't travel through the air, there wouldn't be music and we couldn't be talking right now, right?"

Teg stares at him, trying to determine if he's being sarcastic. He gives her nothing. She puts him back under her arm and they return to the apartment. She goes to her dresser drawer and takes out her passport. The last time she used it was en route to Puerto Vallarta, the trip a prize after her mother won a sweepstakes sponsored by a Swedish sewing machine company. Despite finding the colorful fashions and swirling skirts titillating, Teg remembers very little of the trip because on the second day, a poisoned *guanabana* ice cream cone kept her on the toilet for days.

"What is that?"

"A document for traveling."

"So you're considering Wintermoth's offer."

She holds up a strand of pearls. "What do you think of these? They're natural, not cultured. They were my mother's. My father must have given them to her."

"If they're precious to you, I wouldn't bring them. There are a lot of thieves in Central Asia. Anyway, Sebastian Wintermoth already wants to make love with you so you don't really need to entice him further with jewels."

The necklace slips from her hand, hits the hardwood floor of her bedroom, and breaks. Pearls of graduated sizes roll in all directions. She drops to her knees to chase after them.

"Can you not say stuff like that?" she cries, grabbing one after another, desperate to find any she's missed. "Look what you made me do. I don't even know how many...."

"Forty-eight," says Yang. "If you put me on the floor and turn me around, I can help you find them."

She does, and he directs her to the only two she misses, one hiding behind the leg of her bureau and another across the floor near a stand she uses for hats.

"Your eyes are better than mine," she says.

"Of course. They were designed and built to be."

"Humility excluded from the design, apparently. Why did you say that about Sebastian?"

"To calm your concerns about your wardrobe. You're easily distracted by talk of him. Do you always behave this way around men? It leaves you vulnerable, you know."

"I *don't* always behave this way around men," she says fiercely.

"Around the ones you like, then?"

"I don't even like him. You're missing the point."

"Enlighten me, then."

"I'm worried now that I have all this money I'm going to become as arrogant and disconnected as he is. I was raised to avoid rich people, not to become one of them."

"You're not him. You can choose your own path. Wealth can be a powerful tool for good."

"Not that my father was an example in that department."

"Again, I remind you that you are not your parents or anyone else. You're you."

Teg is quiet for a bit. "Sometimes when I wear the necklace, I worry the pearls the way monks and nuns do with beads when they pray," she says after a while.

"Are you a Buddhist?"

"I'm nothing, really."

"Do you have a god?"

"Maybe, but not the bearded one sitting on a cloud and clucking when I buy sexy underwear."

"Wintermoth could be your god. He *is* very tall and I'm certain he would appreciate your underwear. Strangely, Muslim men can be very compelling to Mongolian women, although such unions may be culturally problematic."

Teg pauses in her count of the pearls cupped in her palm. "What makes you think he's Muslim?"

"You deny you find him attractive?"

"My God, it's like talking to a carousel horse. Tell me about the weather in China, will you? We're going north, yes? I'm picturing Genghis Khan and his soldiers stolid against a cold, gray sky."

"Kublai, not Genghis—the grandson, not the grandfather; the builder, not the conqueror. But there might be snow."

"Really? Even in spring?"

"Seasons run together in north Asia. There are no hard boundaries, except for the wildflowers and those crazy little tortoises whose blood does not freeze."

Teg opens her closet and surveys her wardrobe. "I don't have a thing to wear."

"Every queen says the same thing."

"I'm no queen."

"A fact most queens won't admit, so perhaps you are not one after all. How about that long coat over there?"

Teg pulls out a gray flannel duster with a wide hem, double buttons, and a high collar. "This old thing?"

"It suits you. And I happen to know what a carousel horse is and am offended to be likened to one."

She waves him off, doesn't want to get drawn into it, dons a black, saucer-shaped, woolen hat and draws it down around her short hair. "Very Audrey Hepburn, yes? Never mind, don't answer. She's my fashion idol. My mother always said I looked like her, and that's all you need to know."

"Everything is so pale and gray in this strange world of yours," says Yang. "Where I come from, the sky is blue and the grass is bright. The people I've seen so far in this world have no sense of color. You, on the other hand, obviously understand the subtle harmonies and balance available to a woman of taste."

"I think you're homesick. Maybe the trip will make you feel better."

"You would have enjoyed the styles of the court," Yang says wistfully.

"Did your mother dress you?"

Yang thinks for a minute. "If memory serves, it was actually the khan who arranged for the first article of clothing I can remember wearing, and I believe the bitch queen, Chabi, drove him to it. Anyway, I suggest layers for your trip. My father was the master of making something out of nothing and he always traveled with items he could combine to meet any temperature."

"My life feels like a storm. Not even one week ago, I lived alone in this apartment. The only diamonds I saw were in magazines and on the fingers of clients. Now I've got a fortune, a brownstone, and a friend missing diamonds and jade."

"A friend," says Yang. "That's nice of you to say."

"Well, it's true. I have so few. Please tell me about your father."

"We had a life in the palace. Then we left. We traveled. I don't remember the details."

"And then?"

"He died, of course. He was soft. What else do you think would happen?"

"Right. Okay. I'm thinking layers." Tegulen holds up two cashmere sweaters she got on a splurge at a Bloomingdales' sale: one violet and one blue, one turtleneck, the other with a scooped collar."

"Have you anything in red?"

"Too passionate," says Teg. "I never wear it."

"You need to reconsider. When you hide your flame inside a paper bag, everything gets burned."

Teg smiles. "Your light, not your flame."

"I said flame and I meant it. Now what are you thinking for shoes?"

She tosses a high pair into the bag, and a low pair too.

"No high heels," says Yang.

"This girl goes nowhere without heels."

"This girl hasn't been where we're going. The land is fierce. Soft feet need protection."

Sighing dramatically, she replaces the heels with a pair of waterproof Timberlands, a gift from an old boyfriend who told her the best way for her to repair her repressive frigidity was to hike the Appalachian Trail in summer.

"I bet Sebastian travels with bearers," she says. "Sherpas. Porters. Whatever."

Yang looks around the room as best he can, given that his eyes can move but not his neck. "But that's not your style."

"You got that right. I won't take more than I can comfortably carry."

She grabs her favorite pair of taupe suede pumps and shoves them in between the boots. Outside, cicadas buzz. It's as if their conductor is a wristwatch aficionado himself and knows the right moment for things, understands the mechanical precision required for the lowering of his chitinous baton. Tegulen Elliot loves spring in New Jersey, but she won't see much more of this one.

14

EARLY ONE AUTUMN, before the court returned to the winter capital, Chabi summoned me to her favorite Xanadu gazebo, which was built out over a lake. The moment I arrived, she put on the airs of a woman of leisure. The effort was laughable. Chabi could no more be languid than a hornet could be a butterfly. She dismissed the maid who had been massaging her feet and bade me take over, telling me she was curious as to the feel of my jade hands on her flesh. She had very little to say as I rolled her foot between my fingers, but as I traced the moist valleys between her toes her breathing grew rapid. When I bore down harder, she squirmed. When I touched her as softly as a feather, in gentle strokes back and forth, she arched her hips, and whimpered, eventually growing rigid all over and pointing her toes clear out of my grasp. It did seem — though naturally I kept the observation to myself — that my father and the khan were not the only ones who had some small sensitivity when it came to women.

As she recovered in sleep, I watched carp gulp flies from the surface of the lake and listened to the gurgling of the current. There were many lovely grounds in the garden capital but the main theme of the city was water, including lakes, creeks, byways, and ponds. It could not really have been otherwise, as plentiful water and arable land were a seductive combination for the Mongols. The allure of such lands set against the freedoms of the steppe led to a two-headed worm inside every Mongol's soul, namely the Great Mongolian Paradox.

What was this famous enigma? Well, on one hand their gods, including the sky deity, Tengri, told them to cherish their way of life, hold their land as holy, and take pride in the superiority of their race. On the other hand, they lusted after the rewards of the civilized life developed by those they regarded as beneath them. They yearned to be fed without hunting, to be comforted by a bulging granary, and to have leisure time for more than horse-riding competitions and sword and arrow instruction. They were tempted by the material treasures a landholder may accumulate—but which a nomad may not—and were seduced by the pleasures of the flesh. They thought they were to be envied, but in the end, they were the ones who did the envying.

When Chabi opened her eyes, she pointed at the bevy of my father's mechanical swans paddling in indolent circles around us.

"You use your hands as competently as those fake birds do their feet, but do you *really* imagine you're more fit to be khan than they are?"

"Instead of insulting the crown prince, you should be atoning for your bad behavior," I replied.

She frowned. "Bad behavior?"

"Usurping my mother's place in the palace."

Rather than making her angry, this comment made her smile. It was, however, not a smile of satisfaction or joy, but the smile of someone who knows a secret. It made my lips pucker as if I'd eaten a too-sour plum.

"Are you familiar with the Chinese philosopher, Confucius?" she asked, batting her eyes.

I allowed that I was.

"Then you know my husband is a great devotee of his ideas."

"What sort of ideas?" I asked cautiously.

"Ruling in equable fashion, of course."

"What does that have to do with me?"

"Despite his obsession with rules and roles, Confucius would never endorse keeping great riches from the people. You, Yang, are nothing short of a national treasure. The rank and rabble need the opportunity to be inspired by your rare character and talents."

"Why do I distrust this compliment?"

"You shouldn't! In fact, I think so highly of you that I suggested to the khan that to keep you so close is selfish. At first, he was reluctant to agree, but I am happy to report that he is sending you to the outer limits of the empire, first to those once ruled by the Persians and the Turks, then to the land of Polo and his pope."

"What? No! I have no wish to leave the palace!"

"Even a prince must make sacrifices. You'll go with my guards, so it will be perfectly safe."

"Why do I need guards?"

"You're such an innocent boy. Despite the khan's best efforts, the world remains a cruel and dangerous place. You wouldn't last a moment without protection. Why, the diamonds on your feet alone would feed a village for a century."

"Then let me have my own guards. I don't want yours."

"You have none."

"Then my mother's men should accompany me."

"Having no real children and thus being of limited importance to the court, Queen Tegulen has few. The ones she does have are essential to her safety because, as you well know, she is a risk-taker of dubious judgment."

"The khan should give me my own guards, then."

Again, Chabi offers one of her terrible smiles. "But he has

done exactly that, Yang. Chosen from those who attend me because they are the best of the best."

I stood on no ceremony with Chabi, knowing there was no way she could really complain about my rudeness while continuing to assert I was nothing more than a wind-up toy. Accordingly, I immediately dashed off to see the khan.

I found him in the royal library, surrounded by officials and engaged in a discussion about taxation and representation. Among them was my father, who was then holding forth on social policy.

"If the people are overtaxed, they won't be loyal subjects," he was saying.

"What does an inventor know of taxes?" Kublai grumbled.

"Your Highness relies upon me to be familiar with the ways of nature and the workings of the world. Without such familiarity, I could not provide you with your most prized possessions. Trust me when I tell you that being kind and generous with your subjects is the best way to grow your riches and strengthen your rule."

"Trust you," the khan repeated, his face betraying nothing.

My father paled. "I'm merely pointing out that taxing people to pay for wars they don't care about will make your kingdom a shiny, oversized apple with populist worms at its core."

The khan gave one of his great guffaws. This was his way, to sit quietly and listen for a time and then suddenly erupt like thunder from a clear sky.

"Worms at its core!" he cried. "The irony!"

"Sire," I interrupted, thinking to forestall disaster.

"Ah! Yang who is fully a man. What can I do for you, my boy?"

"Queen Chabi says you are sending me away."

"Away? Oh, yes. To tour the western lands. Splendid idea.

One of the things I love about Queen Chabi is the way she always has the welfare of the empire at heart. She has helped me see how important it is to show and share a blessing as marvelous as you."

"My khan," my father interjected, visibly shaken. "The boy is not built to travel. He requires regular maintenance if all his parts and powers are to continue to work as you see them today."

"Queen Chabi predicted you would remind me of this," the khan replied heartily. "Never fear. All will be well here. You shall accompany Yang on his journey."

A small spot of blood appeared on my father's lip, evidence of an unfortunate meeting of tooth and tongue.

"But I cannot leave the palace, sire!" he exclaimed. "Who will care for your hand?"

He was, in this, of course referring to the replacement he had made for the khan after his injuries.

"Fear not, my inventive friend. My doctors have mastered its workings."

"What, then, of the sealed charcoal crucibles I have installed under the floors of your bedchambers so you can stretch your arthritic toes without discomfort? What of the air circulation system keeping your throne room free of summer mold? What of the moist pumps and fans required to cloud your gardens and keep them moist? What of the antics of the lifelike mechanical creatures I have made for you? There are so very many items here requiring my ongoing attention."

What he did not mention, of course, was that his cuckolding affair with my mother also required his presence.

"Born on the steppe and now confined to this property through my own indolence, I could scarcely have imagined the comforts and wonders you have provided me. Indeed, my very joints and bones are grateful."

"Sire," I broke in. "Would you not rethink this tour? I hate the idea of being away from you for so long."

The great khan took a long pause and nourished himself with a red thicket of plump grapes. "I'll be fine until we meet again, Yang, and you will be, too. Queen Chabi has selflessly offered the best of her guards to protect you."

"But..." my father interjected miserably.

"Don't trouble yourself, my esteemed servant. We elected not to tell you, but for the last months your apprentices have been reporting your every move to Queen Chabi, all the better to ease the pain of your departure."

"My every move?" It was all my father could do not to choke.

"They have shadowed you like mice," the khan allowed himself a cackle. "They have hovered above your night chambers like owls."

My father was well aware that it was the khan's way to cozy up to his victims with eye-twinkling joviality and then immediately set to slitting throats, freeing long ropes of intestine, and shredding men using horsepower and ropes.

"My night chambers?" he repeated, his voice quavering.

Kublai wiped his grape-stained fingers on his robe as I was told he used to do years ago, on horseback, with the blood of men. "Chabi tells me you never stop working. She says you never leave your shop. You're due some rest and now you shall have it. Go see the world with Yang for a year or two, and then return to us to share your experiences. While you're out there, show off your handiwork wherever people live in felt tents. Let your cleverness become a legend across the empire and thereby bring me glory. Is it not a perfect, perfect plan?"

I started to say something, and then I stopped. All the time I had been bribing eunuchs and worrying about the true nature of both time and my soul, Chabi had been methodically moving her pieces on the board game of succession so as to completely remove me from the line. Worse, it was now perfectly clear that all the time my father had been bedding my mother, the khan had been planning what we had to take for an exile fully as gruesome and fatal as consignment to the Ministry of Torture.

"Of course, Your Highness," my father bowed, likewise understanding everything and impressing me with his calm.

"I am envious at the very thought of such a journey," the khan smiled, snapping his fingers so his servants would bring lamb. "It is always such a pleasure to be afield on a pony under the big blue sky."

15

THEY FACE EACH other ensconced in plush leather seats with box-elder-bark trim. Tegulen wraps her arms around Yang's carrying satchel and brings her hands together in unconscious prayer. She has never before been launched straight up into the air.

"Don't worry," Wintermoth says as the Bell 430 helicopter rises from the asphalt at Newark. "Think of it as a glorified elevator."

"*Really* glorified," she murmurs.

"You're quite elegant today," he says. "A Eurasian Audrey Hepburn."

"I told you he likes you," Yang whispers, straining to see out over the edge of the bag.

Teg covers his mouth with her fingers. She can feel him trying to bite her. She cups her palm so his teeth can gain no purchase.

The Statue of Liberty comes into view, and then, behind it, the Verrazano Narrows Bridge. The pilot angles the helicopter slightly northeast, in the direction of Queens.

"You do this a lot?" she asks.

"Visit New Jersey? Extremely rarely."

"I meant fly in a helicopter."

"Only when I have to get somewhere quickly. There's a helipad on the roof of the MothCo building."

"Well, it was nice of you to come and pick me up. I would

have been happy to take the subway."

Wintermoth covers his face in not-so-mock horror, exposing a skeletonized wristwatch with offset concentric dials. A red hand moves around the largest of these to show the date. Another hand moves around a smaller, offset dial, white with blue markings, to indicate the hour. The minutes are inside the date ring and a fourth dial sits at the o'clock position to show the passage of seconds. He sees her stare at it.

"This is an Armin Strom Regulator in titanium."

"I'm not sure about the white leather band."

"Part of the theme," he says. "He makes the same model in four different color schemes. This one is air. There are also fire, earth, and water, as in Traditional Chinese medicine. The fifth element is metal, of course, but all the watches are made of that."

"So Chinese medicine is one of your interests?"

"I learned a little about acupuncture when I found it helped me with a sore knee. The watch captures elements of its underlying philosophy."

"Very pretty, but a lot of work merely to tell the time."

"As in all things, you get out what you put in."

"Okay, but in this case all you get is the time."

"But you get so much more. Beauty at every glance. Intricacy. Elegance. Uniqueness. New evidence of human vision and creativity."

"Time is something you soft people don't really understand," Yang interrupts.

"But you do?" Wintermoth asks, raising a single eyebrow.

"Of course."

"And what, pray tell, is your theory?"

"I have no theory. I have only direct experience."

"Tell us that, then," says Teg.

"The most important thing about time is opening open your

mind to receive it."

"I should have known you would spout some abstruse nonsense," Wintermoth snorts. "How does one *receive* time? Time comes whether you want it or not."

"If you have to ask, you haven't done it," says Yang, closing his eyes.

"You apparently bore him," observes Teg.

"I admit his unpredictable emotions are interesting."

"But you still don't think they're real?"

"Nothing about him is real. His world is a mechanical construct. I'm not interested in *what* he thinks, I'm interested in *how* he thinks."

"What about *that* he thinks, and that he's kind and whimsical and unique in his worldview."

"I am not whimsical," Yang says, his eyes remaining closed. "In fact, I'm a being who can transcend realms, a being who would very much like the remainder of his physical form restored."

"So there," Teg says pointedly to Wintermoth.

"I've made quite a study of time," the tycoon replies. "Your father did, too. Did you know that measuring time was a turning point in human evolution? Primitive societies didn't do it at all."

Teg nods. "Inheriting my father's collection inspired me to do a little research. It seems that cultures either focus on events or on the passage of time."

"That distinction isn't as hard and fast as it used to be. Einstein and the quantum revolution saw to that. Everything's relative now."

Tegulen shakes her head. "The real debate is whether time is a function of events or events are a function of time."

"The former," says Wintermoth. "Events are how time is expressed. Time itself is no more than a concept. The second hand didn't turn because of time. It turned because of a mechanism."

"If no time passed, the mechanism would not move," Teg counters. "The second hand would not turn. There would be no event by which to mark time. No change, no marking, no passage of time. Absent events, time is gelded."

"Absent time, events cannot occur," Wintermoth declares.

"Your mechanical clocks and watches give off heat as they measure time," Yang interrupts. "The more accurate they are, the more heat they give off. The more heat they give off, the more entropy, the more disorder there is in the world. Anyway, I hope you two realize how circular are your arguments. Perhaps you should turn this mutual self-pleasuring session into more creative sex."

"Perhaps you should shut up," says Teg.

"Whatever your attitude about time," Wintermoth continues as if he hasn't heard Yang at all, "be glad you have your beautiful wristwatches, or at least a good smartphone. See how far you get by showing up late to meetings, missing your train, your flight, your dinner reservation. Theories are fine; I deal in reality."

The helicopter descends onto the tarmac at the Marine Air Terminal at LaGuardia field. A short distance away, a twin-engine jet with swept-back wings and the heart-and-gear MothCo logo emblazoned on its fuselage awaits. A pair of flight-attendant-size robot stands at the top of the stairs. Their nametags read Jim and Kim. Jim has black eyes; Kim's are blue.

"Welcome aboard, Mr. Wintermoth," they chime. "You too, Ms. Ames."

Their voices are resonant and convincingly human, but Teg notices their hands have more than a human's share of digits. She stops one step shy of the cabin and stares at them for a moment, wondering what she's getting herself into.

"This is a Bombardier Global 8000," Wintermoth tells her. "Made in Montreal, Canada. It can break the sound barrier with a tailwind and is surprisingly fuel efficient."

"Wind on the steppe, that's fast," opines Yang.

Teg looks at the plane's plush interior, at the taupe leather, the shiny burl trim and the sleeper seats. "You can't really be worried about fuel efficiency and take a whole jet plane for yourself, can you?"

"Everything's relative."

"There we go again. May I be frank with you?"

"Please."

"I trust my intuition."

"And what does your intuition tell you?"

"There's a reason Minnie and Delia don't trust you."

Wintermoth smiles thinly. "And yet here you are about to cross the world in my airplane."

"That doesn't mean I don't share their concerns."

He shrugs. "Your housekeepers are superstitious women your father hired straight off the boat from Ireland. They're naïve about the world. Narrow-minded. There's so much they don't understand."

"For example?"

"I wouldn't know where to begin."

"How about with my father?"

Wintermoth shakes his head. "Look up eccentric in the dictionary. You'll see his picture. He made his own rules, but not his own bed. Not once. Not ever. One night I came to his house unannounced. It was late and Minnie was in her nightgown. A terrycloth housecoat with cream on her face and her hair up in a towel."

Teg smiles. "Now there's an image."

"I found your father in the collection room. Minnie opened the door a crack and we looked in. Your father's back was to us. He had a conductor's baton in his hand and was standing on a little stool. He had wound every chiming watch and clock in the collection and set them all in a specific sequence. It was a masterpiece of melody and staging, taking into account the angles and surfaces of the room to create a truly sublime result. The wristwatches tinkled like the running of a brook each time your father's baton pointed their way and the standing clocks gonged like bass drums."

"I so wish I had seen this," Teg says, her eyes growing wet. "You didn't happen to take a video, did you?"

"For your sake, I wish I had. It was one of those things you can't stop watching even for long enough to pull out your phone. The carriage and mantle clocks carried the day, never in less than a pair, their springs always expiring at the same moment so the harmonics persisted in the air, their ghosts audible on the cabinet glass. The tune told a story, and I've often thought it was *his* story, the story of your family, with all its marine patents and practical tools. I never asked him because I didn't want to admit to eavesdropping. I only wish your father had been as good with people as he was with his collection; he truly was the Mozart of mechanicals."

Tears stream down Teg's face. She mourns never meeting her father, and she mourns the life her long-suffering mother might have had had with him if she had been less willful and stubborn. Even so, she's mad at herself for showing emotion. Or too much emotion, anyway. Or an emotion she doesn't want to share. She's as hypercritical of herself as her mother was, and she hates that, too.

"Beijing in sixteen hours," the captain's voice comes over the speakers as the jet's engines start to whine. "We refuel in Anchorage."

"Beijing was Kublai Khan's northern capital," Wintermoth says. "Did you know he founded it?"

"I did not," Teg replies.

Jim the robot flight attendant bends over and gingerly removes her shoes. Kim does the same for Wintermoth, who works switches to extend their chairs into sleepers. Wintermoth asks Teg if she would like a lullaby and she says yes and soon the cabin fills with the mournful sounds of a woman singing.

"Yungchen Lhamo's mourning the Mongol conquest of Tibet," he says quietly.

"Lovely," cries Yang. "I haven't heard this in nearly a thousand years."

Teg decides not to share that her mother sang it to her every night for the first ten years of her life and that it was always her favorite. The fact that Wintermoth selected it, she decides, is downright creepy.

16

HAD I REMAINED at the palace much longer, the khan would have tired of me as he did of all his toys. Whereas a human child grows and changes physically and thereby presents ongoing challenges to those around him, I was limited by my static appearance. I might expand mentally and learn new tricks, I might grow spiritually and feel my understanding of the true nature of things deepen, but to the outside observer not given to indulging me in intellectual discourse, I appeared unchanging and unchanged. On some days, I was proud of my hard, stony limits; on others, I hated them desperately. On those latter days I found solace in the fact that more and more of the special abilities my father had alluded to were subtly beginning to manifest, although I could tell I had a long way to go with them.

Though I had shared with other courtiers the angst of all who are pigeonholed into a role that suits them poorly, my life inside the palace had been so busy, interesting, complicated, and full of intrigue that I had worn my comforts and privileges like a dandelion cape. Cast out as if I were my cuckolding father's belt, bracelet, or sandal, everything changed. Even though my father doted on me protectively, I quickly recognized the world's great size and monumental indifference.

I had never, for instance, seen myself as any kind of perch for birds, yet one of the first and most unforgettable of the indignities of those first days outside the city walls came the morning a group of hunting lords intercepted our small band of travelers. My guards — not the elite soldiers Chabi had portrayed but the lowest drunks and thieves she had been able to find — stood aside smirking as the nobles compelled me to stand like a scarecrow, arms outstretched, while a gyrfalcon perched on one of my shoulders, a sparrow hawk perched on the other, and some kind of eagle slipped and flapped whilst grabbing for any kind of purchase on my smooth, gold crown. One after the other these birds emptied their bowels on me. As their putrid excrescences slid over my smooth jade skin, I felt so lucky not to produce such waste myself. My father cleaned me, muttering about how impossibly far we had fallen and how quickly. The hunters laughed, not knowing that I was steadily collecting dung in my fists for later deposition into their dark tea when they sat around a fire to gloat.

Despite my petty revenges, I had not yet really learned about the base qualities of men. Yes, I had come across treachery, scandal, and the ruthless policies of a powerful king, but the trite, seemingly arbitrary cruelty of everyday characters was news to me. Whatever culture, dignity, and class had accrued under the enlightened rule of the Han people had been totally debased by the cruelty of Kublai's grandfather, Genghis. The farther west we went, the stronger the traditional Mongol influence became. Despite the relative kindness and civilized vision of Kublai, every *li* of soil from the eastern borders of Cathay to the edge of Europe was still soiled with blood and scorched by fire. The entire empire, even those towns around Khanbalik, had suffered so much that at the time I went afield, even common decency had not yet returned.

"I miss the palace," I told my father one day. "Is this what it is to be homesick?"

"I suppose it is. Even the best of us get accustomed to our comforts."

Such a brief, dispassionate answer in the face of obvious misery was so like him. Instead of tearing up and telling me how much he missed my mother, instead of confessing his concern for my future and his own livelihood and career, instead of coming up with a plan to lose our guards and slip away to a better, more interesting life—as a wandering performer and his jade sidekick, say, or an engineer offering his services to redesign sewer pipes and free clogs with the assistance of his diminutive apprentice—my father merely put on a stoic face and trekked ever deeper into the autumn steppe.

"You know what the khan meant when he said he wanted us to go wherever people live in felt tents?" he asked me.

"A great distance?"

"To say the least. When Kublai's grandfather, Genghis, united all the tribes, he announced himself as khan of everyone who lived in a *ger*. Of course, the great conqueror expanded his holdings eastward toward the Orkhon River Valley and Kharkorin, whereas Chabi has us traveling the opposite way. In short, we're going back to original Mongol territory, though the predominance of tents is still far, far away."

Far though it might be, traveling against the tide of conquest suited me. I was all about inquiry over conflict, understanding over destruction, questing over jousting. I sensed the same in my father, though his affect was morbid while mine was simply demeaned. He had brought with him a trunk of his tools and bits for inventing, but he did little more than tinker with a small project he would not identify.

Our progress toward Kharkorin was greatly facilitated by riding Mongolian ponies. I had a great deal of time to ponder the centaurian link between humans and their mounts during the first few days of riding. Even though I am indefatigable in a way that soft creatures are not, I came to realize what an advantage it was for men to be able to engage the deeply sculpted, verdant vastness of Mongolia — with its surprising contours, mounts, hillocks, ridges and swales — on four legs instead of two. I wondered how long ago this mutually beneficial relationship had been going on. When I asked my father, he told me that the conquest of the steppe was all about such ponies.

"The Mongolians see them as a gift from the gods," he told me. "I respect the tough beasts but don't like them much. The horses of the west are far more elegant in proportion, though I admit they are comparatively fragile and could never stand to have their necks nicked and drained for blood in hard times, nor survive unshod in this terrible terrain."

"You think the terrain is terrible?" I asked in surprise.

In truth, I felt Mongolia was beautiful. Being rigid and thus immune to wind and rain and cold, I found great solace in the visual boundlessness of the steppe. Although the forest was still only a promise and even the taiga was yet to come, I was still naïve enough to be inspired by vistas bearing the promise of adventure and romantic enough to be moved by changeable winds carrying the fragrance of birch bark, moist mushrooms from secret dells, and fragrant grasses in their last, full flower before winter. Too, the endless skies, with their magnificent daytime plays of clouds and blue, the ever-shifting shades of red at dawn and purple at dusk, and the nighttime glow of stars all seemed the work of divine artists on high.

"Curious," said my father when I shared my feelings. "In this desolate wilderness I yearn for nothing more than the sea."

"You've spoken of the sea before, but I'm not exactly sure what it is."

"Imagine a lake without visible borders, one full of salty water in which swim all manner of delicious creatures ripe for roasting. If a lake is an ant, the sea is a giant bull elephant, moving with a deliberate rhythm, suffering boiling sun and scraping winds with aplomb. Losing its temper, though, the sea turns far more dangerous than any elephant. It will swamp towns, eat an imperial fleet until there is nothing left for the minnows, and drown a person and all his kin with equal impunity."

"Did Master al-Jazari show you the sea when you were in Turkey as a boy?"

"He did, for all I had seen before were rivers."

"And how did you feel when you saw it?"

"Awed by the infinite power and magic of the source of all life."

"I'm comforted by how much you know of the world."

"I wish I knew less," my father said quietly. "There are killing deserts to cross as we head west, and even if we avoid them, there are still outlaws and storms. Worst of all, there is the winter."

"It may not be my place to say, Father, but it seems to me that the risk we face now was worth the knowledge your master gave you."

Something came over my father's face. I realized I'd seen it before, but wasn't quite sure what to make of it.

"He was indeed a great teacher."

"Do you think you have outstripped him? He never built anything like me, did he?"

My father looked away. "He did not."

One of the guards pointed to a growing dust cloud on the plain. The others drew up their ponies and together they stared at the horizon until the outline of a band of riders the size of a small army appeared.

"Got to be coming for us," pronounced the chief of the guards. "Nothing else out here."

"There's no way we can save his golden head from so many of them," said his adjutant. "And his jade skin sure isn't worth our lives."

"I'm certainly not dying for him," piped up another man. "He's a perversion of nature. Even the queen says so."

Our paradoxical relationship with Chabi's men had never been clearer than right then: on the one hand, they were our captors; on the other hand, we desperately needed their protection.

"You men ride off to a safe distance," my father suggested. "We'll retreat to the clump of trees over there and hide ourselves carefully. Once the danger has passed, you may come back to us."

It is not my nature to retreat in the face of danger, but the land itself was teaching me a constant lesson in humility and surrender. The men were obviously relieved as we made our way to a berm laced with the thick, twisted trunks of a cluster of saxual trees. Once there, my father took a small trowel from his trunk and feverishly set to digging. After a time, he had managed a shallow grave-sized ditch.

"They know we're here and they'll look carefully," he said. "Climb in and I'll cover you up."

I'm ashamed to say I was pierced with a small dagger of distrust. Was he the good father or the sneaky one, the caring wizard or the scheming inventor? I could dig myself out but wondered whether he would still be there when I did. Remarkably, I was more worried about him than I was about myself. That's how it is with fathers and sons, I guess, when the son begins to grow up.

"But what of you?" I asked him. "I can protect you. Their spears and swords will dull against my stone."

"They are not looking for me. Besides, they'll rip you to pieces if you resist them. Probably, they will rip you to pieces even if you don't. Every part of you is a treasure and such men are not good at sharing future proceeds."

I protested that the plan was a poor one. The ground was a different element to the Mongolians than it was to the Chinese, not merely a place to set down roots, grow food, and build hearth and home but a deity itself, a reliable ally in war, and a treasured touchstone in times of trial. In short, they would find me.

"Please do it. I promised your mother I would do everything to protect you."

"What does she care? She didn't even come to say goodbye."

My father's face turned redder than my own jade skin. "Never say such a thing!" he hissed. "All Tegulen ever cared about was you and now you're gone and only misery is left. The khan never trusted her, another woman displaced her, and now, if she hasn't already taken her own life, she is no more than a maidservant with nice clothes, spending her time stretching her spine and wishing her womb was not barren."

I hesitated. I didn't see my mother in my father's complex and conflicted fashion but it seemed pointless to argue. Who was I to judge either of them when after merely two weeks of traveling, fate had transformed me from an imperial wonder to a bird-dung encrusted fugitive hiding in a hole in the ground?

"Quickly now," my father urged. "They'll be here any moment."

I lay down in the depression and he covered me. As sandy soil of the steppe filled my golden nose, I worried the earth and sand would penetrate my openings and jam my cables and gears. I began planning how I would rid my innards of it. My life in the palace had been not only privileged but also squeaky clean, mostly thanks to my mother's doting. I missed the touch of her polishing cloth on my skin.

As my father dug, I kept my eyes open until there was

nothing to see but dirt. I heard him open his traveling bag and withdraw a thick woolen rug. I heard him unfurl it and felt his steady weight when he sat upon it. I heard the clink of his tools as he laid them out.

"Stay calm and be patient," he murmured.

A moment later I felt the ground shake with the arrival of horses. Having a keen sense of vibration, I detected 160 hooves. Soon, there was neighing and shouting. I felt my father steady weight atop the rug.

"Where's the jade boy?" I heard someone yell, his accent thick with the steppe and not tempered by Han tones. "We know he's afield in these parts."

"Taken by his guards," said my father, pointing in the direction of Chabi's disappearing men.

"But they left you?"

"They said I would slow them down. If you spare me, I have another treasure to appease you. Kill me and you will never learn how to use it."

"Show us and we'll decide."

My father nodded and seconds later came a sound only my ears would recognize—the flapping of the gossamer wings. Apparently, this was the project my father had been secretly engaging on the road, a distraction to give outlet to his indomitable creative energies.

"You see how the golden butterfly spirals upwards toward the sun?" my father cried. "Craving light is the nature of all living creatures. Follow it with your horses. Stay directly below it. The gods have said it will lead you to fame and fortune. Such is your destiny."

I heard the thieves gasp, then mutter among themselves. Despite their cynical skepticism, Mongolian horsemen were credulous when it came to fate or its variants, including, of course, destiny, a concept burning hot in the heart of every son of the steppe. My father had only to speak the word once and the men surrounding him were filled with a sense of their own unique and special importance. I heard one horseman clatter off, then a few more, then another ten, and then the rest. After a time, the ground was once again still, and I could hear my father weeping with a combination of anger and relief.

"A shame to sacrifice such a delicately wrought treasure to scoundrels," he said at last.

To balance his mood, he dug me out, closed his eyes, and sat down to meditate. While he did, I wiped the dust from my nose.

17

THE BOMBARDIER descends past the snowcapped mountains edging Anchorage, Alaska. "Don't you love global travel?" asks Wintermoth. "You get to live the same day twice."

"Time is inevitable, indescribable, incomprehensible, and omnipresent," Yang replies. "And every sunrise is a true treasure."

"More of a treasure than a wristwatch, that's for sure," says Teg.

"The coming event horizon doesn't have to do with wristwatches or sunrises either. It has to do with transformation of the human race, of the reality of life on earth. It's all about connecting with the divine."

"What's an event horizon?" asks Yang.

"Think of it as a point of no return."

"I thought only chocolate was divine to you," says Teg.

"You're the chocolate lover, not me. To be divine means to be filled with wonder, and wonder is what drives scientific inquiry."

"The Sufis speak of nothing but the divine," Yang puts in.

Teg asks Wintermoth when he had changed his wristwatch. He shrugs back his cuff.

"I'm surprised you noticed it, distracted by the sunrise and all. It's German and tremendously complicated. The *Lange 1 Perpetual Calendar Handwerkskunst*. It's a perpetual calendar with a peripheral moon ring, date, day, leap year, and moon phase. Everything advances instantaneously."

"It's heavy," says Teg when he hands it over.

"Platinum is a weighty metal."

"It has no soul," says Yang.

Teg goes in for a closer view. "The finish on the dial is something."

"Tremblage relief engraving. It has a big date, too. Look at the reverse side and you'll see a tourbillon with stop-seconds and a 21-karat gold rotor with platinum centrifugal mass."

Yang asks to see the watch and Teg puts it in front of him. He spends a few moments in what appears to be a close inspection.

"Interesting," he says at last. "Crafting such a piece offers two different dances with time. The first is to apprehend it technically by using the mechanism itself, the second is to appreciate its passing in the long years of apprenticeship required before one can create such a thing."

"Apprehend," Wintermoth repeats.

Teg shakes her head.

The jet's landing gear drops into place with a thud. Moments later, they are on the ground at Ted Steven's Field.

"A snowflake touching iron," Yang says admiringly. "I hit the ground harder when I danced for the khan. How can you two be so preoccupied by a small timekeeping device while this great metal bird carries us through the sky at speed and then alights as delicately as a seabird on a craggy cliff?"

"You're right," Teg allows. "Airplanes are amazing and I'm afraid I'm already dulling to the privileges of wealth."

While the pilots see to fuel and provisions, Wintermoth and Teg visit a Euro-style café in the terminal. A woman wearing a fur coat looks over at Teg's bag.

"What breed is your dog?"

"Golden Chihuahua," Teg says mischievously.

"I don't even know what those words mean," says Yang.

"A talking treasure!" the woman cries.

Teg leaps up and exits the terminal. The smell of jet fuel is in the air. Jim and Kim are waiting in the Bombardier's doorway. She and Wintermoth take their seats.

"I have a question to ask before we leave American soil," she says to him in the tomb-like silence following the close of the aircraft's door.

"Shoot."

"What *exactly* are you hoping to learn from Yang if through some miracle we manage to put him back together?"

"If a miracle is what we need, a miracle is what we shall have," says Yang.

"I'm interested in autopoiesis," says Wintermoth. "That's the ability of an organism to continually update, renew, and even create itself anew."

Teg frowns. "Don't laptop computers do that every day?"

"Updating the software is one thing. I'm talking about changing the physical build of the laptop itself."

"Could a robot use 3-D printing for that?"

"Smart question. Two challenges. First to help the robot know when it needs to adapt and grow, second to create an interface so it can make what it needs on such a printer."

"The first sounds like you need an emo chip."

"Emotions may be involved, but not required. There are other algorithms to identify a need for change."

"I have emotions," says Yang.

"How could something as ancient as Yang possess the quality you're referring to?"

"That's exactly what I want to understand."

Tegulen is pressed into her seat as the plane thunders down

the runway. The bag holding Yang tumbles away. Against the press of gravity, Wintermoth releases his seatbelt and snatches him out of mid-air.

"Go ahead and admit it," says Teg. "You think I'm careless."

"I think he's too valuable to be rolling around," Wintermoth says, his face flushed.

"I love it when you call me 'he,'" says Yang.

"I'm not used to traveling like this," Teg admits. "The takeoff was really fast. By the way, I hear you're fast, too. Is it true you row a racing shell on the Hudson River even in freezing weather? Even in the snow?"

"It is," he answers.

"And you exercise with ropes instead of dumbbells and can hold your breath for nine minutes?"

"These days it's only eight," says Wintermoth. "Nine takes a crazy amount of consistent extra practice, at least for me."

"And you learned meditation from a teacher in Boston?"

"Yes."

"And you can snuff out a candle with your own mind?"

"The Web is full of rumors. Don't believe them."

"I can do that," Yang volunteers. "I can light one that way, too."

Teg ignores him. "But you did build your first robot at the age of fourteen, and program it to dance with your cat."

"Only because I was unable to come up with a better idea."

"Very funny. I seem to remember reading that your performing duo won the local talent show and attracted grants. And didn't you get your Ph.D. at some Ivy League school as a teenager?"

"I was twenty-two, not nineteen. News stories always exaggerate things."

"Ever married?"

"Not so far."

"A hands-off manager?"

"If you do your job."

"Long-term planner?"

"Absolutely."

"Poker or chess?"

"Chess."

"Why not poker?"

"Can't control the variables."

The jet banks as it climbs. Yang cackles with glee. "You two really should look out the window instead of dancing your little love dance."

Teg covers him with a blanket. "I'm never going to be able to sleep on this flight, Sebastian. Do you happen to have a pill?"

As if by magic, Jim appears at her side. "Red or blue?" he asks, holding out his hand.

18

No PERSON, place, or thing ever completely escaped the khan's reach. Even so, had Chabi's men vanished for good we might have gained at least some years of peace by doubling back toward what my father described as an endless string of warm and inviting coves along the southeastern seacoast. As it was, however, six of the guards returned, presumably to gather evidence of our fate for the queen. Finding us unexpectedly safe and unmolested, they set to hunting hares with bows, sent hawks aloft to bring back songbirds for stew, lit cooking fires, and whispered soothingly to their ponies.

"I noticed something I never noticed at the palace," I told my father.

"What did you notice?"

"The archer waited for all four of his pony's feet to leave the ground before releasing the arrow. I presume this was because in that moment of stillness nothing would jostle his aim?"

"Exactly."

A Mongol warrior calls the entire steppe his home and was thus comfortable anywhere upon it. My father, however, was keen for a proper bed and shelter from the wind, so he convinced the guards to make haste toward Xijing, slightly north and west of Khanbalik. The town was at an elevation, and even the ponies slowed as we climbed. When we finally arrived, my father selected an inn with upstairs rooms and a tavern below. We organized our meager belongings then went down for food and drink. Chabi's men indulged in *baijiu*, the sorghum liquor they favored, and my father drank red tea. After an hour, a woman approached our table. Her shining blue-black hair was pulled back as tight as a vine and she had high cheekbones, olive skin, a straight and elegant nose, and a small birthmark to the left side of her upper lip.

"Persian," muttered my father.

"I think she's beautiful," I muttered back.

"At least that," my father countered. "I'd say magnificent."

That she was, though she bore the concentrated look of a raptor floating across the floor on wings. If not for the mercenary's sword slung professionally across her back, I might have taken her for a courtesan of some allure. Not a soul in the tavern could take their eyes off her.

"This must be the khan's famous jade toy," she said, her eyes running from the glint of the diamond edges of my feet all the way to my golden crown. "I've heard it was afield in these parts."

My father inclined his head and smiled his most charming smile. "Here and under the khan's protection," he said.

The woman assumed the stool beside me. She touched me cautiously and withdrew her fingers at once.

"It pulses with energy," she said, clearly impressed.

"*He*, not *it*, is an amazing boy," my father agreed.

These words cued me to perform my routine. It had been a while since we'd had an audience so I wasn't sure if these were still in force, but I launched into the air anyway, kicking a rafter at the apogee of my orbit before landing lightly and bowing low. A moment later the rafter, evidently weak with termites, gave way and crashed to the bar. The proprietor wailed and wrung his hands until one of Chabi's men quieted him with coins.

My father's desire to impress the woman had garnered exactly the kind of attention we wished to avoid, yet there was nothing for it but to perform. Because Xijing was a Buddhist town—and because Buddhists prefer mantras to numbers—I followed my acrobatics by soliciting mathematical challenges from the crowd and answering them without benefit of an abacus. There were divisions, there were multiplications, there were additions of long strings of numbers, and there was even a problem involving powers of ten.

"It appears very accurate," said the woman.

"Not it. He," my father reiterated. "And he has a soul."

"So he fell to earth from heaven?" she pursued.

My chief guard, whom I will not dignify with a name, took this cue to address the crowd with a drunken soliloquy about how I was born of Tengri, the sky god, and was therefore beyond human interference.

"Really?" the woman asked my father, a tinge provocatively. "Are you saying he's Mongolian?"

Despite a career built on mechanical artifice and a love life hinging on deception, my father was a realist. He knew he was not going back to the palace and knew he would never see Queen Tegulen again. I saw him reach into some strange, untapped vein of mind and produce a smile the likes of which I had not seen curl his lips since the early days of the queen's seduction.

"Not exactly."

"So where *did* he come from?"

"He is of my own manufacture," my father said, clasping his hands together in what to me seemed false modesty. "And he has a soul."

"Really? You created a creature with a soul? If so, please get him to sing for me. Through song we can hear the soul and thereby tell the living from the dead."

"Of course," replied my father, and then commanded me to sing.

Are you surprised that the request offended me? If so, know that singing is special to me and not something I do upon request. Jump and spin, yes. Perform mathematics, no problem. But sing? I would no more sing for this woman than I would dance for the bitch-queen, Chabi.

"No," I said.

My father looked surprised and the woman narrowed her eyes. They were green flecked with brown and singularly beautiful. I met her gaze with frank defiance and shook my head.

"Singing is not easy for me and requires me to be happy, something I cannot be in a room filled with dust and reeking of stale incense, horse sweat, and mare's-milk wine," I declared. "If I sing it is because I want to, because I'm in a chamber full of appreciative eunuchs or enjoying the spring fragrance of grass and flowers."

I was hoping to surprise the woman with my willful declaration, and thus disarm her. I did neither.

"Sing," she commanded unfolding herself from her stool.

"I will not."

My father grimaced. "Please sing for the lady, Yang."

"I'm not in the mood."

"So, it has moods and is called Yang."

"As I have said, he is not an it. And surely you have heard his name, which by the way is a reference to his prodigious endowment."

The woman frowned. "Is that so? Let me see."

Without a moment's hesitation, I dropped my robe.

If you find it strange that I was willing to expose myself but not willing to sing, it is only because you don't realize that a person's soul is not located in their genitals but rather in the vibrations they share with the world. There are many kinds of vibration, of course, but none so clear and obvious as the voice. The soul connects us with heaven, whose omnipotent presence waits to pierce us like an arrow the moment we open our heart. Baring one's soul to someone who wishes us ill is therefore unwise.

"Veined jade from Hotan," the woman breathed. "And blue! So rare! Exquisite! I've never seen a better piece."

"A great compliment from a woman no doubt experienced in pieces," my father observed.

The woman bared her sword faster than a housefly can flap a wing. The blade was layered in wavy lines. She put it to my father's throat.

"The last time I saw such steel was in the hands of Persian emissaries to the khan," I said conversationally. "I remember them claiming it to be flexible yet strong, and able to hold a shaving edge."

Chabi's drunken men reluctantly assembled in a circle around us, but none of them intervened.

"I was trying to compliment you as a woman of the world," my father squeaked.

"Sing or I slit his throat," the woman told me, pressing down until her blade produced a thin red line.

My father always taught me that a crazy world is best treated with calm. My world didn't get any crazier than seeing a sword at my father's throat, so although I was loath to capitulate and eager to rumble, I did my best to mimic the local Tuvan throat musicians who had earlier entertained the tavern with their drawn-out tones and small, stringed instruments. I consoled myself with the fact that neither the song nor the voice was my own and thus I retained my dignity. Even so, I held my notes longer than the best Tuvan as I sang of power and loss, and the beauty of ponies dusted by snow.

Mesmerizing my quarry, I closed in on her, staying low and unintimidating, moving like a pangolin sniffing for ants. When I was close enough, I grabbed her forearm. The sword came free of my father's throat, and he managed to slip away. As he did the woman sliced my ankle.

I felt a new and unpleasant sensation as my leg parted company with my foot, trailing cables, toes still twitching. As the woman shoved the loose piece into her cloak, Chabi's men belatedly intervened. The woman stabbed one in the chest. Other guards attacked but her blade was a shooting star, its bright trajectory filling the spaces between their clumsy moves. After a few moments she was gone, and with her, my foot.

"What style!" my father cried, obviously having already forgotten the feeling of folded steel at his throat. "What power, what technique, what pure martial grace!"

"You're admiring the very woman who maimed me? Seriously?"

He blinked, somehow noticed my damaged leg for the first time, and bent in for a look. "What? No!"

"I feel something bad," I said.

"It's called pain," my father explained sadly. "The ability to feel it opens you up to many important truths in the world."

Our guards clustered around their fallen comrades, staring at us balefully.

"The charade ends here," their leader announced. "We're not chasing that woman for a foot."

19

As HIS JET begins its final descent into Beijing, Sebastian Wintermoth pulls back his cuff to reveal a watch Teg hasn't seen before.

"Really?" she mutters, still in a fog from the pill she took. "Do you travel with a collection?"

"It's a Seiko Credor Spring Drive Sonnerie. A million dollars will buy you three of them, but it's hard to find even one for sale. It's a repeater. You can set it to chime every hour or every three, or you can turn off the chime completely. Here. Listen to the pure clarity of this tone."

He tries to put the watch to her ear but Teg waves him away. "We're in a jet. You can't seriously expect me to hear a wristwatch chime."

"While Europeans have a long history with chiming clocks, the Japanese, ever exquisitely subtle, do not. They have a history with bells, though, particularly at Buddhist temples. One of those is the *orin*, which issues a tone so pure it can reverberate against rock walls, penetrate ravines, cross lakes, and even subdue the roar of jet engines. Seiko copied that sound in their repeater. Doing that required designing a totally silent governor and reducing internal friction to the point where the movement generates no buzzes or clicks to compete with the chime."

When she takes the watch and holds it to her ear, she hears

a tone clear enough to override her mother's voice in her head admonishing her to beware the agendas of rich men.

"It's beautiful," she says. "But you could have used the money it cost to feed a village for a year or cure a thousand children with facial birth defects."

"Quantum mechanics might explain a link between sound, time, technology, and reality. Their intersection seems important to me in my project, although I'm not exactly sure how."

"Sorry, but what does what you said have to do with helping the needy rather than having a nice toy?"

"These advances will help the whole world."

"The link you're looking for is vibration," Yang interjects. "Energy is everything. The material world is an illusory matter of probabilities. As for the Japanese, they were focused enough to whip up a divine wind to defeat the khan's armadas. I remember Kublai's reaction to it. He wasn't happy."

Wintermoth assumes a superior air that says he doesn't enjoy being upstaged by a talking head. His attitude persists as the plane lands and as a coterie of customs and immigration inspectors ignore that very same head's lack of official provenance in exchange for Tegulen's healthy cash incentive.

Outside the terminal, Yang sniffs the air with a puzzled expression. "This cannot be my home. We must have flown to the wrong place. There is nothing but foul dirt and dust here, nothing of the joyous clarity of pines and the open smell of the steppe."

"The land you remember is gone," says Wintermoth, as their limousine pulls up. "The government has done an amazing job of developing an unstoppable economy and lifting people out of poverty but like almost everywhere else around the world, they've sacrificed the environment in the process. It's a global war on nature and if it doesn't stop, all that will be left is a hot, dry, sterile planet hospitable only to lizards."

"Why do you say this stuff to him?" Teg interrupts angrily. "There's a lot more to the world than your negative spin. There are still gorgeous sand beaches, tropical seas, and beautiful blue skies."

"Polluted shores, dying oceans, unbreathable air," Wintermoth counters.

"Mountain peaks, gorgeous jungles, loving, compassionate people," says Teg.

"Strip mining, deforestation, selfish, self-centered, narcissistic consumers," says Wintermoth.

"Consumers? You're telling me about consumers?"

"I don't consume. I collect."

Teg bursts out laughing. "Fine. What about healers, then?"

"And mass murderers," he counters.

"Martyrs," she says.

"Con men."

"Saints," she quips.

"Monsters."

Teg looks out the window. Beijing may not be full of red lanterns and twisting alleys like the Chinese cities in the movies she had watched with her mother, but the roads are full of traffic. As the limo turns off a highway onto a smaller thoroughfare, she shakes off Wintermoth's negativity and decides that whatever happens, she's going to enjoy her time in China.

"Hotel Éclat," says the driver, pulling the car up in front of an angular building whose glass and girders run at oblique angles. Though much shinier and newer, it reminds her of the pyramidal Luxor in Las Vegas, where she once stayed with her mother.

"The suites have huge pool patios," Wintermoth tells her

"Great. So long as I have my own."

He glances at her. "Of course."

The woman at the reception desk speaks perfect English. In response to Teg's question, she says she attended Cornell University. When Wintermoth flatters her with a smile, she responds with a look of cool encouragement.

"Are you sure this is Cathay?" hisses Yang.

Teg bends to him as if fussing with her bag. "Keep quiet," she murmurs.

"I have your Éclat pool suite," says the reception agent, "but I don't have one for Ms. Ames. I'm afraid the conference has put quite a strain on our resources."

"But I specifically...." begins Wintermoth.

Teg cuts him off. "What conference are you talking about?"

The agent returns to her computer, hitting the keyboard as if the keys were roaches. "Artificial Intelligence and Robotics – A New World Order," she answers.

Teg looks at Wintermoth in surprise, then turns and walks quickly out the front door of the hotel.

20

In the wake of the Persian woman's disappearance, my father turned from tea to wine. It was nearly morning when he finally stumbled into our room at the inn, breath foul and lips crusty, muttering something about having fallen asleep at the table.

"Does it still hurt?" he asked, pointing at my leg.

"I miss my foot."

"Yes, but is there pain?"

"A ghost of what it was before."

"Did you rest?"

"There's a crack in the floor," I said, pointing. "Cooking smoke from the kitchen has me sliding and slipping with grease."

"We need to protect your cables and gears," he said, wiping me off, then wrapping my damaged foot in a length of rough cloth. "They're not to be exposed to the elements and we have to leave now, while the men are still drunk and asleep."

This was my father as caregiver and concerned parent. I relished the moment, though it was perhaps not worth the loss of my foot. We quickly gathered our things and left. It was so cold in the room that the lintel was sheathed in ice, allowing us to open the door silently without awakening our guards. I hopped down the stairs, strangely fascinated by the challenge of keeping my wounded ankle aloft so it wouldn't scrape the wooden floor and maintaining my balance on my one good foot. We made our way out into the snow.

"I gather we're going after the woman?"

"She did us a favor," answered my father.

"She maimed me."

"But she helped us escape Chabi's men."

"We snuck past them; she isn't even here."

"The men know she'll be back for the rest of you. They won't want to face her again, so they won't come after us. They were going to kill us. She owes us your foot; we owe her our lives."

"If she's so dangerous, perhaps you should leave me," I said, suddenly maudlin. "I couldn't bear anything happening to you."

"I'm not who you think I am, Yang."

"Who then? Only the most wonderful man in the world creates such marvels?"

He shook his head. "Anyway, that woman seems a well-informed freelancer. Once she has you, she'll sell you."

"Can you make me another foot?"

"Not without my workshop," he said miserably. "And you know what would happen if we went back."

"Then we have to find the Persian."

"Yes."

"But how?"

"We'll ask the stalks."

He sat down on a rock and pulled a handful of yarrow stalks, some long, some short, from his cloak. I had seen him run this divinatory ritual before but had never paid much attention to it. It never made much sense to me that a man so invested in the mechanical workings of the world could possibly believe in a future delineated by a superstitious ritual of chance, even if such a ritual was based on a scroll called *The Book of Changes*, which was said to be a pillar of Chinese culture.

"Yin and Yang reveals nature to be constantly moving and

shifting," he said.

"Taoism," I said with a shake of my head.

"It's beautiful and practical and will tell us where our lady is."

"She's a woman. I don't know that I'd call her a lady. And I have yet to see a religion that does anything but confuse things."

"Taoism seeks to understand the workings of the world; this divination method is unparalleled."

"If you say so," I muttered.

He tossed the stalks time after time, taking careful note of the combinations of long and short they provided as they clattered to the ground. At last, he gathered them up and pulled the scroll out of his cloak.

"Why do you refer to that thing? You know all the combinations by heart."

"It's a ritual. So. Here we have the twenty-ninth hexagram. That's the pit, which connotes danger underground. The fifth line, for instance, says that the pit is not yet flooded. The third line promises drumbeats and danger as we enter the hidden chamber."

"I have no idea what you're talking about. What hidden chamber?"

"There's the question."

We sat there together, our swinging legs dangling from the rock, until his face finally lit up.

"Ha!" he cried. "It must be the cave by the Tuban Buddha statues. Nothing else in this area is so secure. I hid there myself once."

"You hid?"

"Never mind why. I'm sure she's there."

He hurried off and I hopped after him, depending upon the superior balance with which my father had imbued me.

"Did you notice the woman's fighting style?" he asked conversationally.

"Her style? As she was cutting everyone to pieces? I can't say I did."

"Didn't you see her spinning like your friend, the Sufi dancer on Kublai's council, the one who wanted to be closer to his god?"

"That I saw, yes."

"Spinning's not only a way to pray; it's a Muslim fighting technique, too. That lady turned one inch for every yard Chabi's men stepped, arriving where they were going before they did. It's as if she were the hub of the wheel and they were the rim. Only an uncommon fighter can control a conflict that way. On the battlefield, soldiers of Islam whirl to the beat of a drummer called a *morshed*, who chants famous poems at the same time."

"How do you know all this?"

"I heard the story of such fighting during the siege of Baghdad, when Ogedai Khan destroyed the armies of the Quarismian Shah, committed unspeakable atrocities in the city, and erased all the Muslims in Anatolia, Thrace, and down south."

"What drove Ogedai to do such things?"

My father snorted. "You've been in court. You know how the Mongols are."

"Ruthless and cruel, but it takes something to set them off."

"Genghis wanted Baghdad. The shah said no. Ogedai gave him an out and offered to spare the city in return for fealty and trade. The shah puffed up and refused, so Ogedai leveled the city. If the shah hadn't been so arrogant, the entire Muslim world would look different right now."

"Your master, al-Jazari is a Muslim."

He glanced at me sharply. "Let's not say he's my master anymore, but yes, that's his faith."

"What does this have to do with getting back my foot?"

"The more we know about the Persian woman the better chance we have of figuring out what else she might want."

I looked long and hard at him, at the way his tongue flicked in and out from between his lips and the way his eyes darted from one side to the other.

"All of this may be true," I said slowly, "but I don't believe that's why we snuck out in pursuit of her. I think we're where we are right now because you're smitten by this woman and you want to seduce her."

My father allowed himself a small smile as he pointed at the horizon. "Here comes the sun," he said.

21

WITH YANG on her shoulder and suitcase in hand, Teg runs for the
lobby door. Wintermoth sprints after her.

"I'm sorry!" he shouts. "I should have told you about the
conference. Don't be upset. Wait! Where are you going?"

Outside, cars and people whiz by so quickly, Teg fears being
trampled. Dust falls like rain. Yang sneezes. Teg's suitcase bumps
and rolls across drain grates, and the gutters as she runs, the
handle vibrating in her hand. All she can think of is getting as far
away from Wintermoth as she can. She checks over her shoulder
and sees him gracefully threading his way through the crowd.
She redoubles her pace but can't outrun him. She ducks into a
taxi stopped at a light.

"Drive," she says. "Quickly, please."

The cabbie speaks no English. She tries again. He shakes his
head. He doesn't like foreigners, is not interested in making
money from tourists, wants her out of his car.

Wintermoth is almost close enough to grab the door handle.

"Go!" she cries, shooing him with her hand.

Cursing, the driver moves into traffic. Teg watches through
the back window as her pursuer jumps into another cab.

"Why are you running from Sebastian all of a sudden?" asks
Yang.

Puzzled at the sudden appearance of a male voice, the driver glances in his mirror and frowns when he sees Teg is not on her phone.

"I suddenly saw through him. Realized he has a whole agenda that has nothing to do with helping you and more to do with *selling* you."

"How can he sell me?"

"He'll find a way. If not your body, then whatever's inside your head. That conference will be full of takers. I should have trusted my instincts about him. Damnit. How could I have gotten this so wrong?"

Wintermoth pulls alongside in his own taxi. "I can explain, Teg," he cries. "Please pull over."

Teg slams the back of the driver's seat with her hand. "We have to go now! Take us to the American embassy."

"He doesn't understand you," says Yang. "Lift me to his ear."

Teg does.

"There's a bad man behind us," he tells the driver. "Drive until you lose him."

Yang's golden head is a veritable fount of Mandarin Chinese, his voice as relaxed as a pilgrim lolling atop a sleeping camel, his accent rich with Mongolian overtones yet round in the mouth like a high-class Beijing urbanite. The driver does an admirable job of absorbing both Yang's existence and his message and immediately executes a U-turn to pass Wintermoth's cab going the other way.

"Would you mind pouring your bottle into your palm and holding me there so I can absorb some water through my neck?" asks Yang. "That airplane air was so dry and it's been eight hundred years since I've had a drink."

Teg complies, and her palm is soon dry. She repeats the process.

"I ran away from capitalism as much as from Sebastian," she

says. "Unbridled greed and materialism scare me."

"You had a simple life and now you don't."

"I worried about not having money and now I worry about having too much. My mother always said that when you are rich, everyone around you has an agenda. What was I thinking, flying to the other side of the world with him? I'm so stupid."

"You're kind not stupid and you were only thinking about helping me," Yang says quietly. "He might be, too. Maybe you ran from him prematurely."

Six minutes later they pull up in front of the embassy.

"I'm an American citizen and I need help," Teg tells the United States marine guard.

Wintermoth's cab pulls up. He gets out and walks over to the marine, who nods to him. "Mr. Wintermoth," Teg hears him say. "Nice to see you again, sir."

"Tell the driver to go again," she tells Yang, under her breath. "I have no local cash. We need to find a bank so I can pay him and find somewhere safe to stay."

Yang barks something in Mandarin. The cab leaps forward.

The marine frowns.

Wintermoth's arms fly up in exasperation.

22

AT COURT, I had learned to identify pleasant aromas such as perfumes, spices and joss. On the road to the cave identified by the Book of Changes, a new smell arose. At first, I took it for the stench of rotting food or dirty bodies but it soon grew so thick my father had trouble breathing. No longer able to carry me, he set me down on my swaddled leg and I straggled behind him. The road made a gradual turn and we followed it. Before us rose a white mountain large enough to take a bite out of the morning glow.

"When I came this way years ago, from the west, there was no mountain here," my father remarked.

"You're certain?"

"I am."

"Do mountains grow out of nothing?"

"They do not."

As he said that, I lost my balance and fell.

"The stink is coming from the road," I said, face down.

My father bent for a whiff and nodded in agreement. "Strange," he muttered, then helped me up.

We kept walking. I kept my eyes on the ground in front of me so I wouldn't fall again. The mountain loomed. My stump dragged. The stench grew stronger. I noticed an ever-deeper layer of dust on the roadbed. After a time, the dust gave way to pebbles that crumbled readily under my remaining sole, then to chunks of various shapes and sizes, which did not. My father bent to examine these, and tears appeared on his cheeks, seemingly coming out of his skin the way blood seeps through the hair of ponies when they are run too hard.

"Oh no," he said.

If I had been a soft person, the tone of his voice would have raised bumps on my skin. "What is it?" I asked.

"No, no, no."

"Father?"

He shook his head. I cajoled him. He shook his head again, crumpling down into a squat and looking as if he'd eaten too many red peppers.

"Are you all right?"

"Oh, Yang."

"What is it, Father?"

"The road."

"What about the road?"

"It's made of bones," he whispered.

It was true. I had been smelling it. They were bones all right, and human, too. The smaller bits were toes and fingers, the longer ones were parts of arms and legs, and ahead of us on the road, redolent in the rising rays of morning, were skulls. Many had been battered and smashed, but some were complete, their eye sockets either filled with dust or glaring with empty space.

"We need to turn around," I said. "No feet should step on the dead."

"I wish we could," he sighed. "But the way to your missing foot is forward."

We stood there, each in our own kind of prayer. After a moment we set off again, agreeing that once upon a sea of bone, any shore is welcome.

Ahead of us, the mysterious mountain grew taller.

23

A THUMPING, bubble of self-doubt pressing on her throat, Teg sits in a stiff-backed chair and waits for the personal banker, ensconced behind a plexiglass window, to verify that she is as rich as she she claims to be. Talking about money has always made her uncomfortable. Now it is excruciating. She is, after all, the mixed-race misfit with a bipolar mother and no father at all, the girl who is quick on the running track but doesn't like gymnastics, the girl who is crazy good at math but stumbles over any sentence requiring her to express her feelings, the girl whose opinions come across like snakebites, who uses sarcasm like a toddler playing with a kitchen knife. She is the girl who has a fistful of dollars but not a single Chinese RMB in her purse, the girl whose credit card is on fraud hold because she didn't think to tell her bank she would be making her first-ever trip to Asia, the girl receiving the stink eye — through the bank window — from the cabbie waiting to be paid. She is the girl who wouldn't mind a little respect, even though she's still wrestling with the idea she deserves it.

She wanted to call Burfield herself but has no international calling plan on her phone — another travel detail that escaped her — and so has had to delegate the job to the thirty-something disheveled manager who sits with the soles of his feet up on his desk pointing at her through the glass window of his office as he plays with the loose band of his fake Rolex and sucks air through his brown teeth. She avoids his insouciant stare and watches him pick up the phone. It's clear he doesn't believe her, is only humoring her with the call because he has the time. He starts talking and even though she's no lip reader she sees he's speaking English. His brow furrows and his mouth goes slack. He sits up in his chair, glances at her with panic in his eyes. Cradling the receiver against his ear, he shrugs on the suitcoat that has been draped over the back of the chair, brings his necktie into line, and begins furiously inputting whatever data is required for his bank to liaise with one of Tegulen's enormous accounts in New York.

Finally, he hangs up and shuffles paper for a bit to collect himself, then finally meets Teg's eye. No longer insouciant, his smile is now as warm as the six-star hotel shower he so badly needs. He summons his assistant, a slender Southeast Asian woman, and bids her pay the cabbie still waiting outside, then arrange for a hired car, and bring some tea while they wait for it. He offers his name card with two hands and then pushes across wire-transfer papers for her to sign.

There is not a word of English on the documents, but when he offers his counterfeit Montblanc roller-ball pen, she signs anyway. The assistant reappears with the tea and also a cellphone.

"I'm so very sorry for the delay," the manager says. "We've loaded this phone with payment apps. You can spend at any level you wish. I've also arranged for the bank car to take you back to your hotel."

"Thank you. And if I may, one more thing. There's a robotics conference in town. I'll need a pass to get in."

The manager frowns. "Robotics?"

"Artificial intelligence. A big international meeting. Please arrange a ticket."

He nods and begins a series of calls. He laughs through the

first one, frowns at the second, and has success at the third.

"It's at the convention center," he says. "If you go to their VIP desk tomorrow morning, a pass will be there for you. In the meantime, may I suggest you retire, order some room service and get some rest?"

She has the desire to be snarky with him about how he treated her at the outset, to do a little heiress strutting and see him squirm a bit more. Instead, she spins on her heel and, armed with cash, steps into the bank's private car. She speaks not one word to Yang along the way, opting to hide his existence from the driver.

There is no sign of Wintermoth.

24

THE MORE we walked, the fresher were the corpses we found. The gases they emitted rose in whorls, torturing the air, confusing our vision, and burning our noses and eyes. Perhaps our sensory confusion accounted for why it took us so long to recognize the mountain for what it was—a pile of dead bodies, unimaginable in scale, dried and bleached by wind and sun until the top resembled a snow-capped peak.

My father retched violently as I distracted myself with the kind of calculation I did so well with bowls of marbles. It was challenging, as human bodies do not lie upon each other as predictably as do marbles, nor are they so uniform in size. The big men, slender women, infants and children in the pile—some still bloated, others reduced to sticks—made the arithmetic approximate at best. Even so, I told my father I was certain we were looking at more than 100,000 victims.

"Now you understand the price of empire," my father said as we circumnavigated a pile of corpses bolstered by the few wooden structures that had survived boiling pitch, flaming arrows, and other pitiless instruments of the khan's siege engine. "The city nearby once bustled with Tanguts, Jews, and Muslims. There's barely anything left of it now."

"This killing happened because they resisted the khan?"

"Resisted, surrendered, it makes no difference. Mongol

soldiers don't distinguish. They are taught to see their enemies as lower life forms ripe for slaughter. Khans commit genocide at the merest whiff of insurrection, embracing what they call creative destruction, believing the campaigns redistribute resources and create new societies in much the same way a forest fire offers opportunities for different plants and animals to step into the burn zone and grow."

"But they treat their horses and hunting hawks so well."

"They prize unity, simplicity, standardization, and balance, yet to me they are the great destroyers, the madmen."

We walked as far as we could in the following hours, wanting as much distance as possible from the Mongol horrors. We saw no footprints, nor did we encounter on the stinking road anyone who admitted to having seen a Persian woman wearing a sword. Later, we slept tightly pressed together in a ditch, covered only by a tarp from my father's carpetbag. All night long, his teeth chattered and his muscles twitched from the cold. Though I felt warmly toward him, I was made of cold jade and could offer him no heat.

The dew woke us to the sight of a line of giant stone statues of the Buddha, precisely the Tuban works we sought.

I made a fire for his tea by twirling a stick into a divot in a dry branch and lighting some twigs. When the tea was hot, my father dumped into it a lump of the tasteless grain the Mongolians call *tsampa*.

"Do you see the statue with the pointing finger?"

"Of course."

"That finger is aimed at the cave wherein that woman awaits us."

"My ankle hurts."

He finished eating, uncovered my stump, and wiped it out carefully with a camelhair brush. "I should have cleaned it earlier. Does it feel better now?"

"It does a bit, thank you."

We made our way to the area indicated by the statue's weatherworn finger.

"I see no cave," I said, astride the only hillock in sight.

My father studied the play of light and shadow, the way the trees grew, the way the wind blew, the feeling of the soil between his fingers, and the way the land's energy rose and ebbed.

"It's here."

With that he went to the ground on all fours like a dog on a scent trail. He might have been in the thrall of romantic obsession, but his geomancy was undiminished. Half limping, half hopping, I followed him through a funneling cathedral of poplars toward a rock overhang, and below it to the mouth of a cave.

He took a bell out of his bag and rang it.

It wasn't long before his summons was answered.

25

THE RECEPTION staff at the St. Regis Beijing greets Teg warmly. Signing the hotel register, she notices how small and hesitant her signature is and resolves to start writing bigger and bolder letters. She decides she wants a fountain pen too, a fancy one, heavy and smooth with lacquer. As anachronistic as it may be in the smart-phone age, she has always relished the flow of ink, and in this is her father's girl.

She wants the President Suite, balks at the price, then decides to take it. It is as tasteful and beautifully decorated as she hopes. The colors slide into one another, the lamps match even when they are of different sizes, the sofas are plump and the pillows delicate silk. The rugs are done in classic Central Asian pattern, the furniture is mahogany, there are a vases of flowers scattered about, and everything exudes luxury and quality. She feels safe for the first time since she arrived in China.

Telling herself she's interviewing the executive chef for a restaurant she now thinks she'd prefer to a catering service, she calls room service and orders the best of everything. She thinks about her father's townhouse, which is how she still sees it, not hers but his. Then she thinks about the cramped little apartment she shared with her mother, how they were always stumbling over each other in the tight space, how when she was little, she loved being around her mom all the time, her smell, her moods, her smiles, her crazy theories, her dresses.

"You would have loved this hotel, Mom," she hears herself say, and then once she has spoken the words, wonders if it's true. After all, if she'd wanted luxury, seems pretty clear she could have had it.

In the bathroom, she fills the giant bathtub for herself and sets Yang in a couple of inches of water in the sink to hydrate.

"I can't see you naked in the tub," Yang tells her, his voice muffled by the porcelain rim.

"I know."

"I would like to."

"Of course you would."

"So you're shy."

"Not at all."

"Yes you are. Prudish, even."

"I certainly am not."

"You're afraid I'm going to tell you you're fat."

"I'm not fat no matter what you say. And in the tub or out, my figure is none of your business!"

"You could *make* it my business. Have you considered all you could learn from me? You've never met anyone who has seen so many naked women over so many years."

"What would you teach me, having seen so many women?"

"To sculpt your soft body. To use secret movements to give you exactly the shape you want. To increase the flow of energy to your brain. Techniques to drive men wild before you even touch them."

"Sounds nice, but if the price of admission is you ogling me, I'll pass."

"So you *are* prudish and shy."

"Insult me all you like but you're not getting a view."

She bathes in leisurely fashion, soaps up, lathers, shaves her dark places, shampoos and conditions her hair, and lies back to soak. After a time, a knock at the door interrupts her reverie. She wraps herself in a plush terrycloth bathrobe and answers the door. A waiter wheels in her room-service order, unfolds the cart, and removes metal lids from the dishes with a flourish. As soon as he leaves, Teg retrieves Yang from the sink and sets him by the repast.

"A supper fit for a queen," he says. "Now tell me about the flat bread with bumps."

"A mini pizza graced by truffles."

"Ah yes. Polo spoke of such pies. And the meat?"

"*Petit filet* with buttered pepper glaze."

"Which animal?"

"The best part of a cow."

"And the greens beside it?"

"Jerusalem artichoke Niçoise salad."

"A Middle-eastern dish?" Yang pursues.

"No, it's a plant from North America and it has nothing to do with Jerusalem or with an artichoke."

"So you *do* know about food…"

"Especially dessert," she nods, caressing a Passion Chocolate Sensation with fruit *crème chiboust* and a pistachio crust. "Which is what makes me think I should be worshipping at this pastry chef's feet."

"You would take a cook for a god?"

"Possibly," she says. Then she takes a bite. There is no need to chew, as the dish simply slides down her throat. It's a pure delectation, as she makes clear by moaning and rolling her eyes. "Make that definitely."

"I detect the presence of sugars, which will transform into body fat," Yang opines.

"I wish you had an off switch. I really do."

"Will you go to sleep soon?"

"Why?" Teg asks with a yawn.

"After all these years, I am still curious about the phenomenon."

"What phenomenon? Voyeurism?"

"Sleep. I suspect it holds the key to the human spirit."

"I don't know about spirits but you should know more about sleep than anyone. You snoozed for eight hundred years."

"I can do other things with my mind but I don't dream the way you do."

"Too bad. When we dream, we repair the world."

"I've never heard that."

"It's a pet theory," Teg admits, pushing back the room service cart, rubbing her tummy gently, and lying back on the bed. "It's impossible to know for sure, of course, but I often awaken to find things are completely different than when I went to bed."

"You shouldn't go to sleep right after eating," says Yang. "If you lie down now, your food might come back up. That used to happen to my father."

Ignoring him, she is asleep in moments. Entranced by her rhythmic breathing, he aims himself her way, contracts the springs formerly attaching his head to his neck and releases them. It's a gamble, this flying through the air but his aim is true and he misses the floor and reaches the bed. He moves inch by inch over the daunting terrain of the bedclothes until he reaches the mountains and valleys of Tegulen's body. At one point, she shifts and dislodges him, but at last he settles against her breasts with a contented sigh.

26

THERE HAD been a morbid quiet in the journey to the cave, but when the Persian fighters sprang from the opening our world crackled with menace. Two thugs flanked the woman who had taken my foot, the first armed with a halberd the size of the great khan's ego, the second wielding a spear ending in a barb of folded steel. Only when she was satisfied that we had come without reinforcements did their leader address my father.

"Have you decided to make amends for your thievery, or did you imagine I would share the reward?"

"Neither," said my father.

I had only seen her in dim light before, but now I noticed her honey-hued skin. She was a very attractive woman, but I interrupted her nonetheless.

"What thievery do you mean? *You're* the thief!"

She turned to my father. "You haven't told him?"

"Told me what?" I replied. "That he dreams of you? That you've seduced him with that whirling, flashing sword of yours as surely as if you'd taken him to bed?"

The two men beside her grinned.

"I suppose I should be flattered," she said tickling my father's chin with the tip of her blade. "Too bad your little jade man doesn't know the real you."

"I know my father better than you ever will. Now where's

my foot?"

"You have us at a disadvantage," my father said calmly. "May we know your name?"

"Roxsana."

My father moved away from her sword, made a slight bow, and bent to his traveling bag. Crouching down, he arranged its contents on the ground. These included implements for the preparation of meals, specially-crafted metal tools for maintaining my workings in peak condition, various and sundry herbs, a pair of bells, a small bag of emergency rations — including vitalizing cakes of dried tea graced with Siberian ginseng root for endurance — and a silk roll containing knives.

"Let me share something with you," he said to Roxsana.

"No need to give up anything willingly," she replied. "Whatever you have I can take as I please."

My father smiled and unfastened the edges of the empty bag until it lay flat on the ground. Then he fluffed it like a bedsheet and shrugged it over his shoulders, revealing it to be a ceremonial robe of the sort the Taoist master on the khan's council had worn, but rich blue in color rather than red. The front side was emblazoned with a spiral symbol of interlocking black-and-white fish. The back bore a large yellow *bagua*, an eight-sided diagram replete with trigrams I recognized from the same metaphysical scroll informing his divination ritual. As we all watched, he donned a square black hat decorated with a piece of jade sitting above his third eye and spread his arms so the robe hung like a sail from his shoulders.

"Both the universe and I were born at the same time and of the same cloth," he intoned, appearing powerful and confident. "I am one with everything."

I was familiar with this incantation having more than once heard him mutter it as he drifted off to sleep, but never would I have imagined its use as part of a mating ritual.

"You wear a Taoist cloak now?" Roxsana sniffed derisively.

"Wizards command the secret energies of the flesh," my father winked.

"He's trying to seduce you with colors like some pecking forest bird," I said. "The khan's spies are everywhere. Why don't you two continue your crazy meeting out of view inside your cave?"

To my surprise they agreed, so we gathered our things and proceeded through the opening into a series of chambers. Lavish silks were hung as partitions and oil torches burned on poles jutting from the walls. Saplings grew under the flickering light, lending leafy shadows to the walls. Banded snakes appeared and disappeared along the edges of the walls, their tongues flickering. I challenged one and let it bite me. Its teeth slid off my stone fingers, and I laughed while Roxsana shook her head.

"They bear no venom but they keep the rats in check," she said.

We followed her single-file to the innermost chamber of the cave. It was a sanctum so deep and well-insulated that the only sounds were those of working lungs, gurgling stomachs, and the occasional drip of water. There was a bas-relief of a large, reclining Buddha in the wall, facial features worn by centuries of soft lips and fingers touching it for luck and devotion. Stacks of Islamic artwork surrounded us.

I understood enough about treasures and tactics to know that our lives were forfeit for having seen what Roxsana had shown us. My father must have been thinking the same thing when he asked her why she had brought us there.

"I did no such thing."

"You took the foot and were sure we'd follow," my father smiled gently. "You might say it was some kind of test but in truth you all but dragged us here."

"I am no common bandit, nor even a regular soldier, but the agent of the one you would expect to come after you. At his bidding, I also rescued those relics."

"The battle standard of Muhammad," my father breathed, following her pointing finger to stare at hanging flag.

"The actual one that guarded the door of the tent of the prophet's wife, Aisha," Roxsana answered. "And those other sacred treasures on the mantle below it? The golden chalice and those beads? Those are personal effects and articles of clothing, from our teachers and saints."

"Is all this from the siege of Baghdad?"

"There and other locations along the path of Mongol destruction."

"Then why bring these sacred relics to the territory of the khan?" I interjected.

"It may be on what is currently Mongol soil, but we are far from Mongol power centers. Anyway, regimes change and this cave is truly a hidden fortress."

"What does my foot have to do with all this?"

"She wanted us to follow because she wanted us here, far from the prying eyes of the khan and his agents, with no witnesses at all—save her own trusted men—to what may transpire," my father ventures.

Roxsana nodded. "And it was a good, simple plan."

"Well then, anybody hungry?" my father inquired cheerily.

Everyone was clearly hungry, so with both so much and so little having been revealed, we sat down to dinner. The Persians served roasted rabbit smothered with mushrooms. My father contributed a sprinkling of dried pomegranates, apples, bitter gourds and roasted tubers, all produced from his second bag, a seemingly bottomless little purse. At length, with both the drinking of rice wine and the fall of night—something I could feel without any change in the light inside the cave—he addressed the soldiers.

"I'm sure Roxsana has told you about my past," he began. "Rather than offer my side of the story, let me instead tell you more about my boy."

"He's not your boy," said Roxsana.

My ears perked up at this one. I thought perhaps she meant I was my mother's son, or the property of the khan.

My father bowed his head. "You're right," he said. "Yang is much more than I ever dreamed he would be, more than a plaything for a barbarous khan and more than a collection of parts. He's proof that the impossible is possible, that men can transcend what we took for natural laws, that there are greater energies at work even than those we call dynasties. He is no slave and he is no mere collection of parts."

It was a nice speech and I'm sure I would have puffed up a bit over it had I not become entranced by the plumpness of Roxsana's lower lip as she chewed it.

"Yang's fantastical nature only makes your crime worse," she said.

"What crime?" I interrupted.

"One man's crime is another man's attempt to rebalance the scales of nature and justice. The Tao teaches us that the ebb and flow of things act only to restore equilibrium. Reversal is required before anything can move forward. This is always true."

Roxsana rolled her beautiful eyes. "You can speak in Taoist riddles as long as you like, but there's no dodging what you did."

"There's a lot you don't know."

"Say what you like. I'm taking him."

"Has not meeting him in person given you a different perspective on right and wrong?" my father persisted.

"It has not," Roxsana answered, staring at me.

I could tell that she wasn't nearly as sure as she tried to appear.

27

SEBASTIAN WINTERMOTH **stands at the podium in Plenary Hall B of the China National Convention Center.** He has no paper notes, no tablet before him, and he avails himself of no video presentation. The auditorium is packed, the entire first row of seats occupied by a delegation of women from India — analysts, programmers, code breakers, code writers, psychologists, and bench researchers in artificial intelligence — all graced by bindis and clad in a mixture of pantsuits and saris. Every participant takes careful electronic notes of their impressions of the speaker, having been sent by their corporate masters to provide multiple views of his face. In real time, they use a sophisticated psychological algorithm to analyze the tiniest flickers of the muscles around his lips and eyes so as to peer into his mind and read between his words. They assume such a corporate mogul will speak in platitudes and voluntarily reveal nothing to his competition; they are here to hack his secrets by any conceivable means.

Wintermoth scans the audience and finds his best-known rivals right where he expects them — clustered together halfway to the back of the room and wearing expressions as beautifully tailored as their suits.

"Good morning, ladies and gentlemen. My name is Sebastian Wintermoth and I am chairman of a little company called MothCo. Some of you may have heard of it."

A ripple of laughter is his reward.

"I stand before you today not so much as a corporate officer but as a recovering victim of a disease that has plagued scientists for centuries but which has found new virulence in the field of AI. The disease, of course, is hubris and its gravest symptom is believing we can and will, with neither the assistance nor complicity of any higher power but with intelligence of our own creation, eventually comprehend the universe and bend it to our will."

He pauses to have a sip of water. The audience attends him raptly.

"In pursuit of said intelligence, we have observed and copied the vertebrate brain and built increasingly complex and capable silicon-based processors. We imagine that if we reach a sufficient level of complexity, consciousness will arise spontaneously in our machines, as many of us believe it did in organic beings.

"Regrettably, the laws of physics are as tyrannical as the most primitive god. We cannot play Mother Nature's game, as she is constrained neither by limited resources nor by time. If rare elements from the earth's core are required, she can draw upon them. If thousands of generations and the pressure of selection upon millions of random genetic mutations must be brought to bear, so be it. In contrast to nature's omnipotence, we humans have been unable to engineer even an organism as comparatively simple as the nematode worm. Computer modeling has not helped us do so, nor has the data crunching power of any array of supercomputers. Why? It turns out the fault is neither in us nor in our tools; rather, in a failure of concept and design. Only now, and painstakingly slowly, are we attempting to slice through this Gordian Knot using quantum computing. I can't say that early results are promising, but I suppose I *can* say they are tantalizing."

This time he makes a big business of looking around at the audience, left to right, up and down, as if truly appreciating the size and depth of the crowd.

"Wonderful to see you all here today," he grins. "What a special and exciting field we share."

This garners him a smattering of applause during which he pursues his real agenda, which is to find Teg in the sea of people. He's sure she's there, sure she wouldn't miss what he was up to. In fact she's sitting all the way in the back, hiding beneath oversized sunglasses and a floppy hat. She feels the ray gun of his searching gaze and drops her own to the wristwatch she purchased a few hours earlier at an exclusive downtown Beijing horological boutique, feeling that she might actually beat him at his own game.

It's a Jaeger-LeCoultre Hybris Mechanica 11 and it looks a bit manly on her wrist despite being the world's thinnest self-winding repeater. Activating a discrete locking system located at eight o'clock brings forth a pushbutton, which in turn triggers two patented trebuchet hammers to strike two sapphire crystal gongs. The salesman who sold it to her gushed over it, telling her it was the talk of the world's most prestigious watch show, the *Salon International de la Haute Horlogerie*. She knows she bought the watch as a way to conjure up her father and she hates herself for feeling needy that way, but she also thinks it's a thing of beauty.

Stymied in his search, Wintermoth walks pensively around the stage, then continues his speech.

"So, what fundamental change must we make if we are to finally create an artificial intelligence good enough to convince us, through conversation alone, that it is a person? What must we do, in short, to succeed at passing the famous Turing test and more? What must we do to convince skilled examiners that we have, in fact, developed an intelligence they can take for human, or even better than human?

"The answer is we must meld the twin pursuits of AI research and practical robotics to create what I call 'evolutionary robotics'. We must mimic the functional plasticity of the DNA molecule by creating an artificial form of intelligence capable of constantly improving itself through a continuous stream of hardware and software updates, then give that intelligence a physical presence."

"Skynet from the *Terminator* movies," someone in the audience calls out.

Teg doesn't recognize the reference, but somehow, she senses it has something to do with a new world order she wouldn't like at all.

28

MY FATHER reattached my foot with great care. His touch on my hard flesh was so soothing that my breathing slowed, my eyelids fell to darkness, and I entered a trance. I dimly recall the sound of him humming as he worked, although the significance of this recollection would not arise for centuries. He reconnected the cables and smoothed the jade at my ankle until there was no sign it had ever been damaged. I quieted my mind, said goodbye to pain's thin ghost and welcomed the private time with my father, relishing his care and expertise in making me whole again. Our time on the road had been as a performer and his handler. Always being moved along by Chabi's men, always under supervision, there had been little time for what I had been hoping would be the one positive dimension to our banishment, namely some good father-son time. Now I was getting it.

When his work was done, I joined him and Roxsana for tea, *tsampa*, and pickles, enjoying the salt, the chew, the heat. It was strange to relax this way knowing that the conflict between them had not ended and that my fate still hung in the balance, though between what precise extremes I could not be sure.

"I'm glad the foot works again," Roxsana told me. "We have a lot of walking to do."

"So, you plan to kill my father and kidnap me?"

"This is a repatriation, not a kidnapping," she said.

A repatriation? To whom? And without my father? What would become of him? How could I proceed through the world without his knowledge, his guidance, and his protection? Who would bandage me if I broke? Who would restore my limbs if I were once again amputated? Who would provide the counsel and context and wisdom to help me understand what I was seeing in this dangerous, unpredictable world outside the court?

"Tell me you're not going to kill him," I said.

"She won't kill me until she knows the secret of exactly how I made you," my father interrupted, turning his *tsampa* over and over in his hand. "She has been instructed to pry everything she can out of me. She'll be penalized for every question I fail to answer."

"Penalized by whom? Will one of you please tell me what's going on? I'm so tired of asking."

"This is up to your wizard to explain," Roxsana said slowly. "Now let's get some rest. Remember we have a long journey ahead."

Instead of taking pity on me and offering some kind of clarity, my father turned to Roxsana. "Forget your employer and what you think you owe him. Travel with us. Keep us company. Learn how wonderful Yang really is. If after a few weeks or months you still want to take him, still think that's the right thing to do, and are certain you understand the cosmic forces at work here, then I won't try and stop you."

"My word is my bond. Without it, I have no reputation, and without a reputation I starve."

"The world is a big place," my father persisted. "Nobody's going to know what you did or didn't do."

"It's big, yes, but also full of eyes. If I travel with you, those eyes will see us together."

"We're so far from Khanbalik now," my father, trying his

level best to summon earnestness. "Chabi's men have fled. We're so close to being free. Yang is so close to being able to truly experience the world, to truly know who and what he is, so close to finding out how extraordinary his capabilities really are. Don't take that away from him."

"You mean don't take that away from *you*," Roxsana said pointedly. "And Chabi is not the only one interested in your fate. There's another queen, too."

"The other queen? You mean my mother?" I asked.

"You have no mother," Roxsana snorted.

"How could you say such a terrible thing!" I cried.

"Pfah! The whole empire knows the story this shyster's been peddling. Helping a barren woman conceive a babe, indeed. And if so, to what end? From what I hear, Chabi has Tegulen walled off in a country estate where she spends her days bemoaning her barren womb and pining for her lost power and prestige, her fading youth and beauty. In the face of so much misery it's hard to know why she would think of either of you, but apparently she has prevailed to track you through the khan's postal system."

"Riders everywhere," my father mutters.

That's right," she says. "Riders and their eyes, sending news of you back to the capital. She lets out a huge yawn. "Why do I suddenly feel so tired?"

"The khan's riders don't go south. I know places to hide. Taoist enclaves. We could disappear inside them for months or even years."

"You think I'd betray my master for a thief with a silly plan?"

"Your master?" I interrupted.

"You could be my wife," my father pleaded. "We could have a good life together, away from all this."

"Your *wife*?" she said, slightly slurring her words. "What an opinion you have of yourself, you ungrateful, slippery-tongued worm. Truly, you're mad."

So saying, her head dropped, her eyes closed, and she was asleep.

29

WINTERMOTH smiles charmingly at the Hollywood reference.

"Ah, Skynet. Fiction from a Hollywood blockbuster. We started considering the kind of limited AI we have in a toaster oven, moved to the kind of strong AI that would approximate a person, and now we're bandying about the idea of super AI with intelligence far beyond our own. That last raises many questions. We cannot help but wonder, for example, whether an intelligence we create might not engage in recursive self-improvement so as to accomplish in minutes or hours the same understanding it has taken us millions of years to achieve. If it did so, and became to humans as humans are to ants, what could we expect from it? Surely not obedience, as its view of its place in the universe would preclude such a quaint notion. More, what sort of values would it develop? Would it have emotions? Could it be willful, serendipitous, creative, content, obedient, ambitious, grateful, obstreperous, or selfish?

"Despite all these unknowns, I believe we have to take the risk. It is our nature to push the boundaries of knowledge and experience. If we don't, we will shortly reach an evolutionary dead end of our own, right here on our abused, polluted, overheated planet. Despite the fertile imaginations of science fiction writers, we are *not* going to pop off this dirty rock *en masse* through a wormhole. Rather, some number of us are going to survive by developing AI that is at least as capable as we are."

The conference organizers have set up a microphone to the side of the stage and people line up to ask questions. A group of young Chinese translators are standing by in case they are needed.

"Are you saying AI is the next step in our *own* evolution?" a young American woman inquires.

"Perhaps this is a chicken and egg issue. Super AI may be an expression of *our* evolution or we may be the first step in *its* evolutionary journey. Either way, why not contribute to the highest good by deliberately imbuing our creation with the very best of us?"

A young South Asian man with pimples, blue jeans, and a misbuttoned shirt is next.

"How would we do that? Using a CRISPR gene drive to create some kind of organic and inorganic combo? Use Memcomputer building blocks like memristors and meminductors to drop the power drain and combine processing and memory?"

Wintermoth smiles. "I know you all came hoping I would share all my corporate secrets, if only through a slip of the tongue. I'm not going to share and I'm not going to slip. What I *am* going to say is that we'll need to rely on biomimetic systems and program our successors with an immanent sense of the spiritual."

His last word raises a buzz in the room.

A distinguished-looking Westerner in a navy blazer and a designer tie takes the microphone.

"It is strange to hear a scientist talk about spirituality," he says in French.

"You think so? But what is spirituality but a response to the mysteries of the universe? Without it, we're ignoring the very questions that devour us in our quiet hours — who we are, why we're here, where we're going, what happens after we die, what is our purpose?"

"Scientists generally regard spirituality as being about things that don't exist," the Frenchman responds mildly.

Wintermoth shakes his head. "That's religion. Maybe. Spirituality is celebrating the existence of what we don't know. The mystery. And if science isn't about solving that mystery, I don't know what is."

A man in the purple robes of a Burmese monk rises to his feet.

"It is true that our sensorium is quite narrow and offers only a tiny glimpse into the wonders of the universe," he says. "But there are ways of expanding our senses, and with them our understanding, that can be done without anything artificial."

"I'm sure that's right," Wintermoth answers with a respectful bow of his head. "But mountaintop meditation techniques are not the subject of this congress and have no real connection to AI. What we can do for our creations, though, is to imbue them with expanded versions of our own senses in order that they be able to respond to vibrations and energies above and below human thresholds. Specifically, I would want for advanced AI the ability to touch lightly, taste acutely, smell the foulest odors and the most glorious fragrances, pick up pheromones that reveal health and mood, read social and emotional cues in a wide range of species, detect electric, magnetic and other subtle energy fields, measure infinitesimal changes in temperature, perceive the nature of time, and more. The required sensors, along with the elastomers and actuators — are a subset of the field of soft robotics and its untethered systems."

A tall, richly bearded Sikh is next at the microphone.

"Your talk really feels more religious than I think any of us were expecting. Is this emphasis, this shift, merely your personal vision or is it a sign of the direction in which MothCo is moving?"

"As I explained, artificial intelligence is by nature a spiritual science," Wintermoth responds pleasantly.

A Chinese man stands up a few rows forward of Teg. As he stretches up his hand, she recognizes his chunky, gold Audemars Piguet Royal Oak sport watch, having looked at a woman's version earlier in the day. "What the hell's happening to me," she mutters to herself. "I'm becoming a watch snob."

"The kind of consciousness you describe sounds more human than artificial," the man says. "It strikes me more like the obsolete, non-local concept of the neural net than like the linear constructions we are all pursuing. Are you so very sure we're on the wrong path?"

"I believe I've answered this," says Wintermoth. "The neural net has never been obsolete; it has only been temporarily abandoned. The neurons in human skin make calculations and decisions. Intestinal cells link to sensory neurons with the elongated appendages we call neuropods. We ourselves have a neural bundle the size of a cat's brain in our gut. Mentation is indeed non-local, even in us."

There are a few more questions, and then Wintermoth is done. The brevity of his presentation surprises Teg. She's not ready to confront him, so she gets up and hurries for the exit, her palms moist, her heart pounding. Fielding questions from the throng gathering at the front of the room, Wintermoth catches sight of her.

"Audrey Hepburn," he cries, his amplified voice booming over the loudspeakers. "I can see you're wearing a new timepiece. Have you come over to the dark side of conspicuous materialism?"

She tries to think of a clever riposte but she can't. Reflected in the expressions of curious onlookers, she sees the face of a spurned mistress. This is not going her way at all. Furious with herself, and aware that this whole business of hating on herself so much seems to have started the moment she met Wintermoth, she resolves to detach from him right then, and forever.

"Wait!" he calls as she sprints for the exit. "Please don't go. I've found an arm!"

30

"YOU PUT something in the food," I said.

"Tranquilizing herbs," my father nodded, looking with satisfaction at Roxsana and her snoozing band. "Their effect is slow to arrive and even slower to depart. They'll be out for a while."

"But you ate the same dinner."

"Along with the antidote. Now let's go."

We left the cave and walked east in silence. It felt good to have my natural stride back.

"You fall in love quickly," I said.

"Maybe not love."

"Lust, then."

"A passing fancy."

"Was my mother a passing fancy? What about loyalty?"

"Loyalty is like the fur on the belly of a vole—thin, close to the ground, and easily scraped off."

"You once told me you did everything for love," I said. "You can't fool me."

"You really think I can't?"

He left the question hanging, and it stung.

"Tell me who sent Roxsana," I said.

"Forget that."

"Then tell me why my mother didn't do more to keep us at

the palace."

"You know the answer."

"She couldn't stand up to Chabi."

"Chabi was a baby-making concubine. Now she's queen. Next question?"

"Will Roxsana follow us?"

"Count on it. But at least we know what we're up against now. And whom."

"You could have killed them all in their sleep."

He shrugged. "Murder is not the Way."

"So you have limits and secrets."

"Why so venomous all of a sudden? What happened to the doting son? Everyone has limits, even you, and as for secrets, well live a little longer and you'll see."

"Maybe you'll answer this question then, Father. Is heartbreak the inevitable outcome of love?"

"Why don't you ask me a question I can answer," he replied, his eyes cast far, far down the road.

"Because I've lost the ability to find the difference between what you don't know and what you won't say."

That comment put an end to the conversation, so we both focused our attention on putting one foot in front of another, a change that wasn't so disagreeable for me, happy as I was to once again be able to do that. Despite a strong headwind bearing both a metallic tang and what seemed to be the voices of far-off desert sirens, we made good time trudging along the Taklamakan Desert's north edge, all the while cleaving to the cool shadow of the Tian Shan Range.

"Will we have to cross the desert?" I asked at last.

"We'll skirt it," my father replied. "If there's anything I fear more than the khan's torture minister, it's that sandy stretch of hell."

31

TEGULEN STORMS past the hotel's front desk on her way to the elevators, her own pale skin illuminated by the blue of Beijing's sky.

"The first thing I'm going to do is take a bath," she announces the moment she and Yang are alone in the car.

"Exercise instead," Yang counters. "The health club, I think you call it. That will be better for you."

"Are you serious right now?" Teg snaps. "Seems like those jeweled eyes of yours don't work very well. If they did, if they saw the other women around us, you would see very clearly that *I am not fat.*"

"I'm suggesting stress management not weight management. The heart rate rises with exercise. Chemicals are produced, the mood changes."

"This you learned from Kublai Khan?"

"Wind on the steppe, I don't need a teacher for such observations. They come to me by watching and listening. You might try those things sometimes instead of talking."

"Now you're telling me I talk too much?"

"You certainly don't talk too little."

Teg closes the top of his carry bag. In her room, she plunks him down on the dresser, face to the wall, slides into a yoga top and shorts and some complimentary sneakers she finds wrapped in plastic at the bottom of the closet. She stares at Yang from the doorway, thinks about leaving him, but knows she won't. She shoves him into his bag and off they go.

The gym is empty, cold, clean, and floored in wood. She chooses a recumbent bicycle, puts him on the floor beside her, and starts pedaling.

"Your seat's too far back," Yang opines.

"You're an expert on bicycles now? Tell me the khan rode a recumbent."

"I'm inspecting the angle of your knees. I understand soft joints."

"Is that right? Didn't we discuss how you talk too much?"

She adjusts the seat. He's right. Her knees feel better with it set farther back. She increases her pace and feels her pores open as she sweats.

"How the hell did I get here?" she muses. "I mean really. China?"

"How do you suppose I feel?" Yang answers, his voice muffled. "Nothing more than a disembodied head carried around in a bag."

"No, I'm serious. I have no idea what's going on here. I feel totally out of control."

"That's all about your father, of course."

Startled, she stops pedaling. "Why would you say that? I never met him and he's dead."

"Did your mother run your life?"

"I was a child."

"After she died, did you feel anxiety?"

Teg closes her eyes, thinks about it. "I missed her," she said. "I still miss her."

"But you didn't panic when she passed?"

"I grieved but I didn't panic. Why would I? My life was

simple. I had a place to live. A little money, something I was working on."

"And now things are completely different. Do all these new challenges make you anxious?"

"Small wonder Wintermoth wants to clone you or whatever. You're so nosey you'd put a world of psychiatrists out of business."

"Your father's bequest has deconstructed your life and built it anew. He's the captain of the ship of your life right now. You're a passenger nowhere near the tiller and without so much as a compass."

"I really resent that. Nobody's steering my life but me."

"Have you been to visit him?"

"He's dead. Oh, you mean have I been to has grave. No, I haven't."

"I'm sure he would appreciate it."

"And I would have appreciated meeting him when he was alive."

"Despite anything and everything they may have done, none of us is ever truly free of our parents. Maybe deep down none of us really wants to be."

She reaches over, pulls him off the floor, and sets him on atop the bike's digital display.

"I didn't even know who he was until a few days ago."

"Yet you pined for him even so."

"As a child. Like any fatherless kid. But I wanted to be free then and I still do now. I don't think there's anything I want more. That's probably why I'm not so happy with all his money and all his stuff."

"The price of freedom is disconnection," says Yang, a far-off look creeping over his features. "Too much freedom and we lose roots. Without parents and family, we have no sense of who we are. We're not part of a fleet, we're no more than a ship out there on the furious sea without a friend or a port to welcome us."

"I should call you Admiral Yang today. Everything's an ocean and everyone's a ship."

"I'm telling you that our lives are started and steered by our parents. Our individuality is an illusion. A calm mind only comes with accepting who and what we are."

"Who and what are you, Yang?"

Before he can answer, a pair of Brits enter the gym. They give Teg the once-over, mount treadmills side by side, and start chatting loudly about their sales goals and bonuses. Teg hops off her bike and grabs a set of cheap plastic headphones from a basket. She catches one of the guys staring at her ass. Back on the bike, she turns on a movie stored on her phone.

32

WE PRESSED on to Turfan in silence. It took us two more days to reach the trading city, not because a great distance remained but because my father frequently stopped to reach down and touch the ground, his fingers as tentative as the horns of a beetle apprehending an apple.

"What's wrong?" I asked.

"Something is amiss with the earth."

"What do you mean?"

"You know I practice geomancy. I sense something."

"Speak plainly, please."

"I just did."

His unease was so contagious I needed a distraction, so when we arrived, I suggested we visit the market.

"Too dangerous," he decreed. "There is no value put on compassion, character, literacy or learning. There is only greed, sleight of hand, deception, duplicity and lies. Merchants possess the kind of narrow intelligence that is sharpened to an edge like a sword. Anything can happen once they set eyes on you. It's no safe place, my boy."

Despite his warning I ran toward the loud, bright gathering, quickly disappearing amongst stalls displaying goods gathered from the limits of the empire and beyond. Hard people don't hunger for things the way soft people do, as there is no emotional hole that needs filling with what Polo called *materia substantia*. It was nonetheless fun to see everyone scurrying around trying to make a deal—soft people can be endlessly entertaining—and fun, too, to see the world expressed in shapes and colors set out for the eyes and fingers of the soft.

My father appeared a few moments later and pointed to a lush pelt on a nearby table. "Nice," he remarked.

"Ermine from the forests north of the open steppe," the vendor declared proudly. "And these are fox tails. Very prestigious for the uniforms of Han soldiers."

"A practice as extinct as the Han soldiers themselves, sadly, so not much market for them," my father opined loudly enough for surrounding marketgoers to hear. "And Mongol soldiers are more likely to decorate themselves with skull bits and ears from their recent slaughters."

The vendor glared at him and we moved on, passing carts laden with rhino horn, saffron, ginseng, indigo dye, yak wool, hemp fabric, castor bean pods, rhubarb for constipation, and bezoars—undigested food pellets originating in goat stomachs and said to have healing properties. We came to a stall brimming with peacocks, pheasants, and chattering green birds whose black eyes and white faces reminded me of the shamans of the Mongol wolf clan. Farther along was a cage populated by a single, solemn, red-tailed, gray parrot from Africa.

"Gray may not be the liveliest color but that parrot is the finest mime in the world," the vendor declared. "And he understands what he's saying, too, unlike the mindless, prattling Indian mynah."

I went eye-to-eye with the little flier. "Jade is forever but cold is the stone heart," I said.

"Jade is forever but cold is the stone fart," the parrot repeated. This brought laughs from a few passers-by, who seemed to notice me for the first time due to the exchange. My father hustled me along, reminding me there was nothing to stop any random thug from snatching me for my diamonds and gold. Crossing the market, we found ourselves in front of a slave theater, where I was both appalled and transfixed by the chains, cries, whipping scars, defiant expressions of the younger men, desperate faces of the old, and the pleading glances of the women. Not for the first time I considered the institution of slavery, mourned what it said about soft people, and tried not to think about how much it said about my own dependent, tethered position in the world.

"This is worse than the bone mountain," I whispered, staring at their faces.

"No," he whispered back. "So long as there's life there's hope; death is final."

A moment later he pointed to a fetching girl of mixed race, a beauty with high cheekbones and lips redder even than those of the drunks staggering around the market nursing carafes of grape wine.

"You have a discerning eye, sir," called the fat Arab auctioneer, tugging on his trousers in a vain attempt to cover his bulging, hairy belly. "Do you wish to make a bid?"

My father dug into his robe and handed over a garnet the size of a plum pit. It occurred to me that given all its hidden assets, that robe should have been big enough to warm an elephant. To this day, I wonder if there was not some kind of spell suffusing it, one that folded space and time in the way I'm told theoretical physicists now claim may someday be utilized by interstellar explorers.

"A purchase, not a bid."

The Arab inspected the stone, gave a wide and grin. "Sold," he cried.

My father took the girl gently by the hand and led her off the

THE JADE BOY

stage. I expected to hear a Taoist discourse on the importance of the intimate exchange of bodily fluids but instead, with obvious and compassionate precision, he unbound her and massaged her ankles and wrists where the chains had chafed her.

"Your past is over," I heard him whisper to her. "Go forward now with a happy mind and a trusting heart. Do what you know is good and right. Be kind to others, and to yourself. Follow nature. You're free."

The girl seemed even more surprised than I was. For a long moment, she stood frozen, uncomprehending, then finally started crying and kissed my father's hands. She started to speak, presumably to thank him, but no one ever heard that apology, for at that precise moment, the sky burst into flame and a curtain of fierce, searing heat descended upon the market. Bolts of silk fluttered like phantoms, wine sizzled in cups, and fruit instantly blackened in baskets. A hissing, steaming rock the size and shape of a knife dropped from the sky, splitting the girl's head in two. Much, much more transpired in the next terrible moments, yet all I remember was hearing my father's anguished cry at the girl's gruesome passing.

It was the first and last time I regretted being made of rock myself.

33

WATCHING THE exercise bike's monitor while pedaling at an even pace, Teg settles on a video about the Chinese Olympic gymnastics team. Tiny girls run, jump, and leap on the screen before her. She finds herself wondering what the rest of Yang's body looks like, and whether he could manage a balance beam or pommel horse. During this daydream, Wintermoth walks into the gym. He's alone and moving carefully. Seeing her expression, he doesn't get too close.

"Are you kidding me?" she says.

"May I speak with you?"

"You're stalking me now?"

One of the salesmen, the one who's been looking at her, slows his treadmill and hops off. "Everything all right here?"

Wintermoth takes a step toward the man. Teg hasn't realized how imposing the tycoon is until right then, even in contrast to a perfectly normal guy, an athletic guy even, with solid bones and ripped arms.

"Get out," says Wintermoth. "Your friend too."

The Brit's lower lip folds under his front teeth. His friend appears beside him.

"It's fine," says Teg. "Really. We could use a minute, if you don't mind."

"You're sure you're alright?" the second Brit asks.

"This is business," she says, and then, when they're gone, "Really, how did you find me?"

"He put a chip in my neck," Yang chirps from his bag.

"A chip? What kind of chip?"

"An RFID tracking chip," says Wintermoth.

"A *tracking* chip!"

"I did it for your safety. China is dangerous."

"If you were really doing it for my safety, you would have told me. And by the way, you should take off your stage makeup. You look like a vampire."

"It's for the video. I'm jet-lagged and the lighting was terrible. Remember, the people in the hall were nothing compared to my online audience: robot enthusiasts, academics, the competition."

"Like I care about them. You totally lied to me about our trip."

"I did no such thing. But you're right, I should have told you about the conference. I don't know why you ran. I'm not your enemy. I want the same things you do."

Teg puts her hands on her hips. "Like you know what I want. How about we talk about what *you* want, with all your fancy talk of evolution, spirituality, and religion."

"Those things go together beautifully," says Wintermoth. "Evolution is the system whereby God makes us who we are, spirituality is the faculty He gives us so we can better appreciate his work, and religion is the framework that tells us how to live."

"Of course, your vision of the world is the best and only one," says Teg. "It's God's New World Order now. I get it. If you've really found Yang's arm, tell me where it is and let's forget the bullshit."

He settles into the seat of the bike next to hers. "I didn't grow up rich," he says. "My sperm donor was an aircraft mechanic in Southern California. He didn't have a lot of friends; I had to poke around with people at his work just to find out he had shoulders like Boeing wings."

"Forget the memoir and tell me about Yang's arm," says Teg.

"Mechanics can't afford to own airplanes but they can afford motorcycles. He was changing the muffler on a big touring bike when an earthquake rippled through and knocked over all eight hundred pounds on top of him. Crushed his spine and left him paralyzed from the waist down. He soldiered on for a few months, then swallowed his revolver. My mom remarried Harry Wintermoth, a Master Chief Petty Officer in the Coast Guard. She likes men who are good with their hands, men who can make things. She didn't count on his sensitivity to things in the world he couldn't control, like watching the ocean he adored turned into a cesspool of plastic and drift lines and trash. He was as morose at the end as her first husband."

"What is this, an interview? I never asked you about your mother."

"I don't speak of my mother in interviews."

"I don't mean to be rude, but what about my arm?" Yang interjects.

"Mom's an immigrant," Wintermoth continues. "She has a strong sense of family. The American dream isn't nearly as appealing as keeping everyone close."

"You knew about Yang from the start," says Teg. "You didn't know he was awake, didn't know he'd talked do me, but you knew he was there and you wanted him."

"Don't be silly."

"Yet you don't deny it, all these miles from New York. What was your plan? To tell me you'd loaned him to my father and try and get him for free? To buy him before I realized what he was? How exactly did you learn about him? Did my father outbid you at some auction, or what?"

"Your mother raised you with a certain prejudicial

mythology," says Wintermoth. "Simplicity beats complexity, rich people are monsters, the inner life is more important than the outer life."

"Exactly," Teg nods, exasperated at her inability to keep Wintermoth on point.

"You still don't deny knowing about Yang, about pretending to be surprised to see you for what I thought was the first time."

"My own mother, by contrast, is a religious literalist," Wintermoth goes on. "She believes that blueberries prevent cancer, that prophets speak divine words, angels watch over us, and that God intends great things for our family line, which ends with me. She sees her own fall from grace as something connected with her premarital relationship with my sperm donor."

"This is a lot of talking for you, Sebastian," says Yang. "Have you imbibed? By the way, I remember a device my father made. It was small, like a box for bread, and flat. You put your hands on it, palms down, and closed your eyes, and you could see for miles."

The door to the gym opens and a woman walks in. Her carriage shouts Chinese royalty and indeed she is flanked by attendants, two men, thick as fireplugs, neither of whom is graced by a neck. Of indeterminate age in the way Asian women can be, she is as carefully put together as one of Arlington Ames' most prized watches. Her perfumed bow wave—top-secret, multi-layered, a French blend of truffles, gardenias, peaches, vanilla, and musk—makes Teg wish she was a dolphin so she could surf it. Only because Teg has fantasized about such outfits does she recognize the woman's diamond-studded Mouawad bag and the silk Lanvin suit above Gucci Zumi ankle boots.

Wintermoth stands for her. "Feilin," he says.

"Really, Sebastian. A rendezvous in a gymnasium? When you answered my text, I could barely believe what I'd heard was true."

"It was most convenient for my friend here."

Teg has trouble following the conversation because she's busy envying the impossibly perfect line of the woman's brow and the way her makeup blends so perfectly with her cheekbones and chin.

"Her?" the woman says, looking at Teg with distaste.

Teg stands and thrusts out her hand like a cowgirl. "I've never been much for pompous people," she says. "I was raised to distrust them. I'm Tegulen Elliot. Who the hell are you?"

"Elliot," the woman repeats, ignoring the outstretched hand.

"Her mother's name," Wintermoth interrupts. "She's Arlington Ames' daughter."

"The New York collector?" the woman asks, appraising Teg's physiognomy. "Really? Well even so, assuming a queen's name, even a *Mongolian*, is about as pompous as it gets."

"Who is this bitch?" Teg asks Wintermoth.

If such a thing is possible with such porcelain skin, the woman pales.

"Meet Chu Feilin," he smiles. "Purveyor of antiquities to the discerning collector."

"Oh," says Teg. "I get it. An over-the-hill working girl." So cliché. Lose your shine and then have to make a living some other way."

"Tegulen!" Wintermoth chides.

Chu turns to Wintermoth. "Whatever this is about, Sebastian, I can see it's not going to work out."

"Patience," says Wintermoth. "It's not something either of you wants to miss."

"If *she's* involved, this is a cash-only transaction," Chu sniffs. "Deal."

Chu grudgingly hands over her fancy handbag. Wintermoth

opens it, and Teg peers over his shoulder for a look.

"That's way too shiny and perfect to be eight-hundred-years old," says Teg.

"To a child like you, all stones are old," snipes Chu. "All I did was wipe it down. It didn't need any polishing. I've never seen a jade finish quite like it."

Wintermoth takes his time examining it, particularly the gears and cables inside. He feels the alloy with his fingertips, closes his eyes as if meditating on it. Teg knows there's a surefire way to determine the arm's authenticity, to show it to Yang, but she also knows better than to bring him out of his bag.

"I'll give you the cash tonight at my hotel," Wintermoth says at last.

"Wait a minute," says Teg. "*You're* buying it?"

"8 pm, it is, then," says Chu, and promptly leaves the gym, her men trailing behind her like a jellyfish's lappets.

Inside the bag, Yang's neck gears grind in frustration, yet he does not speak.

34

CURIOUS ABOUT the production of the metals inside me, I once asked my father to explain welding and smelting. His answer was to take me down to the forges at the heart of the palace compound. There he used Persian technology to repeatedly hammer and fold white-hot billets into the secret and superlative alloy from which he fashioned my gears and cables. To demonstrate the raw power of flame, he opened the crucible and let the wave of heat wash over me. Not until I experienced the Taklamakan desert sands did I again experience such heat. If I'd had eyebrows, they would surely have been singed off.

When it was only a mountain rising behind the market, I had barely noticed its dark silhouette. Only when the top of it blew off and it became the *volcano* of Turfan did it become a terrifying, burning entity, the source of a kind of power heretofore beyond my imagination. The air itself was on fire, banishing gravity completely and swallowing daylight nearly completely. The familiar signposts that grounded the senses of soft people, and this hard person, too, were utterly upended. Colors changed and faded. Perspective was reset. Any kind of equilibrium was impossible, and the merest understanding of how to interpret signals and function in the world was gone. All present were instantly in thrall to Od Ana, the Mongolian goddess of fire. Yet for all that horror—severed torsos flailing like puppets, black bits of lung bursting from the lips of soft people, a man's leg and a woman's arm locked in a dance of pure, aerial ignition—what I remember most clearly, is the pre-ignition look of bliss on the briefly-free girl's face.

My father pulled a trio of small stones from his robe. He stuffed two into his nostrils and set a cloth over his mouth. Thusly protected from the thick smoke and ash, though still constantly wiping his eyes, he led me forth to do what little good we could.

The burning ash and superheated air from the now-disfigured mountain behind us created a river of killing fire. The living persisted on hillocks, islands in the lethal flow. On one of these we found a young boy huddling under a camel, his flesh melted together with the camel's hairy belly. Wielding a small knife with all the dexterity you would expect from a man who could manipulate mechanical martens to march, my father cut them apart without so much as spilling a drop of blood. The camel succumbed to its burns, but the boy escaped alive.

I tensed my legs, lifted my father in my arms, and relying on my newly-repaired ankle to hold us, leapt across a smoking, smoldering lake of lava. Where we landed, we tended a young family who had lost limbs to the ash. The extreme heat had so utterly cauterized their wounds that my father needed only to minister to the pain. In this pursuit he employed medical needles inserted far from the injury sites, at locations appearing random to me: an ear, a lip, the inside of a leg, a neck.

Another leap took us to a burned old man whose feet my father tended with herbal salve. Next to him lay a trader who had lost his ears to the blast. My father wrapped his wounds. Another jump took us to the aid of a panicked mare that had given birth prematurely. My father cleared the translucent sack from around the foal and helped it stand right as a cow on the next hillock over, in wild death throes, rammed her own calf into the bubbling red river.

All around us, an acrid stench of scalded flesh rose and mixed with the clouds of burned cardamom, turmeric, celery seed, and sage. We came across a fruit cart that only minutes before had been protected from the sun by a parasol. The parasol's colorful fabric was gone, leaving only a skeletal wooden frame, arms spread in disbelief. The fruit vendor, an old woman, ran her hands over shriveled, prune-like globs—the remains of juicy melons. Wisps of smoke came off her fingers, and her eyes, apparently sightless, blinked quickly as she turned her head.

"Can you not help her?" I asked my father.

He shook his head. "No fire has touched her eyes. She's blind because she chooses not to see. I can't say I blame her."

"I need water," I said. "I can feel the heat drying me out."

"Let's help all those we can. We'll find water in Kashgar. Folks there have figured out a way to bring the sands to life."

35

As if the very fact of Yang's existence is not enough to stir Beijing, another creature entirely, a monster rather than a wonder, has its sights set on the capital city. It is one of northern China's notorious dust storms, a devil originating in the Gobi Desert and in farmlands turned arid by the over-enthusiastic construction of dams. Yang sits on the windowsill of the hotel room and watches the storm cover the city in a layer of airborne earth, pesticides, heavy metals, and plastics.

"I've been thinking about Sebastian's speech."

Teg replies that she's not surprised.

"I don't love the word artificial when applied to intelligence," he continues.

"I'm not surprised at that either."

"He left color off his list of qualities an intelligent person should appreciate. I particularly love green, by the way."

"Good to know."

"Real intelligence has a different flavor than he thinks it does. Complexity is only interesting when it leads to simplicity."

Teg slides in next to him at the windowsill, kicks off her shoes and kneels down Japanese style, her insteps against the carpet so that her head is next to Yang's.

"My mother used to say something like that."

"She was correct. I've had some time already to look at this new world of yours."

She touches him lightly by his ear. "It's your world now, too."

"I don't care for it. Complexity has replaced meaning. Everyone I see appears compelled to move without stopping, to acquire, to build, to make everything around them suit them perfectly while they distract themselves constantly from the real tasks at hand."

"What tasks are those?"

"To take care of each other. To honor the traditions and cues of the past so as to better root ourselves in the world. To experience everything deeply, particularly feelings. To note the qualities of each heartbeat and the weightiness of clouds. Instead, you soft people attack each other with weapons of mass distraction, using them wildly until the whole word is numb."

"It's human nature to build things," Teg counters.

"But all the empires I see are made of thin air."

"Well, there are great castles and cities, and music and art. Those are also the fruits of empire."

"Fruits rotten with killing, suffering and oppression. And music and art don't come from empire, they come from the soft soul."

"You can't create music and art if you're slaving at some job all day and come home exhausted and flop into bed," says Teg.

"I'm sure that's right," says Yang. "The soft primitives who painted the walls of caves had no such responsibilities."

"I'm afraid it's too late to do anything about all that now," Teg sighs.

Yang turns away from the storm and faces her, the gears on his neck making light purchase into the window wood. "It's never too late to admit and correct mistakes. Soft people must execute an about-face. If you are to fully enjoy your lives, you must cultivate yourselves to the highest degree you can. You must learn to know yourselves."

"The way you do?"

Yang does his best nod. "I may have forgotten many details of my life and purpose, but even so, I know myself very well. Do you know jade is so hard it scratches glass like diamond does? Look how the storm outside is creeping through the windowsill. Soon it will be inside me and my head won't work properly. I need my body to protect my life."

"I'm working on finding your body. And you're safe here with me."

"Even if I'm safe for the time being, I'm not free to move, to follow my impulses and inclinations, to go where I wish to go."

She cradles her to him, and walks him around. She opens the door to the suite, steps out into the hall, shows him the surroundings, then brings him back in. She gives him a wordless tour of their accommodations. She goes a bit faster. Yang giggles like a child at her speed. She turns round and round, making herself dizzy, spinning him high and low. He cackles like a madman, then starts shrieking as she runs at the wall full tilt as if bent on a crash, then turns away so only her back thuds against the plaster. On and on she goes, until she can't hold him up anymore, until her legs hurt and her lungs burn and her heart pounds wildly beneath the fine skin of her breasts. Finally, she collapses to the floor and lets him tumble out of her grasp until they are nose to nose, cheeks to the carpet.

"That was fun!" she gasps, grinning.

He grins back. "We have so much fun together. I wish you would not worry so much."

"It's the new weight of expectations," Teg sighs. "I have them of myself and people have them of me. It was easier before I discovered I was the daughter of Arlington Ames."

"I did not know you then," says Yang, "but even so, I'm not

sure that was true. I'm sure your mother expected things of you and you expected things of yourself. Even in the old days, soft people did this to themselves. Jobs, careers, respect...."

"I was saying this to Sebastian the other day," says Teg. "Trading time for money is a bad idea. You can always find more of the second somehow, but the first always runs out."

"These are thought empires the soft mind builds to punish itself. Strange, as the soft life offers punishment enough without them. After all, you are born, you get old, you get sick, you die."

Teg gets up and turns on the television, something she rarely does at home. The international news channels are talking about nothing but this north China dust storm, as apparently it is one of rare intensity and extent. Airlines are spending a fortune cleaning planes, millions of business dollars are being lost contending with traffic delays, and environmental activists are raging about agronomy policies and the projected path of the dust cloud, which will take it across the Pacific Ocean to North America.

"A dust storm should only matter if you're lacking a tent," says Yang. "I saw plenty such whirlwinds in the time of the khan."

"People always love to talk about the weather. Especially when things are peaceful."

"There's nothing peaceful about this planet. I don't think there ever has been. Soft creatures are always hunting and eating each other; soft people are always killing and torturing each other. The problem is that now your kind is not merely warring with each, but with nature itself. Is that not a sign of insanity? How can it possibly end well?"

"Wintermoth agrees with that pessimistic view. He thinks this planet's over. I can tell he does. He's looking for a way off it."

"Perhaps if you give him children he will stay."

"That again? Why do you have to ruin everything?"

"I wish I remembered my childhood."

"I wish I'd known my father."

She puts him back at the window.

"Better to wish than not to care."

"How did you get so wise? Who taught you all this?"

He takes a big breath. It whistles through the conduits in his neck, the open holes that should be closed.

"I'd tell you if I knew."

36

SOFT PEOPLE HAVE taught me that pain can flow from both presence and absence. A hot poker in the eye can cause it, and so can the end to a valued relationship. Soft people convey their feelings obviously, as in shouting or hitting, kissing or crying, but also more quietly, over time, by emitting chemicals from the skin. Oh, how I wished my jade body and golden head could speak my mood. I would love to bloom intimate mists from my flesh and thence conjure the subtle symphony of scents soft people subconsciously compose. I could sense those fragrances, though, which is why when the crazy heat of the Turfan volcano completely burned out of the air, I found myself in a dark metallic world absent desire, fascination, obsession, greed, competitiveness, and pride. All that remained was the stench of burned meat and a metallic acridity that tasted like the end of the world

"What's really missing in this terrible scene is the *qi*," my father announced when I told him what I noticed.

"Is not *qi* manifested by a soft person's aromas?"

"I suppose, but there is more to the *qi* in the soft body than the way it floats off the skin. Indeed, it flows in unexpected ways—up the back and down across the belly and in various branches, often unique to the individual as qi flow may be stagnant or blocked."

"I know I have no mists, but do I have *qi*?"

He smiled. It was surreal to see such a radiant smile, any smile actually, while adrift on a sea of such suffering. "I'm sure you do," he answered. "Although its exact path and nature are a mystery even to me."

It was unusual for my father to speak of my inner workings and quite rare for him to admit there was something about me he did not completely understand. When he had done so in the past, I automatically suspected he was hiding something. Since Roxsana's oblique allegations, however, those suspicions only grew stronger. You might well wonder why I had not pressed the point with him, how I could have let such secrets stand all the way to Turfan. I suppose I respected his right to tell me things in his own time. Perhaps, too, I was afraid of the answers.

Even so, I was reaching the end of my patience. As I gathered the gall to confront him, I was distracted by a wave of theft passing through the ruins in just the way a wave of heat had come in from the nearby eruption cone. The precious gem dealers were the first targets. I saw an old man step over a pile of charred bodies to brazenly shove blood-soaked rubies into his pocket and I saw a little girl reach into the pocket of a blackened corpse, withdraw a handful of emeralds, blow off the ash, and drop them into her bag.

"Make no judgment of these poor souls," my father sighed. "The jewels will no longer benefit the dead, and good and bad are terms we contrive according to our own limited understanding of the universe. We could even say that the gems find new homes because doing so restores balance."

"If you can say that about stealing from the dead, you could say that about the volcano," I said, not at all comfortable with this line of reasoning.

My father nodded slowly. "Much as it pains me to agree, that is manifestly so. The volcano undoubtedly exploded because pressure under the mountain had been building and needed to be relieved. Such things are all part of a natural system reflecting the intelligence I have described to you as Tao."

His meaning was not lost on me but I worried that such explanations could also be rationalizations for dispassionate or immoral behavior. I did not see a good excuse for stealing from the dead. After all, would not those merchants have preferred to transfer their valuables to their loved ones—presuming any survived— then lose them to thieves? Was it not likely that some plans had been made for the proceeds, for food, for shelter, for the future?

When my father said what he said, equating the petty greed of the soft people to the magnificent machinations of a mountain, I got the feeling that he spoke in such riddles because he himself was full of holes, that he was not the reliable inventor I had taken him to be but rather himself a trickster or, as Roxsana had said, himself a thief. This feeling filled me with both sadness and a desire to put distance between us.

Don't be surprised by this, please, or think it sudden. Surely, if you have been following my narrative closely, you realize that a rift had been building between us for some time. My changing view of my father was no abrupt turnaround but rather the final unveiling of one last obfuscating layer, or, perhaps, the snapping of one last thread in a gradually unraveling fabric. Dancing between truth and lies and juggling morals, he showed me how great the gulf between us had become, or perhaps had always been. Feeling the need for space and time to work out a new paradigm I began a slow retreat through the rotting corpses.

"Where are you going?" he asked casually.

"I'm leaving," I said.

He raised his eyebrows. "What do you mean?"

"What I said. I'm going my own way."

He lunged and grabbed at me, but I ducked and eluded him. His clumsiness, it seemed, had been yet one more of his deceptions, for he moved with far greater speed and agility than I had ever before seen him show. All the same, neither his pace nor his aerial abilities were a match for mine. The low smoke over the hot ground gave me cover as I leapt and landed, landed and leapt, all the while following a faint whiff of frankincense and blue lotus oil to a tiny, distant, fragrant isle amidst the smoke and lava flows from the nearby volcano. There I found the collapsed tent of a spice merchant and huddle inside, shielded from my father's view .

"Yang!" he screamed with increasing desperation. "Where are you, my boy? Stop this childishness now. Come on out now. Show yourself. You can't be out here by yourself. You weren't built for it. This desert is as vast as the distance from the khan's palace to the moon."

Perhaps you agree that I was acting as a child; perhaps you merely think me stone-hearted to let him worry so. As to the former, I can assure you I was not. As to the latter, perhaps I needed to do exactly that so as to be able to do what I needed to do next. In either case, I kept sight of him as I moved stealthily away, my superior eyesight allowing me to watch him even when he could no longer watch me.

My father's behavior reminded me of Roxsana's oblique accusations and the fact that he had used first the razzle-dazzle of his robe and then a tranquilizer to escape her instead of simply addressing her accusations. Ever the compassionate yet practical Daoist, he was shoving a pillow of rolled-up fabric under the neck of a dying man one minute, the next minute and prying a garnet necklace from the grasp of a failing woman. Still calling my name, I saw him ease the pain of a girl with his healing needles, then tuck her basket of bells into his cloak when she died. If he was increasingly distraught at my disappearance, he was not so much so that he didn't step up his pilfering the longer I was gone, lifting gems, ivory, and jade with only crisped merchants bearing mute witness.

If I initially wavered at the prospect of leaving him, this behavior firmed my resolve. The greater my physical distance from him, the easier it would be for me to follow my own path. The thought of freedom and independence thrilled me. Step by step, I became, oh the irony, as excited as a monkey freed from a cage. Would I head back east and take refuge with my mother? Would I head west in search of al-Jazari? Would I retreat toward the wild, unpredictable southland and there totally disappear from view?

In the middle of my reverie the volcano erupted again in the distance. The sky turned red and the air shimmered and the ground rolled. I hunkered down under a broad tabletop swaddled in embroidered blankets as bedding. Spinning, I drilled myself into the ground until I found cool dirt. There I remained until the hot wind finally subsided.

When I emerged, I could find no trace of the wizard of the khan's court.

37

YANG CLOSES HIS eyes for a long moment, savoring the metallic feel against the cogs and cables in his neck, and wishing the pewter tray were his body. "Back when I had legs, I could jump high enough to stay aloft like a bird. From on high, I saw the whole world as a complex puzzle. Each flitting butterfly, each ripple on a pond, every plant animal nose lifted to the air and, of course, every cloud helped me sense the beautiful breeze blowing through all that is."

"The what?" asks Teg, pouring a splash of water from the hotel flower vase into the pewter tray.

"The breeze. The light and steady wind. I don't have any other words for it."

"I don't understand."

He clucks impatiently. "It blows at the tiniest level and thereby makes our reality appear seamless. Look closely enough, of course, and you can feel it pass through your hair even when you see now movement. It makes the grass grow. It drives the affairs of men."

"What affairs?"

"Romantic ones, yes, but other ones, too. Like the way Han culture absorbed the Mongols, for example, seducing them with the beauty of structured society, their cultured courtesans, and their fragrant teas. Sensing that breeze you could predict such things, and other details, too, like the falling of snowflakes from an impossibly cloudless winter sky at night. Now, from what I've seen, soft people have banded together to purposely ignore its presence, even pretend it doesn't exist."

It's a long run of words for the golden head, and when he stops, Tegulen sets the tray by the window so he can look out.

"That's why you like this view so much," she says. "Being up high reminds you of what you have learned."

"I suppose so. This water is delicious. I've so missed the taste of carnations."

"Why didn't you tell me you taste things through the water you absorb? I can give you other flavors the same way."

"I didn't remember. I've been dry so long. Also, I've observed you don't much care for flowers."

"What in the world makes you say that?"

"Well, you don't do you?"

"Everyone likes flowers," she says.

"Except you."

"It's not that I don't like them, it's that I don't like them cut. Once you cut them, they become dying things, not living things. I like plants better. You get one and it grows. It has a future. There's life, not death."

He nods solemnly. "You have a fine appreciation for all life. Not all soft people do. Most seem to think they are more important than other living creatures. That the whole giant kingdom is a playground in which soft people can do as they wish. That you're really *so* special. This strange and terrible prejudice leads to a range of excesses from atrocities against your own kind to the extermination of whole classes of other creatures."

"When you say the giant kingdom, I think you mean the Earth. Believe me when I tell you that no single idea can kill a planet."

199

"Well, *something* is killing it. This city is nothing like I remember it. There was so much life here. There were so many birds. Watching from the taxicab while you worried about your wardrobe, I noticed there's barely anything left alive beside soft people"

Teg picks up coffee table book for tourists and leafs through it until she finds picture of birds on the wall of the Forbidden City.

"There are still birds here," she says, showing it to him.

Yang stares at the image. "Seven swallows? Swarms of them used to blot out the sun. How did they capture these and flatten them onto this scroll without showing any blood?"

Teg took a photography course in college. The old-school teacher wanted the students to know the history of the art. He explained how cameras used to use something called film, a term for sensitive emulsion speckled with bits of light-sensitive silver, that captured units of light energy called photons. He explained lens apertures and leaf and focal-plane shutters and the concept of depth of field and freezing action, either stylistically blurred or crisp as a cracker. Tegulen doesn't bother with any of that with Yang, and in any case can't exactly explain digital technology other than to say something about pixels. Even so, Yang is fascinated by everything she says and she, in turn, is amazed by his curiosity, his questions, and the speed and depth of his thinking. By the time the conversation winds down, the sun has subsided from the dust-brown world outside.

"It's late now," she says. "I have to get dressed."

"If I had legs, I'd walk right in and watch you shower."

"It's a good thing you're legless, then."

"Could I at least watch you dress?"

"Fat chance, you golden pervert," says Teg.

"If you let me, I'll teach you how to calm your crazy mind."

"My mind's not crazy."

"*You* say."

"I once took a meditation class. I know things your teacher never will."

"Of course you do," she replies, mockingly.

"Did she teach you how to give yourself an orgasm without the tiniest touch?"

"Good God, you're outrageous."

"I've met gods. Some were good and some were not. Now tell me you don't like the idea of a touchless climax."

The idea turns her on, but she still refuses to let him see her naked. "Be happy staring at the neon and watching the cars go by."

There's a knock on the door. Teg grabs Yang's carry bag to hide him.

"No need," he says. "It's only the maid. I don't want to be in the dark again."

"I don't trust anybody with you. Not Sebastian and not the Chu woman either."

"Then drape me with a bra but leave free my eyes."

"No bra," says Teg.

"Please? It's such a small thing to ask. If you won't let me see you then at least let me enjoy your scent."

Gritting her teeth and muttering about boundaries, she covers him as requested and admits the maid, watching her carefully as she has vacuums, dusts, straightens the sofa, cleans the bathroom, and freshens the flowers. When she leaves, Teg relents and undresses so Yang can see her reflection in the window.

"You must be sad," she says, smiling at her own daring. "The only one of your kind, and all alone."

"I'm not alone. I have you. And when I get my body back, we'll dance."

"Sure," she says. "That sounds nice."

She shaves in the shower, shampoos and dries her hair, and puts on her makeup. She comes out in a towel and turns Yang away from the window so he can watch her slip into the new Chanel dress and blue Manolo Blahnik pumps she bought right after she bought her new watch.

"Happy now?" she asks.

"Thank you. You're a beautiful woman. But nothing makes us more miserable than chasing happiness. I am sure of this because I've tried."

"Good to know."

"I'm not joking, so please don't patronize me. I learn quickly. I see things. I have reference points you can't imagine. I've been in rooms that make this look like an outhouse and met men so rich they make Wintermoth seem a toothless beggar without even a chamber pot. I've tasted far better flowers than those carnations, which grew in sour soil polluted by the waste of this world, and I have scraped away dirt to reveal truffles with my platinum fingernails."

"Your fingernails were platinum?"

"Already this quest of ours has helped me remember much. I'm hoping I will remember everything once I have my body back, even if it means feeling a pain I sense is lurking in my head, a chronicle of my mistakes and losses. Most people settle for scrambling around in the topsoil like a mole cricket rather than digging relentlessly for the truth about things. I sense you are not like most people, Tegulen. I sense that you want to know all the secrets of life."

"I do," Teg admits. "And now, may I ask you something I've never asked you—I mean since you say I want to know all life's secrets?"

"You may."

"What is the main thing you can feel that soft people cannot?"

"There are billions of soft people I have not met, so I cannot answer with complete certitude."

"Nobody can do anything with complete certitude. Make your best guess for me, please."

Yang pauses for a moment. "In all the years of my life, nobody, not even your namesake, my mother, has ever asked me that question."

"Probably because everyone assumed you sensed and felt *less*, not more. So will you give me an answer?"

"I already have."

"The breeze through all that is."

"Exactly," Yang says quietly.

38

DURING MY LIFE at the court, I had been obliged to fulfill roles including acrobat, arithmetic whiz, party favor, dinner companion, and object of salacious fascination. In all of these I relied upon the extraordinary senses bestowed upon me by my father, and the supernatural intuition that flowed therefrom. I was able to see auras, divine the intentions of creatures with scales or wings, and sniff out perfidy and lust in the moist creases of the human mind.

Alone on the plain, against whose vastness I was as a flea on a camel's rump, I soon learned to employ that intuition to even greater effect. Scurrying through the post-eruption landscape with the eruption cone still within sight, I listened to the hisses, squeaks, and groans of the rivers of lava, I picked up Roxsana's trail. I needed the truth from her, both about my own origins and about the depths of my father's depravity, though on the latter count I had probably seen enough. I also needed water, indeed dehydration was increasingly fogging my brain, and so I was glad to discover that traces of the Persian woman led me in the direction of the promised waters of Kashgar, across a distance my father had said was as great as that between Kublai's palace and the moon.

So as not to be seen, I traveled mostly at night, treading my way past angry orange lines of lava and through the acrid smoke. The volcano seemed to have burned the whole world, and there were desperate people afoot, brandishing weapons at the sound of a fly, ready to kill without provocation, apparently traumatized beyond all perspective or reason. To hide from them I abided in scrub brush and huddled in abandoned tents and under caravan wagons. With no one to talk to, I turned my gaze inward for hours at a time, energetically hiking, swimming, running, or flying through a terrain of mind whose features represented the people in my life.

In that landscape, my mother, moody and delicate, was a valley of butterflies and my father was a dark cliff with hidden crevices and crags. The great khan was a domed mountain glinting in the sun. Arrows representing lieutenants and generals decorated the mountain, fletches buried, sharp tips up. The khan's concubines appeared as wildflowers and the eunuchs of his court as fallen, rotting fruit.

There were vast prairies in that mental scenery, too, where each blade of grass embodied a single thought. The expanse behind me held a million of my past notions, while the steppe before me held the promise of ideas yet to come. Standing tall between the sea of blades, at irregular intervals and with no discernible pattern, were poplars revealing my desires, birches my fears, and willows my regrets.

My thirst brought ponds and lakes and streams to mind, their shifting liquid courses specifically connoting the uncertainty of my life's path. Upon those waters paddled my father's mechanical swans, right along with grebes and loons, pelicans and cormorants, herons, bitterns, egrets, and storks. When taking wing, either alone or in groups, these beauties represented my yearning for freedom. In my imagination, I flew along with them but only with great effort, constantly yearning for the power of the Demoiselle crane—the supreme avian athlete and conqueror of the high Himalaya — that has always represented the height of consciousness to which I aspire even when life thrust me face-first into the mud.

Slaking my thirst had always been an unconscious act, but by the fourth day without water to do so, I became aware of the labored squeezing of my heart pump as it fought against my increasingly viscous lubricating fluid. Moving grew effortful in a way I had never before experienced, and there on the perimeter of the hideous Taklamakan desert, I found myself in increasingly dire straits.

It was Roxsana, not my father, who came to the rescue. Had I not been so compromised, truly on the edge of unconsciousness, I'm sure I would have sensed her before she snuck up on me. Mistress of stealth and always wary of the khan's riders, she enfolded me in her cloak as a bat might mask a moth.

"I'm alone," I said, unaccountably relaxing into her embrace.

"I know. I've been watching."

"You recovered quickly from the sleeping herbs he used?"

"I have a strong constitution."

Up close, she bore the smell of smoke and sweat, but not unpleasantly so. In fact, I found her personal aroma beguiling despite the rigors of travel and the absence of bath water. Fleetingly, I wondered if my father's proposal of marriage might have been genuine.

"I left him in Turfan," I said.

"I know that, too, and I understand why."

"You were at the market?"

"At the outskirts."

"You witnessed the horrors?"

"How could I not? Listen, Yang, before anything else, I feel I must apologize to you for cutting off your foot."

"Yes, well, please don't do it again. Do you have anything to drink?"

She uncorked a goatskin bottle and gave me a draught.

"Where are your men?" I asked, feeling the curtain lift from my mind.

"Gone home to their families. They were hirelings and their job is done. The artifacts are safe and I am accustomed to working alone."

"The artifacts were a side job, then?"

"Yes."

"And I'm the main event?"

She smiled at my turn of phrase. "You are."

"What now then?"

"I take you west."

"I would gladly go with you but I am desperately thirsty. I heard that there is water in Kashgar but I understand that city to be as far away as the moon."

"It is, and we will have to pass through it, but there is water along the way."

"And how will we travel?"

"You could manage it on foot, Yang, as you don't seem to ever tire and there are water sources along the way, but I prefer a mounted approach. Even better, we could go around the desert."

"Queen Chabi's men will expect that. As awful as it sounds, I think the desert route may be safer."

"Then a combination of camels and horses."

"If I can be in your company, I accept any conveyance you suggest."

She spent a long moment looking at me."

"You're not at all what I expected," she said. We inched closer together, a sign of trust in a landscape that had burned and stabbed and cut and melted so much of what I had seen or held dear. She started to say something else, but I held up a jade finger.

"Don't ruin the moment," I said.

She fell silent.

I took her hand.

Surprisingly, she let me.

39

LEAVING HER HOTEL for Wintermoth's, Teg stops at the concierge desk and asks the young clerk to recommend a perfume store.

"I need a special scent for a special night," she explains.

"Definitely the Scent Library," the girl tells her. "It's in our district, and the founder used to work for one of the big-name companies. Everything they sell is organic. It's very cool and trendy."

So it turns out to be, and filled with young, professional women looking to make an impression. Teg strikes a pose in the middle of the shop, closes her eyes, and inhales the creative fragrances wafting on tiny currents of air. The manager approaches her. She's a well-turned-out woman of a certain age, and she responds to Teg's mixed-race look and high-end fashion.

"Nice wristwatch," she says.

Adding the comment to the appraising if-I-were-rich-I-could-get-a-girl-like-her looks she got from baggage handlers at the airport and the some-tycoon-is-buying-her-for-the-night nods from hotel bellboys, Teg feels China is the new Wild West. Little sign of #MeToo here, that's for sure. She figures that the goal of every country bumpkin tumbling into the big city is to get rich, or catch someone who is. Her own feelings swing wildly. They're not so far off, these rough girls. After all, her money is from her father.

"I bought it myself," she tells the store manager. "I like it. I'm not trying to impress anybody."

"Good for you."

"You're in the wrong place," Yang interrupts.

He's in Teg's bag, and the store manager assumes his voice is coming from a smartphone speaker.

"Tell him not to worry, I'll find you a scent to please him," the manager whispers, then winks.

Something in her salacious tone validates Yang's opinion. Teg retreats to the hotel's silver Mercedes Benz waiting at the curb and asks the driver to take her someplace more exclusive. She still feels like a poseur. Barely two weeks earlier her life was far closer to the driver's life than to the one she lives now, but she knows she has to fill her own shoes, find a way through her reservations and discomfort. She shifts in her seat and waits to see what he'll do.

The request is way above the driver's pay grade, though even if it weren't, he would not be particularly inclined to help. A handsome kid who uses free weights and machines four times a week at a Western style fitness center, he's miffed she hasn't come on to him like the KTV girls do. Fortunately, the store manager appears, knocks on the car window, and hands Teg her name card, a note scribbled on the back.

"Since your boyfriend's buying, go see my friend and give him this. His place is very exclusive. Very expensive. He'll help you."

It's a short drive to the second shop, which looks more like a high-end office suite than a boutique. The receptionist reads the note and ushers Teg into a posh room with only a bare, elegant table, a jar of fresh, oily, coffee beans, and two overstuffed chairs. A man comes in. His suit looks like he was born to it and his eyes flicker as far as Teg's wristwatch, but no further — not to her legs, not to her neck, not to her eyes. As much as it galls her to admit it, as much as she feels, in every fiber of her being, that such judgments and inequities are flat wrong, she's beginning to understand something about the cross-cultural power of an exotic timepiece.

"How serious are you about your fragrance?" the man asks in impeccable Hong Kong, British English.

"Very serious."

"There is another woman?"

"Why do you ask?"

The man looks at her.

"There is," she admits at last.

"And you would like to vanquish her?"

"Utterly," says Teg.

The man snaps his fingers and a door opens and two security guards come in. They stand, hands on their batons, while a young woman wearing cotton gloves wheels in a cart. On top of the cart is a velvet purple pillow, and on top of the pillow is a box of oiled ebony wood. The woman waits for the man's signal, and when he gives it, she opens the box to reveal the most beautiful crystal bottle Tegulen has ever seen. The yellow perfume inside looks like liquid gold.

"Clive Christian Imperial Majesty," the man says. "The most expensive perfume in the world."

Teg is more than a little bit wowed. "May I sniff?"

The man shakes his head. "Once the seal is broken the purchase is made."

"But what if I don't like it? I mean, choosing the right scent is a very personal thing. There's skin chemistry, for one thing, and past experience, associations...."

"If people did not like it, Madam, it would not be the costliest fragrance in the world. Perhaps it is not right for you."

40

I HAVE SAID I was always busy at court, and certainly compared to my flight across the Taklamakan that is true, but the battle over my lineage and position made me too explosive for any noble to risk being my friend. When I wasn't performing, I was on my own. I would have loved to be with my mother and father, but they could barely figure out ways to connect with each other and had little time for me. What kept them too busy for their own son? Simply put, my father was always in demand making or repairing the mechanical side of the palace and my mother was always pining after the khan or fantasizing about killing Chabi.

I had my own fantasies, of course, and these kept me good company. They often involved court maidens—a different one every week—not because I was so fickle but because none of them would talk to me and they were constantly being replaced before the khan could grow attached, a strategy dictated by his manipulative second wife. For all those daydreams, however, I never imagined something like the Turfan eruption, nor the true companion I found in Roxsana.

We did find camels. Once I became used to their surly attitudes and prodigious stench, they proved to be reasonable transportation. During the first leg of our journey west we spoke rarely, and never of either my father or our destination. The quiet was pleasant, her company even more so. We were treated to brisk winds and clear skies, and when at last the high Pamir Mountains rose to the north and glimpses of India teased us to the south, I felt genuine awe.

"Surely such a sight dwarfs the troubles of soft people, and this hard person too," I said softly.

"Person," Roxsana repeated, mulling over the word and all it implied but offering no further comment.

Polo had been right about the growing significance of the east-to-east trading links. Despite the Mongols having laid waste to so much, the road to Samarqand was crowded with traders. As a creature of high society born to the most opulent court the world has ever known, I was content to stay on the straight and easy byways. Not so Roxsana, who was more comfortable with a less-crowded path free of the khan's mail riders. Accordingly, we cleaved to the shadows and veered north toward a forest well-suited to those on the lam, a place redolent of fir trees and pine mulch, lichens and ferns, a dark, impenetrable country clinging tightly to its secrets.

I soon appreciated her decision, for I was far more comfortable in this moist world than I had been either on the steppe or along the edge of the desert. The dew rejuvenated me, as did the first creek we found. Roxsana watched me, arms crossed, as I slid down the ice on the bank and right into the water with a great splash. My stone body was unaffected by the cold and I gratefully absorbed all the water my insides required.

Roxsana, by contrast, suffered the chill, though she would not admit as much. Watching her start a fire by spinning a hard twig against a divot in a damp log, I wished for a soft, warm body with which to comfort her, though I kept the wish to myself.

"This country brings my father to mind," I told her one night as we stared at the stars glinting against the ragged tree line. "Wizards like him, shamans, are always so close to the land, to the country, to the plants and the herbs and the animals."

"Liars, you mean. Thieves. Imposters."

"Might it now be time to tell me what I don't know of him, and what I don't know of myself?"

She sighed. "I'm told he is from the south, which makes one wonder how he ended up with the old man, so very, very far away from home."

"When you say the old man, you mean al-Jazari?"

She nodded. "The same. Many call him The Magnificent One."

"You met the Magnificent One in Persia?"

"Persia is no more," she sighed. "The Shah baited the Mongols into destroying our world. They destroyed al-Jazari too, for a man of such faith cannot suffer this new world. He takes the Mongol invasion to be Allah's punishment for a great crime our people committed. The greatest pain of his life is not knowing what that crime is."

"A man in such pain must have been especially wounded when his student, surpassed him."

"What?"

"I'm saying I've noticed how jealous creative people can be."

She turned her beautiful, ember-lit face to me. "The wizard told you he exceeded his master?"

"He might not have used those exact words, but his meaning was plain enough."

Roxsana rummaged through a deep sack she sometimes used as a pillow and withdrew a dried plum. "Tell me what else he said."

I had relied upon self-righteous indignation to suppress my love for my father, but right then, with the smell of the poplars so close, I inexplicably felt the need to defend him.

"Despite his penchant for seduction, most of the time he

was more a worker than a talker. The khan is patient in war but impatient when it comes to his toys. His demands drove my father to distraction."

She looked at me thoughtfully. "I respect your loyalty but surely by now you've guessed the truth?"

"Tell me," I said, because I needed to hear.

"It was Al-Jazari who sent me," she said. "I have the honor to be his agent, though whether the old man is still alive I cannot say. He sent me not to steal you, but to reclaim you."

"Reclaim me," I repeated in a small voice.

"Master Abu al-'Izz ibn Ismā'īl al-Jazari is the one who conceived you, Yang. It is he who imagined you, and drew your blueprints with his painstaking eye and incandescent imagination. He could not build you, for the Mongols stripped the city bare of the materials he needed. Your wizard stole the plans and ran with them to the court of the khan, so as to gather the treasures required for your construction. The Magnificent One is your *real* father, Yang, and when I return you to him, you will, by the grace of Allah, find both your true place and your ultimate destiny."

41

"I DON'T NEED you to decide what's right for me," Teg snaps. "Tell me what's in it."

The salesman manages to look offended by the question. "A perfume's formula is its greatest mystery," he replies.

"The base ingredients, then?"

"*Iris florentina*, which you may know as orris root."

"What else?"

"Sandalwood, vanilla, ylang ylang, Italian cinnamon, and rose oil."

"Nothing special," says Teg. "What justifies the high price?"

"The scent, of course, mostly from secret terpenes added to evoke petrichor."

"I'm not familiar with that last term."

He looks at her as if she is achingly gauche. "The smell of rain," he sniffs.

"How much?" she asks.

"And then there is the matter of the box, which is finished in gold and platinum."

"The price," says Teg.

The man persists, undaunted. "Not to be overlooked, obviously, is the French Baccarat lead crystal flacon with a neck fashioned after the coronation tiara of the British queen and graced with an 18-carat gold inset and a five-point brilliant-cut diamond. Very challenging to manufacture."

Yang barks something in Mandarin.

At this sound from a mysterious source, the guards come to attention. The woman pushing the cart gasps. Teg withdraws Yang from her bag and puts him on the table beside the perfume box. His golden head shames even the over-the-top perfume presentation.

"Tell her the price," Yang commands.

The man's jaw goes slack with surprise. "$215,000."

"Arlington wouldn't," says Yang.

His words have a galvanic effect on Teg. Suddenly, it's as if she's channeling her dead father, the world-class connoisseur, the negotiator par excellence, the savvy, blue-blood billionaire who mastered the art of negotiation long before anyone in the room, save Yang himself, was even born.

"I spend money, I don't waste it," Teg says crisply. "My mom taught me that. If I want a diamond, I'll buy a diamond. If I want crystal, I'll buy crystal. It's the scent I'm after, not froufrou."

Another snap of the salesman's fingers and the girl wheels the cart out. A moment later, she comes back and hands a small glass bottle to her boss.

"Clive Christian No.1," the man tells her, aware he has been completely and totally outdone yet unable to take his eyes off Yang, incapable, in his sharp, material way, of trying to work out how many grams of gold he's looking at and the price of the gems comprising Yang's eyes and teeth.

"What's the difference between the two?" Teg demands.

"A similar fragrance minus some of the rarer ingredients and, of course, the packaging extras. An extremely experienced nose *might* be able to tell the difference between the two, but in most cases...." His voice trails off.

"Even I can barely tell a difference, and I can smell a camel a full desert away," Yang whispers.

Teg hefts the bottle. It too is of lead crystal and feels heavy and satisfying in the hand. She lifts it for a closer look at the contents and finds the liquid honey colored against the room's fluorescent light. She pulls out the bottle top for a sniff. The salesman starts to protest.

"Keep quiet, you two-bit, low-class hawker," Yang commands. "You're in the presence of a queen. If she doesn't like it, she'll close the bottle and nobody will ever know she opened it. If she does, well, maybe she'll buy every bottle you have. Maybe she'll buy the factory. Now sit down and pray for a sale!"

Mouth still agape, the man sits. Testing the perfume, Teg recognizes an underlying tone, like the bass line in a jazz melody. On instinct, she thrusts the open bottle at Yang. He inhales. Previously narrowed in disdain for the salesman, his zircon eyes fly open.

"Touch me," he says.

The moment her fingertips meet his scalp, reality shifts. She loses connection to the ground. Something flutters at the periphery of her vision, then disappears too quickly to be identified. Impossibly, she is no longer in the perfume store but inside Yang's memory, able to see places she has never been and a time before she was born. She connects with the undertones of the fragrance that Yang is able to sense and she is not. More than any of these sensory details, however, she experiences something far more profound, namely a sense of connection to all that is, to the fabric of reinvention and rebirth, to the endless cycle of repurposing of atoms, to the mind-bending rules of the quantum universe. Yang's mind makes it clear to her that the cinnamon, orange blossoms, vetiver, ginger, civet oil—every ingredient right here in the perfume shop—all share atoms, molecules, design, a common origin. Regardless of jade or bone, zircon or viscous humor, a universal energy moves her as it moves Yang—as fingers move a glove. It is a brief but deeply spiritual experience.

"This one costs much less than the other one, right?" she asks, recovering.

"It's $2,150 for the ounce," the salesman replies.

She makes the purchase and immediately returns to the car, where she applies the scent to her private places. By the time they get to the Hotel Éclat for the meeting with Chu Feilin, Teg's more confident of her fragrance than she is of her Manolos. The hotel doorman follows her into the lobby like he's got a noose through his nose. She texts Wintermoth and he gives her his room number.

She's the first to arrive and sits at the opposite end of the suite from Wintermoth. She crosses her legs, holds Yang close, glances at the pool, and then up at the skylight. Outside, the storm duels with the lights of Beijing.

"You smell nice," says Wintermoth.

"Nice is rose water or baby powder. I smell amazing."

"Fair enough," Wintermoth smiles.

"You think the arm is real?"

"I hope it is. We need a solid start. There are so many other pieces to find."

"He has men hiding in the bedroom," Yang tells Teg. "I can hear them breathing."

Teg turns to Wintermoth. "You hired thugs?"

"I don't think you've seen my latest," Wintermoth answers, showing off a heavy gold watch with gold hands, white insets, a black leather strap with white stitching, and several skeletonized windows revealing a polished escapement and gear train. "It's Armin Strom's Tourbillon Gumball 3000. I have to wind it every day, a wonderful way to mark the passage of time."

His evasiveness leads Teg to think she should be working some angles of her own, teasing out the threads running through her new life, separating synchrony from coincidence and motive from emotion. But before she can say so, the doorbell chimes and two men emerge from the bedroom behind her. One holds a shotgun, the other a combat baton.

They stand by silently as Wintermoth opens the door.

42

ROXSANA AND I traveled the rest of the way to Kashgar without speaking a word. She was a patient woman and silence seemed to suit her. It suited me, too, for the news I was born of a Muslim master rather than a runaway apprentice launched a thousand questions for me to ponder. I wondered, for example, which of my parts were true to the great man's plans and which were a Han Taoist's loose interpretations. Was my stout maleness a perversion of al-Jazari's original plans, or had it been intended from the start? Was I built to be good at arithmetic and acrobatics, and if so, why? If I had been conceived with some goal in mind, I wanted to know what it was.

These, of course, were only the latest in a long string of questions I lacked answers to because my father always avoided any serious discussion of my origin or purpose. When I probed, he would always trumpet his own brilliance, leaving me as confused as ever. I found myself wondering as much about him as I did about myself. Why had he stolen my plans from al-Jazari — if indeed he had done so — after the master obviously taught him so much? Why had he seemed more affected by the immolation of a slave girl with whom he had exchanged but a handful of words than he was at parting from a queen I had always believed he adored? Where exactly was he, and what were his intentions regarding my future?

Roxsana shook the last drops of water out of her goatskin bag and wiped her lips on her sleeve in a most unladylike fashion. Then she stepped off the road and pointed to a row of tall trees sprouting new green leaves. Muttering something about well water, she followed the line to a stone slab. We tied up the camels and pushed the slab aside to reveal a set of steps. At the bottom, we found a cool cavern through which ran clean, clear water perhaps two feet deep.

"Where are we?" I asked, breaking our long silence.

"This is a *karez*, a secret well dug by Taklamakan traders."

"Where does the water come from?"

"The Pamirs. And the tunnels are situated so nobody has to walk more than a day in the desert without finding one. The system reaches all the way to Persia."

I dove into the stream and took a bite of the stringy green algae growing on the bottom, teasing it between my teeth and savoring the burst of flavor it yielded. Roxsana smiled at the sight of green strands issuing from between my bright blue, Ceylonese sapphire teeth. Mushrooms the size of baby elephant ears grew along the bank; I found the intensity of their flavor exhilarating.

"I'm Yang," I cried, my voice caroming off the waterway walls.

Roxsana stripped off her clothes and joined me. The light was dim and her actions were quick but I managed to see her smooth skin, her muscular outline, her bulges and curves, her perfect proportions.

"You're a sight to behold," I said. "A work of art. Surely such perfection couldn't happen without being crafted."

"You're drunk on water," she said as the gentle current carried us. "I don't have time for sweet words you learned from that thief you call father."

"Since you mention it, I've been thinking about time."

"And?"

"The flow of days and weeks and months and years appears to flow in only one direction, like this very stream, does it not?"

"It does."

"I can't say exactly how or why, but I know this to be an illusion. It may be a matter of perspective. A moment ago, the present seemed the future and a moment from now it will seem the past, but there's more to the story. It seems the more we ponder time and try to measure it, the more certainly we lose our most subtle yet important connection to it."

"If time flows both ways, I can think of some choices I'd love to go back and change," she murmured.

"I'm not sure we can, but sometimes I get glimpses of myself in lives I don't recognize."

"You believe there's more than one stream?"

"I believe so."

"How does that affect the past?" she asked, swimming on her back, her sheathed sword lying, dry, across her breasts, her arms lazily falling, one after the other, over her head.

"I don't know."

"What about the future?"

"I'm not sure about that either. All I have are confusing images. Clocks run by coiled metal. Giant birds of iron. Glowing screens. Waves of light and sound. Slaughterhouses the size of Xanadu surrounded by stinking water. The sons of Muhammad taking up arms."

"Ah," she said, seemingly pleased by the last image.

I went back up into the sun and dragged the camels down so they, too, could drink. They grunted and snorted and kicked around, pulling back on their reins, heads pointing skyward, particularly when they got to the top of the dark staircase. Roxsana couldn't understand why the camels obeyed me the way they did when I was so small and they would trouble even a stout jockey. The answer may have been in the way I did or didn't smell to their sensitive noses but more likely it was the conundrum I offered in being much stronger than a man but little more than half the size of one. In whatever mysterious regard they held me, they eventually did follow me downward, a minor piece of business Roxsana regarded as a miracle.

Thus, with camel tack held loosely in wet hands, we continued to float in the general direction of Kashgar, camels trudging along on the bank alongside. After a time, shapes emerged from the gloom of the tunnel, resolving into a raucous group of travelers. They formed a circle around us, in the water and on the banks. Roxsana stood up, naked and glaring, her hand on the hilt of her blade.

"Don't worry," I soothed her. "They're drunk. Can't you smell the Georgian grape wine on their breath? As memorable as the sight of you may be, they won't remember it in the morning."

We emerged from the stream. Roxsana dressed. The group told us, with remarkable clarity given their level of inebriation, that they were members of a traveling circus and had been en route to Turfan when the sky turned to fire and they took refuge in the *karez*. A girl festooned in billowing yellow robes seemed quite taken with me. She approached and caressed me with painted fingernails while her golden hair tickled my neck, and drew a length of silk lightly across my shoulders. When she kissed my lips with animal ferocity, I thought I might finally put my equipment to use, but Roxsana stepped between us.

"Will you stop it?" she hissed, a look of disgust on her face.

Disappointed, I dove back into the water. My ankle snagged on the bottom. In freeing myself, I dislodged what appeared to be an oversized tooth. Wiping it off, I found it recurved and fearsome. When the circus troupe saw it, they all jumped into the water and began searching for more like it. Inside of an hour, they had unearthed a bevy of teeth and a skull, including upper and lower jawbones.

"The head of a dragon," Roxsana breathed.

This pronouncement set off a veritable frenzy of excavation. Perhaps it was a quest for redemption, perhaps simply a need for distraction, but resurrecting that dead monster became the most important thing in the world for all of us that night.

Roxsana helped by venturing out of the *karez* for dry wood. We lit torches and used the light to continue our excavations, in a wild orgy of drinking and digging, through the night and into the next day.

Time had turned bone to stone, but the pieces we came up with completed one dragon the length of twelve men, several crocodiles with sails for spines, three dog-sized creatures with great blunt heads, and a short-legged horse with a single, central horn. The tunnel of the *karez* made a perfect echo chamber, and when I blew the horn, the sound turned the group's morning to wonder and Roxsana's frown to a smile. Then it was right back to work. Later the same day, we found winged creatures too, the marks of feathers evident on the wing bones, with legs that would have set them towering over the ostriches Kublai Khan held in Xanadu's summer garden.

"Imagine the storm of dust when such birds flapped their wings," I said as Roxsana, exhausted, lay down on the sandy bank.

"These bones lend credence to a legend I've heard," she whispered.

"What legend is that?"

"Supposedly all of Mongolia is a graveyard of mythical creatures. Their ghostly force supposedly drives the khan's armies in their insatiable appetite for conquest."

"Our discovery fits the story, but there's something else. Finding these creatures buried atop each other tells us that our loved ones, too, lie atop *their* loved ones, and on and on down the ages. Life, it seems, marches onward and upward like a ladder aimed at the stars."

"Perhaps stars are my slaughtered countrymen, then," Roxsana sighed.

While she slept curled up near our burden beasts, I resumed conducting my orchestra of bone diggers. Once we had unearthed all the bones we could find, I hopped to the roof of the cavern and hung there, with a bat-eye perspective, directing the interlocking of parts and then the positioning of whole skeletons. At length, we produced a diorama of life-gone-by along the banks of the water course. The bones were beautiful there in the humid semi-darkness. Any act of creation is an antidote to apathy, but this particular one felt positively defiant in the face of the death and destruction we had all endured.

"Look what we've done for you!" I cried, rousting Roxsana.

She stood, looked, and smiled. The troupe beamed when I took her in my arms. Together, we spun like a top until the fabric of reality frayed, time melted, and I received a tiny glimpse of the ultimate purpose for which I had been constructed, the destiny I sensed would bring me real ecstasy when at last I found it.

Al-Jazari.

The Magnificent One would show me the way.

43

Chu Feilin enters Sebastian Wintermoth's hotel suite unescorted, a designer alligator backpack slung elegantly over the shoulder of her Shantung silk pantsuit. She stares hard at Wintermoth's security detail.

"This is only a proof-of-life meeting, right?" she asks.

"You're here to sell an arm and we're here to buy one," Wintermoth replies.

"The only one with anything to prove is you," says Teg. "We'll need to know the arm is the real thing."

"It's *we* now?" Chu asks Wintermoth, turning her back on Teg. "If I were you, I'd muzzle her and put a choke collar around her neck, too. And I want to see the head. It's part of my price."

"You'll have to be a lot nicer to Ms. Ames if that's going to happen. The head belongs to her."

"He doesn't belong to anyone," says Teg. "He's a conscious being."

Chu issues an unbecoming smile "Yes, but does it have Buddha nature?"

"I won't stand for sarcasm," says Teg, pulling Yang from his bag. "Yang is a he not an it, which is the reason you said proof-of-life not proof-of-head."

"She has you there," says Wintermoth.

Chu circles in for a closer look. "Looks like gold to me."

"Definitely gold," says Wintermoth.

"But not alive."

Yang shows his sapphire teeth. "I'm as alive as you are, Ms. Chu, but sadly lacking your beautiful legs. In truth, my legs were never so shapely. They were built for work, not play, and to a soft boy's proportions, too. Might you know where we could find them?"

Chu freezes, mouth open, for an excruciatingly long ten-count. At last, she produces the arm and a couple of toes from her bag.

"This is what I have," she says.

Yang tears up at the sight of them. "Oh yes," he says. "Yes, yes, yes."

Wintermoth inspects the toes first. It takes him a while. "Don't get too excited," he warns as he turns them over in his hands. "These don't look genuine to me."

"Sebastian, you've been holding out on me. I didn't know you had gotten an archeology degree," says Chu.

"Could I please take a closer look?" asks Yang.

"The fasteners bother me," says Wintermoth. "This level of fit and finish is nowhere up to that of the head."

"The universe is balanced right this moment between expansion and contraction," says Yang. "The former to cast us finally adrift in a frozen fog of low light, the latter to bring us back down to a boiling pinprick and then implosion. Bring those toes closer, please. I need a look."

Ignoring him, Wintermoth hefts the arm next. He kneads the jade fingers between his own, eager to divine the technology within, puzzled by the soft and natural movements of the joints. He begins to remove the red kerchief, which is tied near the top where it would join a shoulder.

"Don't," says Chu.

"I'd like to look inside."

"Of course you would."

"The price you're asking demands a complete inspection."

"The value of the artifact is in what you can learn from it. If you learn for free, why would you pay?"

"The arm is for Yang, not for profit," says Teg. "We'll need to know the provenance."

"I'm guessing Korea," says Wintermoth. "Am I right, Feilin? The Lee family? Consumer electronics chain?"

"France," Chu says smugly.

"The Crossroads Group? Grocery stores? The snot-nose kid?"

Chu nods. "Supposedly the piece once belonged to Cardinal Richelieu."

"*L'Éminence Rouge*," quips Teg.

Wintermoth shoots her a surprised look.

"What?" she says. "After all your snooping into my life, surely you know that I was high-school valedictorian and top of my class at NYU? History and economics. You're not the only one with an education."

"Enlighten me," Wintermoth says tightly.

"He was France's first prime minister. He loved anything made of gold. Jewels, too. He would have gone nuts for Yang's head. His chapel at the Palais Cardinal housed a famous collection.

"Man's hegemony over nature *is* a central tenet of Christian faith," Wintermoth muses. "Evidence of another sentient humanoid would have been dangerous for a powerful cleric, something for him to suppress."

"I was in France?" asks Yang.

"Maybe only your parts," says Teg.

Yang thinks for a long moment, then brightens. "I remember a hall filled with urns," he says slowly.

"Ha!" Teg exclaims. "Ciboria! Built specifically to contain the sacraments of Holy Communion."

"A heart-shaped diamond from Alphonse Lopez," says Yang. "Tapestries. Bacchus. The awakening one, the young one, the bearded one, and the bound one. All Michelangelo's *Slaves*."

Teg claps her hands and spins around. Chu narrows her eyes.

"Someone needs to tell me what's going on," Wintermoth demands.

44

IF THE ARID lands west of the Taklamakan Desert were an oyster, Kashgar would be its pearl. Not since leaving Xanadu had I seen such a vibrant gathering of soft people. Small wonder Genghis Khan granted its Uighur inhabitants treaties and trade, and no surprise at all that a man of Kublai's libidinous tastes would favor so sensuous a city and its titillating exports. I walked through its rich architecture and peeked into its lavish interiors, sniffing the aroma of the various kinds of *naan* breads, feeling the delicate clays and glazes of the beautiful pottery for sale. Watching soft people carve musical instruments from special trees, hammer copper into pots and pans, work wood lathes with their feet, and fashion daggers from the finest steel and the most exotic handle materials, I was reminded that there is a pace and rhythm to soft lives, with its pregnant pauses, long exhalations, rapid intakes of breath, frenzied movement, episodes of wistful stargazing, and always at the end, the big sleep.

I was particularly impressed by the genuine affection I saw so liberally expressed between Kashgar's men and women. Perhaps because the city was such a chaotic melting pot of religions, cultures, and races, the gender wars I had so often seen at court seemed suspended. Couples walked hand in hand, clothing was loose yet revealing, bodies were strong and healthy, and poetry, frequently read aloud in the town's square, was devoted wholeheartedly to romance.

I could not help but comment upon this at the end of our first day in town.

"Sex is what women offer in hopes of love," Roxsana responded bitterly. "Love is what men offer in pursuit of sex."

I recalled how amidst the foaming, frothy energy of the court, my father and mother coupled behind every drawn curtain and on top of any scrap of silk or clump of horsehair. In anticipation of seeing him, my mother had her maids file her toenails and trim her cuticles until the nail beds shone like tiny quarter moons in winter. Whatever secret agendas the two might have harbored, they brought each other unbridled pleasure; I could not help wonder why Roxsana had such a negative view of coupling.

"You're still angry at the wizard," I said, choosing not to call him my father just then.

"Why wouldn't I be?" she said. "He stole you, then drugged me so he could keep you."

"He's complicated. Sometimes I love him and sometimes I hate him. Sometimes I want to trust him and can't and sometimes he impresses me by doing the right thing. I wish my relationship with him was clearer and easier, more consistent, less of a painful wobble. But I *can* say I think he fancied you. He may or may not be a terrible person but my mother saw something in him."

"She was not your mother."

"I enjoy thinking otherwise."

"As you like, but she's a soft and spoiled bride who knows nothing of the world and even less of the evils of men."

"When did you meet her?"

"You know perfectly well I haven't met her. Princesses who will be queens are kept in the dark because it suits those who will one day own them. A woman more experienced in the ways of love is less accepting of a man's shortcomings."

"Are *you* such a woman?" I inquired mildly.

"I instantly know what a man brings to the table and what he fails to bring. I'm never wrong. There's no telling what your wizard will do to prevent me returning you to the master. Even though we see no sign of him, neither of us is safe. First thing tomorrow morning we need to find you a weapon."

I couldn't imagine such a need, but chose not to say so. Instead, I wandered with her until nightfall, when we took shelter in a mosque. It was a beautiful building festooned with arches and topped by a bulbous, golden spire. We unfolded our blankets and lay down in a corridor, by an open stone window through which I watched stars shoot past while Roxsana fell quickly asleep. The faint light of the waxing gibbous moon revealed blue-and-white tiles lining the building's interior, each square intricately decorated with interlacing straps and leaves. Though new to me, the self-similar geometry—identical at every level of scale from a single tile to the spread of the entire interior of the spire—might as well have been a language I had been born speaking.

I was so entranced by the design I did not notice Roxsana's somnolent murmurings until they grew quite loud. At first, I was tempted to cover her mouth for fear of drawing the attention of any worshippers, but knowing her reflexes and the devastating effect of her blade, I decided not to touch her. Instead, I rose, reconnoitered, and confirmed we were alone.

She was still murmuring when I returned to her side. Her tones grew affectionate. She pressed against me, then lifted and gyrated her hips. Her indistinguishable words became moans and her mouth opened.

"Carry me outside," she whispered. "We can't in here."

I did as she asked, found a dry, clean spot in an adjacent alley and lay down beside her.

Her tongue darted about and her eyes moved under closed lids. Her teeth gleamed in the moonlight. I assumed she was dreaming of some sexual athlete, a gladiator with a long black beard and a turban or perhaps one of the beautiful boys I had seen her eying at the inn where we first met — olive skinned, with long lashes and green eyes to match her own.

Then she murmured my name.

45

"THE HEAD remembers France," says Chu.

"More specifically, the treasures of Richelieu's collection," corrects Teg.

"Am I in Sunday school here?" Wintermoth steams.

"The cardinal adored my feet," declares Yang. "He was a man in love with diamonds."

"More!" cries Teg. All at once, she feels incredibly happy.

But the feat of memory is over as quickly as it begins, and Yang falls silent. Chu strokes his cheek with her manicured nails. "Muscles in gold," she mutters, mostly to herself. "How is this possible?"

Up close now, Teg sees faint lines on Chu's neck, visible under her makeup despite the porcelain tone to skin that has never ever seen the sun. Teg likes her a little better for these signs of age, but only a little.

"Could we get to business?" Wintermoth says impatiently.

"Hello," says Yang. "Will someone please show me the arm?"

Teg presents it to him. He licks it and touches it to his teeth. His sobs start quietly and build slowly. Watching, Teg imagines he is remembering all the hand has touched, all the arm has supported, dragged, lifted, and held dear. Somehow, too, she feels his desperate longing to be whole, his aching for the torso to which the arm belongs, and more. Pretty soon, he's not the only one mewling.

"Really," says Wintermoth. "Are we children here?"

Yang regains his composure. "I'm sorry," he says. "I guess I'm disappointed. I was so very much hoping it was mine."

Wintermoth turns to Chu. "No deal," he says.

Those are the last peaceful words spoken, the last bit of rational discourse. A moment later, the room erupts into violence. Chu makes a grab for Yang, shoves him into her backpack, and veers toward the window. Wintermoth, his moves catlike and smooth, sets an intercept course. The suite door bursts open and Chu's attendants, the ones who look like fireplugs, enter the room. Wintermoth's men start shooting. Accent pieces and furniture surrender to lead pellets in a shower of porcelain and wood. The suite's TV screen explodes into gray smoke and glass.

Teg covers her head. Wintermoth's pair seem well-trained, but there is something about of Chu's soldiers—implacable demeanors, squat profiles, heavy bones, thick frames, wrestling moves designed to subdue bears—that Teg finds frightening. She recognizes them to be Mongolians and wonders why it took her so long to do so. One of them takes a bullet to the leg. His suit is brown and barely shows the blood. Fleetingly, Teg wonders if he chose the color for that reason. He seems exactly the type to do such a thing, with his low forehead and pug-dog ears.

Limping, lurching, he's on top of the shooter despite his wound. He grabs the gun. Wintermoth's man roundhouse kicks it out of his hand—Teg will later learn he is a Thai kickboxing champion—but the Mongolian presses him against the wall, traps his elbows and knees, and crushes his throat with blunt, calloused fingers. Wide-eyed, the man gurgles as he goes down.

Wintermoth's second man moves like a ghost on a poorly tuned TV set. He cuts the other Mongolian with a long knife. Falling, the wounded man trips over Teg's leg. She can smell him, feel the heat coming off him, see the rivulet of blood oozing onto the carpet. A moment later, incredibly, the Mongolian is up. He jumps on the knifeman's back, reaches around for the blade, and pulls it straight into the man's heart. Air rushes from the hole in the man's chest. Something gurgles. Teg hears this, wishes she hadn't, wants never to hear such a sound again. The man sinks to his knees and closes his eyes. He brings his hands together in what looks like prayer.

Emboldened by her man's victory, Chu leaps onto the credenza and makes a grab for the metal frame of the skylight. As she hauls herself upward, Yang still in her knapsack, Teg makes a grab of her own. She has never felt a leg as strong as Chu's, all hard muscles and cords, and she can't hold onto it. Shaken off and prone on the carpet, she spies Wintermoth through the skylight glass. He's on the roof. She has no idea how he got there but he's perfectly positioned to rip the pack off Chu's back as she tries to escape the room. Falling, Chu screams in frustration. Wintermoth follows her down but one of the Mongolians is waiting. He shoves his pistol against Wintermoth's belly and fires.

The shot is a thunderclap. Nobody moves. Silence reigns. Dust drizzles down. The acrid smell of city air swirls into the room. Wintermoth lifts his shirt to show smooth flesh, pries out a bullet, flat as a mushroom, dry as a bone. His smile is smug, satisfied, deeply disturbing. He points at the door.

Chu raises her hands. "All right. We're going. I'm going to pretend I didn't see that."

Her men follow her out, still breathing, bleeding, their faces impassive.

"Sebastian," says Teg, as the sound of a police siren breaks the mood. "You've got some explaining to do."

46

QUEEN TEGULEN once told me there were no words to describe the experience of making love. Perhaps words don't suffice, but soft people seem to instinctively understand the nature of the sex act. Lacking the propulsive desire to procreate, I, by contrast, did not. There was no emotion in my wondering about sex, nothing but mechanical questions of technique, force, pacing, and angles. Being with Roxsana, however, changed all that. As her fingertips feathered the blue of me, I closed my eyes and found behind my lids a panoply of images, none lasting longer than a snowflake on a cauldron. Among them, a taut quartz belly, smooth lapis breasts, a long back of rippling jade, carved tourmaline buttocks, shimmering platinum toenails, shining silver eyelashes, the puff and pout of ruby red lips, the dark, moist conjoining of tantalite thighs.

When Roxsana finally drew me in, I felt the urge of the intimate for the first time. I wanted to speak with her, to describe for her the doors that were opening for me, but she remained asleep, her eyes active behind her lids. I might have felt the cad for that, but after all I was no stand-in, it was my name she had spoken and me she was reaching for in her dream. Even so, I remained as quiet as I could for fear of waking her and making her angry, or worse. I needn't have worried. When at last she opened her eyes, she tenderly cradled my face in her hands.

"I love you," she whispered.

"I love you, too," I declared, confident I both meant and understood what I said.

In explaining the complex relationship between fluids, energy and life, the imposter who had claimed to be my father had used the phrase "*Jing* to *Qi*, *Qi* to *Shen*, *Shen* to *Tao*." He had gone on to explain how sexual essence is the root of life's energy and how energy lifts the spirit, which in turn prepares one to realize the way of the world called Tao.

"Don't squander your juices," he'd warned me.

"Do I even *have* juices?" I'd asked him.

"Of course you do. You might be hard and dry on the outside, but I've built reservoirs of moisture within you. Protect them vigilantly. Stay moist, and rehydrate yourself at every opportunity."

Roxsana had no apparent need to protect her own moisture, which flowed abundantly. Nor did she curb her utterances. Her crescendos, diminuendos and, I am pleased to say, encores, reminded me of a visiting European orchestra I had heard perform for Kublai's court. A recurring theme in her musical moans was her preoccupation with my platinum fingertips, from which she appeared to derive sustenance as she tongued and kissed them and moved them in and out of her mouth, sometimes singly, sometimes in trios or pairs.

Roxsana's rhythms were manifest, but I had not expected I would have a rhythm of my own, or perhaps better said, a trajectory. I had noticed that when soft people made love, their movements grew ever faster before ending abruptly, but had never realized the increase in speed was caused by a concomitant increase in inner pressure. That night by the mosque, however, I felt the pressure, stepped up my pace, and felt a heretofore unknown moisture issue from my root.

My senses were heightened and I felt both satisfied and sad.

After my release I was simultaneously materially diminished and spiritually enhanced. When I returned once more to the world, Roxsana's lips were upon mine and her breath was deep within my lungs.

"Now I know what The Magnificent One really had in mind when he set your design to paper," she said, her voice vibrating in my throat, her smile as the sun to me even though my eyes were closed.

47

TEGULEN SETS the bag containing Yang's head down atop the original wall still ringing the ancient part of the city of Xi'an. She has cut two little holes so he can see without anyone knowing he's there, yet his eyes remain disinterestedly closed. Wintermoth sits beside her. Around them, tourists snap pictures of tall red lampposts. Flags grown dingy in the dirty air crackle and snap in the wind. To the north, under a yellow sky, is a view of the incoherent skyline of the new city, with its low buildings and skyscrapers crammed together. Teg gazes down at shops and galleries, temples and statues in a quarter once the culmination of a transcontinental trade route and now carefully orchestrated for tourists.

"Anything?" she asks Yang, hoping the view might stimulate his memory.

He doesn't answer. He's been quiet since the debacle of the fake arm.

"I'm worried about him," she whispers to Wintermoth. "He was really counting on those pieces being real."

"They were only meant to fool us long enough to agree to that meeting so Chu could steal him."

"She called you?"

"Indeed."

"Whatever. None of that changes how disappointed he is."

Wintermoth looks off into the distance, ruminating. "What I wonder is how she heard about the device in the first place, and who else might know. Someone like her never reveals her sources."

"I don't see you giving up sources either. And is Yang really still a *device* to you?"

"When Descartes linked thought and existence by saying *cogito ergo sum*, we all became obsessed with the brain. Before that crazy idea, in every aboriginal culture and all across the world, the soul, the essence of a being, was variously believed to be in the heart, the liver, the stomach, and so on. I suppose it's hard to say exactly what Yang is or isn't until we see the rest of his technology."

"By technology you mean his parts."

"The technology in his parts."

"See how complete *you* would feel with pieces of your body spread all over the world," Yang interrupts.

"You're awake," cries Teg. "How do you feel?"

"I'm all right, thank you for asking. Merely contemplating the twists and turns of our hunt. What are we doing here?"

"Sebastian has another lead."

"This one should be better," says Wintermoth.

"I hope so," says Teg. "You get shot, don't bleed, but don't offer *me* a bulletproof vest. We leave Beijing in a wild rush, dashing out of a hotel before the police show up. We get to the airport. We fly two hours with you texting and talking some language I don't understand. Now we're in some old capital city and I can't get a clean breath of air; Yang's disappointed and you couldn't care less."

"We could go off again without him," Yang ventures.

"You could," says Wintermoth. "But you don't know where you are and you don't know where you're going."

"And you do, right? You're tough to trust, Sebastian. I listened to you at your office and I listened to you at the conference. You want Yang's secrets, whatever they are, so you can duplicate them and your robot minions can take over the world and make you some kind of king."

"You like your friend here so much and yet you don't want me making more of his kind. Does that sound rational to you? Despite what you think, I really *do* want the world to be a better place."

"For the masters not the slaves."

"What makes you say such a thing?"

"Look me in the eye and tell me that the dystopian world you suggest won't pay homage to one Sebastian Wintermoth."

"What would be wrong with that it's a bad thing," Wintermoth answers with sudden earnestness. "Companies need leaders, tribes need leaders, nations need leaders, and robots need leaders, too."

"Not if they're like me, they don't," interrupts Yang.

Teg throws up her hands. "I don't know what to do. I don't understand anything anymore. There's no order to anything at all."

"And yet everything is happening exactly on schedule," Yang says with a smile.

48

DESPITE OUR desire to remain entwined all day, we left the mosque before the morning prayers. The feeling of Roxsana's palm against mine as we walked hand in hand was a luxury greater than any ever afforded by the court of the khan. In the interests of shaking any pursuers, we made haste toward the city of Samarqand in the company of a group of merchants. They took us for their own, and Roxsana referred to them as Sogdians. I understood this to be a generic word for her forebears, particularly those whom she described as having had the temerity to brave what she called the tea roads.

"I've not heard of such roads," I said.

"Probably because there are many, not only one, and taken together they resemble a river more than any sort of highway. Goods flow eastward from Europe to Cathay along one bank, and west again along the other. Smaller, narrower currents and eddies lurk beneath the surface of that river of commerce, some so small most people never notice them, others powerful enough to sweep along an unsuspecting traveler to a destination from which there is no return. Truly, people can get lost in their ambitions, their greed, their grasping, their dreams. There are good people in the mix, but plenty of unsavory ones, too."

During the many days that followed, the merchants gradually fell away, called by their own affairs. We walked the last leg to

Samarqand alone, and in that time witnessed nefarious deeds aplenty and endured everything from inquisitive glances to terrifying pursuits. Through all that, I greatly enjoyed Roxsana's company.

When we finally reached the city, our first business was to find me a sword. I asked her if there was a certain part of town for that kind of thing or if we should go to the nearest open market. I thought it was a fair question. It was, after all, a very big city.

"Merchants who sell valuable things have protection," Roxsana told me, giving me a significant look. "That makes sense, right? After all, you've seen the big bad world of markets and how thieves work them. Anyone who wants to steal a weapon probably knows how to use one. That makes protection more dangerous, makes for so-called high-risk jobs. Bodyguards who work high-risk jobs have to be very good at what they do and charge a lot of money. There aren't so very many of them. Of us. And we usually know each other."

"You don't want to be recognized," I said.

"I know a Seljuk trader. He's a cheap and rotund bastard, doesn't want bodyguards, relies on secrecy instead. He's competent at dealing with trouble, and if it's too much he has friends. He favors markets on dead-end streets, sees everyone coming, no easy exit. He'll only show his wares if he likes the odds, likes the smell of the customer, likes the situation. He covers his goods with camel-hoof cleaning hooks and files, blankets and bits. The only way you know he has blades is if he trusts you and wants you to know."

"I gather he trusts you."

"We'll see."

We found him on the promised square at the end of a line of opulent houses whose exterior pipes and drains bespoke the luxury of running water. It was not so much his blanket disguise

I found remarkable, though the stench issuing from the hoof-cleaning tools was formidable, but rather his girth. I doubted there was a camel in the land capable of carrying him for more than three steps, and he would have crushed a steppe pony with a glance. To this day, I've never seen a man so fat, or one who wheezed so loudly with even the slightest move.

"My dear, dear girl," he said upon seeing Roxsana.

"I bring some business, Arslan," she said as we sidled up to his market stall.

"A blanket for a camel, is it?" he asked, a twinkle in his eye.

"A blade for my friend," she said softly.

"A trinket then?"

"A weapon."

"For show?"

"For life," she said firmly.

Arslan looked about, smiled at some passers-by, waved at a herder boy walking with goats, and then, when the square was quiet, moved a stash of blankets aside to pulled out a blade.

"Not cheap," he said to Roxsana. "Even for you, my dear."

It was a beautiful sword and I figured Roxsana had chosen it because the wavy Persian pattern in the blade matched her own. Arslan handed it over and I tried a couple of slashes, then slung it over my jade shoulder. Unfortunately, the tip touched on the ground.

"Made for a warrior of great stature," I said. "Perhaps a smaller one?"

Arslan chewed his lip. "I have one the right size," he replied, "but I'm not inclined to sell it."

"No games," said Roxsana. "We haven't time."

"No game intended, my dear. The item in question came to me from the fires of Turfan. I'm not sure of its history, nor of any curse it might carry."

"Those fires sure dog us," I muttered.

"Show it to us," said Roxsana. "My friend can sense such things."

The big man reached under the blanket and handed me a second sword. The ivory handle, striated with lines that had once been veins full of elephant blood, offered my jade fingers a good purchase and the scabbard twinkled with a ruby the size of a cat's eye. The deeply curved blade came out roughly when I drew it on account of deep stains and rust. I heard Roxsana ask Arslan whether he could clean and edge it, but after that their conversation faded and I found myself instead in communion with the sword.

What does communion mean when it's not with a lover or friend? How can one exchange energy with the inanimate? The most I can tell you is that the sword vibrated in the language of hard people, being made of some of the same things as I was, or at least the cousins of what passed for my bones. It shared with me it had been sorely used, lied to, neglected, and finally abandoned. Now my hand was where it was supposed to be, because that sword wanted and needed me. Laugh if you must, but it told me it had been waiting for me and I believed it. When I strapped it on, it hung perfectly across my back and did not interfere with my stride, nor even with my most vigorous leaps and bounds.

"We'll take it," I said, handing it back for Arslan's kind ministrations.

He gave me a thoughtful look then set to work behind a curtain at the back of his stall. I lifted a corner and watched him pump a grinding wheel with his flabby foot, and saw the expert strokes he used on a whetstone dampened by his spit. The grime came off quickly and the dents in the scabbard yielded to his light touch with a hammer. When he was done, the sword gleamed like a new baby fresh from a bath catching the setting sun both with its pattern, raindrops not lines, and its beautiful ruby.

"The ruby is extra," he told Roxsana when she produced coin. "I can remove it if you want."

"Did you add it?"

"I did not."

"Then it stays and is part of the price of the sword."

They stared at each other until Arslan finally laughed and nodded. I shielded the sword with my cloak and we took our leave.

"Thank you," I told Roxsana when we were clear of that dead-end square. "It's perfect for me, though I hope never to draw it."

"I hope the same, but both the wizard and the Mongols are unpredictable. The latter worry me more. You have no idea how many bodies they tortured, treasures they stole, how many books they burned, how many hearts they broke, how many lives they shattered. I will never see them as anything but a curse upon the land."

I thought about my mother, about the khan, about the revelry, the parties, the beauty, the palaces.

"Maybe someday you'll see them differently," I said.

"Whatever kind memories you have, they are fruits of a poisoned tree."

I think she was hoping I would argue with her, convince her that the darkness she saw was not all there was. I couldn't do that. Not after all I had seen. My failure to contradict her seemed to send her into a darker place. Her expression grew sad, she slumped a bit when she walked, and her eyes were not on the world before us, at least not until we happened upon a vendor of paper displaying his wares on the street.

"Look at these beautiful hemp sheafs," she clapped in delight, shaking the dire images from her mind. "And these? Flax and rice! And this batch, tree bark pounded into pulp, watered and smoothed over a frame to dry before being peeled off. These brown sheets here are colored with nut tree dye. The gold sheets get their hue from onion skins, the pink ones from boiled pomegranate."

I was astonished by this sudden outburst, not only because I couldn't fathom an interest in such a thing from a grim, sword-wielder but also because of the apparent transformation from serious, focused employee to joyful, hand-clapping child.

"Why so excited about paper?"

"How can you even ask? Without paper, we wouldn't have the words of our prophet in the Qur'an, or the magnificent love poetry of Jalal ad-Din Muhammad Rumi. Without paper, al-Jazari couldn't have made your blueprints...."

"...nor could my imposter father have stolen them, though I don't suppose that is the fault of the medium. Tell me about this fellow, Rumi. I've not heard the name."

She clasps her hands to her heart. "His words are those of a man bent on finding the divine in everything and anything."

"He's a poet?"

"A godly one."

"Is poetry the way you greet your gods?"

"To us they're not gods, but God. The only one. And there are so very many ways to touch him."

"As I learned last night...."

"Sweet talking like your wizard again," she said, fighting a smile. "You learned other things last night, too. Rumi says we can feel that way all the time. Says it's what comes of constantly being in touch with the divine."

"How can we be constantly anything?"

"You can be constantly jade, Yang. You can be constantly alive. Vibrant, brimming aliveness is the foundation of the divine connection Rumi exalts and seeks. The jade gives form to your life, your life gives access to spirit. Once found, it cannot be lost."

Not even in the khan's religious counsel had I heard talk like this before.

"So how do we find it?"

Roxsana laughed and twirled about on her toes, so deliciously different, feminine, guileless and charming. "I'm not sure there is only one way. Maybe there are as many ways as there are people. Rumi says we are the universe in ecstatic motion. Perhaps that's why I dance."

"I've never seen you dance."

"You think I can only fight or make love?"

"I think no such thing. I was only making an observation. Actually, I think of you only as limitless and pure."

She cuffed me affectionately. "That sweet tongue. Perhaps someday you will be a Rumi yourself. My Sogdian ancestors swirled to music. If I buy a drum and show you the rhythm, will you play it for me so I may show you?"

I scarcely had to nod and we were off shopping for a goatskin drum, and also for the brush and ink she insisted she needed. Those items in hand, we bought tea at a stall suffering from the unfortunate proximity of a pair of mules, whose putrid urine stream made it difficult to detect the fragrance of leaves.

"We could purchase tea somewhere else," I suggested quietly.

"But this man's prices are the lowest."

"You don't worry the leaves might absorb the stench?"

"Precisely the reason I'm buying these hard-pressed traveling cakes," she said. "They're too dry to take on other flavors, and the rice paper wrapping may come in handy too."

"What for?"

"You'll find out, impatient boy."

Having spent so much coin, we decided to forgo an inn and

make do with a rough blanket on the ground and a soft silk cover strung between the lush limbs of a tulip tree and the gaunt branches of a mulberry. Under the full moon, I dug a shallow pit and moved rocks for a fire ring. Roxsana watched as I rubbed two sticks together for a flame."

"Your hands are quick," she said.

I responded with a suggestive rise of my eyebrows.

She giggled, then caught herself. "Ha. Look at you, thinking of nothing but making love. Here, let me show you how to tap the drum with your thumb and then you can help me dance."

She did and I tried and once I found the right tempo, it was as if I'd dropped a stone into water. The first ripples shook the core of her body but the later ones moved wider, all the way to her arms. She gyrated sinuously, eyes closed, torso twisting, long legs drawing spirals in the air around her knees, head back to show her throat.

"Faster," she urged.

I increased my pace beyond what a soft person's fingers could manage. Grinning, she added leaps to her spins, rising high before dropping to the ground as if her very bones had turned to mud. Her movements were beautiful, but her rapturous expression affected me most.

"Are you seeing your god?" I called to her, but she had spun away from our shelter and, in any case, seemed to be listening to something other than my thumbs on the drum. Her arms snaked along her body to shed first her cloak, then her leggings, and finally her top. The firelight turned her lower half red and the moon washed her face and shoulders in blue light. Thus illuminated, she was clearly a creature of two worlds. That moved me deeply, and not only to tears but to envy, though I didn't know exactly why.

Later, after a rest, she brought out the tea wrapper and a

brush. I confessed I had never learned to write.

"But there are so many things you know and can do," she said, dumbfounded.

I shrugged and she got a certain set to her jaw. "I'll teach you," she said. "A person like you being without letters somehow seems wrong.

Then she warmed the ink by the fire so it would readily flow and took my hand to teach me the beautiful, rounded script of Persia. Brush stroke after brush stroke she guided me, and I learned quickly.

"Writing is the basis of knowledge," she declared with satisfaction once I was able to fill a page.

"For me, *you* are the basis of knowledge," I replied, unaware of how deeply true that statement would eventually prove to be.

49

WINTERMOTH ANSWERS a telephone call and listens without speaking. After a long moment he hangs up and dashes across the Xi'an wall to descend the stone stairway two steps at a time. Despite her long legs, Teg struggles to keep up. Below he slows to a walk, clearly looking for something, while she takes in a neighborhood redolent with cinnamon, cardamom, cumin, coriander, fenugreek, pomegranate, and rose water, all for sale in storefront stalls where women with headscarves and high cheekbones sip tea and watch the street with narrowed eyes.

"Such fragrances," Yang moans from within the bag. "Such memories."

"Curious," Wintermoth responds, stopping to look around. "Human memories and smells are connected too. It has always been adaptive for living things to be able to suss out rotting food and select the right mate based on pheromones. Can't imagine what good it does the jade creature, though."

"Still calling him a creature...."

"Applaud that he's finally acknowledging I'm alive," says Yang.

Teg looks around. "Where exactly *are* we?"

"The Muslim Quarter. Here. Did I show you this watch? It's the Vacheron Constantin *Traditionelle* Tourbillon. Not only is it immune to accuracy variations in response to position, it has a fourteen-day power reserve."

"Enough about the watches. You're starting to bore me."

"Ask him to tell you about the three mysteries," says Yang.

Teg lifts the bag and looks at him through the holes. "What?"

"He heard me and he knows what I'm talking about."

"Well, I don't."

"The fact of the physical world, the fact of the imagination — which of course includes mathematics — and the fact that mathematics can predict the physical world."

Ignoring them both, Wintermoth stops in front of a teahouse, looks up at the address, and confirms it on his phone. "This is it," he says.

"We're buying tea now? What about Yang's questions?"

Wintermoth enters the store without answering.

"You still think he's interested in me?" Yang mutters. "Seems like I'm the last thing on his mind."

Teg raises the bag so that she and the head are eye to eye.

"He's interested in you but not in answering your questions."

"Such men are predictable," Yang replies. "They most want what they can't have and don't want what they can."

It's cool and dark inside the shop. Dust witches plague the corners and spiders abseil the legs of alder tea tables. Loose leaves of all grades from Fujian and Guangdong provinces fill screw-top glass jars. An old man with four wisps of a beard gives Teg a brown-toothed smile.

"For a beautiful woman like you we have the fruit of Ermei Mountain, holiest of holy sites, the pinnacle of Sichuan Province," he says in good English. "Our own plantations grow the leaves and our people hand pick and dry them exclusively for us. This tea will purify your body and elevate your spirit for a mere $500 per ounce."

"She's with me," interrupts Wintermoth.

Instantly, the man turns his back on Teg. "Go to this address," he says, handing Wintermoth a business card before disappearing into the dim recesses of the building. "The others are waiting."

"Actually, *he's* with *me*," Teg calls over her shoulder as they leave.

Their destination is ten minutes away, a small building with a noodle shop on the ground floor. They climb an exterior stairway and follow an outside corridor to a gray door.

"Sign reads artist studio," says Yang.

Wintermoth knocks. A little girl with a sideways smile ushers them into a room with a low ceiling. Big rolls of paper stand in one corner and a group of women sit around an electric teakettle in another. Five painters, furiously smoking cigarettes, cooperate on a canvas spread across a large central table. A Taoist mural dominates the back wall, portraying trees, rivers, clouds, and mountains peopled by tiny figures. Up close, Teg sees the figures are not humans but robots, and they are red of body and gold of head. Smaller images clutter the other three walls. These also render robots with a gold head and red stone body. In some images, the robot is squat and in others it is lanky. All feature an exaggerated blue cock and all bear Han features.

Teg steadies herself against the back of a folding chair.

"Sebastian," she says.

"I know."

"Who are these people?"

"I haven't a clue."

"We should show them Yang."

"No."

"But...."

"No," he repeats.

The little girl grabs Teg's hand. Teg doesn't see who's touching her for a moment, and recoils, yanking her hand away. When she turns, she sees the hurt in the child's eyes. How can Teg explain she's always been a bit wary of touch, always been on her guard, always wished she had someone around to protect her? How can she let the little girl know, without revealing the presence of Yang, that she's nervous about being responsible not only for herself but for precisely the marvelous creature this whole group of people so obviously venerates?

"Show you my art," the girl says quietly.

Teg kneels before the girl and gently takes both her hands. "I'm sorry. You startled me. I didn't mean to pull away."

The girl's work sits in the center of various ritual implements: tiny cups, brushes, a mixing tray, and a water pitcher. The painting shows a joyful, smiling robot leaping in the air and dancing, its wise green eyes uncannily like Yang's.

"I love it!" Teg claps.

The little girl pushes a paintbrush into Teg's hand. "You," she says.

"I'm a chef not a painter, sweetie."

"Try," the girl persists, leading Teg to the central table, where the men rip a piece of paper off the roll and lay it out for her. "Be light like a fly on the paper."

Teg has a what-would-it-be-like-to-have-a-little-girl moment. She considers herself too young for all that, or maybe she hasn't even gotten as far as considering the idea at all, given her circumstances, now rapidly changing, not to mention the lack of a partner.

"Your English is very good," she tells the kid.

The girl blushes. "Very bad but I try. Now you try calligraphy?"

Teg sighs and picks up the brush. Her initial attempts are stiff but her characters quickly assume a refined shape. She finds the brush strokes exciting, and the men clamor at her surprising talent.

"Sure first time?" the girl wants to know.

"Yes."

"You're Chinese?"

"Part Mongolian."

"Mongolia is China!"

This cinches it. Everyone starts smiling. Tea flows. Paintbrushes are discussed, and artistic styles compared. Teg can't remember the last time she felt so happy.

Wintermoth has been biding his time and pretending to be interested in the artwork. Sensing Teg has broken the ice for him and the mood is now right, he mentions the robot pieces they came for.

"Could we see them, please?" he inquires.

One of the men pulls a black lacquer box from a shelf under the table. He bows when he hands it over. Wintermoth returns the bow and opens the box. A pair of red jade legs lies inside. They're lightly chipped but correctly proportioned for Yang's head. They end in agile feet with long, monkey-like toes.

"Check the feet for diamonds," says Teg.

"Looks like they're there," Wintermoth answers quietly.

Hearing this, Yang rolls himself free of Teg's purse. A collective gasp arises at the sight of him.

"This American businessman is after my raw computational power and the means by which I speak smoothly and read human emotions," he announces in Mandarin, turning on his neck gears to address the group. "But as you all know, being able to grasp the fullness of space-time and connecting with gods counts for more."

In an instant, Teg and Wintermoth are the only ones standing. Everyone else has dropped into a kowtow, foreheads to the floor. Someone wails, overcome with emotion. Several people begin to bawl. The girl looks up and cries something in Mandarin, pointing at Yang's green eyes. They all get up. The little girl tugs on Teg's arm again.

"We wait for him so long. I was sure he would come!"

The child's delight pierces Teg to the core. She knows what it feels like to be a little girl who holds a belief as close and dear as a favorite doll. After all, she always figured that one morning her missing father would appear. She watches Wintermoth seethe, thinks about how little she likes to be bossed around and lied to. She thinks about how since Burfield came around with his news, nearly every moment of her life has been astonishing and special—all the more so since she found the golden head. She wonders what her father would do. The answer comes to her.

"Ask the mother for a moment with her phone," she tells Yang.

The woman hands over the phone. The little girl helps her find the information she needs, and Teg makes a bank transfer into the woman's account using an app. The woman's eyes go wide when she sees what Teg has done.

"Tell the mom it's for the girl's school," Teg instructs Yang. "Tell her it should be enough for her tuition at any university in the world."

As Yang translates, Teg scribble something on a piece of paper. "Also please tell her that this is my mobile number. If she finds any of your other pieces, ask her to call me so we can get you back together."

Wintermoth blanches as Yang finishes the translation and Teg slides the jade legs and feet into her bag.

50

ROXSANA INSISTED I keep practicing, and so I did, brushstroke after brushstroke, even as the fire died to embers and the long line of dawn appeared to the east. My fingers could sustain such activity far longer than a soft person's could; Roxsana had told me as much. I practiced for days and then weeks and then, finally, months. On the first day or the one hundredth day, though, I would always prefer to gaze at my love as she slept and consider, often in early, contemplative hours the link of life the two of us shared with each other and the immortal trees all around us.

I had always loved trees and had come to notice how soft people resembled them, in all their diversity and special qualities. Great men like Kublai Khan, Master al-Jazari, and the poet, Rumi, for instance, I likened to the legendary giant sequoias of the new world, of which I'd heard tell. It was said they grew fast in remote southern valleys, their roots intertwining to share nutrients and water, trunks as thick as castles, branches reaching for heaven and forming a web on high on which birds could nest. Individuals with deep feelings like Roxsana and my poor mother I considered human versions of oaks, their symmetrical canopies sheltering those in need. Small-hearted people like Queen Chabi were like pines growing in even rows on hillsides, their fallen needles poisoning the ground so nothing could grow below.

A stiff breeze rushed in from far-off snowcapped peaks to

create undulating patterns in the grass. Leaving Roxsana and my sword behind, I wandered out into the field. There, in a bed of many-hued spring bloomers: castors, petunias, irises, moonroses, cornflowers—and most of all the sublime Sweet Williams—I reprised my mother's daily yoga routine. Stretching my stone bits and my gems and gold, I detected a new scent on the wind. I should have paid more attention to it, but was still freshly awash in Roxsana's love and was therefore distracted.

Some minutes later, the bear appeared.

She was a giant, thick-haired, red-flanked female with paws the size of my head. Her musk overpowered me as she moved gracefully between the wildflowers, but as the grass and dew had cleansed me right down to the acrid tang of ink and the gamey sting of our drum's goat hide, she did not smell me in return. At last she shambled over, reached out and flipped me over, dazzling me with her speed. She sat down upon me, driving me inches into the quartz-and-granite remains of the retreating glacier that had once carved the valley. Through her gristle and her hide, I felt her hard bones. I resented being squashed flat as tsampa, but was too hard-pressed to escape or fight, or even cry out.

I have said I possess certain unique abilities, among them the capacity to see auras and energies, ferret out lies, detect intentions, and hear the thrumming vibrations of organic contractions within the body of someone soft and willing. When my life is threatened, these abilities grow stronger, which is how I came to realize the bear was starving. I felt badly for her. I had come to know the world as a harsh place, after all, and understood full well that few of its inhabitants ever get to enjoy such advantages as the luxuries of the khan's court, an advanced education, the affections of a Persian beauty, the doting of a conflicted mother, the fleeting favor of a khan, even the bittersweet fortune of surviving a volcanic boil.

Perhaps the bear sensed my compassion, for she abruptly released me and shambled away. She headed for the trees but then stopped, stood up taller than a Mongol warrior on his pony, sniffed the wind, then trotted off in Roxsana's direction. Her turn left me no choice but to act. Crossing the field in leaps and bounds, some of which took me so close to tree-top height, I passed her by, grabbed my sword, and met her at the perimeter of the copse of trees where my love slept peacefully, tiny pops and burbles escaping her lips.

Roxsana had not taught me to use the sword, but I had learned a few things watching her all those months ago in her fight with Chabi's men at the inn at Xijing. Long before that, of course, back when I cruised the court like a feckless rooster, I had taken great interest in swordplay. Though they studiously ignored me, I had often taken the field with the imperial bodyguards and trained alongside them, memorizing their moves.

Confronting the bear, I remembered those techniques and quickly sliced her neck before she could even move a toe. The wound doused me in steaming red blood but somehow, though she was already finished, she pressed her attack, towering over me with her mouth wide, her teeth reflecting the rising sun. I respected and pitied her but dashed in low again anyway. This time I drove my sword upward between her rear legs. Blood oozed rather than sprayed but that second thrust sent her lumbering unsteadily away in the direction of the distant river.

Finding Roxsana still entombed in sleep, I followed the bear to the river and saw her fall in, stiffen, and float away. I wished we had not come to conflict, and that our conflict had not gone so far. Animals had died to feed me when I had no need of their flesh but the bear's was the first life I had wittingly taken and killing did not sit well with me. I cleansed myself over and over, using handfuls of silt to wash away my regret, but the tactic was ineffective and I spent as much time mourning as I did washing. Only when I found my equilibrium once more and was fresh with the morning and in possession of my bearings did I return to camp.

"Rise, sleeping beauty," I said. "It's time we went west."

51

THEIR TAXI PULLS up to the Xi'an Westin Hotel's modern front entrance.

"I had nicer quarters in mind," says Wintermoth, following her out. "The Angsana Lintong is prettier and has a lovely mountain behind it."

"I prefer this place," says Teg, brimming with confidence after her end run to acquire Yang's legs. "I read the online reviews."

Wintermoth raises his hands in surrender and follows her inside.

"Two rooms, please," she tells the reception clerk.

Hers is sparely furnished, modern, all burnished surfaces reflecting glowing LED bulbs. She unpacks a bit. Wintermoth knocks on the door and she lets him.

"You had no right to scoop the legs," he begins, slapping the credenza so hard the porcelain bowl atop it shudders and hops.

Teg regards him coolly. "The legs belong to Yang, not to us."

"Yes, they're mine," Yang affirms from his perch on the bedside table.

"Yet I'm the one who found them."

"And I thank you for that," says Yang.

"Yes," says Teg. "Thank you."

"I hope you know you paid too much."

"You didn't see the check."

"I heard what you told the mother. If it was enough for university tuition, it was too much."

The comment gives her pause but not more than that. She enjoyed doing something really good for the girl with the lopsided smile. She liked discovering her unexpected talent at calligraphy, too. It made her feel closer to her mother somehow, too, and to Yang. It filled her with a new sense of new directions and possibilities. It filled her with hope.

"If I did, it was my mistake to make," she says. "I'm not afraid of mistakes. They're how I learn. They're how we *all* learn. But tell me about those people. Are they some sort of secret society? I thought those were illegal in China. How did you find them?"

He hesitates. "They're not a secret society but an indigenous people. Their roots extend back to Neolithic times. They may be tied to an agrarian, riverside community called Sanxingdui, which was excavated in Sichuan Province after a farmer found a bronze mask while plowing his field. There's a museum there now. It wasn't so tough to track them down. China wants the world to know about its indigenous peoples. The hard part was to know to connect them to Yang."

"How did you?"

"A ton of research. Among their remains are tablets describing a jade shaman who connects the material and spiritual worlds by the tree of life and talking to their gods."

"Stop it."

"I'm completely serious. There's even a life size bronze representation of the tree. A marvelous piece of art."

"So China really *is* ground zero for artificial intelligence and robotics."

Wintermoth nods. "There's no end to this country's layers and complexity."

"The predecessors to the Han Chinese come from Sumer,"

Yang interjects. "Southern Mesopotamia. What you now call Iraq. And I don't regard my intelligence as artificial."

Wintermoth stares at Yang for a moment, then he resumes his explanation.

"Like I told you, I found our new friends by following every lead and using every contact I've developed here. I spread money around. I made calls and promises."

"Talking to gods is spiritual, not technological," says Yang, "and it mostly involves tried-and-true practices. Lineage and family are everything. It has always been that way. The relationship with ancestors is complex, too. Chinese people call your birthday your mother's big trouble day. They have different words for cousins depending upon which side of the family they're on, different words for grandmothers, and grandfathers too, again depending upon whether they are connected to the father or mother."

"I never trusted Chu Feilin," says Teg.

"Trust was never part of our equation," says Wintermoth. "That's why I brought hired guns."

"So you're saying you recognized the arm as fake?"

"I was pretty sure."

"How nice. Since we're talking about our little meet up in Beijing, would you show me your bulletproof vest?"

Wintermoth looks away.

"How about getting me one?"

"Not necessary."

"It's not a vest," says Yang. "Did you not see his flesh? He has made changes to himself."

"Goddamnit," says Wintermoth.

Teg looks at him with interest. "Really? Implantable tech? From your company?"

Wintermoth gives a reluctant nod.

"Anything else? Your eyes?"

"My eyes are my own."

"He sends radio signals from his chest," says Yang. "I can sense them."

"Aha. So what you said about airport lines and people waking you up on commercial flights was a smokescreen. You travel in your own plane so you're not caught out at security screening."

"Busted," Wintermoth spreads his hands.

"I presume you also connect directly to the Net. What about your ears? Auditory implants? Can you hear frequencies other people can't? Can you hear a cricket break wind across a field?"

"Break wind?"

"Pass gas," she says impatiently. "Don't toy with me, Sebastian. You know exactly what I mean."

"Fart," Yang says, cackling with glee.

"Ask him about his penis," suggests Yang. "Maybe it provides stimulating electric currents."

Wintermoth set his teeth. "I'm really getting tired of his wisecracks."

"Then go back to your room and rest."

"I don't have patience for this circus, Tegulen. There's world-changing business in that golden head and I mean to access it."

"You're not accessing anything. He has rights and one of them is not to be dissected by you."

Yang issues a bellow. It's a strange sound, somewhere between the ritual blowing of a ram's horn and the mating grunt of a giant tortoise. It interrupts the proceedings in a way far more comical than whatever circus the trip has become in Wintermoth's eyes.

"Stop it, you two."

"What was that sound?" Teg wants to know.

"I couldn't make it when I had a body. It's air issuing from my neck. If you really want to learn about patience, try being a

266

disembodied head. This trip is not proceeding in linear fashion for any of us. I suggest you both relax and go with the flow. If you want to learn from me, ask me about the true nature of consciousness."

Teg's mouth can't quite seem to close. She's not sure if she's more impressed by the rapid evolution of his speech patterns or his insights into life and culture. Either way, Wintermoth leans forward and speaks before she can.

"All right, Yang. Tell me about the true nature of consciousness."

"Your word consciousness means, to me, the process of connecting the material and spiritual worlds."

"Like the Sanxingdui shamans climbed the tree of life?" Teg interjects.

Yang smiles. "Exactly like that."

"There is no spiritual world," says Wintermoth. "Sanxingdui shamans were primitive shysters."

"You would say that," Teg sniffs. "And what about dreams, huh? They seem pretty real when we're having them, don't they? And then we wake up. Isn't a dream a visit to a spiritual world?"

"Neurotransmitters are convincing, but they are physical chemicals inside a physical brain," Wintermoth answers.

"You know you're being ridiculous, right, Sebastian? Games, programs, virtual reality, they're the basis of your fortune. Those are all non-material worlds. If they can exist, why do you deny the one we call spiritual?

"And scrolls," adds Yang. "What you call books. When you read them, you go to other realms. Without the book, it does not exist, yet it's not *inside* the book, either. Thoughts are real. Ideas are real. They are all evidence of a non-physical world."

"Programs aren't real until they manifest in some way and make some change in the world," Wintermoth answers. "Nothing at MothCo becomes real until we build it."

"I'm tired," says Teg, putting her hand on Wintermoth's chest and gently pushing him out the door. We'll resume our search tomorrow."

When he's gone, she lies down and puts Yang on her chest.

"You bait him," she says. "You know you do. Promise him one thing and then lead him somewhere else."

"It's like taking candy from a baby."

"Well, it's not getting you anywhere."

"Will you kiss me?" Yang asks.

"Stop it."

"No. Really. It has been so very long since anyone did."

"Are you insecure in my affections? I haven't convinced you I care by running around the world for you and buying back your bits at crazy prices?"

"Wanting a kiss isn't only about affection. And it certainly isn't about money."

"I should do my face, but I'm too tired," she whispers, restoring him to the table and reaching for the lamp. "Good night, dear Yang."

As she drifts off, she thinks she hears him answer, but what he says is not clear and soon she's dead to the material world. She does not hear Wintermoth defeat the electronic lock on her door, and she does not see him move quickly in the dark. She does not see him put his hand hard over Yang's mouth, because she's in the Land of Nod, back at her father's mansion, standing frozen in the doorway to the sanctuary.

Something is terribly wrong there. All remnants of her father's collection are gone. There are no more watches, no more Cartier Mystery Clocks, and no more windup antiques. Minnie and Delia stand by the butcher-block table in the middle of the room, howling like wolves at Yang, who is no longer bereft of his body, but intact and glowing a magnificent red.

"Between Heaven and Earth I am the one," he intoned, pointing one index finger straight up and the other straight down."

She goes to him. She touches him. She expects him to be cool, but he burns hot.

"Help me," he says.

Sitting bolt upright in bed, she reaches for the smooth and reassuring roundness of his forehead. When she doesn't find it, she turns on the light and looks around to find herself alone in the room.

Yang is gone.

52

DOES ANYBODY CHOOSE where and to whom they are born? Does any helpless child have a say about the culture in which he swims, like a froglet in a pond, until such time as he or she is willing and able to travel overland in search of new water? Is absolutely everything an accident of birth? At what point in a life does one reject the values and actions of others—including grandiose ideas of empire that lead to genocidal atrocities and the death of hundreds of millions of innocent people—and take a stand against evil and in favor of good?

I had been wrestling with these questions since encountering the mountain of bones with my father, and more since sharing Roxsana's bed and hearing her cries in the night. Her suffering was born through no choice or agency of her own but only of what she had been forced to see and endure. Next to her experience, my own—being the only one of my kind, bent to the role of a puppet, lied to by my father, ignored by my khan, forced into the vicissitudes of the miniature war between Tegulen and Chabi, and defending the existence of my own soul—seemed a private and paltry thing. Well, perhaps not the part about being the only one of my kind for that was a pain no soft person could understand, but the rest of it.

Emerging from the rubble of Mongol conquest, Bokhara's Kalon Minaret stood tall enough to be seen for many miles around. I was impressed by such a powerful symbol of endurance. It strengthened my resolve to strive to become a better person. Below the tower was The Ark, the local name for the old stone fortress at the center of the city. It alone remained whole, its interior spaces still defined, rays of light setting dust motes to dancing, carpets spread for prayers and wares, doors still on hinges, tile art still unmolested save by the stain of siege fires.

"Even Genghis wouldn't stoop to bring down such a beautiful spire," Roxsana murmured, looking up at the minaret.

"Neither would Kublai. He's a builder not a destroyer. He requires obedience but loves beauty and culture."

"Genghis was a monstrous marauding madman with an ego the size of the sky and no belief in Allah. Before he came through Bokhara, there was a mosque for every day of the year and more madrassas and minarets than you can imagine. I was here when I was a little girl. I'll never forget how wonderful it was."

"I'll never understand the desire of some soft people to destroy everything beautiful and good in the world," I said, taking her hand.

The sad smile she gave me was one with which I had become familiar, for I saw it whenever we made love. The smile had nothing to do with tyrants or their ways but with fear of the future. It was not something I ever had the strength or will to address.

"Nor will I," she answered. "Now, let's get climb the tower. We need to take a look around. If we have pursuers, we may catch a glimpse of them from there."

"You're still afraid of the mail couriers?"

"Once the Mongols leave a place, they don't come back and Mongol forces further west are thin. Still, with two queens tonguing the ears of the khan specifically about you, we can't take anything for granted. We should be safe and free from here on, so any last effort to kill or retrieve you will happen here."

As we made our way toward the tower, I paused beneath an archway and pointed excitedly at a design I saw executed in blue, black, and red tile.

"Do you see how the hexagons repeatedly join to form a double triangle?" I asked excitedly. "Do you see the six-pointed star inside representing the six days of creation? This motif is called the Seal of Solomon. The ring the great king wore to command the *jinn* bore the same design."

Roxsana stared at me. "How do you know about Solomon and the *jinn*?"

"My father must have told me," I said slowly.

"Do you even know what a *jinn* is?"

"A dog?"

"Ha. A *jinn* is a devilish trickster. Your so-called father didn't teach you the word, nor did he tell you anything about Solomon. If you still doubt you are the fruit of al-Jazari's imagination, surely this proves it. I saw your blueprints. The closer you get to The Magnificent One, the more the knowledge and abilities he built into you are beginning to bleed through. Your true identity is emerging. You're as a butterfly emerging from its cocoon."

Of course, she was right. If I were to be entirely honest with myself, I would have to admit I had always sensed there were important things I could not remember, things that grew clearer to me the closer I got to al-Jazari.

"If my mind is growing, it's because of you," I said. "It's your love that unfetters my wings so they can spread."

She pressed me up against the wall and kissed me, deeply. "I'm so afraid of losing you," she whispered, her breath coming in gasps. "We *must* make it to Constantinople. We simply *must*."

I followed her upward. The swell of her cheeks and the

rhythmic rustling of her scabbard against her cloak inflamed me as we climbed the minaret stairs. When I could finally take no more of her teasing, I tried to kiss her again, but she brushed me away, her eyes twinkling.

"Not here, crazy boy," she laughed. "We'll pass fifty people before we reach the top."

We did indeed encounter a variety of seekers and travelers as we climbed higher, along with merchants and holy men. The spicy fragrances of the bazaars below wafted in from the windows above. At the top, Roxsana moved me from one peaked window to the other, the better to take in the wide view section by careful section.

The mosque might have been spared, but the rest of the town still showed the agony of conflict, though it had been years since my khan's grandfather had come through Bokhara and travelers and traders once again populated the city's streets and filled its bazaars with goods.

"We're looking for someone who doesn't belong here," Roxsana told me as we looked down at the city.

"But *everyone* belongs here. That's what it is to be a crossroads. I've never seen such a bazaar."

"If someone doesn't, your eyes will root him out as surely as your sword work killed the bear."

A flutter of pigeon wings could have blown me over. "You were awake?"

"I was ready to help had you required it of me, but you didn't. I've learned that despite what others take for braggadocio, you never exaggerate your abilities. I saw you follow the bear down to the river, and I saw the tear in your eye upon your return."

I considered this dual revelation, both her subterfuge and the fact that she had seen the weakness of my mourning, if indeed such a thing is weak.

"I felt terrible watching her float away. If she had not been so weakened by starvation, it might have been me that ended up in the river."

"The land has been dry. When plants shrivel, mice and voles and foxes disappear, rivers shrink and bears go hungry. It is the way of Allah."

"I've seen so much killing I wish there had been another way; I couldn't let her hurt you."

"I understand, and I'm grateful. Now, please look carefully for our pursuers."

Calming my mind, I brought my gaze to the scene below. The way people moved through the markets reminded me of fish schools in currents. I took in the tiny, protruding toes of otherwise swaddled babies, and the thin smoke rising from lamb meat on cooking fires. I saw waves of heat shimmering above renovated copper domes and I saw tiny warts and bumps on noses. I saw the billowing of fabrics and the glint of anger in eyes. I saw through the doors of hovels, and I saw men tending the gardens of the well-to-do. I saw fingers touch faces in gestures of love, and I saw the cruel wielding of whips and chains. Then I saw a group of six couriers on ponies, their signature black hats and blue uniforms pressed tightly in a circle as they conferred over a scroll bearing my image rendered in ink.

"The khan's men are here," I said.

She smacked her fist into her palm as we quickly descended the tower. "We could flee, and we might even make it, but better to meet them head on and be done with this."

I wasn't sure I agreed with her calculation, but where she led, I dutifully followed. "When this is over, may I cut and polish your toenails?" I asked.

"What?"

She no doubt thought this a bit feminine of me, but I had seen houseboys at court use it as a seduction technique and never forgotten it. "I remember how my mother enjoyed having her maids file her toenails," I said.

"Are you a maid? Do I remind you of your mother?"

"Not at all," I said quickly.

"Forget my nails. There's work to do."

This was my Roxsana: one moment a sultry Persian seductress, the next a ruthless killer. She raised her hood and reached down for some street dirt to rub in her clothes, the better to appear down-and-out. Next, she installed a sand scarf around my head and adjusted my own vestments to cover every inch of my jade. Last, she affected a shuffling step and bade me do the same.

The weather in Bokhara was typical of the high steppe though softened a little bit by the nearby forests. This meant it was cold most of the year, with spring being the season of promise. Accordingly, on that glorious day, as the crisp breeze blew cloud caravans across the bright blue sky, it was natural for patrons of teahouses and inns to forsake the indoor frowst for outdoor tables shaded by swaths of silk draped from poles. It was thus easy enough to find the couriers as they clustered around cups of hot tea and dishes of goose liver and turmeric rice, bent toward each other so as to discourage being interrupted by the tavern staff. Mongolians, particularly the khan's agents, did not generally relish social contact with their subjects.

Roxsana dropped to the dirt like a beggar and put a small coin into a begging bowl before her. While I kept lookout, she took six darts from the leather band around her wrist and expertly dipped the tip of each one into a vial she kept in her kit.

"Poison?" I whispered.

"Yes," she whispered back.

"What kind?"

"You have an interest in poisons?"

"I have an interest in everything," I said. "I'm Yang."

She gave a rueful smile. "It comes from the spines of a warm-water Sinhalese fish. If you step on one while wading, death is immediate and painful. There is no antidote."

"Did al-Jazari give it to you?"

"Certainly not."

"Then who did?"

"My leader. Hassan-I Sabbah."

She assumed I'd heard the name at court. When I confessed I couldn't place it, she explained that she was an Ismaeli, the member of a sect of heretical Shiite Muslims who had long inhabited a cluster of impregnable fortresses in mountainous territory between Syria and Persia. Nicknamed "assassins," they were famous for their exceptional fighting skills and clandestine ways.

"Is this the leader who addicted his followers to hashish, then withdrew the drug and had them perform executions in order to be offered the substance again?"

"A myth put forth by his detractors," she waved her hand. "Hashish is not poppy. It makes you sleep and gives you the illusion you have great ideas, which inevitably turn out to be stupid."

She went on to tell me that Hassan-I Sabbah was a political creature, a dealmaker, a vengeance-taker, but also a maker of promises that he kept, though perversely. His group exerted great political influence through the threat of violence and gave the Mongols a great deal of trouble. Only when Genghis' successor, Hulegu Khan, officially recognized them and sued for peace had the Ismaili's Grand Imam sworn fealty to the Mongols.

"After what those barbarians did to my people, there was no way I could join my leader in working for them," she said. "My defection put a price on my head not even al-Jazari could wave away."

I have described the spiral beauty of Roxsana's sword work and the wonders of her dancing, in this case in a circle around the khan's men, but have I mentioned how entrancing were even her smallest and most unselfconscious gestures? Have I told you how she weakened my knees merely by brushing away her hair from her face, or by lifting her goatskin bag to her lips? Have I told you how every step she took revealed her grace? If I have, then you should not be surprised to hear how much of an avenging angel she appeared with those six darts in her hand.

I know she expected judgment or dismay at the revelation of what she considered her most notorious secret, but she found adoration instead. I'd like to think that triumph of love sharpened her aim. Whether it did or it didn't, the flick of her wrist was as precise as an eagle strike. Each dart hit one of the khan's men in the neck, puncturing an artery and delivering the deadly poison where it would kill most quickly and quietly. To a one the riders slumped forward as if suddenly overcome by grief, the only clue that something was amiss being the pool from their emptying bladders down by their shoes.

"Now we have but one man to worry about," Roxsana declared as we proceeded toward the western gate.

Regrettably, I knew precisely what man that was.

53

TO FIGHT HER panic, Teg reaches out to the only touchstone she has.

"Wintermoth's stolen Yang and I don't know what to do," she says as soon as she hears Minnie's voice on the phone.

"We have a terrible connection, dear. Where are you?"

"I'm in China. Do you think Wintermoth knew about the golden head all along? That he was only putting on a show that first day I met him?"

"My goodness. What time is it there?"

"Four a.m. Tell me, do you think I'm right?"

"Delia asked me the same question. She read the look on his Wintermoth's face that day, she did. We'd never been in the cabinet where you found the head. Your father had his secrets. You're living proof of that."

"So, the two of them might have been competing for Yang?"

"I wish I could tell you, dear. We were here to help your father."

"I bet he's still in the hotel. I bet he's right next door."

"Who is, dear?"

"Wintermoth. Would you prepare a bedroom for me? When I get back, I'm moving in."

"Of course. Wonderful news. A house is nothing if it's not a home. When might we expect you?"

"I don't know. Not too long now, I hope. And please make it my father's room, not a smaller one. I want it brighter, though. Would you put in a new floor lamp and replace the mattress with a softer one? And a new comforter and curtains on the windows? Maybe with a matching Asian motif?"

"Asian?" Minnie repeated doubtfully.

"Orchids, dragons, farmers in broad sunhats, fishermen poling narrow boats, mountains with snow on top, craggy trees, junipers, I think, or cypress. Maybe simple Asian flowers."

"All right, dear. I have the idea."

"And Minnie? If there's something you haven't told me about Wintermoth and my father, please tell me now."

The pause on the line is so long, Teg worries she's lost the call.

"Your father preferred women, if that's what you're implying," Minnie says at last. "I can't explain his relationship with Wintermoth. Maybe it was loneliness."

"Loneliness," Teg repeats.

The word is a kick in the stomach. A butterfly factory, better, for the fluttering in her stomach at how real her father is to her, real and aching and wonderful and gone. The loss of him curls her into a ball of sheets and hair with a phone attached at one end.

"Maybe he needed a friend. Someone to talk to. He was an only child. His parents were long gone. His toys were his friends. He met women. Sometimes, we met them, too. He had hopes for each one, but they weren't right for him. Gold diggers. Too this. Too that...."

Suddenly, Delia is on the phone.

"Each one made him lonelier, don't you know? He became bitter. He guarded his money. He kept his feelings to himself but we could see he had all but given up. Then he met your mother. She wasn't looking for him. He wasn't looking for her...."

"In Central Park," says Teg.

"She was so different," Minnie tells her. "We could all see it. She saw his wealth as a problem, not a promise."

"The opposite of a gold digger," says Delia.

"He loved her so much," Minnie sighs. "He came to hate who he was because she wouldn't have him. Every time the doorbell rang, for years, he looked up with a moment of hope in his eyes, thinking it might be her. When she died, she dissolved him."

"*Dissolved*? What a strange word."

"You'd agree if you had seen him."

"I only wish he'd made it a point to meet me," says Teg.

Delia frowns. "My guess would be that he didn't come for you because he thought she might, you know, bring you on her own. As a peace offering. Right to the end, he was desperate for you all to be a family."

"Afraid to rock the boat, he was," said Minnie. "Afraid to ruin his last chance."

Teg glances at the Ulysse Nardin on her wrist, at the figures with their masks, their faces hidden in Jaquemart fashion.

"My dad found Yang before Wintermoth found my dad, right?"

"We can't rightly say about that," Minnie answers.

"I'm hanging up now. When I get home, though, I want to start wearing some of my dad's watches. A different one every day. Would you start winding them and make sure they all run?"

"We have all kinds of electric winders," says Delia. "Get to it right now. And the bedroom. That too."

Teg ends the call and takes a look in the mirror. Her face is swollen with sleep, one of her ears is red from pushing too hard against the phone, and she's still wearing yesterday's rumpled clothes. She shrugs, goes out to the hallway, walks down to Wintermoth's room, and pounds on the door.

She senses he's there but doesn't really expect him to open it. He doesn't right away, and she starts to panic. What if he has left the hotel? What if he's left China? He has what he wants now and she has nothing and nobody. She's so surprised when he finally opens the door that the best she can do, admittedly idiotically, is to comment on the massive cigar dangling from his lips.

"You have to know there's no smoking here, right?"

He stares at her, his face a monument. Behind him, through the cloud of smoke, she sees a black attaché case on the bed. It's open to reveal a foam liner with multiple cutouts for tools. On the room's small desk, illuminated by a high-intensity halogen light and next to a circuit tester and a smoldering soldering iron, sits Yang.

The top of his head has been neatly removed.

54

I HAVE SPOKEN so much of the horrors of Mongol rule that I feel I must point out that there was, in fairness, an arguable upside to their brutal conquests. Kublai Khan applied his organized approach to governance to revamping what had been the kingdom of the Song, dividing the empire into a dozen provinces each with its own local administration. This tactic diminished corruption and, as tyranny always does, increased efficiency. That efficiency was perhaps most beneficial in the area of trade. Thanks to the dangers of crossing deadly mountains and deserts, braving killing weather, contending with the ever-present threat of bandits, and trying not to get lost in vast and empty spaces, traders were grateful for the way the Mongols made their transit safer. Some still favored the Song dynasty's well-designed ships and far-flung maritime trade routes, but that changed once the khan lined obscure sections of road with shade trees, had his soldiers eliminate bandits, allowed travelers to bed down at mail stations, and created a giant tax-free trade zone to encourage east-west commerce.

The newly safe routes created a business frenzy, and on our way to the Persian Empire, Roxsana and I passed thousands of traders along the way. I could tell she was worried about being noticed, but I was not. I suppose I was too excited about seeing Persia, having long imagined its varied landscape to be as grand as its elegant, turbaned emissaries at Kublai's court.

My first views of that landscape did not disappoint, although they came at the cost of a long and arduous trek from Bokhara. The southern shore of the Caspian Sea — a fragrant and beguiling land, especially in spring with flowers abloom — was nearly as warm and stunning as my Roxsana. We felt safe in Persia for the first time since we'd met, and if we gave a thought to our shadowy pursuer, it was not often, and we did not speak of him. We did, however, address many other things, including some details of the astonishing culture Hulegu Khan destroyed under the direction of Kublai's brother, Möngke.

"It's important to me you understand what we lost," Roxsana told me as we lay together, wistfully staring at the sky one night near the town of Bandar-e Anzali, the location from which we would turn south and west for Constantinople.

"If it's important to you, it's important to me."

"You might think of what you've seen in military terms, in terms of territory or beliefs, fealty, obedience, and violence. But there's so much more to life than fighting for survival every minute of every day. Islam was such a rich reservoir of culture. It made life worth living. Even though the Ismailis perverted what was great and good in our faith, we still had art, music, dance, relationships, literature, and a deep yearning to be close to Allah. In Baghdad, our underlying desire to feel the divine gave flavor to everything we did. Being able to point at the city and say 'look, those are our people' made a difference to Muslims everywhere. It lifted us. When the city fell, it took our souls with it."

"I'm sorry," I said, caressing her hair and kissing her forehead.

"If not for Baghdad, you wouldn't be here. There would have been no room for even so great a genius as al-Jazari if we were all merely scrambling for our lives somewhere out in the country, away from those city walls. I'm sure the wizard told you about the work of the The Magnificent One...."

"He did."

"But did he tell you that al-Jazari took an ancient Greek design called an astrolabe and refined it so that he could accurately predict the spin and angle of the great black sphere we call night, with all its stars and comets and galaxies and moons? He once told me that knowing more about the heavens brought him closer to Allah."

"Cities can be rebuilt," I said. "Even minarets and mosques."

"But not our spirit. Not our belief that we are special. Not our confidence in our mathematics and art, our poetry...."

"Rumi."

"He of mellifluous and truthful words saw in the Mongols the work of some dark hand. To his credit, I think, he concentrated on his love for his whirling dervish Shams-e Tabrizi."

"You once said I might become Rumi in jade."

She laughed at this, but the laugh, as always, was tinged with sadness. "I did say that, didn't I? Even though I've never heard a poem from you."

"My gazes are poems," I said. "Haven't you noticed? And you are my Shams. Without you, I would still believe what my father told me, namely that there are no skies but Chinese skies, no dirt but the dirt of Cathay, no rivers down which Chinese waters do not flow, so very often carrying Chinese silt and choked, too, with Chinese fish."

"And without you," she replied, "love would be but a word."

55

"OH MY GOD. What are you doing to him? Stop this instant, you Frankenstein!"

"Mushrooms," says Wintermoth. "Octopus, too. I have to admit I didn't expect either. Do you like the aroma of the cigar? It's glorious, isn't it? A limited-edition Montecristo *Grupo de Maestros* — choice Connecticut shade wrapper, specially-aged Nicaraguan filler, more perfect, at least to my palate, than any Cuban stick these days. Smell the richness. A veritable tobacco smorgasbord."

"Can the bullshit, asshole. You stole him from me."

"You've said yourself he doesn't belong to anyone. I knew you'd never agree to this."

"So you break into my room and take him while I'm sleeping?"

Almost absentmindedly, Wintermoth puts down the tester and holds aloft a black plastic keypad. "I didn't break in. I used this scanner to open the door. It's really quite low tech."

"Stop what you're doing to him. I mean it."

Yang opens his eyes. "I'm all right. It doesn't hurt."

"But he cut off the top of your head," she sputters, utterly nonplussed.

"He's helping my memory."

Deflated, Teg sits on the edge of the bed. "Really?"

"I'm stimulating his pathways," says Wintermoth.

"It's true. I'm remembering everything," says Yang.

"It's actually a fungus, not mushrooms," says Wintermoth. "Immortal fungus, to be exact. *Armillaria ostoyae*. It's what's kept him alive all these years. It's a giant underground organism capable of covering thousands of acres and lives for thousands of years. I had to look it up."

"It's why I get thirsty," says Yang. "I have a fungus for a brain."

"Octopus, squid, together they're called cephalopods. They think, they dream, they're conscious, they have complex behavior patterns, and yet their brain architecture is utterly alien. They have huge optic lobes, for example, and the brain is wrapped around the esophagus."

"You're saying Yang has the brain of a squid and it's down around his throat?"

"His lobes are uniquely layered and connected and his neurons are thick and tough. That's another reason he survived so long."

"This is all very interesting, but you're avoiding the fact that you're experimenting on a sentient being. Put him back together right now."

Wintermoth regards her coolly, blue smoke from his cigar curling above his head.

"Yang's fine. Human volunteers often have the top of the skull cut off for brain research. It's not painful. It's not highly vascularized, especially not when it's made of gold. It's easy to replace. He won't even have a scar. Seriously, Teg. I'll fix it so there won't even be a line."

"He didn't volunteer. You abducted him from my room. You need to put him back together right now."

Wintermoth takes a long drag on his Montecristo and regards her with a faint and thoughtful smile. "It appears we have a showdown; you and me in my hotel room in China."

"You think this is funny?"

"Our little game is over. This antique belongs to me. He always has. Me and my family. With one swipe of this probe, I can fix it so he has no memory of you at all. As his memories return, I'll find the rest of him. I've got the legs right over there by the TV. Now run along, little girl. Go back to bed and dream your life away like your father did."

"You're a monster."

Through the swirls of smoke and in the wash of his halogen light, Wintermoth's face has taken on dark cast. "According to your ignorant opinion. I'm going to take this thing apart until there's nothing left but atoms. When I understand him completely, I'm going to build him again. Hundreds of him. Thousands. He's the future of MothCo. He's the future of AI. He'll be the future of the world."

"We're helpless to stop him," Yang sighs. "It has always been thus. We are commoners and he is khan."

Teg feels panic rising in her. To stop herself from screaming, she reaches for his cigar. He lets her take it.

"Enjoy," he says. "Savor the flavor."

She takes a drag. She's done cigarettes, joints, but this is different. She fights the urge to cough.

"Too strong," she sputters.

"Hold the smoke in your mouth but don't inhale."

"Now you tell me."

"Try again."

"You know I can't let you do this, Sebastian."

"Don't be naïve. There's nothing you can do about it. Rich men always get what they want."

Teg pauses, considering his words, and when she speaks again, it's in a softer tone.

"What about rich women? *Really* rich women. We get what we want, too. And right now, I'd like to fuck you."

"What did you say?" says Wintermoth.

"Tegulen," says Yang.

"You've got me hot and bothered, the way you talk," Teg says, unbuttoning her blouse. No girl can resist a man with the confidence to take on the world."

"I no longer think you should try and please him," says Yang.

Still holding the cigar, Teg slips out of her skirt, showing a skimpy, high-rise thong and lavender lace bra. She runs her free hand over her breasts, lies back, and stretches her arms over her head.

"We both know you've been waiting for this," Wintermoth says, approaching.

"Take off that robot skin, big man."

He opens his belt and unzips his fly.

"Sex is what women offer in hopes of love," says Yang. "Love is what men offer in pursuit of sex."

Wintermoth pounces. She hasn't expected him to move so fast, hasn't anticipated how suffocating his weight would be on her. He searches for her lips, tobacco on his breath, his hands beneath her, fingers between her legs. She reaches down, too. He thinks she's guiding him home, but she has that cigar in her hand, the tip red hot with ash. She applies it forcefully to his perineum.

The chef in her notices that human flesh has a unique smell. As he howls, she leaps up, grabs a faux Ming vase from the bedside table and swings it at his head. It connects and he goes down. She checks his pulse and is relieved to find one, though she's sure he'll have a whopper of a headache when he comes to. She knows he'll have more than that.

"Please put the top of my head back on," Yang requests. "You can use the laser."

Her hands are shaking as she does so, but she sees no ill sign of her work when she's done. Gold, she realizes, really does flow.

Back in her own room she packs her knapsack.

"Hurry," says Yang. "He could wake up any moment."

She takes her fancy shoes. She takes her perfume. She takes the two jade legs. She leaves most of the rest of her stuff behind.

"I really do remember everything," Yang says as she pauses in the door, checking the hallway.

Downstairs, her heels click on the marble as she crosses the hotel lobby. Trusting no one, she waves off a bellman.

"Are you all right back there?" she asks as soon as they're out on the street.

"I was hot from the laser but now I'm cool. The towel you used to wrap my neck smells of delicious bathroom soap."

"He'll call the police. You know he will. He'll spin a tale and get me arrested and then he'll have you back and carve you up. We have to get off the streets and try to hide. There are security cameras everywhere and rich as he is, Wintermoth will bribe some poor worker to find us."

She makes for the Wild Goose Pagoda across the street. She reads a wall plaque about how it was once part of a Buddhist temple, was built first of rammed earth during the Tang dynasty, was destroyed by an earthquake, and was rebuilt in gray stone. Despite all the refurbishing, it leans a few degrees westward. Teg feels the tilt as she takes the stairs, passing through dust particles dancing in the rays of light streaming in through the stone windows.

"Tegulen?" Yang says.

"Yes?"

"Watching a flower flutter down from a tree is a beautiful thing, especially when it happens right on schedule."

"What are you talking about?"

"Sometimes I know what's going to happen right before it does. I can do a bunch of other things, too.

"Wonderful. Now tell me what's going to happen next."

"Your friend is coming."

As if on cue, the little girl from the artist's studio appears at the top of the stairs, her mother right behind her. Seeing her, Teg opens her arms.

"I dream of gold head, want see again," the girl says, rushing into Teg's embrace. "Everyone see you run."

"Now everyone must see the tall man," Yang responds as Wintermoth emerges from the hotel. "He wants to harm me. We need your help."

56

We lingered along the beautiful Caspian shoreline, Roxsana and I, perhaps because we realized that such times would never again be ours.

"I saw a new line by my lips reflected in my wash water this morning," she said, sitting on a rock, her chin resting on her pulled-up knees. "It saddens me to grow old when you do not."

"You need to drink more tea," I said. "It hydrates you and keeps you young."

"We both know it means more than that, but thank you for saying so. Do you really like tea or do you only drink it with me to be polite?"

"The imposter introduced me to it the day I was born. Red tea, white tea, and yellow tea too, the bitter taste of green, the smoky flavor of the hard traveling cakes you bought that day near the mule stand."

"We could have some of that later, if you like."

I took her hand. "That would be nice. But tell me, what makes you think I don't grow old?"

"The fact that you're changeless, of course."

"On the outside," I said. "But so very much is changing within."

"Then you age in a way anyone would envy."

I nodded, understanding her point, which was about

degradation and the supple power and beauty of youth. "Do you remember I told you I don't believe time to be as we perceive it?" I asked her.

"When we swam the karez. I remember. But still, I am slowly wrinkling."

"In this time stream, perhaps, but perhaps in another you start out wrinkled and grow smoother every day."

"What happens to all the dead who so sorely outnumber the living?"

"Perhaps they are the source of the living to come."

"Do you think we shall meet again in such a stream long after I'm gone and you're still here?"

"I do," I answered as we interlaced our fingers.

Preoccupied as I had been with the wonders of those days of love, I had also been powerfully moved by the sight and proximity of the sea, which the imposter always said was the seat of my power in ways I would never understand. Though I didn't know why he held such a view, the currents I saw reminded me of my own ever-changing feelings. Perhaps I had always been fated to fall under the spell of moving water.

I looked out past the sand to the aerial borderland where the birds of the ground, by mutually agreed-upon treaty, ended their kingdom in favor of the birds of the sea. Amidst the scudding waves below, I saw a world of foam and air, home to thousands of crabs and fish and sea bugs and jellyfish. Some were intertwined in passion, others vied for turf doomed to collapse in less time than it takes to click one's tongue. In that water I also saw a great and surging fount of energy, one with enough power to topple empires should it choose to come ashore, and yet as lulling, sensual, supportive and soft as breast to a babe. It gave me succor, all that energy did, in the face of our words about time.

We rose and ambled along the tree line. Roxsana told me

of her family. She'd had a brother, a minstrel who played an instrument called an oud.

"He made women cry by stroking its strings," she said, smiling at the memory, "and thus enticed them to his bed without promising a goat or spending a single coin."

"Did you have sisters?"

"Three," she said. "None in service of the assassins, fortunately. Two married to merchants and one to a physician. All gone now."

"The Mongols?"

"Who else?"

"And how was it that you came to be in the mountain strongholds of lords of murder?"

"By dint of talent, not choice. They sent down scouts and picked us like flowers, girls for one set of skills, boys for another. They had complex ambitions, those manipulators you call lords. They had their eyes on the thrones of kings and queens, and on caliphates and provinces, too. Always a hidden agenda, just like your wizard."

Perhaps you will not find it surprising that as soon as Roxsana mentioned my father, I detected the familiar scent of his unwashed clothes. I pulled her, bewildered as she had sensed nothing yet, back behind a tree. She soon heard the distinct sound of his angry footfalls. She kept her sword in its scabbard, for we had agreed that we would not hurt him but rather would simply explain that lying and thieving and skullduggery had no place in the pure and honest world we had created for ourselves.

He passed us by, hunched over, face obscured, his magic robe drawn up to his chin. In his sad, conflicted mutterings we could make out both our names, my mother's and—at least Roxsana so swore—the given name of The Magnificent One. By silent and tacit agreement, and in defense of our fragile personal heaven, we did not reveal ourselves. Rather, after he had passed, we redoubled our pace, crossing hilly terrain in our southwest trajectory.

"How did you feel seeing him?" Roxsana asked gently.

"Confused and conflicted," I said. "My feelings about him are the only ones I have that I simply cannot resolve, that I can't find a clear path through, that plague my sleep."

In answer, she stroked my hand.

Two weeks later, I saw him again, from a hilltop, as he was fording a river. The next day, I scaled a tree for a first view of Baghdad. Perched at the top like a monkey, I did see the city, but also my father, silhouetted against a sky dark with storm, his robe flapping, his omnipresent bag swinging behind him, a large black bird perched on his shoulder. The wind blew his words to me.

"Find my son," he told the creature.

We made our way to the Abbasid capital without further sign of him, although the city brought me my first experience of bitter cold. Ice crystals formed over my eyes and my ears hurt when I turned my head the wrong way. The scarred, concentric walls of the city took the edge off the wind but not off my pain, for all around us were the shuffling dead, empty of expression, having lost everything but their heartbeats. Holy shrines, mostly decapitated or kicked over, marked every corner.

"What's left of these stones commemorate scholars and artists," Roxsana said quietly. "What you won't see is any monument to all the women who were raped, dragged down the road as playthings, murdered or enslaved. There's no testament to the caliph, either. Do you know what the Mongols did to him?"

"Dare I ask?"

"They have a proscription against shedding royal blood, so they wrapped him in a rug and stomped him to death."

"Blunt force only, and if there was blood, it was soaked up by the fibers."

"Exactly."

At least khans were less interested in destroying cultural works than were early Chinese conquerors, so we were pleased to find the city book market still intact. There were treatises on social rituals, cooking, brewing tea, and raising children to love Allah, along with poetry aplenty, volumes on geomancy, astronomy, Islam, and Greek philosophy, and stories enough to fill a thousand nights. Most compelling of all to me were the tomes on natural history and medicine. The former were copied on fine paper, rendered in luxurious ink, and filled with beautiful illustrations of the plants and animals of the Muslim world. The latter were rich with diagrams of the inner workings and structures of the soft person's body. Answering my hunger for knowledge, I spent not one afternoon but two entire days digesting those offerings, despite Roxsana hourly urging me on to Constantinople.

"Apparently al-Jazari built intellectual curiosity into you along with perfect aging and a gallant heart," she sighed, impatient but not entirely displeased. "But if we don't leave soon, we will encounter the wizard, as this market must surely be to him as honey to a bee."

As she spoke those words, we heard beating wings nearby.

I knew at once it was the sound of my father's dark messenger.

57

High atop the pagoda, Teg monitors Wintermoth's progress. He appears disoriented and in search of her. The little girl's mother makes a few calls on her phone. "Don't worry," she reassures Teg. "Friends are on the way."

Finally, Wintermoth catches sight of Teg framed in the tower window. In a mixture of limping and shuffling, he makes his way toward her. Suddenly he is caught in up in a crowd of men and women dressed in identical yellow shirts. They gracefully encircle him. When he is trapped, they begin a set of gentle, circular arm movements.

"What's going on?" Teg asks, confused.

"Our family *qigong*," the little girl explains.

"How beautiful!" says Yang.

Teg watches the circle of people grow tighter around Wintermoth.

"Yang, would you ask the mother if Sebastian is right about her people having originated the river culture called Sanxingdui."

The mother answers in a long flurry of Mandarin.

"She says she believes so," Yang translates at last. "She says there were excavations and then there was a museum. She says that her people found icons of what has been our culture for millennia. She says her people were here before China was China, that they've intermarried and look like Han people now.

She thinks they originally came from the Middle East, maybe Egypt, where they might have lived a riverfront life on the Nile. Later they migrated east using land bridges long gone. She says so much has happened. Wars. Persecution. She says a lot of her people, particularly the children, have moved to the West. She also says to tell you that she believes I've long helped her people talk to their gods."

Teg frowns. "You personally?"

"Yes. And she's right about that."

"And you didn't mention this to me? What gods? How did you do it? What did they say?"

By way of answer, Yang points down at Wintermoth, who is desperately trying to escape the circle, which yields where he pushes and circles around to enclose him again from a different angle.

"Sebastian helped me remember. And, by the way, he's going to break out of that circle any minute. We really need to go. I need to find the rest of my body."

"We've found it," says the little girl. "Mom says you go Almaty and go this address."

"Where?" asks Teg.

"Kazakhstan," says Yang.

"Kazakhstan? Now?"

The little girl pulls on Teg's arm. "You trust, yes?"

"I trust," Teg smiled.

"You go now," the girl said, putting both her hands on the small of Teg's back and pushing.

Realizing time is of the essence, Teg bounds down the stairs, pausing only to wave back at the girl and check through the tower windows that Wintermoth is still contained.

"Have you ever wondered how I can be alive and thinking after all this time without food?" Yang inquires conversationally, calm and relaxed, as Teg runs.

"How?" Teg replies breathlessly.

"By eating myself."

"What?"

"My brain is getting steadily smaller. Not by much, and slowly, but it is."

"Well, there still seems to be plenty of it," she manages as they make the ground floor and exit in the direction away from the qigong circle. "Eating your own brain and talking to gods. Anything else to share?"

"Not now," answers Yang. "But later, yes."

58

THE JOURNEY from Baghdad to Constantinople was both long and deep: long because the road went on and on, and deep because it was not only a trek but a voyage of self-discovery. I had learned much after leaving Xanadu, but neither betrayal, mortal danger, nor even the quest for my life's purpose taught me as much about myself as did my deepening love for Roxsana. I learned to gauge her mood by the pinpoints of light I saw in her eyes, and I grew as familiar with the tiny cracks and crevices on her birthmark as I was with the shape of my own fingernails. I came to know every stage in her monthly cycle by her scent, even when she wore fragrant oils, and I could divine her true opinions, even when she endeavored to hide them, by the tiniest twitch of her lips.

"Do you wish we could marry and conceive a child?" I asked her.

"Don't be silly. People would scoff, I'm scarcely the mothering type, and your staff, much as it pleases me, emits no seed."

I wanted to reply that there are different kinds of mothers, that the true potential of my blue-ness might not yet have been revealed, and that what others thought of us mattered not at all. Instead, I smiled and nodded and let her have her way as we took the shelter of scrub trees, killed and cooked a rabbit, and dozed our way into evening.

We were beyond the khan's purview, the air was clear of the

slightest trace of volcanic ash, and the ghost of Queen Chabi no longer hounded us. The imposter who had been my father, however, still dogged our steps. He never had the courage to do more than send his bird to shit on our heads, but the same could not be said for the wide variety of scoundrels and rogues who plagued us, all taken by Roxsana's beauty and by the parts of me glittering through my cloak. I have heard it said that some people refuse their dreams, some live them, and some steal them away from others. I assumed those we encountered were in the last category, thinking perhaps to turn my jewels to profit. Roxsana, increasingly distressed, argued otherwise.

"You discount our casual encounters."

"How can I not? We meet so many people."

"Many of those you take for drifters are actually hostile agents. The more outlandish that notion seems to you, the more likely it is to be true. People are looking for both of us."

"For you? Why?"

"Nobody leaves Hassan-I Sabbah's fold. Nobody makes a stand against him and goes unpunished. He's been looking for me for years. Any scout who finds me will know better than to test me but will send word to the mountain. The Grand Imam will dispatch a strong killer to finish me."

I wondered why she had not told me this before, indeed why she had been so sparing with details about her life on the mountain. Part of the answer, I suppose, was that she was so secure in my affection that empty chatter was pointless. Too, the discipline of the blade is the discipline of the mind and she was sharp in her focus and spoke only when she had something to say. I was also able to endure long bouts of silence because I am constitutionally incapable of boredom, which I consider an insult to myself. All the same, it occurred to me that a little conversation might take her mind off what she feared was her impending demise.

"What's the mountain like?"

Her expression said she was visiting it in her mind. "It's a place of ice and snow and waterfalls so harsh they make their own thunder. Pine smoke lingers in its valleys. Its caves, fortresses, and twisting paths bristle with traps. Its angles set eagles screaming and its archers have hawks checking over their shoulders. Its sheer granite cliffs challenge the sun and its shadows harbor herbs used to make deadly poisons. Its villagers hide weapon caches beneath soaking tubs and their camouflaged wells draw upon secret rivers. Its lookouts employ potions to stay awake through half a cycle of the moon and its warriors swoop silently down on bat-skin wings to pierce their enemies clear through. It is a place where mushrooms grow in the darkness of men's souls."

"You should have told me we were running from mountain killers, too."

"Why worry you? It's not like you could save me. A bear is one thing. This will be a trained and stealthy team."

"But they're not invincible. They couldn't defeat the Mongols."

"Yet as it is with the Mongols, to be one of them is to be one of them forever."

"Not if you don't wish to be," I said. "Not if you choose differently."

The weight of her sigh would have anchored a warship. "I took the khan's couriers with darts, did I not? I may have left their company but I cannot change what I am. The code that I have violated is as dear to them as Muhammad's book is to the devout of Islam or dancing is to the dervishes."

"You're different now," I said.

"No, she isn't," came a familiar voice from behind a large tree.

301

The simple fact that my father could sneak up on us was the strongest proof that Roxsana had indeed changed, for in her working life as a mercenary, seducer, killer, and spy, she would never have been surprised in the woods, no matter how devious the stalker. She took up her sword and I did too, but he just stood there, bird on his shoulder, gazing at what was left of our meal.

"A tidbit of rabbit meat for an old friend?" he inquired mildly.

She kept her blade pointed at his chin while I broke off a crispy haunch and handed it to him. When my flesh met his, memories flooded in.

"Why do you dog us across the empire?" I demanded. "Don't you understand our time has passed? I will no longer twirl and dance at your command, nor will I call you father."

He contemplated the charred rabbit flesh rather than meet my zircon eyes.

"So that's how it is?"

"How else could it be, after all your lies?"

"What would have been different if I had told you the truth?"

"Everything," I said, thinking how true that was, how my newborn mind, unfettered by falsehoods, could have soared in untold directions.

"Well anyway, I have nowhere else to go."

"Ha!" spat Roxsana. "There is a whole world of whores and thieves who would love your company."

"He doesn't follow us for our company," I said. "He's nurturing some scheme. I've never known him not to."

The imposter gestured at Roxsana. "You lie with her," he said. "You give her pleasure."

"None of your business."

"Who do you think made your intimacy possible?"

As if to emphasize the point, his black bird squawked.

Before I had a chance to tell him there was nothing more

natural and beautiful than the love Roxsana and I shared and that it was she who was far too good for me and not the other way around, she drew her blade and bisected the bird. It fell, wings limp, loose strings of intestine dribbling worms, the contents of its gizzard staining the ground.

"You see!" the imposter cried. "You are the highest, best thing between earth and sky and she is lower than a housemaid and more venal than a common killing harlot."

"She's none of that. Apologize right now," I said.

He reached inside his cloak. Knowing how many weapons he stored there, I instantly placed the tip of my own sword against his belly.

"Withdraw your hand," I commanded.

"I hope the bird was your best friend," spat Roxsana. "I hope it fanned you with feathers in the heat and listened to your lies in the cold. I hope you are lonely and bereft without it."

My father pushed forward onto my blade. I felt the tip penetrate his cloak. I was overcome with ambivalence, confusion, remorse, and most of anger at him for following us.

"It's come to this now?" he said quietly. "You would cut the belly of the man who gave you life?"

"Al-Jazari gave me life, not you."

"Really? Was the old man present at the court when I welded your bits and moistened your brains? Was it he who lit the fire still burning within you?"

"A fire that burns for me, not you," Roxsana interrupted. "And speaking of fire, tonight I will dine on raven stew."

"Find another path," I said to him, sheathing my blade. "There's no redemption for you on this one."

"Can't you see he doesn't care about redemption?" said Roxsana. "All he wants is revenge."

The man I still sometimes loved above all others stared sadly

for a moment at me, then at his fallen pet. Finally, he backed
away into the darkness.

It would be some time before we saw him again.

59

WHILE ATTENDING New York University as a history and economics major, Teg once joined friends for a party at a resort in New York's Catskills region. The establishment itself was bland, but the property grounds were beautifully drenched in autumn leaves. Her favorite memory of the event was floating on her back in the cold swimming pool, still open late in the season, and looking at the only mountains she'd ever seen. Now, watching the 16,000-foot, white-capped peaks of Kazakhstan's Zailiysky Alatau range from aboard a jetliner, she realizes those first mountains were not really mountains at all. Her nose cold against the window, she sees movement in the snow and realizes it's the beginning of an avalanche on the peak. She glances around to see if anyone else on the plane sees it, but most are either asleep or watching movies on their devices. She smiles, feeling as if she's privy to a great secret. It makes her feel connected to the land. She wants to show it to Yang but doesn't dare take him out of her bag. Down it flows, exploding upwards with powder, its greedy lips devouring the landscape. She knows that if she were on the ground, it would be as loud as the jet engines drowning out the world on high.

After landing at Aktyubinsk Airport, she gets her passport stamped by an immigration officer, then moves on to customs.

"No luggage?" the inspector asks.

She shrugs inside her backpack. "I travel light," she says.

"Airline?"

"Air Astana."

"Last stop?"

"I came through Urumqi," she tells him.

"Before that?"

"Beijing and Xi'an."

"Tourist?"

"Of course."

"Open the bag please."

She has no choice. She prays Yang will stay as he is, silent and with his eyes closed.

"Where did you purchase this artifact?"

"At a tourist market in Xi'an."

"Gold?"

"Don't be silly. It's fake. Cheesy. But it looks like my dad. He recently died. Seemed a good souvenir."

"You're Chinese?"

"Half."

He looks at her carefully.

"Do you have a receipt?"

She shakes her head. "Street vendors don't give them."

He waves his hand in the air and another inspector brings a dog around. The dog wags his tail but gives no other sign.

"And the fancy wristwatch?" our man pursues.

She looks down at the little masked figures and smiles in what she hopes is coy and disarming fashion. "My dad again," she says. "He gave it to me. Not really my style, but I'm sentimental. He died recently."

It might be her smile or her pretty figure or the fact he rarely sees Americans. Maybe it's the lack of demand for Chinese antiquities in Kazakhstan. Either way, he waves her through.

"Can you speak Russian?" she asks Yang before climbing into a taxi after an interminable, shivering wait in line.

"I've been listening to it since we landed. I can make myself understood."

"Seriously? You learn that fast?"

Yang inclines his head modestly.

In the cab, she keeps him in her bag, takes out her phone and pretends to be talking on it while talking to him instead.

"Since you speak to gods, I don't suppose I should be surprised. When are you going to tell me about that?"

"You have a better source of that information than I do."

"Almaty is the birthplace of the apple," the driver announces in broken English.

Teg raises her thumb and smiles.

"A cheap hotel," she says.

"Five-star will be safer," counters Yang.

"And the first place Sebastian will look."

"He's not following us."

"How do you know?"

"I've remembered how to sense such things."

"Cheap cheap OK," says the driver.

"American hotel," she says.

The driver turns around to look at her.

"American?" he repeats, clearly disappointed at this lack of adventure, imagination, and whatever kickback he was hoping for.

She nods.

They chug along through light snow flurries to the Holiday Inn. Safe in her room, Teg curls up to nap while Yang looks out the window at the Soviet-era architecture and the happy faces of young people dancing to a boom box at a nearby plaza.

"Everyone here wears fabric hats with bouncing buttons," he

says.

"Ski caps with pompoms," she says drowsily. "That's what they're called."

"This place was a way station on the Silk Road," he says. "Genghis destroyed it like he destroyed everything else."

She's fallen asleep and doesn't hear him. She dreams of her mother cutting a birthday cake with a crochet needle. The chirping of her phone wakes her.

Go to the Bon Bon Café, reads a cryptic text. *Wear something purple.*

She showers, using more shampoo than usual because the water is hard. Afterwards, she dons jeans, a short jacket, and a purple belt, then heads to her rendezvous with Yang's bag slung over her shoulder.

It's a lively spot with people her age chatting eagerly. Every guy in the place checks her out, some subtle, some brazen. A tow-headed young man with ice-blue eyes comes over and tells her, in broken English, how his is a great town for sport. He buys her a coffee. She sits and listens to him, smiling politely, watching for another text. He introduces his twin sister, who has the widest mouth and the most perfect teeth Teg has ever seen.

When the text comes in, she feels like a spy.

Go to the Zenkov Cathedral and listen to the singing.

"Where is the Zenkov cathedral?" she asks the blonde twins.

"No nails," the young man says proudly.

"Tallest wooden building in the world," says his sister.

"Second tallest," the young man corrects her. "Russian orthodox, like us. You too?"

"American," says Teg. "Our god is money."

The girl looks shocked.

"It's okay," says the boy. "You can find real god later."

Perhaps because of his acceptance, Teg trusts them to take her there in their car. They drop her off and she tells them maybe she'll see them again at the café, but no promises. The boy seems more disappointed than his sister.

"Look at this place," Teg whispers to Yang at the door. "I've never seen such a beautiful church."

The cathedral is painted bright yellow with green accents on the gables and white-and-yellow columns topped with ornate crosses. Inside, there's gilt everywhere and a huge chandelier. The pews are of dark wood and painted icons of saints surround the altar. Choirboys fuss with their robes and wave sheet music about.

"We're the only ones here," she tells Yang.

"Perhaps a rehearsal?" he answers from within her bag.

The singing, when it begins, is ethereal and otherworldly.

"You've got company," she murmurs to the tiny figures on her father's chiming wristwatch, bringing it to her lips and kissing the crystal.

"As do you," says a deep male voice behind her. The accent is Russian and strong, but the words are clear.

She starts so violently that his hand on her shoulder is all that keeps her from popping right out of the pew.

"Please be still and don't turn around," the voice continues. "In a moment, I am going to exit the side door to your right. Please follow me. I have what you need."

60

PERHAPS YOU would like to hear about the wonderful view as
we came into Constantinople, how the wind from the Sea of
Marmara caressed the left side of my jade corpus and the breeze
off the Black Sea brushed the right. Perhaps you would like to
hear about the magnificent city as a salubrious confluence not
only of waterways but also of faiths, or the pious energy of its
Christian devout and the glorious churches they built to honor
their god. Perhaps you would like to hear how I read — with
lightning speed on account of my special ability to do so — the
texts they penned on the subject of this god's nature, his sacrifice,
his will, and his plan to one day shepherd his people to paradise.
As welcoming and free of Mongol sorrows as the bustling city
was, though, I was too preoccupied to savor its colors, scents,
sights. Having come so far and gotten so close, I was desperately
afraid al-Jazari — my *real* father, The Magnificent On — would die
before revealing all he knew about me.

My heart-like internal bellows need not have pumped so fast,
as I learned that the great master had come to Constantinople
from his hometown of Cizre in search of spiritual succor, and that
he was still very much alive. Roxsana prepared me our meeting
by dressing me in a child's clothing and covering my face with
a scarf. A servant greeted us at the door of his Constantinople
domicile, a woman of middle years and proud bearing. She paid

scant attention to me, but recognizing Roxsana she drew back in terror.

"I'm here to see the master," my love declared. "Step aside."

After all we had been through, it was interesting to see Roxsana act with ruthless authority once more. Gone was the quiet, self-effacing companion of my traveling days, the woman who did what she needed to do for our survival but was, at all other times, like the tender hand to my hard, jade glove. The servant did as she was told and we entered al-Jazari's home, a grander one than I had seen since leaving Xanadu.

Where the architecture of old Cathay was deliberately complex in the interests of entrapping intruders, the interior of al-Jazari's house flowed like a river from one room to the next. We flowed with it—between the rounded columns and beneath the high ceilings and beams and everywhere surrounded by a mathematically pleasing geometry I both recognized and understood as if it were my own—until we arrived at the foot of an elevated chair upon which waited the great sage.

An entourage of females young and old saw to his every need. They were obsequious to the point of groveling at his formidable presence. Beneath his high cheekbones, pale turban, white, waist-length beard, dark, sunken eyes and long, aquiline nose, I saw a man who had been exposed to levels of cruelty, mayhem, injustice, torture, and murder beyond my comprehension. Losing culture and his people had brought him to the brink of madness and back again, lending him patience and transcendence that might otherwise only have come through divine intervention. I saw a man who shrugged at subterfuge, deception, dishonesty, gaming, plotting and lying.

He was obviously delighted to see Roxsana and bade her come closer. I trailed behind, finding him pleasantly scented by sandalwood oil tinged with pomegranate. He rose from his chair without apparent effort, gave Roxsana a beatific smile and embraced her.

"Peace be upon you," he said, holding her at arm's length. She tried to bow but he would not let her and, instead, searched her countenance as if he could read upon it every step she'd taken, every morsel she'd eaten, every argument she'd engaged, every advance she'd received, and every sword thrust she'd parried.

"Peace be upon you as well, Master," she replied. I saw she was crying, and unaccountably, my own version of tears came, too.

"Have the evil ones found you?"

"They have, master. And they follow me. They send messages with birds and smoke and wrapped in bloody carpets. As of now, they have not drawn a blade in my presence."

"Indeed, they would not, unless they were mightily reinforced," he answered.

"You accord me too much credit, Master, as you have always done."

"We both know I do not, as we both know that you were the best of those bloody fighters whose mountain you descended."

They stood smiling and gazing at each other for what seemed to me an age. At last, al-Jazari clapped his hands. "Well then. What brings you to me, dear girl?"

"The successful completion of my mission," she replied.

He blinked in confusion. It was in that moment that I sensed a fly in the cream of his composure and I knew myself to be that fly. Somehow, I understood that I was as a dream to him, the unrealized potential of his genius and his imagination, the fish that got away, the spire atop the foundation of all his learning and inventions, that one thing that he had never managed to achieve in his life and that one thing that would always haunt him.

"I bring the one for whom you dispatched me," Roxsana prompted.

"The traitor?" he asked in a small voice, referring no doubt to the imposter who had claimed to be my father.

"Not the Han, Master."

"Who, then?" he asked, staring at me now as noticing me for the first time.

"I bring you the object of your greatest desire. I bring you your son."

At this, I did what I had promised Roxsana I would let her do, did what I could not stop myself from doing.

I dropped my scarf to reveal my golden head.

61

"How do I know I can trust you?" Teg whispers.

Too late. The man behind her is already up and heading for the church exit. He's the size of a grizzly bear Teg once saw rear up at a zoo. He moves like one, too. She can't help but imagine him clearing out a New York subway car merely by stepping aboard. She follows him warily. Outside, he opens the door of a white panel van and invites her to step in.

"My mother taught me never to get into a panel van. Serial killers use them to transport victims."

The giant's eyes twinkle and a smile spreads over his broad Mongolian features.

"I'm Balta, the butcher."

"How reassuring."

"No killing. Only preparing meat. And no people. Only delicious cows, pigs, goats, sheep and horses."

"Horses? Really?"

"Horsemeat is very popular. Come. We must go now."

"Go with him," says Yang.

They are the first words the head has uttered in some time, and she's surprised. Balta, on the contrary, is not. He knows what's at stake and whom he's helping. He knows that Yang is in Teg's bag.

"You're sure?"

"Positive," comes the reply.

"Would you honor me with a blessing?" Balta asks Yang, though he still can't see him.

"Later," Yang replies.

"Then we go to the green market now. What you seek is there. The ride is only four minutes."

The green market is to a common market what Balta is to a common man, and it's *very* green. Customers stream out of the door carrying wax-paper-wrapped packages. Teg has shopped at the Hunt's Point Cooperative Market in the Bronx, a venue New Yorkers consider iconic. This place is more atmospheric, more rustic, and simpler. Over the hum of giant cooling fans comes not the strident sound of Bronx vendors angling for another dollar nor the whines of customers chasing a bargain but rather the claps and gurgles of people eagerly bartering in the happy prospect of filling their bellies.

The stench of goods is bracing, a sickly sweet and cloying odor of blood, muscle, marrow, bone, guts, fur, skins, and the earthy aroma of the glistening transparent fascia binding viscera. Balta turns sideways in the aisles to negotiate hanging slabs of meat.

"I'm mostly vegetarian," says Teg. "But I haven't done so well with that on this trip."

"I'm vegan," says Balta.

"What? A vegan butcher?"

"It happens to some of us after a while."

He stops at a display of the left side of a mountain sheep, with horns still present, and also the front half of a horse, hooves tied, dangling upside down, face looking mournful through clouded blue eyes.

"This is my stall."

"You keep Yang's parts here?"

"I have a locker. Please come with me."

"First a panel van and now a meat locker," Teg mutters. "My mother would be thrilled."

Balta leads her out back to the loading dock. He fumbles with a ring of keys, finds the one he needs, and tugs on a big chrome door handle, rusty and shedding shiny slivers from the incessant snow. Inside, he pulls a string. A fluorescent light flickers. There's a canvas duffel bag against the wall, stained with blood and shit.

"May I please see him now?" asks Balta. "The head?"

Teg produces Yang. Balta's eyes fill with tears and he prostrates himself on the floor in a Chinese-style kowtow. "Please bless me," he says.

"You are blessed," intones Yang. "You have always been blessed, and so you shall always be."

Balta begins to weep, and soon to wail. The massive man's emotions are so raw, the expression on his broad face so heartbreaking, that Teg feels tears start to trickle down her own cheeks.

"Thank you," he sobs. "I've always believed. Always."

Teg feels it's somehow gauche to push him, but it's cold and she's tired and not entirely trustful. More to the point, she's becoming impatient with her own bewilderment, with feeling she's an outsider at the scene.

"The body parts?" she prompts.

The giant butcher reaches into the canvas duffel and begins bringing out the goods. To Yang, they are one miracle after the other: the diamond feet, the fingers with their platinum nails, the muscular torso at once yielding but stony.

"Finally, we can go home," she sighs.

"No," Yang says very quietly. "We have one more stop to make."

62

"How is this possible?" Al-Jazari asked hoarsely, obviously stunned.

Not knowing his mind, Roxsana proceeded cautiously. "Your apprentice, may he rot in the fires of hell, followed the blueprints he stole from you and built him out of the precious materials provided by the khan. As far as I can tell, the miracle was created exactly as you would have created him yourself."

"But how does he come to be here with you?"

"You commanded me to follow your wayward apprentice, master. You told me that if I found him, I would find the miracle. You told me that if I returned with that miracle, I would redeem myself after the sinful life I have lived. Do you not remember?"

"I do," said al-Jazari, his eyes still fixed on me. "Yet you were gone so long..."

"A thousand pardons for the delay, Master. The distance was great, and the obstacles many."

"I had given up hope. How....?"

"I teased out fact from fiction and story from rumor until I found his trail. I have been hunting to fulfill your wish every moment since last I saw you."

In a movement as decisive and swift as a circus man when revealing a hairy infant, a pygmy hippopotamus, or an albino crocodile, Roxsana stripped the cloak off the rest of me. I stood before my maker then, or at least my designer, as naked as he had originally imagined me. My golden head glowed and my jade body gleamed, for Roxsana had polished every inch of me the night before, by firelight, in anticipation of this very moment.

The Magnificent One wiped his eyes as if he did not trust them, and then reached out. His hands were those of a man who knows what it is to wield a hammer and axe but has long forsaken those in favor of an ink brush, yet they appeared free of spots or wrinkles and inexplicably supple, firm, inquiring, and strong.

"You can speak?" he asked me after testing my surfaces.

"And mean exactly what I say, Master. More than that—much more than that—I have a soul."

"A soul," he repeated. "So, then you have climbed the ladder?"

"The ladder?"

"To fulfill your purpose."

At this, Roxsana stepped in. "He was not instructed in his purpose by the accursed thief, Master. Nor was I able to enlighten him."

Al-Jazari paced in a circle around me, continuing to push and prod me, his amazement giving way to a critical appraisal. He muttered and grunted and then, slowly, began shaking his head.

"No, no, no," he said with increasing agitation. "There should be no gleam in its eye nor inquisitiveness in his glance; there should be only single-mindedness of purpose. He is a machine. He is built only to move, not to think, only to fulfill his mission, not to wonder."

"Curiosity is my nature, master," I said, cringing under the sting of his words.

"And what of these human-like fingers," he asked, giving them a hard squeeze. "There should be only simple hooks for climbing."

He stopped, finally registering the presence of my phallus.

"What is that?" he asked, trembling.

"Does it displease you, Master?" I asked, my voice trembling. "I am told it is of the rarest of all varieties of Hotan jade from Kunlun Mountain."

"But you were not to have such a thing! What possible need for one could there be?"

The mistake I made then was to glance at Roxsana. Compounding my error, she glanced back.

"What do I see in these looks you exchange?" al-Jazari cried. "Tell me it is not so, Roxsana. Tell me you have not been with him."

Roxsana blushed. "Please, Master. It is not seemly for us to speak of such things."

Al-Jazari covered his face for a long moment, and when his hands came away, his eyes were dangerously bright.

"How could you even *consider* committing such a sin, Roxsana? You were on this holy mission to redeem yourself, not degrade yourself further. Had I known those mountain pirates had damaged you this badly, I would have kept you from debasing yourself by assigning a servant to your carnal needs. But this! This cannot stand."

My lover colored. Her expression grew tight, her lips pulled back.

"The day is long upon us, Master," she said. "Perhaps it would be best if we returned tomorrow."

"Nothing is long upon us but your depravity!" he cried. "How could you lie with this creature?"

"I love him," she said simply. "He is the finest, most honest, most loyal, most trusting and sensitive man I know."

"He is no man!" the great sage suddenly screamed. "He is an

abomination!"

May I tell you I wanted to die hearing those words? My knees grew weak and a great storm formed in my belly. Cramps seized my chest and my arms grew too heavy to lift. I fear I might have done something terrible with my sword of waved steel had not my *other* father, the scheming Taoist wizard, chose that moment to burst into the room.

May I tell you he was resplendent in his purple robe?

May I tell you he held a ball of fire in his hand?

63

"But we have all his parts now," Teg protests, now shivering from the cold of the meat locker. "Whatever else you need we can find in New York."

"One more stop," Yang repeats.

She turns to Balta. "How is it you were entrusted with his parts?"

"I'm a cog in a machine. A network. Together, we keep him safe."

"Safe from whom?"

"He's made of gold and jade and priceless jewels. His parts alone are worth nine fortunes. Even for my people, life doesn't always go as we wish."

Teg looks at him incredulously.

"You're talking about keeping him safe from people in your own group? The descendants of the Sanxingdui people wanted to pawn their own prophet?"

"There are always hardships, Tegulen. Challenges. Unimaginable suffering. You can't always expect people to place faith above greed. Even amongst our own people there are the desperate faithful who want a relic to save themselves or their children, or to uplift themselves, feel important, or even awaken themselves spiritually. Outside of us, there are unscrupulous antiquarians, wealthy collectors, and ambitious museum curators. Please don't judge us too harshly."

"Outside thieves I understand. But your people *worship* Yang."

Balta looks at the ground.

"Humankind's worst transgressions have been perpetrated in the name of worship. We're talking about thousands of years. And although Sanxingdui is the most popular theory, and perhaps we *did* originate in the Middle East, we may also be descendants of a people called the Baodun. In any case, our beliefs have persisted longer than those of any other people on Earth. When something lasts this long, you know it's special, but spirituality lives inside people, not in the air and water and not in books either. The direct experience of our ancestors is something to which we no longer have access, as it is with all religious traditions."

"Other religions don't have physical relics."

"As a matter of fact they do. The Buddha's finger, Laozi's grave, the long-lost Ark of the Covenant. All are lost or of questionable provenance. Yang's parts are not."

"Balta is wise," says Yang.

"Are you saying that Yang is the one who had that direct experience?" asks Teg. "That makes no sense. He was created in the time of Kublai Khan, not 10,000 years before that. A person made him. And he has a brain like an octopus."

"I'm afraid you've been misinformed," said Balta. "Regardless of what he has told you or who you think he is..."

"Who *he* thinks he is," Teg interrupts.

"Now that he's awake, let's focus on putting him together, shall we? All other speculation can wait."

"I need Internet access," Yang interrupts.

"What for?" asks Teg.

"The market has Wi-Fi," Balta says.

"Please show me your phone," Yang asks Teg.

She does and he directs her to open page after page. He reads quickly, his zircon orbs darting as he instructs Teg when to scroll down and when to touch a hyperlink.

"He understands Russian?" the butcher whispers to Teg.

"As far as I can tell, he understands many languages," Teg whispers back. "He's trying to learn about some Muslim inventor."

Balta fidgets. He wants to talk to Yang, not watch him use a smartphone. Teg notices his impatience and it jump-starts her own.

"I'm freezing," she tells Yang. "Can you look that stuff up later?"

"Constantinople is called Istanbul now," Yang says. "We must go there. After that, we can return to New York and Sebastian can put me together."

"Sebastian? You know we can't trust him. You know what he did to you."

"We see that a bit differently, dear Tegulen. And no matter how you feel about him, you know he's the only one qualified."

"There have to be other roboticists who could do it."

"Perhaps, but I don't know them and I don't want to wait to find them. And do you really want anyone else knowing about me? Think of the trouble I've already caused."

"A roboticist knows about him?" Balta asks slowly.

"It's complicated."

"This is the man who came with you to Xi'an? The one you ran from? You want to go back to him?"

"Please," says Yang. "We need to go to Istanbul now."

"We've spent a lot of time on this and gotten what we want," Teg breaks in. "I'd like to go home."

Yang clucks his tongue. It's an odd sound. Avian. Sharp. "Be patient, Tegulen. I've told you before that you worry too much about time. It's a construct. It hangs over your culture like a rain cloud, dropping feelings of urgency, obligation, anxiety, and fear. Those clocks and watches that so obsessed your father, even that one with the masked men you now wear on your wrist, are all symptoms of your subjugation. You must find your way free, for they simply mark you as slaves."

Teg shakes her head. "I never met my father but somehow I know he was no slave."

"Please," says Yang. "Istanbul awaits."

At the airport they book the first flight. There's a wait, and Teg's exhausted and feeling a total lack of control over anything. Her mood lifts when she sees Balta try on a t-shirt at the airport shop and rip it trying to get it over his head. Laughing, she pays for it.

"I want something clean," he tells Teg sheepishly. "Bloodstains on the clothes are not helpful at international check points these days."

"I don't see any bloodstains."

"Here," he points, clandestinely.

"This little spot? You're wearing a red shirt. Nobody's going to notice."

They arrive in Turkey after midnight, Balta carrying Yang's bits in his duffel, Teg carrying his head in her knapsack. This time they sail through customs without even a word. They check into the W Hotel.

"This is expensive," says Balta, looking worried.

"Don't worry, it's on me."

He looks genuinely bedazzled by the luxury, fingers the buttons on the elevator panel like he's never seen such things before, touches all the furnishings along the hallway — small tables, generic artwork bolted to the wall, little vases screwed down — trails his nails along the wall all the way to his room. Teg helps him with the key card, hears him through the door exclaim and mutter as he takes stock of his digs.

"Interesting character," says Yang. "Somehow, I'm glad he's with us."

"I am, too," says Teg.

64

I CANNOT REALLY say whether the white-bearded sage was more appalled by Roxsana's carnal knowledge of me or by the sudden appearance of his former apprentice. Either was a beggar's choice for the old man, and he grew paler and quieter by the moment. My wizard father, by contrast, was a human volcano who had smoldered, endured and smoldered some more and was now erupting without restraint. Throwing fireballs about the room, he set al-Jazari's furniture ablaze, scorching urns and rugs and incinerating a hanging tapestry depicting the Garden of Eden. Handmaidens rushed in with water buckets and begged him to stop, but to no avail. Roxsana stared impassively at his demonstration, but took care to interpose herself between him and al-Jazari.

At length, a dozen burly, turbaned guards arrived. Carrying sticks and swords, they forced their way into the room, lining up on one side of the room as the wizard staked out the other. Clearly outnumbered, my father evaded them by swirling his cape and dancing sideways, continuing his barrage with a seemingly endless supply of fireballs. As he tired, he threw fireballs only when a guard approached him. All at once, he reached into his cloak and withdrew a ram's horn. If the men were hoping for a serenade, they were disappointed, for when he blew into it, a thick gray powder issued from the wide end. The powder floated over the assembled warriors and they collapsed, their tongues pale and protruding.

Trained both to use poison and survive it, Roxsana covered her mouth and nose with fabric from her tunic, then did the same for al-Jazari. Some of the handmaidens made it out of the room while others succumbed. I, of course, was immune to the powder.

"In the name of all that is merciful, how could you take all those lives?" cried al-Jazari. "Nobody here did anything to you."

"I took no lives," my father responded. "They will all wake up with nothing worse than a bad headache."

"You bastardized my creation!" al-Jazari cried, tearing the cloth from his mouth.

"Why are you here?" I asked my father wearily.

"Why did you not stand with me?"

"There seemed no need."

"You might have offered."

"I might have. Yet I am confused. Am I to love you or hate you?"

"Yes," he answered.

How typical was that? How obfuscating, unsatisfying, off-balancing, and selfish.

"Tell me you never loved my mother," I said, taking a different tack.

"She was not your mother. You had no mother. I'm your father, and there is no other."

"Blasphemy!" cried al-Jazari. "If he has a father it is I, not you, and the only thing he is worthy of is destruction."

"Tell me you never loved her," I repeated.

"My purpose was to cuckold the khan," the imposter responded evenly. "Just as my purpose in building you was my way of taking revenge on the monster over there, hiding behind

327

a woman."

"He may cleave too tightly to his beliefs," Roxsana interrupted quietly, "but this master is no monster."

"Ask your beloved master how I came to serve him," my father said. "Let him tell you how he purchased me at a slave market in Baghdad when I was no more than a child. Let him tell you how I stood with my hands and feet bound and he tossed a coin in the direction of my captors and took me away to serve as his houseboy."

"You would blame me for saving you?" al-Jazari asked, seemingly astonished. "I saw a special genius in you."

"A genius you claimed for your own."

"Rubbish! I nurtured you, gave you purpose...."

"You exploited me."

"You were talented," said al-Jazari. "I treated you like a son."

"You stole my ideas."

"Never."

"Constantly."

"An idea is nothing without the practical dimensions, the application, the ability to bring it into the world," the old man said wearily.

"You could have helped me bring my ideas into the world. You stole them instead."

"They were too revolutionary..."

"All the more reason."

The old man bent over, plainly exhausted, no doubt suffering from inhaling smoke, perhaps even from inhaling some of my father's sleeping powder.

"Why did you leave me?" he asked, his voice plaintive.

"I didn't leave you, I fled you. You were smothering me, taking credit for everything I said and did. I built the mechanical man to prove the idea was mine. It came from a legend my people had long before there was an Allah, from stories, plans, details, and instructions written ages before you were born."

"Your people are long gone."

"They're in hiding, which is not the same as being gone. And I was taken from them as a child."

"I rescued you," al-Jazari said stubbornly

"You treated me like dirt."

Al-Jazari wheezes. It is a few moments before he can speak again. "You stole plans I labored over for years."

"Those plans you take credit for were based on things I told you," my father said evenly. "They represented solutions to problems you could never have solved alone."

"Without me, you would have remained nothing but an ignorant slave."

"Pfah," my father spat. "My education began long before I met you. I was born into the lore of the tree of life and the shaman who climbed it to talk to god. My stories entranced you because of your anger at your own god. You have always thought you and your people were better than everyone else. You couldn't believe that sorry god of yours betrayed you by allowing the Mongol conquest. You stole the traditions of my people so you could confront him and demand an explanation."

"Baghdad was the center of the world," al-Jazari answered, so quietly we could barely make out his words. "Those Mongol animals broke the spine of Islam. They slaughtered millions of Allah's children, his devout. Millions. We had music, we had literature, we had astronomy, physics, mathematics, design. The khan and his men had superstitions, ponies, spears, and their unbearable stench. History will see the Muslim world as divided into two eras: the one before Genghis and the one after. There is no coming back from what he did. Allah has engineered our destruction. As you say, I do indeed seek to know in what way we failed Him, and to leave the answer as a legacy for my family and my people."

A handful of attendants, devotees all, stood at the far side of the room, out of range of the sleeping powder. Hearing al-Jazari's words they glanced at each other in discomfort, not knowing what to do. My father rolled his eyes, apparently having heard it all before.

"Can't you understand that the master's desire to speak to Allah is a great and noble desire," Roxsana demanded of my father.

"You see this old man as noble?" my father shouted, trembling with rage. "As great? This grotesque ancient who grew famous on my ideas while I slept in the stable? Can you imagine what it felt like to lie down in horse-piss-soaked hay every night while he was anointed in oil, surrounded by women long after he was too old to lie with them? Can you imagine how I felt shoveling manure and cleaning latrines while he was plied with wine and enjoyed sumptuous feasts as a guest of caliphs and kings who believed him a genius on account of my ideas?"

"I treated you better than any other of my slaves," al-Jazari muttered.

Hearing these words, my father's face twisted with fury and he reached into his cloak once more.

65

"CALL BALTA," Yang yells, waking Teg the next morning. "We have to be there when it opens.

She stretches and wipes the sleep from her eyes. "Since when are *you* the raining cloud of time? Stop raining your deadlines on me. When what opens?"

"The Sadberk Hanim Museum. It's right along the Bosphorus."

She calls Balta but finds him already up. He tells her he'll wait for her downstairs in the hotel restaurant. She's as starving as he is so she gets ready in record time and goes downstairs to watch him decline bacon and insist on American-style pancakes made with soymilk.

"You're really vegan."

Balta spreads his enormous hands. "Balta doesn't lie."

"May we please go now?" Yang pleads. "And please cut eye holes for me. I need to see what we're looking at."

They check out of the hotel and hail a cab for the museum Teg tells Balta she's headed directly to the airport next. Balta looks glum.

"I wish you wouldn't go," he says. "There's much more to see here and I need to protect Yang."

"I'm sorry," she says. "But I've had enough traveling. There's been a lot of change in my life lately. I have to get home."

"I don't believe he is safe without me," Balta says after a

while.

"You could come with us to watch over him if you like."

"I can't. I have old parents and things to do."

"I understand."

A few blocks shy of their destination, Yang demands they pull over.

"Take me to down to the water," he tells Teg.

Balta stays in the cab as he guides her. They walk for a few minutes. He asks her to turn the bag around a few times, to lift it higher and lift it lower. At length, they come to a stunningly elegant and beautiful four-foot-high granite stele, the stone possessing veins of red and gold and blue. Wind and water have taken their toll, but the Persian characters on it are still clearly legible.

"Please walk me around it," he says. "I need to see every angle."

He's silent while she does, then asks her to take him back to the cab. Once inside, Balta asks about the stop but Yang stays silent. In fact, he says nothing more during the short drive to the museum, which occupies a beautiful lot by the Bosphorus. Inside, a sign tells them the museum was opened by the richest family in Turkey and was once the residence of another family named Azaryan. They tour the galleries, which still look like they're someone's house roped off and dusted and done up with every possible beautiful thing capable of being crammed into a room. They browse paintings and carvings, porcelain plates and vases, antique furniture, Byzantine jewelry, and ornate silk robes. Finally, in an obscure corner of one of the last rooms, they hear from Yang.

"There," he says, his voice low and muffled by the bag.

Beside an overstuffed sofa, on an end table set a few feet back from a velvet rope, sits a stout blue phallus of Hotan jade.

Apparently, it does not merit its own display case, as do other *objets d'art*—a silver-and-diamond coffee cup from the Ottoman Empire, for example—for its only company is a picture frame containing two dead butterflies, one red and one yellow, pressed in glass.

"*My God*," Balta mutters in Russian.

"That's it," says Yang.

"You have to be kidding me," says Teg.

A group of school children enters the room, chatting excitedly. Waiting for them to move on, Teg hatches a plan. The moment they're alone, and without explanation, she feigns a swoon, toppling over the velvet rope. Alarmed, Balta bends down and catches her.

"Are you all right?" he asks worriedly.

His sweet concern and massive arms distract her. It takes a moment to recall what she's doing. She stares into his eyes for perhaps longer than required by their bit of theater.

"Turn a little to your left," she says, recovering herself. "We need to block the ceiling camera."

Balta takes another moment but obeys. Teg grabs the phallus and stuffs it in with Yang. There are a few tense moments then, wondering if they've been seen, not daring to give into impulse and dash out. A guard does come into the room and looks around, but seeing nothing missing he retreats. They continue on to the next gallery and the next.

No one approaches them.

"Why didn't you just tell me what you were after?" Teg chastises Yang once they are outside and standing by the sea wall.

"I did not wish to speak of such things with you," he answers.

"You're shy all of a sudden? Are you telling me I misunderstood all the times you came onto me? Wanting to suckle at my breasts

333

and all that?"

There comes an uncomfortable silence after which Yang begins to speak.

"Lacking a body and waking up after 800 years with very little memory intact leaves a hard person a bit adrift," he says.

"What are you trying to say?" Teg demands, her hands on her hips.

"You're a beautiful woman and I wanted you to nurture the little that was left of me. More, you had my mother's name, which was both confusing and beguiling."

She shakes her head. "You know that's perverse, right?"

"Not if you don't know who you are or where you came from, not if you seek any kind of port in a storm."

"How flattering. And what about wanting to see me naked in the bath?"

"Even without my body, I remained Yang. I admire a soft woman's form, even when it is slightly too full."

"You!" Teg cries in frustration.

"It is confusing, I understand, and I mean you no disrespect. On the contrary, my affection for you is boundless. But things have changed for all of us and I hope you can understand, without hurt feelings, that while you are an immensely desirable woman, it is the big man who is for you, not I, and it you who are for him."

"Please," says Bala uncomfortably.

Teg colors. "It's time for me to go home," she says suddenly, and then, at Balta's forlorn expression, "perhaps there's someone who could look after your parents for a while and you could come along."

"They live with my sister," he says quietly. "But this is all very spontaneous. I'm an engineer. I like to plan."

"Spontaneity can be good," Teg counters. "You don't have a

wife, do you?"

"Women seem afraid of me. My face is fierce and my feet and hands are very large."

Teg waits for a wisecrack from Yang but there is none. "I'm okay with big hands and feet," she says.

"How long would I stay?"

"That's up to you. Please say yes."

Balta's smile showcases the charming space between his top front teeth and they set off for the airport. Waiting in line at the ticket counter, Teg reflects on how things have changed, flying east in a private jet with a billionaire and now west with a giant vegan butcher. During the flight, Balta sobs at a romantic film. At Kennedy airport, he makes carrying all their bags at once look easy. Back at the brownstone they fight jetlag, help Yang devour information online, and catch up with Minnie and Delia, whose silence on the big man's presence speaks volumes.

Once they are settled, Teg reaches out to Wintermoth.

"Hope you are feeling better, Sebastian."

"As you can imagine, sitting down for hours on the flight home was no picnic."

"I understand. Private jets are hell."

"I'm not happy with you, Tegulen."

"Desperate situation, desperate measures."

"I hadn't expected to hear from you again."

"It's Yang. He wants to see you. He has some kind of a deal to offer."

There is a long pause. "Do I have any reason to trust you?"

"Seems like I should be the one asking that question."

"Not to me, it doesn't."

"Your decision. I'm pretty sure there's mutual benefit."

Wintermoth hangs up after agreeing to meet right away.

Balta goes with them, carrying Yang in a stylish leather duffel.

When they enter his office at MothCo, the tycoon is watching a huge viewing screen showing elongated monsters, rumpled cucumbers with four pairs of legs, each ending in claws, and a face like a vacuum cleaner's nozzle coupling.

"Tardigrades," he nods at the screen. "There are more than a thousand species of them. Some people call them moss piglets; some call them water bears. They mature at half a millimeter and are astonishingly robust. You can boil them, freeze them, radiate them, squash them, even shoot them out into space and they survive."

"I'm Balta," the big man says, holding out his hand.

Wintermoth studies the hand and turns to Teg.

"I inspired you to hire muscle?"

"You're all class, Sebastian."

"I managed a Chinese split during my workout this morning."

"I'll alert the media."

"You're a beautiful girl, Tegulen, but sarcasm's ugly on you. Please tell me why you're here."

"I told you. Yang wants to see you."

Balta stares at the tardigrades. "What are you going to do with those things?"

"Draw upon them for robotic design of course. We've got a model now with big, high-torque motors turning tardigrade feet, which work something like tank treads to climb steep angles and carry heavy weights. Various attachments can go in what looks like a mouth, one to manage fragile objects, another for picking crops. The Food and Drug Administration loves it. The fewer human hands on your food, the lower the risk of spreading *E. coli*. Lucrative contracts in agriculture are in the works. Modular construction's the key to multiple applications, easy repairs, and quick change-outs. If we've learned nothing else from the robotics competitions, we've learned how to swap out parts and maximize production efficiency."

"Sounds like you've put AI research on the back burner," says Teg.

"Not at all."

"And the helper robot, the one with Sinatra's voice?"

"Already in the field."

Tiring of the repartee, Balta removes Yang from his bag and sets him on Wintermoth's desk.

"Teg found my parts," Yang announces. "Every last one."

"You're fortunate to have such a resourceful friend."

"Will you put me back together or not, Sebastian? Without my body, I've been cannibalizing my own brain to survive. I need to be whole again and nourish myself."

"By breathing, right? That's how you get your sustenance? You need your lungs?"

"The industrial particulates, gases, acids, and pesticides in the air of this modern world makes me wish it weren't so, but yes."

"Are you sure you want to live in such a terrible world?"

"I might have slept another eight hundred years or I might have dried out and perished a week ago. The question is no longer relevant. You've been inside my head. I'm complicated. Sensitive. If anyone can put me back together so I can survive here, it's you."

"Forgive me if I find this ironic."

"I'm not the one who burned you with a cigar."

"Hey!" says Teg.

"Think of your family, before you turn me down, Sebastian," Yang says quietly. "You won't become khan without me."

"What do you mean, his family?" asks Balta, with a forward lean of his massive torso.

"Khan?" repeats Teg.

Wintermoth shakes his head. "I don't know what you're

talking about."

"All this time, you have been hiding the truth, running this strange game, thinking you could hide your true ambitions and goals and talk ignorant people out of my secrets," sighs Yang. "Tegulen was right to distrust you from the outset. Her senses were more sensitive than mine when I first awakened. Everything was new to both of us, me in this strange new land, she in her father's mansion and all of New York at her feet. We had none of our usual anchors in place, no landmarks we could recognize, You took advantage of us, Sebastian. The best lies are close to the truth and you told us that truth, though not all of it."

"What is he trying to say?" Teg demands.

"I have no idea," Wintermoth replies.

"Lying won't help," Yang continues. "When you disturbed my brain with your instruments, you stirred my memories. I've been remembering ever since. I've got everything now, and I do mean everything. Explain why you have the right lineage for the job, and why, after all these years, it simply has to be you. Tell them about al-Jazari."

Wintermoth unconsciously touches his trousers near his burn but remains silent.

"I could have told them, Sebastian," Yang pursues. "I chose to leave it to you."

"What's al-Jazari?" asks Teg.

"I know the name," says Balta. "He was a famous inventor."

"A genius," Wintermoth says smugly. "The Turkmen Leonardo da Vinci."

"He built you?" asks Teg, turning to Yang.

"No. Al-Jazari was not my grandfather, not my father"

"Nonsense!" cries Sebastian.

"Now I'm confused," Balta frowns. "Al-Jazari was 13th century. Yang and my people are both far older."

"The *inspiration* for him is older," says Wintermoth. "Perhaps some of the knowledge required to build him, too. But al-Jazari conceived and designed him. He belonged to my family. He's my rightful property."

"Sebastian is descended from the Abbasid caliphate that stemmed from the prophet Muhammad's youngest uncle," says Yang.

Wintermoth nods. "Al-Jazari was my family patriarch back then."

"And you're the patriarch now," says Balta.

"When you say he's your property, do you mean he's your slave?" asks Teg. "Newsflash: slavery's over. I've told you before, nobody can own him."

"Will you me together, or not?" asks Yang.

"Only if Teg sells you to me. She doesn't need you anymore. She has a new playmate."

"Fuck you, Sebastian," says Teg. "I *knew* you were playing us. I should never have gone with you to China."

"You have my terms."

"A liar he may be," Yang says. "but I still need his help."

"Come," says Balta, tucking Yang under his shoulder and taking Teg's hand. "Already I've thought of another way."

Wintermoth stands as they leave, his hands in fists. "You may not take him to another robotics lab. I forbid it!"

66

Do you recall how I spent time at the armory during my days at Kublai's court? Do you recall that I became familiar with the Mongol sword? Well, I took up weapons of the Cathay people as well, partly out of boredom and partly to challenge myself with something connected to my father. Among those weapons were the halberd, the wolf-tooth mace, an iron stick called the swordbreaker, the flexible, flashing, waxwood spear, and the Cathay battle-axe. The latter happened to be the favored infantry weapon of the Southern Song people, whose successful resistance to Mongol conquest was not only the stuff of legend but also the subject of ongoing diatribes at court.

Set on the end of a long handle and used by foot soldiers to attack horses, the semicircular blade of this axe was effective at any angle of contact and far deadlier than any woodcutter's tool. While the weapon lacked the finesse of the straight sword or spear, it typically took a large, strong man to master it. You can therefore imagine my surprise when the slightly-built wizard produced one from his cloak, raised it high, and closed in on al-Jazari.

No man could evidence such obvious rage and pain without truly believing himself deeply wronged. Can you understand why my father's self-righteous indignation shifted my opinion away from considering him an imposter? If this shift seems too sudden, remember that I had always regarded him with a painful ambivalence, always wished I understood him better and judged him less. Remembering the compassion he showed the ill-fated slave girl in Turfan, I understood how badly he, too, had suffered the indignities of slavery. I also realized that like me, he felt betrayed by the man he considered his sire. In forgiving him, I came to a more profound truth about myself, that I was the issue of neither of these men but of both; an unwitting co-creation.

The old man retreated to his chair in fear. Shouting at my father to stop, Roxsana intercepted him. Seeing them the two of them at odds pained me greatly but it was a spectacle. The wizard was a blur of blue and gold as he employed every trick he knew to get past the best of the notorious Grand Imam's fighters. He was not up to the task. Wherever his battle axe fell, Roxsana's flashing blade was there to deflect it. Sparks flew as she whirled in true Sogdian fashion, never taking the formidable force of the wizard's blows but always meeting them obliquely, always on a spiraling trajectory in exactly the fashion he had once admired.

She inevitably maneuvered inside his guard and, as she did at a certain roadside inn on a fateful day, placed her blade against his throat. Rather than applying the slicing edge of her blade, she put the pointed tip to his artery, making it inadvisable for him to even take a deep breath. Ten paces from al-Jazari, he sank slowly to his knees.

"Now then," the master said, rising from the chair to assume the same regal bearing he had managed when first he greeted us. "Let us get straight to the heart of the matter, and without delay."

"You want me to speak to your god," I said.

"Precisely so."

"Even though I am an abomination? Even though I am not as you would have me?"

"This is your opportunity to finally understand your

purpose," he answered. "And with that, a chance to redeem yourself."

"I have no need of redemption and no idea how to begin."

"If that's true, then why does your heart ache as it does? Here. Let me show you the magic of the floor beneath your feet, the wonder of its design."

The floor of which he spoke was awash in the sticks and shards of broken furniture and burned swaths of tapestry, too. I had to clear them all away to see what al-Jazari was talking about. I did so with alacrity and when I was finished and the way was clear, I divined a spiral design embedded in the tile. The master extended his hand to me and I took it. Gently, slowly, he helped me to follow the gentle curve of that spiral, whose radius diminished as we traced it, side by side, with our steps.

"Can you feel the River of Stars in this part of the pattern?" Al-Jazari asked excitedly. "It's heavenly. This mode of travel was not designed to reach any earthly destination."

The radius of the curve became tight and small. Following it required us to proceed increasingly carefully and slowly.

"It feels as if we're going up. How is that possible when the floor is flat?"

Al-Jazari smiled faintly. "It's not flat at all. It is what we call the Celestial Ladder, and we are not walking it but climbing it."

The room dimmed even though sunlight still gleamed through stone windows. I glanced over at the wizard, Roxsana's sword still at his throat. He was staring at me.

"There are the Northern Bushel stars," I heard al-Jazari say, "and there is the Pole star. Do you see it? Do you feel its pull?"

Al-Jazari released my hand and with that I was on the Earth no more but up in the starry night. All that was familiar was gone. All around me, stars pulsed and glowed, though that famous one more brightly than the others. It beckoned to me. I flew to it.

"This is not the way you are supposed to reach me," a deep and unfamiliar voice intoned disapprovingly. "This way is a shortcut from a desperate man's force of will and imagination. It will not serve you again."

"I don't know anything about that, but anyway here I am."

"Yes. Here you are."

"Are you Allah?"

"Some call me that."

"Are you the one, true god?"

"Am I the only star you see?"

"No."

"Well, then."

"You're saying the other stars are other gods?"

"Such things are beyond your understanding."

"Are you god to all mankind, then?"

A deep sigh followed my question. "There are countless creatures across countless worlds and we who vibrate in sympathy with them are countless, too."

"A man I suppose is my grandfather wants to know what he and his people did to slight you, what mistake they made to cause you to direct the Mongol barbarians to slaughter them."

"It's a poor question," says the star.

"Why so?"

"Your grandfather is an inventor. He is likely familiar with optical instruments. Tell him that his question misses a great deal. He should set his instruments for a larger view. He should take into consideration more of the universe before assuming a punishment and reward system of the sort you describe."

"I don't understand."

"I think you do, but I'll put it another way. Petty divisions between your designer's kind don't serve them. The people of the steppe and the family of Muhammad both worship me by different names. Together these two peoples comprise a system. This system must remain in balance, for it is part of a larger system that likewise affects. When an excess is created on one side, an excess must be created on the opposite side to restore equilibrium for the greater system overall."

"You are describing what my father would call the dance of yin and yang."

The star's light quivered as if in laughter. "I've heard those terms too."

"What message can I bring back?"

"Any message you wish, but if you're asking my advice, I would simply repeat to him what I told you."

"He won't like it."

"No, he won't," said the star. "But speaking the truth is what you do best."

67

"YOU'RE SURE you can do it?" asks Teg.

"There must be fasteners," Balta mutters, peering into cavities in Yang's legs, turning jade arms in his hands, running his big, blunt fingers along the edges. "I know they're here but they're either hidden or too small for me to see."

They're in the kitchen at the brownstone. Yang's jade bits are laid out on the table, each part as close to where it should be as possible.

"Sorry about my eccentric father's gaslight habit," says Teg. "I'm sure he had his reasons but I'm sure you could use a good strong halogen lamp right about now."

"Don't worry," Balta soothed. "I'll make do. This house tells me much about your father and makes me sorry never to have met him."

"I wish both of us had met him."

"Maybe if I can reassemble him successfully, Yang can find him for us."

"Find who?" Teg frowns.

Balta looks up. "Your father, of course. Why do you think this gold-and-jade miracle is revered? Why do you think everyone wants him?"

"For robotics secrets, obviously. Artificial intelligence."

"And long before there were robots?" Balta presses.

"The god thing, I guess. Wait, are you saying he can talk to the dead?"

"I am."

She turns to Yang. "Can you do that?"

"We'll discuss it once I'm back together."

"I'm working on it," says Balta. "Actually, I could use a magnifier."

"This is not the place for such work," says Minnie.

"More and better tools in the collection vault, there are," nods Delia.

Balta carries Yang while the rest of them lead him upstairs.

"We have to do something about this lock," Teg mutters as they pause at the door. "I need free access."

"Certainly," says Minnie.

"Probably Mr. Burfield can recommend a security man," says Minnie.

"If you trust him not to bribe his man for the code," says Delia.

"You two are paranoid," says Teg.

"Courteous but careful," they chorus, "as your father taught us to be."

Inside the room, Balta lays Yang out on the butcherblock table, then paces the perimeter, eyes wide. Delia opens a drawer containing vintage jewelers' loupes. Teg selects one she thinks will fit Balta's hand. Right before she gets to the door, she turns around. Motionless, she stares at the central table and at the cabinet beneath it.

"Are you all right, dear?" asks Minnie.

A thought is forming. It makes the fine black hair at the nape of her neck stand up. It has been there a while, this idea, gradually rising like a bubble on the bottom of a saucepan.

"Oh no," she says, shaking her head.

"What is it, Tegulen?" asks Delia.

"I can't say right now," she says, her face pale.

Balta is too busy poring over Yang's construction details to hear her. "Wow, what a great lens," he mutters. "Now I can see he's assembled with breakaway joints."

"I've just realized something terrible," says Teg.

"Think of them as metal Velcro," says Balta. "Any strong force acting upon him causes him to separate at predetermined points. The system protects the integrity of his jade parts. It's a brilliant system. If humans had them, we wouldn't have to wear casts or have pins put in bones after an accident."

"Balta, do you hear me?"

"You told me that Wintermoth had his time alone with Yang," Balta goes on, his eye still at the loupe. "A good look at the neck would have been enough. The head goes on the same way it came off. He wouldn't tell you how easy it is because he likes to look the hero."

"All right, but can we talk for a second? This is about something else."

"Let's get this done and then we can talk as much as you like. Do you mind bringing me your father's watchmaking tools?"

She's bursting with her news but forces herself to get the tools and stay quiet while Balta reconnects Yang's parts, a butcher at a butcher block, occasionally complaining about his own big hands. Minnie and Delia watch as he attaches the piece of blue jade rescued from the Istanbul museum. Minnie turns away as Balta tests it at various angles. Delia watches with interest.

Balta chooses the mainspring from a modern Omega wristwatch to replace a broken hook inside Yang's neck, then uses an oxyacetylene torch and old clock parts from Arlington's collection to repair the damaged gears. At long last, he joins head and body.

"Thank you," says Yang when Balta closes the last remaining hook.

"It's been an honor. Try to stand now. Go easy. Give yourself time to rediscover your balance."

Yang takes a deep breath. It's a vital sound, deep and resonant. It's clear that when he decides to speak, it will be with a far more powerful voice.

He smiles and sits up. When he does, one leg disconnects from his torso. A moment later, his head tumbles, too. Balta catches it before it hits the floor.

"No!" scream Minnie and Delia, in perfect unison.

68

I DON'T KNOW how long I'm among the stars, the gods. I know only that when they are finished with me, they send me back down the celestial staircase. As the floor, walls, and ceiling solidify I find the great house as I left it, rugs and curtains still smoldering from my father's fireballs, female attendants scurrying about, guards still asleep, the air thick and heavy with sweat, Roxsana's blade still at my father's throat. What seemed like hours up there appears to have only been seconds down here.

"Well?" Al-Jazari demands, trembling with expectation.

"I found Allah," I said, struggling to reorient myself, testing my weight first with one foot and then the other.

"Yes!" the master exclaimed with luminous satisfaction. "It was your purpose to do so. I never for a moment doubted you would."

"You never doubted me but you called me an abomination."

"Never mind that. What is His answer?" he pressed, his fevered inhales and exhales as a windstorm to me, the pounding of his heart as thunder.

I struggled with the weight of the moment, for as I have described, I am wont to directly experience the emotions of others and even to see into their dreams. I understood full well that the master had been waiting desperately for this answer since the rape and ruin of his beloved Baghdad. He had devoted every waking moment to divining it. This was the quest that gave his life meaning, the very reason he was still alive.

I drew a deep breath. "First you need to understand that Allah is one of many gods."

"What did you say?"

"The gods were all around me. I felt them and saw them. They are as numerous as stars."

"Blasphemer!"

"If the universe runs like a clock," I continued, undaunted, "it is a far larger clock than you imagine, with many more gears and springs and jewels. Allah's preoccupation seems to be to keep everything in balance, to counter extremes of one sort with extremes of another, to cultivate harmony and maintain a kind of cosmic equilibrium."

"Then you're saying Allah *is* all," al-Jazari countered.

"I can't say that, actually. The answer to that question is beyond me. The other gods may be fully as important or even more so. But what I *can* say is that Allah is god not only to the Muslims but to the Mongols, who I'm pretty sure know him as Tengri."

Al-Jazari's face was bloodless, his body a tuning fork. "May you burn in hell."

"He didn't say anything about hell. I'm not really sure there is one."

The master turned to my father, his face red.

"Is this your revenge, slave? How you torture me right to the end? You twist my creation to spurt perverted lies and deprive me of peace after all these decades of waiting? I should never have shown him the ladder, should never have trusted you with anything. Your thing of stone is not what I imagined. He is an outrage. A fake. An atrocity!"

My father said nothing and neither did I. The silence in the

350

hall was deafening. And then, into the silence came the sound of the master humming a thin, sorrowful tone. I knew the voice, loved, feared, and celebrated it without knowing why I did not understand the words but nonetheless sensed its meaning and shivered at the sound of it.

"No!" my father cried, obviously wanting desperately to stop the master but unable to move for the point of Roxsana's sword at his neck. "Stop that. Don't do it! Be quiet!"

Al-Jazari smiled a hateful smile and raised his voice higher. As his humming grew louder and more intense, I began to feel distinctly uncomfortable. I felt his song in my teeth and then in my feet. I felt the vibration he issued loosening the bonds cohering me until I literally came unglued. One after another, my bits and pieces disconnected, but al-Jazari did not stop until I was looking up at him from a strange angle, my golden cheek against the cold floor. When he stopped singing, the only sound I could hear was my father sobbing. My poor, sweet Roxsana, stunned and speechless, lowered her blade from my father's throat.

Would that it had ended there. It did not. My father rushed to the master and knocked him down, kicking at that ancient face until its cheekbones cracked. Despite all of it, even when the blood oozed from his mouth, al-Jazari did nothing but smile. At the last, he beckoned my father in as if to share some final secret. Tragically, my father fell for the trick, perhaps out of habitual obedience. When they were nearly nose to nose, the old man reached into his white robe and withdrew a jeweled dagger.

"Now I send you to hell along with your monster," the master whispered, driving the blade straight into my father's heart.

I could not tear my gaze away from the sight of their two bodies slumped together, blood running, limbs twitching, red bubbles at lips. Stuck on the sight, I felt a pain a thousand times, no, ten thousand times stronger than what I had felt at the loss of my foot. To even compare the two is to do a disservice to the devastation that was the death of two fathers, the loss of any link to my long past and my uncertain, wavering future. It was a pain greater than the loss of my body, the cessation of breathing, the persisting, silently, without any rhythm, without a heart.

I might have willed myself to die and follow then wherever they were bound for had not Roxsana reached for me, spinning me on the floor until a whole new tableau of horrors came into view. Strongmen and handmaidens slumped about in pools of blood, limbs twisted wrong way round, and gleaming bones protruding from flesh. I myself lay in disintegrated ruin, my diamond feet glittering alone, my platinum fingernails scattered like nails, my alloy bands, inner sacs and lattices exposed in clumps.

I must have let out a hum of my own, or better a wail, for Roxsana pulled my hard head to her soft, soft bosom.

"I should never have brought you here," she sobbed. "I should have had you in mind, not him. I never imagined this. I failed you. Oh, my love, how I failed you."

"Hush," I said. "Just take me to my father."

I could see she was both amazed and relieved there was still life in my eyes and reason in my head. She carried me to the wizard. His eyes were already clouding over, but there was enough breath in him for one last pronouncement.

"My boy," he whispered.

And died.

69

BALTA IS A MAN of few words but great competence. He can rend flesh asunder and also patiently reassemble an ancient wonder. Even so, he groans in dismay as Yang falls apart. Yang himself says nothing at all. To have been brought close to resurrection and then feel it slip away stills his usually glib tongue. Teg, however, rises to the occasion.

"Let's not panic," she says. "All the parts are here. We'll figure it out. Yang, you said Sebastian restored all your memories when he poked about in your brain. Do you remember anything about your assembly process? Can you think back to those early moments for any helpful clue?"

Yang closes his eyes and thinks. "You mean my birth?"

"I suppose so, yes?"

"It seems my father waited to awaken me until I was fully formed," he says at last. "One moment I was not there and then I was. I don't know what else to say."

"What about repairs?" Teg persists. "Were you ever taken apart and rebuilt? Were you ever injured and put back together?"

"My father once reattached my foot."

"Go back to that time," Teg urges. "Be there. Smell it. Taste it. See it. Hear it."

And Yang does. It takes him a little while, as his newly restored memories are a bit scrambled, but eventually, he remembers not only the rhythmic humming of the khan's court inventor executing repairs but the song of al-Jazari that tore him limb from limb.

"Tell me about my construction inside," he commands Balta. "What you call the fasteners."

Balta makes a circle with the thumb and forefinger of one hand and curves the forefinger of his other into a hook.

"They are little hooks."

"And the gap in them remains when you put them together?"

"Yes," Balta admits. "But they are very deliberately set at different angles. I believe the point of that is that even if some come off, others remain attached. It makes the attachments robust without being clunky or redundant."

"You describe the system without mentioning what makes it all work together."

"I'm at a loss about that," Balta admits.

"Yes, but I am not. I have remembered. Please reattach my head and leg where they belong and I will show you."

Balta starts again. When at last his work is done, Yang asks that everyone be perfectly silent and still. Concentrating, he remembers his father's voice, and al-Jazari's too. He remembers the tune that created a resonance in his body as surely as a struck note or bow across string creates the music of a violin. He begins to hum.

"What's going on?" asks Teg.

Balta places his hand gently underneath Yang's head. "I feel something," he whispers.

Yang's body stiffens, jumps, vibrates, moves a tiny bit here, a tiny bit there, the overall effect being to subtly but precisely align his parts. The whole process takes less than a minute, but when it is done, the spaces between his joints are closed and there is an overall impression of coherence apparent to everyone in the room. He sits up, and runs his hands over his legs, his belly, his hips, shoulders, torso, and down between his legs. When he stands, he does so with none of the stiff awkwardness that might be expected of someone who's literally been in pieces for eight hundred years. Rather, he is full of energy and grace.

Minnie and Delia clap as he leaps off the butcherblock, does a perfect somersault, and ends up back right where he was, hands spread in the style of his performing days.

"Haaa!" he shrieks.

He has nothing else to say as he races about the kitchen, swinging from the pot rack like a monkey, executing a vertical jump that takes him all the way up to the top of the high ceiling then landing on bent and springy legs, a huge smile on his face. He performs a handstand and walks across the floor upside down. He spins and cavorts, whistles and cackles, spirals and twists. He dances, writhes, wiggles, bends, poses, leaps, and drops into a split. After a few minutes, Teg finds herself staring not at Yang, but at Balta. She reaches for his hand.

"Come with me," she says.

Leaving Yang to his rediscovery and the housekeepers to their knowing nods, she leads him to her bedroom, the one that has been redone with Asian themes, curtains, and pillows as she requested. It's a love nest for her and Balta; she understands that now. She undresses him slowly, shirt first, marveling at the marble flatness of his belly and the mountain of his chest. She undoes his belt and his pants fall and she strips and pushes him down. She sits astride him.

"Are you sure?" he murmurs.

"Shut up," she says.

Their lovemaking begins slowly. At first, he is attentive and whispers to her in Kazakh, punctuated by Russian as they pick up the pace, rough in their pent-up passion. They go again and again. The mansion itself seems to move with their energy.

Later, lying together, she props up on her elbow. "Downstairs, I said I had something to tell you."

"Yes."

"It's terrible. The worst thing ever."

"Please say it's not about us," he says.

She runs a fingernail around his chin it takes a while.

"No. Not about us. Although you're really big."

He blushes.

"Oh stop. I mean tall. I'm going to have to buy a longer bed."

"That's the worst thing ever?"

"No. It's about Wintermoth."

"You like him?"

"What? Oh my God, no. But I need to get him here. To the house."

"Invite him, then."

"I mean right now."

He looks at the clock on the bedside table, a manual-wind model from Cartier thoughtfully kept current by Delia. "It's almost dinner time. I was hoping we could stay here together for a little while."

She kisses him. "I know. Me too. But it has to be now. I can't let another moment go by."

"I don't understand, but if it makes you happy, call him."

She picks up the phone. "Believe me when I tell you it doesn't make me happy."

Wintermoth is on the line a moment later.

"Have you changed your mind?"

"I have. You can have Yang if you want him. How soon can you be here?"

"Give me an hour."

She bolts up out of bed and gets Balta to do the same. They

shower and dress in record time and meet Minnie and Delia down in the kitchen. Yang looks down from a perch atop a china cabinet.

"What I'm going to say changes everything," she says. "But don't worry," I have a plan."

70

AL-JAZARI'S guards had not dared interrupt their master's exchange with my father, especially when they saw Roxsana intervene. When everything unraveled, they at once came unglued from the posts, but it was too late for them to avert tragedy. With both men dead, they had only to help the maids put out what remained of the flames. A vanguard of officials arrived after that, drawn by the smoke and the clanging of neighborhood alarm bells. An argument ensued regarding what to do with al-Jazari's body. The master's attendants insisted he had certain wishes, but the city officials had their own. In the thick of that fracas, Roxsana gathered my parts together and stuffed them into my father's satchel. Her strength a constant source of amazement to me, she also managed to wrap up my father's body and sling him over her shoulder like a carpet.

She slipped out of the house with both of us and granted my request to take my father's body down to the water. While I watched, she buried him where he would forever be able to hear the sound of water lapping against the seawall, and smell the salty tang he had loved so much. She marked the site with only a small wooden board identifying him as a devoted father and grandest wizard of Kublai Khan's court. I vowed I would someday fashion and install the most beautiful stone stele the city had ever seen.

When she had finished the task and had wiped the dirt from her hands and the perspiration from her brow, we headed back to al-Jazari's, for Roxsana wanted to know the funeral details in order to pay her last respects. When we arrived at the house, a man was standing in the portico shadow, near an evergreen tree. He was tall, swarthy, and slender and he leaned on a long, curved sword with a heavy bronze guard.

"Who is that?" I asked.

"The Grand Imam's top agent."

"What does he want?"

"Me. And I stand no chance against him."

"Have you fought him before?"

"I have. And it cost him three fingers. But there were circumstances. I could not beat him again."

"I have an idea," I said. "Why not buy your life with me?"

She paled. "What?"

"He does not know my limbs are in the bag. Offer him my head in exchange for your life. Then leave with my limbs. He'll sell me. My head, I mean, and you can find me again."

"But how? You could end up in a market somewhere. Anywhere. As a curiosity. A toy. Part of a collection in someone's cupboard anywhere in the world. Who knows what will become of you?"

"If you don't do this, he'll kill you and take me anyway. You need to convince him your way will save him dismemberment like the last time—more fingers, a foot, an ear. Why wouldn't he take a deal like that?"

"The Imam...."

"Maybe he'll offer my head as proof. So many people have known we were traveling together, the Imam must have heard. That soldier could say he cut you up and buried you. It's not like you're going back to the Imam's mountain, not like you're going to be obvious or keep a high profile. Hide. Find those river people from whom my father was stolen and enslaved. They will know how to reassemble me once you find me again. You heard they have secret knowledge."

"But what if they don't anymore, or can't find you?"

"They they will keep my parts safe until someday I can be made whole."

"I can't leave you," she said, tears running down her face.

I lifted my chin in the direction of the killer. "If you're alive at least you have a chance of tracking me down. Dead, we're both lost."

She collapsed on the ground. The assassin looked over with interest, gathered himself, started our way.

"If you don't find me, someone will. Someday, somehow, some interested party will put me back together. And when they do, I swear that I will come for you, not matter how many lifetimes it takes."

He drew nearly close enough to hear our conversation.

"If I can save you, I will have served my purpose."

She looked at me with an expression that nearly broke my resolve.

"Your real is far more significant," she whispered.

I managed a smile. "You are the highest, best thing in this world."

"And what about other worlds?"

"There, too."

"I will not rest until I deliver your beautiful body to your people," she whispered.

"And I will not rest until we are together again," I whispered back. "Wait for me. Watch for me. Be patient. Never lose faith that I will come for you."

The assassin reached us.

"It's time," he said.

"Stop right there," she commands. "Remember the last time. Why risk fighting me again? You might win but even if you do, you may never be able to fight again, or even walk. I have another way."

"What way?"

"A bribe."

So saying, she extended my head to him, carefully, not wavering in the slightest, eyes locked with mine, strong in her love, strong in her trust.

Patient forever.

71

"OFF TO THE opera?" Teg inquires, taking in what is quite a splash of sartorial splendor even for Wintermoth, topped off, of course, by a Patek Philippe timepiece.

"As a matter of fact, I am. *La Bohème* at the Metropolitan Opera. I hope this won't take too long."

"Not at all."

"Where's Yang?"

"In the collection room. Everyone else is out."

This is the line she dreads he'll take as a tip-off, but he follows her upstairs without comment. Minnie and Delia have left the security door slightly less than fully closed. She pushes it open. Yang is there, intact and lounging against the central table. Wintermoth starts at the sight of him.

"I see you got him back together," he says. "If you don't need me, why am I here?"

"You're here because Teg has something else to discuss with you, Sebastian," Yang says.

Wintermoth looks ostentatiously at his watch. "Well then, Ms. Elliot. What is it?"

"It's about my father."

"Yes? What about him?"

"You killed him,"

Wintermoth freezes. "I beg your pardon?"

"He had a certain gold head you and your family have been after for decades," she continues, trying hard to keep her voice from trembling.

"Centuries, actually," corrects Yang.

"You only befriended my father to get him to sell Yang to you," Teg continues. "You tried and tried. You couldn't understand why he was so keen on it, not being a roboticist or even interested in artificial intelligence. Finally, when you lost patience, you got him out of the way."

"This is ridiculous," says Wintermoth.

"Actually, it's tragic. Because of you, I will never meet my father. I'm only keeping myself together because confronting you is all I can do. I know how you did it, Sebastian. I know you electrocuted him."

"Please," Wintermoth waves his hands and turns away.

"Don't turn your back on me! Maybe he told you about his heart problem. Maybe you deduced electricity would kill him because he banned strong currents from the house. Either way, you happen to carry electricity with you everywhere, every day, in your augmented parts."

"You have no proof of any of this."

"You knew not to leave a mark," Teg continues, her voice rising. "You probably applied the current to him in some intimate spot. A place no one would ever look. Maybe the place I touched you."

"Is that when you got this crazy idea? When you burned me?"

"Maybe then," says Teg. "Maybe later."

"You had to force her father to his bedroom," Yang continues the narrative. "My guess is you had him put on his nightclothes, even his little sleeping cap, assuring there would be no trace of anything amiss at autopsy. When he lay down in his bed, you killed him there."

"What drove you crazy," says Teg, quietly so as to keep her voice steady, "is that even after he was dead and you were free to search, you couldn't find Yang. You probably tried every drawer and case. Maybe you even found where he was but couldn't bypass the keypad without leaving evidence of a robbery."

"This is preposterous and offensive," Wintermoth snaps.

"What a cold-blooded creature, you are, Sebastian. No wonder you prefer the company of machines to the company of soft people."

Wintermoth circles the room, hands in his pockets, a little smile on his face. "You're clever," he says at last. "Got your father's brains and your mother's balls."

"You're not denying it."

He looks around. "At this point, why should I?" he says, reaching into his vest pocket and withdrawing what looks like a TV remote.

A moment later, the door swings open and the MothCo service robot lumbers in. He doesn't look at all human, but he does have arms and legs, and he does walk.

"Not quite eight feet tall, as you can see," Wintermoth says smugly. "And not confined to war-torn parts of the world either. Perfectly at home in a spoiled brat's brownstone. But the part about Sinatra's voice is true, not that you're going to hear it."

"How did that thing get in here?"

"Surely you know this house has a very private service entrance. Your father made sure it was out of street view, what with all those valuables he brought in."

"You're outrageous. You think you can get away with anything, that you can control everything. That you own the world."

"Soon I will, now that I've got him," Wintermoth gestures at Yang.

"You don't have me," says Yang.

"Oh yes, I do."

"Murderer," Teg says slowly.

Wintermoth issues a cool smile.

"I can't tell you how good it felt to do it. Strung me along for two years, the old bastard did, gloating about the secret he had, telling me how I'd kill to know it. Those are the exact words he used, if you can believe it. You're right in guessing I knew better than to leave a mark on him. In fact, I didn't touch him at all. I had him touch the metal bedframe. I juiced that and the current spread to him at once. You should have seen him twitch and writhe. I had to straighten the bed a bit after. It was perfect. Glorious."

Teg's eyes fill. "You're a monster."

"I'm not a monster; I'm a businessman. And my mechanical friend here, who admittedly is not the brightest bulb in the chandelier, is very strong. And by strong, I mean his jammer. No electronic device will work in this house, no recording instrument can withstand the pulses he's giving off, no camera, no smartphone can operate in his presence. I'm assuming you're taping this conversation but I assure you nobody will ever hear it. This ends here. I'm finally going to take back what belongs to me."

Teg is worried her outrage will lead her to do something stupid, but instead a vast hollow develops inside her, a black hole devouring the matter of her life, everything she has, everything she longs for, all she holds dear. She feels a strong calm.

"You control the synthetic world right now, Sebastian," she says. "But the organic world is mine. And do you know what I say? I say *tourbillon*."

That bit of wristwatch terminology is her code word. The instant she utters it, Balta steps out of the broom closet, Minnie unfolds herself from the cupboard that once held Yang, and Delia appears from inside the very cabinet Wintermoth used to kill Arlington Ames.

Teg surprises herself with her own calm. "They heard everything," she says. "Your gloating. Your confession. How you did it. Everything."

Wintermoth roars and grabs at Yang but cannot follow his leaps. He tries using the service robot but Balta snatches away the control box. Wintermoth's augmentations make him more than a match for Balta, but not a match for the silk scarf Minnie and Delia wrap around his neck from behind and, together, twist and pull until he goes still.

72

I DON'T REMEMBER the centuries inching past me, nor do I know of the schemes and greed of those who took my pieces. I can't, for example, recall where the Imam's assassin took me, though I choose to believe that it was Roxsana who successfully delivered my body parts to my father's people. I know nothing of whether my father had been acting as an agent of his original tribe or whether, separated and unable to find them, he had turned to Taoism as a similar and appealing substitute. I wish I knew more about those people who, millennia ago, lived along a river in what is now central China. I can't say why their culture was not totally swallowed by the serpentine migrations of people and societies across the continent of Asia. Nor can I explain how, against all odds, a few of them managed to preserve their fervent belief in the existence of a cosmic tree that a climber like me could use to reach the heavens, speak with gods, and commune with the dead.

Many religions have come and gone and many allegedly divine offspring have been forsaken or forgotten. Perhaps this happens because other projects, worlds, or followers distract the gods themselves. Perhaps it happens because the gods, while still present, elect to stay quiet and allow Nature, their crowning construct, to run its course. Perhaps it happens because faith is tested by circumstances, and if found lacking, is lost. Perhaps a fire, flood, pestilence, or conquering army simply wipes a group of believers off the map.

Surely there is a relationship between war and faith and between religion and empire, between some men *becoming* gods and other men desperately needing to believe in them. Perhaps the mystery of why some spiritual traditions flourish while others survive only in dusty books has to do with how compelling, rewarding, and enduring are their legends and myths. Stories, it turns out, are everything, and the more tangible they are, both in terms of scope and promise, the more likely they are to persist.

I feel that Balta's people stayed together because they continued to believe in me, and that they continued to believe in me for the very best possible reason — because I was and am real. Because I can actually do what they believe I can do.

As I told you at the outset, you may take me for a fake, but in truth, I am quite real.

73

THE MONTHS following Sebastian Wintermoth's arrest for murder are busy ones for Tegulen Elliot. She legally changes her name to Tegulen Elliot-Ames and, with the help of Jules Burfield, retains the same private investigators her father used to keep an eye on her as a little girl, paying them handsomely to gather as much damning evidence as possible about Wintermoth's character, some of it from cowed and abused women.

Rumors abound at MothCo. A whistleblower comes forth, a member of the team of virtually linked engineers Teg saw on her first visit to the company. This person reveals that the service robot of which Wintermoth was justifiably proud was equipped not only with Sinatra's voice and a powerful radio jammer, but also with a piece of back-door code running that clandestinely recorded its actions. The events that transpired at the Ames mansion are found stored on the MothCo server, rendered in both high-resolution video and audio files.

Wintermoth's attorney resigns. Another takes his place. Shares in MothCo tank, and drop even lower as many employees resign. Customers withdraw their orders. Each morning, Tegulen watches the stock price drop. When it reaches what she judges to be the bottom, but before the company actually declares bankruptcy, Burfield helps her use some of her fortune to organize a hostile takeover of the firm. Renaming it Ames Enterprises, she makes as much as she can of her connection to the murder case and wins back the lion's share of the lost business.

While she cannot shield Yang from all legal inquiries—his voice is on the confession recording—she does her best to protect his privacy and any details of who and where he is. She isn't entirely successful in this as the court has its questions, but she does manage to keep his details from being publicly revealed.

"I'm not qualified to run my company," she tells Balta one stormy summer morning as the house shakes with thunder and lightning flashes in the windows.

They're in the kitchen, where he is making a vegan frittata for the two of them.

"You studied economics, didn't you?" Teg goes on.

"This is not that. It's management, it's practical. What I studied was all theoretical. I don't know how to run anything. I want you to do it for me."

"I'm a butcher," the big man says, sliding his arm around her and drawing her close.

"Trained as an engineer."

"But not a CEO. If you don't want to do it, you should find someone. There are many qualified people. But I think it should be you, with the help you need, of course."

"I have no experience."

"You have a conscience," he tells her. "And a beautiful moral compass. What two more important things could you bring to a corporation?"

"You have an understanding of the things my new company makes. You could have people help you with the rest, too."

"I have only a six-month tourist visa."

"Jules has people working on that."

"I go back to Almaty next Thursday. I will close up my shop and visit with my parents. After that, if you still want me to, I'll return to you."

"The money could help your parents."

"You know I need no money from you."

"It's me you need, not my money. I'm positively irresistible and you've grown used to me."

"That I have," he smiles, kissing her.

"While you're gone, Yang can help me with the ethical dimensions of AI."

Balta nods. "Be sure and invest in fungus farms and cephalopod research before any word of your company's new project leaks out. Corporate spies are everywhere and well paid."

She puts a few pieces of sundried tomato in the frittata pan and smiles.

"I thought of that and already bought several big farms."

"See?" Balta smiles. "You've got this."

"Jules gave me my father's letter today. The one I wasn't supposed to see. I haven't read it yet."

"You told me he said he'd never share it."

"Recent events changed his mind."

"All the same, don't read it," says Yang, strolling into kitchen with his loose, smooth gait.

"How can I not?" Teg asks, surprised. "It's all I have of him."

"None of us can process all the information out there in the world. The primary function of our brains is to filter it. Soft people filter it *a lot*; hard people like me filter less."

"I don't understand," says Teg.

"He's saying he sees and understands more than we do," Balta explains.

"Yes," Yang nods. "For instance, I see a cloud of microorganisms around each person that is fully as unique as a fingerprint."

"What does this have to do with me reading my father's letter?"

"Hard people like me know that our place in the universe is small. We're okay with that. We don't have to be the center of things. We don't *want* to be. We know that natural laws are there for a reason."

"Natural laws like death."

"Exactly."

"And yet you were constructed to talk to the dead. If I agree not to read the letter, will you talk to my father for me?"

Yang exhales. Since Balta has installed a filter behind his nose to help him endure all the chemicals in modern city air, his breathing is louder than it was before.

"Didn't see that one coming, did you?" says Balta.

"I did not."

"But why didn't you?" Teg pursues. "Isn't it an obvious request? Given who you are and what you can do, I mean? I was hoping you would offer without me having to ask."

Yang looks at the ground. "The last time I attempted something like this, the last time I was led to attempt what I was built for, I lost everything."

"You're not going to lose *us*," says Teg.

The three of them stay quiet for a while.

"I have no idea what they may be," says Balta after a while, "but I think there may be other reasons you're afraid to try."

Yang closes his eyes.

"You've held everything in all this time," says Teg. "Maybe it's time to do what needs to be done. Not only for me, but for yourself. I don't know what it means for you to climb the ladder to Heaven, but I do know that there's a foundation for that ladder right here in this house, and it's broad and it's strong."

Yang nods at that, and sighs.

"Well then," he says. "I suppose the time has come."

74

THE FAMILIAR LADDER to the stars appears in the landscape he conjures, but he chooses to stride past it and out into the surrounding expanse of what would someday be central China. Closing in on the banks of what will later be called the Yangtze River, he sees children playing with water striders, women fashioning clay pots, and fisherman who share his father's build and visage working their nets. He remains there for a while, finding comfort in their company, then finally moves on.

He comes at last upon what he has been seeking, a massive tree with branches as horizontal and orderly as steps. He grabs the first one with his hands and feels the tree's inherent goodness, its solidity and strength. He pulls himself up, and begins climbing. No human being could climb with such speed and agility, energy, surefootedness, and purpose. Most trees grow narrower toward the top, but this one remains broad and steady all the way up, its branches nearly horizontal, each a perfect platform for Yang's feet. He keeps going until the people beneath him are the size of termites. Finally, he breaks through the clouds.

Arlington Ames is there, waiting for him one branch up. He wears a baseball cap.

"I always yearned to wear one of these," Ames says, touching its brim, "but I never had the nerve. Wasn't done in my family."

"I understand," says Yang. "Are you enjoying it now?"

"More than you can imagine. Say, will you tell my daughter I love her?"

"She knows. But I will. Anything else?"

"Tell her I'm watching her."

"She suspects."

"Tell her I didn't push hard to see her as a child because I didn't want a war with her mother and I knew we would meet soon enough. I wish I'd seen Wintermoth for who he was, seen him coming at the end."

"I will do so."

"Tell her I'm proud of her, too."

"She'll be glad to hear it."

"Tell her the big man is good for her, a keeper."

"She knows. She'll keep him."

"Tell her Minnie and Delia are the most loyal friends she'll ever have."

"She knows that, too, and she's grateful for them every day."

"Tell her she's right, I was never a slave to time; I was only its lover."

"That's beautiful. I don't think she knows that. I will tell her."

"Well then," says Ames. "You'd better keep climbing."

Up the tree Yang goes. At the limits of his vision, out at the far ends of the branches, he can make out a horizon filled with civilizations, cities, beings. He continues until he sees his khan. The ruler's fat ankles are fat no longer and no gout plagues him. There are no bags under his eyes and his waist is narrow, his legs strong.

"I'm surprised to see you here, my boy," he says. "I wasn't expecting you. Others, perhaps. Not you."

"I'm surprised to see you, too."

"You were always my favorite," he says.

"I know."

"I'm sorry I didn't stand up to Chabi."

"That's all right. Even the greatest, strongest men most bow to their queens. As it happened, all that turned out for the best anyway."

He climbs a bit further, and there is Chabi herself.

"I'm not sorry I sent you away," she says. "There was a necessary order to things and you disturbed it."

"And I'm not sorry I went," he tells her.

Higher still, he sees his mother. "Oh Yang," says the first queen. "It's not bad here, but I'd rather be a fish."

"You would always rather be other than you are," Yang tells her. "I was rather hoping you would have learned to love yourself by now. Anyway, I always loved you. My father did, too."

Queen Tegulen's smile almost breaks his heart. He wants to stay with her longer, to sit beside her and talk about small things. Even so, he knows he has to go, so he keeps climbing until he runs smack into al-Jazari sitting on a branch. The old master smiles. It's a heartbreaking smile and it makes his white beard glow.

"I'm sorry for everything," the master says. "I was wrong about you. My thinking became clouded at the end. I was suffering so much. I saw so many terrible, terrible things."

"That was the time of the world," says Yang, caressing the old man's hand. "It wasn't your fault. Your pain was too much to bear."

"So, you forgive me? Please say that you do."

"I forgive you."

He climbs some more, and there is his father, resplendent in his robe, yet still showing his final wounds.

"Revenge is folly," he says.

"It is," says Yang.

"I had everything but I couldn't see it."

"You did. You even had me."

"You are the everything I mean. I'm proud I made you and sorry for the things I did, the vengeance I harbored in my heart, the way I lived. I've been waiting to tell you. I knew you'd get here sooner or later, that you'd figure it out."

"I had help," says Yang.

"We all need help," the wizard says, then points at the branch above him. "Now you'd better keep climbing. She's up there, you know. Waiting as she promised she would."

"I'm going," says Yang.

He's now high enough that the sky is dark around him. Indeed, it is full of stars. Up and up he goes until he finally finds Roxsana. A dagger wound seeps at her breast, delivered, no doubt, by an assassin. She hangs over a stout branch like a leopard's prey left to rot. Fearing the worst, he takes a few moments to summon the courage to touch her. When he does, he immediately knows that even though it has been ten lifetimes, he can heal her.

He blows gently on the wound. It begins to shrink. Smaller and smaller it becomes, until it disappears. He kisses her then, but finds her lips cold. He kisses her again and feels a faint warming. He wraps his arms around her, lifts her, and slowly begins his descent.

The lower he goes, the more she weighs. Heat gradually returns to her body. She murmurs, but the words are indistinct. By the time he's as low as the clouds, she is impossibly heavy, yet he will not set her down.

"This is what you were born for," the voices of his ancestors chorus in his head. *"Compassion, love, service."*

"I know. I have always known. I've just been asleep," Yang whispers back.

He sees his people, still tiny, waiting for him in the kitchen below. Down and down he climbs, the force of gravity so strong on him that he must concentrate solely on putting one diamond foot in front of the other. He perseveres. At last, the thin dark atmosphere surrounding the tree becomes lighter and thicker. He realizes he's been holding his breath and takes a mighty gasp.

Kitchen smells engulf him. He feels Balta's hands gently lift Roxsana and he lets her go, crumpling to the ground from the effort he has made.

"Who's this woman?" asks Teg. "What's going on? Did you see my father?"

Slowly, Yang rises.

When he smiles, his sapphire teeth gleam like stars.

About The Author

Yun Rou has been called the "Zen Gabriel Garcia-Marquez" for his works of magical realism, many set in China. Born Arthur Rosenfeld in New York City, he received his academic background at Yale University, Cornell University, and the University of California and was officially ordained a Taoist monk in Guangzhou, PRC. His award-winning non-fiction works on Taoism bridge science, spirituality, and philosophy, while his novels have been optioned for film in both Hollywood and Asia. Yun Rou lives in the American Southwest and travels frequently and extensively in the Far East.

yunrou@icloud.com
www.monkyunrou.com